ENCHANTED MESA

To my fitness buddy, Nancy
Best Wishes
Dianne Hall

ENCHANTED MESA

Dianne Hall

iUniverse, Inc.

New York Lincoln Shanghai

Enchanted Mesa

iUniverse books may be ordered through booksellers or by contacting:

iUniverse
2021 Pine Lake Road, Suite 100
Lincoln, NE 68512
www.iuniverse.com
1-800-Authors (1-800-288-4677)

ISBN-13: 978-0-595-38575-1 (pbk)
ISBN-13: 978-0-595-82954-5 (ebk)
ISBN-10: 0-595-38575-3 (pbk)
ISBN-10: 0-595-82954-6 (ebk)

Printed in the United States of America

CHAPTER 1

▼

"I can't remember his face." Tears clouded the woman's dark eyes. "His touch, the tenderness in his voice, yes. But when my mind gropes backward, the face is gone." She did not feel the sewing needle prick her finger but spotted the tiny drop of blood and blotted it with a tissue before it stained the fabric in her lap. "In photos he seems so real, but the instant I turn away...."

"What happens, Korey, when you turn away?" her sister asked.

"I close my eyes and try to find him until my brain aches, but it's no use. The face hides in that shadowy place just beyond the reach of the mind's eye. Yet, he's still with me in hundreds of ways. I see him crumpled into a slouch on the sofa, his face in a book, the lamp gilding his hair. I hear him at the piano even though there is no longer a piano in the house. He sings in the shower.... Oh, Tina, don't look at me as if I've seen a ghost."

Tina said softly, "It's been nearly two years, Korey. Maybe this is your mind telling you that it's time to let go."

Korey set aside her sewing, sucked the pain from her finger. "I know," she nodded. "But I miss him so much." Tears once more threatened to streak the heart-shaped face.

In a tender ray of a spring sun, Tina Goodwin wrapped comforting arms around her sister. "Oh, sweetie," she said, "we all miss him, terribly. We loved him. I understand you still have days when coping is difficult, but those days are becoming fewer and fewer." Tina drew back and looked her sister in the eye. "Korey, he would not want you, at twenty-eight years old, to stop living."

A rusty-breasted robin pecked at the grass in Korey Westerfield's tree-filtered back yard. Lilies of the valley shyly hung their sweet heads in the shade of a leatherleaf viburnum. Through drying eyes, Korey watched jet trails trim the blue sky in white lace. At last she said, "Springtime is the worst. You would think winter would be. Everything dormant; cold dark days and early nights. But now, in this season of rebirth, when the world is vibrant with color and sweet smells, Danny should be here with me."

At times such as this, Tina knew platitudes were of little help. All meaningful words regarding Danny Westerfield's untimely death had been used long ago. Now Tina could only be a sounding board, absorbing as much of her sister's pain as possible while waiting for the day when the passage of time had worked its healing magic.

The sun was warm, and with slender fingers Korey lifted her short dark curls to the breeze. "I will say," she continued, "this is the first spring in several that some of this rebirth seems to be rubbing off on me. I'm seeing the colors again, smelling the smells, feeling the changes in the air. Those things were dead to me for two years." Her smile was promising. "I'm really trying to find my way to better days."

Tina responded to her sister's lighter mood. "Listen, kiddo, some people would not have survived the blow you were dealt. Give yourself lots of points for getting out of bed every morning, working, making it through each day." She rubbed a supportive hand over Korey's shoulder. "Take each day as it is given. Just remember," a grin lit Tina's lovely face, "The Maker knew what She was doing: She made Earth round so we couldn't look too far down the road."

*   *   *   *

Korey dried a dripping hand on a towel as she grabbed the ringing phone. "Hello."

"I was almost ready to hang up. Were you outside?"

"No, Tina, washing dishes. My dishwasher's not working, and the repairman can't come for three days." With the heel of her hand she wiped strands of hair from her damp forehead. "Never again will I take our modern conveniences for granted."

"And I suppose you dined on a TV tray with that hunk on Channel 9 again tonight."

Korey let slide yet another reference to her dining alone. "You're just jealous."

Tina played along. "Don't breathe a word of it to Bryan. Husbands don't take kindly to their wives drooling over handsome newsmen. Hey, I wanted to let you know Bryan and I have arranged our schedules so we can help you hang the quilt in John Wexler's office on Thursday of next week."

"Great. I'm working my fingers overtime to have the quilt finished by then. I've already cleared it with John. He said if we arrive around six, someone will still be at the office to let us in." Korey plucked a worrisome lash from a tired eyelid. "Tomorrow I'm driving to Athens to talk to the owner of an accounting firm about stitching a wall hanging for their office."

"Wow. Your fame is spreading."

"Fame. Word of mouth is what it is. Starting to make me a fairly good living. I have enough work lined up to keep me busy for awhile."

"Well, here's hoping tomorrow means another commission."

"Thanks." A sharp crackle nearly deafened Korey's right ear. "What in the heck was that?"

"Lightning. We've got a storm moving in."

"Springtime in Chattanooga. I thought I heard thunder rumbling in the distance. It's hitting your side of town first."

"Apparently Nashville is really getting it. Tornadoes spotted even." Another bolt of lightning sizzled the line. "We'd better get off the phone. But one more thing. Some night, Korey, I'd like to hear that you had dinner with a man who *isn't* the anchor on Channel 9!"

$$* \qquad * \qquad * \qquad *$$

"Final boarding call at gate 10 for American Airlines flight 1231 for New York's Kennedy Airport. All passengers should now be on board."

Marc Bradberry propped his sturdy frame against the American Airlines counter at gate 18 as he waited for the ticket agent to finish a telephone conversation. Twenty minutes earlier he had deplaned from Denver and sprinted to catch a connecting flight to Nashville. Now he stood on aching feet waiting to hear how long his flight would be delayed because high wind and torrential rain was pummeling his destination.

"I'm sorry, Mr. Bradberry." The agent, cradling a phone on her shoulder, handed him his boarding pass. "Nashville is still experiencing heavy thunderstorms. Your flight has been delayed for at least an hour."

"Typical," Marc mumbled.

"Pardon?"

In answer, his exhausted body could only shake its head before he reached to retrieve the leather attaché case from the floor. He turned on a well-polished heel in search of a quiet corner in which he could endure the unwelcome delay. Finding the passenger waiting area nearly empty, he sagged into a seat in a vacant row with a wall to his back. Regretting that he had been too rushed in leaving Denver to change into more comfortable traveling clothes, he impatiently loosened the knot in his paisley tie and unbuttoned his shirt collar. Unfolding his long legs, he crossed them at the ankles, leaned his head against the wall and let his heavy eyelids slide closed.

After what seemed to be only moments, the calm was broken by a boy, a toy airplane at the end of an orange string weaving along behind his toddler's legs. Engine noises, from deep within the child's young throat, burbled through rosebud lips. Marc's one opened eye stared into two blue orbs set in a cherubic face. Marc stood, glanced around the room. No one seemed to take an interest in the child. A tiny dimpled hand clutched the string of the pull toy as unblinking eyes stared at Marc: Jack looking up the beanstalk, measuring the Giant.

Marc Bradberry smiled. "Say there young man," he said, "someone must be frantically looking for you."

"Jason." The young mother came from nowhere to scoop her wandering son and his airplane into her arms. "This isn't the place for you to be roaming around by yourself." Her frightened eyes softened when she looked into the kind face of the stranger.

"Beautiful child you have there," Marc said.

"Sometimes." She flashed a harried grin. Peeking over his mother's shoulder, with a pudgy hand Jason shyly returned Marc's wave of farewell.

The sight of the boy vanishing around a corner did painful things to the mending heart of the man who watched. He did not want to think how old his own son would have been. Too tired to fight them off, unwelcome memories came to roost in his head. As he again sat and closed his eyes, Marc's mind refused to rest, choosing instead to visit, with punishing realism, that dreadful night eleven months before.

He had done something that night to displease Clare. Later, he had not been able to recall what he had said or done that had filled his wife with such venom. But drunk as she was, anything could have set her off, and he had carelessly tripped one land mine among many with which she had armed her vengeful heart. He had been tip-toeing around those mines for years, but that night one blew up in his unsuspecting face.

She had said, through twisted lips he had weeks before ceased to kiss, "You're so mean! You would've made a terrible father."

He had gaped at her. "You're....not pregnant," he stammered.

"Not anymore," she said through cruel lips.

"What are you telling me!"

"I had an abortion. A male fetus. Three months ago." She stated it as coldly as she would have said, "I rolled the garbage to the curb this morning."

His knees folded like cardboard, and he dropped to the nearest chair. Too numb to think, he muttered inanely, "Clare, you didn't."

"I did." She straightened her rounded shoulders, cinched the belt of her robe as if to show off her slim waist.

As he sat with his head in his hands, a rage like he had never imagined began to burn through every cell. His long fingers dug holes in his scalp as he fought the urge to use those same fingers to grab his wife's slender neck. Tears vented his anger, filled his green eyes as he looked up.

"When could you have done this?"

"I told you, three months ago. You thought I was spending a week at a health spa, remember?"

Dumbly, he shook his head. "Why? Why would you do such a thing to our child? You know how much I want a family...."

"What makes you think it was your child?" she snapped.

If he had not left the house then, he would have choked her and enjoyed doing it. Wisely he had driven to his brother Kevin's apartment where, without speaking to anyone, he had remained cloistered in his own private hell for three days.

He had found a different Clare when he returned home. She had been frantic with worry, she said. Where had he been for three days? Why would she awake one morning to find him gone without so much as a word?

Marc knew it to be no act. In the past, whole days had been lost and never found after Clare's heavy bouts of drinking. She was reduced to heaving sobs, had begged him to forgive her when he told her where he had been and why. But this time he was spent. He had in the past tried to be an understanding husband. Had driven Clare to AA meetings, had discreetly ushered her home early from parties where liquor flowed like water from a tap. And while remaining true to his own marriage vows, he had even overlooked her affairs. But no more. With the death of the baby, one he would have happily raised as his own, had come the death of the marriage.

Only a deep commitment to his promise of "in sickness" as well as in health had kept him from filing for divorce. But even this sense of responsibility had now run its course. Maybe it was that he had departed Denver so physically exhausted after three grueling days of facilitating architectural seminars. Maybe it was Clare's sloshed harangue on the phone last evening. Whatever the reason, on the first leg of his trip today, in a jet liner packed with disinterested strangers, flying east at 36,000 feet above geometric Midwestern farmland, he had made a decision. Divorce was a cruel word, but tomorrow, before going to the office, that word would be spoken by his own lips as he placed a call to his attorney.

Marc Bradberry's eyes popped open and he sat upright in the chair. Seeking a respite from his thoughts, he grabbed his briefcase and followed the concourse to a coffee shop. A waitress with teased hair the color of carrots overfilled his coffee cup. Too tired to complain, Marc wiped the dripping Styrofoam with a napkin and paid the girl. She did not thank him for his business; he did not thank her for the coffee. At a newsstand, he bought a Time magazine before returning to the boarding area. More passengers had arrived during his absence, but his previous seat remained empty. He set the steaming coffee on the arm of a chair, slipped out of his pinstripe jacket, folded it lengthwise and draped it over an adjoining seat. Carrying his coffee, he strolled in his shirtsleeves to the glass wall overlooking a runway. The starless night coated the window, converting the glass into a mirror in which Marc could see little else but blue runway lights and his own reflection.

Too many hours in the same clothes had left him rumpled; the loosened tie hung limply on his shirtfront. His dark brown hair had lost its well-groomed part and acquired a flat spot at the back where it had reposed against the seat of an airplane. He did not note his unkempt appearance in the glass, but in his present state of mind he would not have been interested if he had. Leaning closer to the window, he watched a plane land, taxi and roll its bottle-nose up to a neighboring gate. Fat drops of rain began to pelt the window, distorting the outside world like a wavy carnival mirror.

The rain reminded him of why he was here and he wondered just how much rain was falling in Nashville. He chastised himself for not replacing the leaking gutter on the house before leaving for Denver. Fragrant steam rose to his nostrils, and he gingerly drank the scalding coffee. He hoped Clare would not be at the house to greet him when he arrived. She did not come often, staying mostly at her own apartment, but the excuse that she needed the use of closet space at the house gave her reason not to relinquish her house key. Thinking of his soon-to-be-ex wife, he drained the coffee and crushed the empty cup in a tight fist, kneading the Styrofoam until it was reduced to no more than a wafer before pitching it into a trash can.

Among the constant trickle of arriving passengers, he returned to secure his seat. With the Time magazine in his lap, he removed a leather eyeglass case from an inside pocket of his jacket. The metal-framed eyeglasses lent a scholarly facet to his handsome features. Instead of the architect he was, he now looked professorial, as if he should be teaching Shakespeare at a private Midwestern university. Even with imperfect hair and wrinkled clothes, Marc Bradberry was so appealing to the eye, that hypothetically, if he were to teach at the college level, among the coeds his would surely be one of the most popular classes on campus.

Absorbed in the magazine, Marc was oblivious to the female glances he received from some who sat near him in the waiting area. He read about the continuing woes in the Russian economy; he shivered when he saw the photos of the tangled remains of a plush Asian hotel that had collapsed killing dozens (an architect's worst nightmare); he scanned the reviews of three movies he knew he would not take the time to see. He glanced at his watch. Fifty minutes gone and still no sign his plane would be leaving anytime soon. A vibration drew his hand to his cell phone. He answered a call from his brother. "Hey, Kev, what's up?"

"We're having a helluva storm here. It's raining like crazy, tree limbs down all over town. Mom was worried about you flying in this stuff. I told her I'd check on you."

"Mom usually doesn't hesitate to check up on me herself."

"I told her I'd be calling you...."

Something in his brother's tone alarmed Marc. "What is it?" He heard his brother's intake of breath.

"It's Clare."

"What's happened to Clare?"

"She's here at the hospital, brought into the emergency room nearly two hours ago, just before the rain started. Marc, she's in a coma. Bludgeoned and left for dead on the sidewalk outside O'Grady's Bar on Central Avenue."

Nausea swept through Marc as he thought of Clare lying in a pool of blood on a cold sidewalk. "Dear God," he moaned.

"I'm sorry."

"What was she doing in that part of town?" Marc thought he probably knew the answer to his own question. Weeks before he had heard that she had taken to trolling bars.

"No clue. But she wasn't just walking past the bar. She had been inside for some time." Static snapped over the phone line. "You there, Marc?"

"Yes."

"Lightning. Storm's right on top of the hospital."

"How bad is she, Kevin?"

"Ray Stoner has been with her from the moment they wheeled her in. Ray pulled Phil Davies out of a Kenny Chesney concert to work on her. Phil is the best neuro-trauma man in the Southeast. They're both doing everything humanly possible."

Marc knew when his physician brother was being evasive. "Just what are you telling me?"

"That right now I don't know about Clare's chances." Kevin paused. Then with pain evident in his voice, said, "It doesn't look good."

As Marc stepped away to a more private area, long fingers of his free hand absently worked through the knot in the loosened necktie. The wide gold band on his ring finger reflected the light as he held the phone to his ear. His wife near death, and he felt guilty for no longer loving her. She had many times behaved as the consummate bitch, but she didn't deserve this....

When Marc did not comment on Clare's grave prognosis, Kevin continued, "How rotten, Marc, that I give you this news while you're stuck in an airport, but I thought you would want to come directly to the hospital when you land in Nashville."

"Of course, yes." Marc's tone was subdued. "What more can you tell me about what happened tonight?"

"I spoke with one patrolman who was on the scene, but I can't make much sense of what he told me. As I said, Clare had been at the bar for awhile. Two witnesses said she was alone when she left. According to the bartender, two guys bought her a few drinks earlier in the evening, but they left long before she did. A patron at the bar knows the guys by first names only. The police are trying to locate them.

"The bartender finally refused her further drinks and wisely phoned for a taxi to drive her home. Before the taxi arrived, she slipped away while his back was turned, and a short while later a patron found Clare on the sidewalk."

Silk whistled against cotton as Marc freed the knot in his tie, yanked it through his collar, and wadded it into the pocket of his coat. He was shocked by what his younger brother was telling him—shocked, but not surprised. Clare's flirtation with alcoholic oblivion had been bound to lead to no good. He was saddened by news of her attack. Beyond that, he was angry. Angry with Clare for hanging out in seedy bars; angry with himself for having given up the fight to help her overcome her insidious disease.

"....kinda crazy," Doctor Kevin Bradberry was saying.

"What's that?"

"About the jewelry."

"What jewelry?"

"Marc, I said the motive was obviously robbery. Clare wore several pieces of flashy jewelry. The bartender noted a large diamond ring on her right hand. I'm assuming it to be the one you gave her on your fifth wedding anniversary."

Marc nodded his aching head as if his brother could somehow see him through the phone.

"She also wore a diamond bracelet."

"Hum, I remember that bracelet. A thick circle of gold set with large stones. Her parents threw a party, gave her the bracelet on her twenty-first birthday. Strange," Marc drew the word out as if thinking, "I haven't seen Clare wear that bracelet in years."

"That's what I meant by crazy. Wandering around alone, wearing those things. And if that weren't enough, she was carrying a large amount of cash. There were plenty of people gathered around the bar who saw the thick stack of bills when she opened her purse to pay her tab. She was not keeping a low profile."

"Obviously." Marc's anger began to creep into his voice. "So everything was missing when they found her?"

"Yes. Jewelry, purse, car keys. Even the car." Kevin hesitated, then reluctantly added, "Marc, she had your Austin Healey."

"Dammit!" He said it without thinking, then instantly felt like scum. What did it mean to lose a vintage British sports car when his wife was in the hospital fighting for her life? "Are you sure?" Marc asked. "She hated that car, said it drove like a garbage truck."

"Someone saw her get out of it in the parking lot. A gorgeous blonde in that red car would draw attention. The car's gone. I hate to tell you this, but the patrolman said by now it's probably in a semi on I-40 rolling to California."

"Someone really hit the jackpot tonight. Cash, jewelry, car, no telling how many credit cards. Wait a minute….if her purse was taken, how was she identified at the hospital? How did you know she was there?"

"That's the really eerie part. She made it a big point to tell the bartender her name. You remember Nikol Sims, the ER nurse I brought to your Christmas party? Well, she's on duty tonight and saw Clare's name on a chart. Nikol called me down to ER. I was in the doctor's lounge catching forty winks. Had just come off of twenty-one hours on the floor."

"Kevin, this is making no sense. Why in blazes would Clare go to a dive like O'Grady's dripping in jewels and money and broadcasting her name?"

"I honestly don't know. It's almost as if…."

"What?"

"As if she wanted to leave a trail, she wanted you to discover that she had been in that bar. The bartender saw her put several personalized matchbooks into her purse even though she wasn't smoking."

"Okay. So she wanted me to know she was running the traps. That much seems obvious. What I can't figure is why. Why the flash, the theatrics?"

Marc sensed his brother's shrug. "She's really mixed up, Marc. I don't know....maybe it was a last desperate cry for help."

"Shit. As if I don't feel guilty enough," Marc mumbled. He pinched the bridge of his nose to force the shooting pains from his head. "I think you're wrong. I think she was trying to punish me. Make me out responsible for what she's become. She hates me for going on with my life and leaving her to drown in gin and vodka and whatever the hell else she drinks."

"You've done everything to help her," the doctor said sternly. "Don't beat yourself up over this. Clare's responsible for her own actions. And right now, instead of pointing fingers, we all need to put our energies into saving her life. That said, there is one other matter. It probably hasn't occurred to you, but someone out there has Clare's purse containing *your* address and keys to *your* house."

"Damn."

"Don't panic. I'm only bringing this up because I wouldn't want you thinking of it later and stewing over it on the flight home. I've called the Brentwood police. A patrolman has been alerted to keep an eye on the place and has asked your neighbors to be on the lookout for anything suspicious." Kevin let out a tired chuckle. "Old man Glockner is probably loving it. I'll bet he sits up all night with his shotgun trained on your door. Better call him before you go home or we might be wheeling you in here with your backside full of buckshot."

"The state I'm in, I wouldn't feel a thing." Marc heard his flight called over the public address system. He cleared a lump from his throat. "Kevin, my flight home is finally boarding. I don't know if she can hear you but tell Clare to hold on. Tell her....tell her I'll be there in just a few hours."

"All right. And Marc?"

"Uh?"

"Those few hours....I suggest you spend them praying."

*   *   *   *

Through the open window came the scent of grass freshly mowed. From beneath a wrinkled brow, Marc Bradberry glared out the window without seeing the wide manicured lawn.

What a week it had been. Clare now in her sixth day of coma. Countless updates that stated there had been no change in her condition. No clues to point to the person or persons responsible. Interviews with detectives. Drowning in condolences. Ringing phones driving him from the house to hide for hours behind the lawn mower's growling engine.

Naturally, he did not follow through with the telephone call to his attorney. Now it would be unthinkable to tell anyone of his divorce plans. He grieved as any caring man would for his estranged wife's injuries. But his feelings for her had not changed.

Why then, if he did not love her, was it now so damn difficult to shed the outward evidence of his marriage? He had, after all, been working up to this moment for weeks. As he grabbed the hem of his sweat-soaked shirt and yanked it over his head, the sight of the gold ring on his finger deepened his frown. The discarded tee shirt landed wrong side out on a chair.

Barechested, ignoring a sudden chill, he crossed the room to the dresser and stared for long moments at the raised lid of a small ebony box. Deliberately, he began to remove the gold band. The finger, moist and swollen from exertion, did not freely give up its possession of nine years, but after a few tugs and twists, the ring fell gleaming into the palm of Marc's hand. His blank stare went to the engraved letters circling the inside of the band. MJB ♥ ♥ CDH. A joining of dreams; a wedding of two hearts. But in the years following, sharp tongues and hurtful deeds killed the dreams and broke the hearts.

Marc's eyes were dry as he dropped the ring into the waiting box. With a turn of his wrist, the lid dropped closed.

CHAPTER 2

▼

Traffic was congested, much heavier than she had expected. Idling at yet another in an endless string of red lights, the car smelled of exhaust fumes. Only tepid air blew from the car's air conditioner; Korey rotated the vent to blow on her face. In Chattanooga, spring had pounced on the city with hot sticky paws, and Korey, or more correctly her car, had been caught unprepared. Great, she thought. Last week my dishwasher, now the air conditioner. She made a mental note, as she drove under the green traffic light, to make an appointment with the repair garage.

The clock on the dashboard said she was ten minutes late in meeting Tina and Bryan as she pulled into a space in the small parking lot at John Wexler's law office. Among a few others, Tina's car sat two spaces away. Korey disliked being late, even though the time for their meeting was, in her sister's words, "sixish." After a glance in the rearview mirror prompted Korey to dash her fingers through her thick brown curls, she slid from the car. A swipe at the lap of her fawn colored slacks did nothing to smooth the wrinkles set there by heat and humidity. She opened the rear car door to retrieve the completed wall hanging. Leaning into the rear seat, her low-heeled shoes flat on the pavement, she did not hear or see the tall stranger emerge from the office building and walk to his car.

As the man paused, keys in hand, Korey unwittingly presented him a sight to admire. He observed that the possessor of the wiggling, shapely derriere seemed to be struggling with something in the back seat of her car. Priding himself on being a gentleman, his instinct was to offer his assistance. On further reflection, however, as he took one additional moment to savor the unobstructed view, he decided in this day of feminist independence, being himself singed more than once by a scowl when he had held open a door for one of the fairer sex, he decided to pass on this opportunity.

He did not, as he drove from the law offices, feel a burning in his ears, and therefore would have been startled to learn that he was at the moment the subject of conversation in the reception room of the building he had left behind.

"His wife was attacked in Nashville last week," the receptionist was saying in a low voice. Tina and Bryan Goodwin stood beside the woman at the uncluttered desk in the thickly carpeted waiting room. "He came by just as Mr. Wexler was leaving the office for the day. That's why we're running late. Apparently he and Mr. Wexler have been friends since college. The wife is in a coma," she finished in a whisper as, from his office, John Wexler stuck his head into the room.

"Melissa." John looked to the receptionist. "I'm on my way home. When Korey arrives with the quilt, make sure she gets the check I'm leaving for her on my desk. Goodnight," he said to the room at large as the leaded glass door closed behind him. Through the beveled glass, his shape sinuously floated down the side steps then vanished.

Melissa answered the ringing phone on her desk. With Melissa's attention diverted, Tina said to her husband, sotto voce, "I wonder if John Wexler knows his newly hired receptionist is a gossip."

"Most likely not," Bryan said into her ear, "or she wouldn't still be here. She must be talking about the fellow who was leaving by the rear door as we came in the front. Only got a glimpse of his back. Surely no one we know and...."

The opening of the front door interrupted Bryan's thought, and he relieved his arriving sister-in-law of the weight of the quilt rolled over her arm. As though sprayed from an atomizer, the sweet smell of lilacs blooming near the door followed Korey into the room. The comfortably controlled climate in the office revived her as she closed the door to the heat and street noise.

"Sorry I'm late," Korey said in greeting, waving to Melissa who appeared in no hurry to disengage from her phone conversation.

"We just got here ourselves," Bryan said. "My last class went a few minutes over, then I was cornered in my office by a grad student who chose today of all days to seek my advice." He winked at his wife. "My car is in the shop so I had to hitch a ride with some gorgeous dame I found waiting in the university parking lot."

Tina laughed. "Gorgeous, huh?" Her brown eyes twinkled. "Say there, handsome, that silver tongue of yours just bought you a ride home."

"Okay, you two." Korey grinned. "It's time reality intruded on this mutual admiration society." She stepped toward John's private office. "Let's get to work."

Minutes later, an expertly stitched abstract design splashed bold colors across a section of dark wall in John's wood paneled office. From a slender ribbon at the lower right corner of the quilt hung a sterling silver medallion. The size of a silver dollar, the medallion's scalloped edges gleamed in the room's artificial light. The initials KRW were engraved on the domed center. Korey fingered her initials then wiped the medallion clean of prints.

Tina stood across the room to appraise the work. "It looks great," she boasted. "Your best one yet."

"Thanks." Korey smiled modestly. "Seems each new project is more ambitious than the one before. But I love what I'm doing. When it ceases to be fun, I'll have to find something else." She watched as Bryan folded a stepladder and began packing screwdrivers, an electric drill and other assorted tools into a toolbox. "Say," she said as if reminded of something, "speaking of having a car in the shop, the air conditioning in my car is on the fritz. If I should have to leave the car for repairs, Tina, could you pick me up at the dealership one day next week?"

"Be happy to. I can swing by and get you any morning before I go to work." Tina's mouth took on a sly curve. "The dealership on Brainerd Road?" In answer to her sister's nod, Tina went on, "Stopping in to see Randy, are you?" For a moment Tina received only a blank stare as a response.

"Randy?" Korey hesitated. "Oh, the service manager at the dealership."

"Yeah, the cute one."

"Very funny, Tina. You know how many times I've turned down his offer for a date. Hopefully he's justifiably discouraged. Besides, I haven't seen him in ages. Surely by now he has a steady girl, is married, or is otherwise diverted. Nothing against Randy. He seems like a nice guy, just not my type."

"Seems nobody's your type."

"Tina, let's not go over this again."

"It's just that I don't like to see you snuggle even tighter into that cocoon, close yourself off from men."

"I'm not 'closing myself off.'" The retort was unintentionally sharp. "I see Rob every now and then. Only last week we went out for dinner and a movie."

"Danny's brother does not count. You and I both know you don't have any interest in Rob."

"Not true. I adore Rob. He's been the dearest friend through….everything. And, as you have heard countless times before, I no longer have an interest in forming anything beyond a friendship with a male of the species. Just thinking of the pain of loving and losing makes my heart seize."

The sisters found themselves alone in the room. As though he had stepped out of range of a camera's eye, Bryan, weighted with tools, had stealthily departed. Taking Korey's cool fingers in her own, Tina said, "I understand. And every time I open my big mouth on the subject of you and men and cocoons, I want to slap myself silly. But I worry...."

"Don't," Korey said gently. "I'm going to be okay. I still have some bad days sprinkled among the good, but not nearly so many now. It sounds so trite, and when Danny died I didn't believe a word of what I was told, but time truly is the great healer. All I need," she beseeched softly, as if in prayer, "is a little more time."

✳   ✳   ✳   ✳

Korey pulled the wet terry cloth headband over her damp curls as she came in the back door. Even though the trail near her home was wooded, the canopy of new leaves did little to shield a walker from the unseasonably warm days that had pressed upon Chattanooga. Though much of her time was spent scouring quilting shops for unique fabrics, still, stitching quilted wall hangings was a sedentary occupation, and Korey diligently squeezed a ninety-minute walk into her busy schedule at least five days out of the typical week. This day was no exception. Yet at the end of the walk, the heat and humidity had taken the depth from her customary aggressive stride.

Traveling the hallway to the bathroom, she wriggled out of damp shorts and tank top. While on her walk, memories from another life had accompanied her and now continued to flow through her mind as lukewarm water from the shower head washed perspiration and fatigue from her sleek limbs. She had days like this, days when Danny was again with her from sunup to sundown. A year ago she had sold the large house they had shared, bought a smaller one, thinking she would not see him in every room. But he had followed her, of course, even though this house did not contain his razor or comb, his books, or those ridiculous pointy ears he had worn to a Star Trek party. The piano.

He had never learned to read a note of music but by ear had entertained her for hours at the piano. Anything she requested he seemed able to play, and she had been in awe because she could not peck out so much as Chopsticks.

The piano had doubled as a photo gallery: graduation from university, Danny and Korey in cap and gown on a campus park bench, Danny sideways in her lap, waving his mortar board, tassels blurred on the film. Honeymoon in Aruba, Danny barefoot on the beach, his pant legs rolled to just below the knee, a shell to his ear, laughing at the camera as an invisible wind held onto his sun-streaked hair at the crown. Others, pictures that now her mind could no longer see.

The piano had been the first thing to go. She sold it to a family in the old neighborhood before she had even thrown out his toothbrush. She had wondered at the time if the sale was an impulsive act she would later regret. She had not.

So she had come here to this house she could call "mine," not "ours." Bryan had driven the rented moving truck down the tree-lined street; he, Tina, and Danny's mother, Evie, and brother, Rob, had generously devoted a Saturday to the relocation of Korey Reynolds Westerfield.

The three bedroom house was not new. It had belonged for ten years to a retired couple who chose to give up the changing seasons in Chattanooga for perpetual summer on Sanibel Island, Florida. They left behind a white-trimmed yellow house, freshly painted, located on a half acre planted with gardenias to sweeten the early days of summer; a stand of hickory trees and a large oak undergrown with wildflowers; dogwood trees and azalea bushes to brilliantly herald the end of winter; and, set in an island of emerald lawn, a bed of twelve of the most beautiful rose bushes Korey had ever seen.

Korey chose the bedroom with the best view of the rose garden as her studio. There Rob had built a cutting table and lined two walls with cabinets to store fabrics and quilting supplies. With the addition of a small desk and a loveseat, the room was cozy, not cramped.

Over the past year the house had become a home. A hand stitched quilt, an impressionistic interpretation of flowers in riotous bloom, filled a wall in the living room. Fabrics in broad strokes of peach and leaf-green in Korey's bedroom and adjoining bath spoke further of her love of color.

Inside the house, Korey learned to repair what was broken, paint what was chipped. Outside, she pruned and weeded, watered and fertilized. She erected birdhouses, poured seed into feeders and water into shallow birdbaths. The animals rewarded her for her labors. Each season brought her visitors: rabbits and squirrels, an occasional raccoon, robins by the dozens, bluebirds, cardinals and woodpeckers.

All of this Korey now thought about while soapy water flowed down the shower drain. When Danny died, she had wanted to die too. But nothing remains the same, and though the velvet was gone from life, still, life *was*, on occasion, beginning to peer with a cheery face from behind the dark clouds.

Over the lull of running water, the distant sound of a ringing phone intruded on her musings. She let the water run, knowing the machine would answer before she could dry herself enough to dash for the phone. She massaged shampoo through her heavy dark curls, rinsed until her hair squeaked as she pulled it through her fingers.

Minutes later, wrapped in a cotton robe, her curling hair finger-styled and air drying, Korey played the message on her telephone answering machine: "Ms. Westerfield, this is Marc Bradberry in Nashville. I'm a friend of John Wexler's. I've had occasion to admire the quilted wall hanging you recently made for John's office. In a matter of months, I'll be opening a satellite architectural office in Chattanooga and may have need of someone with your talent. If you're interested in the possibility of stitching a quilt for my office, please call me at 615-555-1979. Thank you."

Korey shed her bathrobe and stepped into a pair of baggy green shorts. She rewound the machine and played the message for a second time as she pulled on a T-shirt—one of several of her husband's shirts she had saved, a relic left over from his college days that now tagged her, in bold red letters across her chest, as a PARTY ANIMAL.

The phone message intrigued her for two reasons. One, because the quilt had hung in John Wexler's office for less than a week—so little time for someone to see it and possibly want to commission one of his own. And two, though she was disinclined to admit this, she was inexplicably drawn to the voice on the machine. The articulate voice had depth, a richness not often heard; a commanding voice, yet personable, sincere. Korey's mind could not hear the voice without conjuring the companion face. Indistinct though that face was, it was enough to stir the imagination of the listener. As she wrote the name, Marc Bradberry, and a phone number on a notepad next to the phone, her mind drew a whimsical sketch of the caller. A face, deeply tanned, turned to her. Under light brows, deep-set blue eyes stared at her from inside her head; a roguish smile, set in a square jaw, brought a reciprocal smile to her lips. A sheet of white note paper fluttering to the floor snapped Korey from her fantasy. She picked up the note she had just written. How ridiculous, she chided as she wriggled her feet into canvas sneakers. A man leaves a message, strictly business, on an answering machine and a demented woman tries to make him out as some sort of Greek god. Girlish foolishness! Maybe Tina was right to encourage her to get out more often, to go places where there would be men. Shaking her head, Korey marched, shoelaces dangling, to her studio where she pinned Marc Bradberry's name and phone number to a bulletin board. This return call, she told herself as she grabbed a pair of scissors and began carefully snipping around patterns already laid out on the cutting table, is one that will have to wait until tomorrow.

*   *   *   *

Korey phoned the Nashville number. "This is Korey Westerfield returning Mr. Bradberry's call," she said to the pleasant female voice on the other end. "Is Mr. Bradberry in, please?" She was asked to hold one moment. The moment stretched to several, and Korey began to fidget in the chair at her desk. Turning a faceted crystal paperweight in a ray of sun, she painted prisms on the wall. Using a pen, she drew circles on a notepad. She tapped the nib of the pen on the desk, nervously, as if the man she awaited would somehow hear in her voice that, the day before, he had been worshipped in a daydream.

"Marc Bradberry."

At the sound of the familiar voice, the pen ceased its chattering. "Mr. Bradberry, this is Korey Westerfield. You left a message on my answering machine regarding…."

"Oh, yes, Ms. Westerfield. The wall hanging. Exceptional work you did for John."

"Thank you, I…."

"Sorry, Ms. Westerfield, I'm in the car, and I believe I'm about to lose the signal. Would it be convenient for you to meet me in Chattanooga next Tuesday? I would very much like to talk to you about a project."

Korey flipped a page in a desk calendar. "I have an opening at two o'clock."

"Two is fine. We'll meet at my new office. It's a little out of the way so let me give you directions."

Korey's pen flew as Marc spoke.

"Did you get it all?" he asked.

"Yes," she said, but she had doubts as she glanced at the inky scrawl on the paper. "I'll be there next Tuesday, Mr. Bradberry."

"Great. See you then. Oh, and Ms. Westerfield, the formality of 'Mr. Bradberry' has me feeling older than my years. Please call me Marc."

"Marc it is then," she said. Before she could extend to him the same invitation, he said something else, but the voice was garbled and after a pause, Korey hung up the phone.

Staring into space, she swiveled back and forth in the desk chair, disturbed by an unrest within her that she could neither identify nor explain.

CHAPTER 3

▼

Just outside the hustle of city traffic, Korey drove in solitude on a two-lane highway, glancing yet again at the directions Marc Bradberry had given her. It seemed she had traveled far enough to spot the red mailbox that would mark her turn. From the cool comfort of her newly repaired air conditioning, she peered along the road and saw, through heat shimmering on the pavement, the mailbox, its rotting post leaning too close to the road. A few yards before reaching the mailbox, she saw a small wooden sign at the entrance to a narrow lane:

Bradberry Associates, Inc.
Marcus J. Bradberry AIA

Korey made a turn onto the paved lane. In places trees grew so close to the winding road, she wondered if two cars could pass. Honeysuckle, in sweet bloom, choked low-growing bushes. A curve to the left, then one to the right, and she was pleasantly surprised to see before her a small covered bridge. Wide enough for only one car, it spanned a narrow stream. Wide boards, some no longer whole, had not seen a coat of paint in years, if ever. She cautiously eased nearer but hesitated to trust the weight of her car to a bridge so obviously in disrepair. Having driven at least a quarter mile on this narrow road, and with nothing in sight beyond the bridge, she wondered if she had somehow miswritten Marc Bradberry's directions and had made a wrong turn. Strange that he had not mentioned the bridge. She inched the car forward, lowered a window, leaned out to look into the stream. Thanks to one of the hottest and driest springs on record, little water trickled under the bridge. She decided to take a chance. Surely, she told herself, an architect, of all people, would not invite others to cross an unsafe bridge! Removing her foot from the brake pedal, her hands crushing the steering wheel, Korey let the car roll slowly down a shallow incline. Thick deck planks rattled, setting Korey's teeth on edge as the car rolled through the shade of the bridge. Emerging safely into sunshine, she looked in the rearview mirror, half expecting to see the gray structure collapse behind her. When the bridge did not even sway, she smiled.

Navigating a final bend in the road, Korey came upon a two-story brick house. Like bees around a hive, workers swarmed over the house. Vehicles of every description were parked helter-skelter on ground that at one time may have been a lawn. Her car dropped off of pavement as she drove through ruts to park in a shaded spot under an ancient oak. A cacophony greeted her when she turned off the car's engine, the noise escalating several decibels when she opened the car door. With purse and portfolio in hand, Korey started toward the house. Strips of untended grass brushed clinging dust onto her navy blue shoes.

An unfamiliar country song blared from a radio, its rhythm beating to sharp cracks from a hammer. Whining teeth of an electric saw chewed through boards and spit out dust. Voices yelled above the din.

Utility vans broadcast their purpose from signs painted along their sides. Hicks Plumbing and Heating; Home Interiors Lighting Co. Korey recognized the name on the truck parked nearest the house: Carson's Glass. She and Jimmy Carson had been friends in high school. Since graduation she had run into him occasionally. Last she heard, Jimmy had joined his dad's business and married a girl from Murfreesboro.

Korey climbed the trio of steps to a verandah that ran the breadth and depth of the house. She stomped dust from her shoes on a section of new board set into the unpainted floor of the porch. Wide double doors, their wood sealed with only a thin coat of white primer, stood partially open. Korey saw no one as she peeked into a spacious foyer. Stepping inside, she noticed immediately that the noise, however loud, was diminished. The country tune on the radio dropped to no more than a steady beat in the distance.

This day was the same as so many others of late, hot and sticky, and the foyer was even warmer for lack of a breeze. Stuffy air hung ripe with odors—wood, paint, and others Korey did not care to identify. Seams in the walls of the foyer and adjoining hallway were freshly taped and sealed, the drywall mud still wet. Hardwood floor, sanded but not yet refinished, met wide molding at the base of walls then hid beneath the paint-spattered canvas runner on which Korey stood. A steep staircase, newels and banister also stripped of the original varnish, hugged the right side of the foyer and disappeared into the second story.

To Korey's left, in a room the size of a small parlor, two men with beefy arms and strong backs were holding a large mullion window. Reluctant to distract them as they eased the heavy glass into a window frame, Korey turned back to the foyer, hoping the hallway would lead her to someone who could direct her to Marc Bradberry.

"Ms. Westerfield?"

She turned at the sound of his voice. As he stood on the bottom step, a friendly smile on his face, she was struck by the fact that he did not look at all like the man she had imagined. His dark hair brushed the header of the stairwell as he stepped down and came forward to extend his hand.

"Marc," she said. Faced with an unexpected shyness, she did not retreat but met his firm handshake.

"So glad you found us," he said, looking into her dark eyes. "The sign on the main road is easily missed. It's only temporary, but will have to do until the danger of a truck knocking it flat is passed." He grinned. "That's sign number three out there now."

Her right cheek dimpled when she returned his smile. "I had no trouble. Your directions were very exact. However, I admit to doubts about following them correctly when I saw all the construction. You had not mentioned the remodeling."

"More like reconstruction, I'm afraid. Sorry about the mess. Most of those here today were supposed to be here the end of last week." Marc leaned closer as if sharing a confidence. "Frankly, with this warm weather we've been having, it's difficult keeping these guys away from their fishing poles."

For a moment, Korey and Marc stood in a foyer lit only by daylight, smiling into each others faces, sawdust suspended in the air around them. At last Korey said, "I may be wrong, but fishing seems to be the Tennessee state past time."

Marc nodded in agreement. "I envy those who have time to sit in a boat or on the riverbank all day. Some of us don't have that luxury. At any rate, wouldn't you know, everyone would show up the same day I scheduled to meet with you. I thought to change our appointment, but I haven't another day free for several weeks. I hope you don't mind if we try to make the best of it amidst the dust and noise."

And heat, Korey said to herself. Already her skin was damp where her skirt cinched it in a wide waistband. "Not at all," she said while wondering how she and Marc Bradberry could possibly conduct business with so much commotion around them.

Marc stepped around her and pointed down the hallway. "There's a small room." He paused. "Well, to be honest, it's more of a cubicle. I'm using it as a makeshift office until my private office upstairs is completed. It's probably the only place where we have a chance of being undisturbed."

She followed him down the hall where he stopped midway to the back of the house. His spicy aftershave pleasantly replaced all other smells. With a gesture of his hand, he invited her to precede him into the tiny windowless room. Two upholstered chairs, the brown fabric nearly threadbare, sat opposite a tan metal desk. Korey placed her purse and portfolio in one chair and prepared to sit in the other. Before the seat of her skirt had even brushed the chair, a telephone, perched on a leaning stack of papers on the desk, jangled close to her ear. She sat to soothe her startled nerves as Marc answered the phone.

As she half listened to Marc's conversation, Korey felt like an eavesdropper, but the cramped room offered little diversion. The walls, like the others she had seen, were unpainted drywall. Two rolls of blueprints leaned in one corner of the room. A metal file cabinet, tan but not quite matching the desk, stood in another corner. A small oscillating fan hummed atop the cabinet, flipping papers on the desk with each swing of its vibrating head. The only object of color in the room, apart from her own floral skirt and fuchsia blouse, was a bright red mug on the desk, resting in a ring of what Korey assumed to be cold coffee.

The room was so compact, Marc could, while talking into the phone, easily reach the door to close it. This he now did, shutting out much of the noise, then flopped into a chair at the desk. Dressed in a pale yellow knit shirt and khaki pants, he seemed to fade into the neutral background as he searched for something in a drawer. With the door closed, the tiny room quickly became stifling, an atmosphere Korey likened to that of a hothouse. She stared at her hands folded in her lap. Finally looking up, she found herself gazing, in the white light of overhead fluorescent tubes, into the greenest eyes she had ever seen. Absently watching her while he continued his conversation, Marc's expressive green eyes held her spellbound.

Before Korey realized he was no longer talking into the phone, he had said, "I apologize for the interruption, Ms. Westerfield, but my secretary in Nashville patched it through."

Disconcerted, she said the first thing that came to her mind. "Korey."

"Pardon?"

"Please, call me Korey."

He smiled as if he were pleased. "Korey it is, then." He leaned forward. "This room is slated to become a storage closet, hence its dimensions. Right now, it's the only room in the place with a door, so I come in here to get away from the noise. The furnishings are nothing beyond serviceable, I'm sorry to say, but I learned long ago that it shows poor sense to place nice things in a construction site. Now then," he said, resting his forearms on the desk, "let's go to the reason you're here. When the remodeling is complete, we will have a large drafting room running the full width of the house at the back. I planned to show you the room today, but the drywallers have scaffolding set up in there and it's a mess. The north wall of the room will be windows to take advantage of the natural light. The ceiling is high, so I would like a large hanging on the south wall to absorb any echoes in the room."

Korey reached for the portfolio filled with photographs of her completed works. "I can show you examples of some of the things I've done."

"No need," Marc said. "I know quality when I see it." He could not say all he was thinking—that he was not drawn only to her talent. He was, in addition, ambushed by her beauty. After the slightest pause, he said, "The quilt in John Wexler's office is enough to sell me on your work."

Korey was taken back by Marc Bradberry's decisiveness. Wasn't the man interested in what this was going to cost? "Mr. Brad...uh, Marc, I can't give you a price just yet. I'll have to know the dimensions, what design you have in mind, things like that."

"I'm leaving that all up to you. I'll give you the size of the wall, tell you the wall will be oyster white, and you can take it from there." He saw that she was not as pleased as he had anticipated. "Is there a problem?"

"No, it's not often a client allows me this much freedom. It's just....I do have other work; a project the scale you want, well, I won't be able to deliver for at least six months." The walls seemed to move closer together as the room grew ever warmer. Korey eagerly awaited the next sweep of the electric fan as a bead of sweat trickled between her breasts. She saw that Marc seemed to be faring better; his shirt was perfectly dry; only his forehead glistened with moisture. She assumed he had become acclimated to working inside this oven.

He waved off her reference to time. "Six months will be fine. This office won't be open until late summer, anyway. My clients don't expect instant results from me, and I certainly don't expect that from you." He wondered himself what he meant, exactly, when he added, "Anything worthwhile takes time."

"I'll make some sketches...." Another ring of the phone cut her off.

Marc apologized to her before answering. Great, he told himself. Bad enough that the day had turned into another scorcher. But he was certain the last thing Korey Westerfield had planned for her afternoon was to be made to sit in this hot box and listen to him yammer on the phone. As if she were reading his mind, he saw her glance at her watch. Determined not to become even more of a jerk in her eyes, he said into the phone, "Say, Pete, someone is with me in the office. Could I call you back? Good. Yeah, four-thirty will be fine. Okay." He hung up, jotted a note on yellow lined paper. It was when he looked up to see her brushing a damp curl away from her face that he noticed the ring for the first time. At the sight of the wide, diamond-encrusted band on her ring finger, something tugged inside his chest. Why, he wondered, had he not seen the ring before? And what was it that he felt at seeing it now? He did not take the time to try to define it. "Listen, Korey," he said as he stood and opened the door, "it's too hot in here to conduct business, and the phone seems to stubbornly have a mind of its own. Why don't you put together some ideas, and we'll make final arrangements some other time?"

The new commission was no longer foremost on her mind, being released from this torture chamber was, and had she known him better, she would have hugged him for his good sense as she whirled into the hallway, purse and unopened portfolio in hand. A breeze coming in the front door touched her everywhere and, though warm, felt cool on her moist skin. "Mind answering a question?" she asked of Marc as they walked slowly down the hall.

"Not at all."

"How did you ever find this place?"

He grinned down at her as they paused on the wide verandah. "It wasn't easy. At least that's what the Realtor kept telling me. I had a good idea of what I wanted, described it to Joe—and waited. It took him two months to locate this house. It wasn't actively on the market at the time but had been, off and on, for several years. Fortunately, someone in Joe's office had shown it some time ago and remembered where it was. The couple who owned it died, leaving no children. A niece in Washington State inherited the property and was apparently in no hurry to sell. No one here seems to remember the niece ever coming to see the place. She was not the easiest person to deal with, wanted much more than the house was worth. After much haggling, she was rid of a liability, and I was the new owner of fifteen acres, a small lake, and a pile of bricks with potential." He laughed. "The covered bridge was free."

Korey had forgotten about the bridge. "Oh, yes, the bridge."

"Admittedly, it doesn't look like much now, but when it's fixed up and painted to match the house…. Actually, that's what sold me on the place. I couldn't resist the bridge."

"It is….quaint."

Dark brows rose over the green eyes. "But?" he asked, though he knew what was coming.

"Well, I was a little nervous while venturing across," she admitted.

"Makes two of us. The first time Joe brought me out here, I had my own reservations about crossing that bridge. After some heavy rains, the creek was nearly overflowing the bank. Believe me, the temptation was strong to leave the car and walk the rest of the way to the house. But—call it a macho thing—instead of letting on to Joe that I was nervous, I just closed my eyes as he drove across. In retrospect, it was foolhardy to take such a chance. The bridge was not in good shape. We've since shored up the floor and done some truss work to secure the roof."

"Thanks for telling me. Now I'll be more comfortable leaving." Behind her a van door slid shut, then footsteps sounded on the porch. A workman, face red from exertion, sidestepped Marc on the way to the front door. Korey glanced at the man, then did a double take. "Jimmy?"

He stopped in the doorway, his look of surprise dissolving into a broad grin. "Hey, Korey. Long time no see. Didn't recognize you."

Korey put a hand on her hip. She teased, "Why Jimmy Carson, I haven't aged *that* much!"

With the back of his hand, Jimmy wiped a stream of sweat from his cheek, wiped his hand on a pants leg. "You haven't aged at all. Just gotten prettier." He winked at Marc. "Used to have a terrible crush on this gal in tenth grade, Marc. Thought she was the cutest thing under the sun."

"Yeah," Korey giggled, "until Sue Ellen Caitlaw moved to town and had a locker next to yours. You never looked at me after that."

"Did too."

"Did not." As she looked at Jimmy she was glad that he had not. His sweat-soaked shirt stretched over what looked to be a good start on a beer belly. His light hair, usually longer, was buzzed to a flattop and only accentuated his worst feature—his ears. With no hair to cover them, the ears flared out at the top, like raised flaps on an airplane wing.

"What are you doing out here, anyway?" Jimmy asked.

"I'm going to make a quilt for the drafting room of this office. I take it you're doing the glass work."

Jimmy nodded. "The whole house. Big job." He looked again at Marc, who was now leaning on the porch railing, hands shoved in the pockets of his khakis. "I'd better not dally too long," Jimmy grinned, "the boss is watching."

Indeed he was. Though, between the annoying phone calls, there had not been much opportunity for conversation between him and Korey while they were in the house, Marc had noticed that Korey was….not shy exactly, but quiet.

Watching her talk to Jimmy, Marc was seeing a woman not only beautiful and talented, but one with a sense of humor as well. The more he saw, the more he liked, and the more he liked, the more he tried to stuff those feelings.

"You probably haven't heard," Jimmy said to Korey, "I'm going to be a dad in four months. How about that?"

Marc did not miss the wistful longing in Korey's voice as she said, "Gosh, Jimmy, that's wonderful!"

"Yeah, we're pretty excited. One more thing—how's Rob doing? Haven't played poker with him in over a year."

Rob. A name to go with the wedding ring. Marc did not know why this should bother him, but it did. What the hell was going on with him anyway? What had he been hoping for—that Korey was single and she only wore that knockout ring to keep the wolves from circling? Bah.

"Rob's fine. He stays busy, like the rest of us."

"Tell him to call me sometime," Jimmy said as he stepped into the house. "Good seeing you, Korey."

"Call me when the baby comes."

"Sure thing."

Marc walked with Korey to where her car sat in dappled sunlight. A breeze high above stirred the leaves in the oak tree. He said, "I'm more than a little embarrassed by the way you've been treated today. You have my word there will not be this confusion the next time we meet."

"Think nothing of it." Korey took dark glasses out of her purse. "I understand what it takes to run a business, to meet deadlines. I'll come up with some themes for your quilt, make a few sketches." She opened the car door, emptied her arms of the things she was carrying. "I'll give you a call as soon as I have something to show you. Next week, perhaps."

"Take your time," Marc said as Korey fastened the seat belt, then started the engine. "As I said earlier, I'm pretty well booked for the next few weeks anyway." As he walked back to the house in a rare moment of silence—no hammers or saws, no drills—he heard her car rattle across the bridge. If he had the sense he was born with, he told himself, he would find a way for her to complete her project without him ever having to see her again.

✳   ✳   ✳   ✳

The buzz, buzz of a busy signal receded as Marc pulled the phone from his ear. One more time, he promised as he none-to-gently set the phone in the cradle. If he could not get through the next time, he was giving up. No phone conversation should last for more than two hours!

She answered in a tear-clogged voice. "Hello."

The voice was unrecognizable; he thought surely he had the wrong number. "Korey?"

"Yes."

Surprised, it took him a moment to respond. "This is Marc Bradberry." He paused again. "I hope I'm not calling too late. Your line's been busy."

"Oh dear, you were trying to get through. I was on much longer than I wanted to be. My mother-in-law was having a bad night of it so she called me. Now *I'm* having a bad night." Korey cleared her throat. She could not understand why she should be telling this to Marc, who, after all, was barely more than a stranger. Still, the dark mood brought on by Evie's phone call seemed suddenly lifted.

Wondering what it was she meant, Marc offered, "Nothing too serious, I hope."

"No, she has these spells and so do I. We console each other, get the tears out of our system, then we're fine." When there was only silence on the other end, Korey at first thought the mention of tears had been a mistake. Was Marc one of those men embarrassed by emotion? But following immediately on that thought was another: Marc Bradberry probably did not have the slightest idea what she was talking about. "You must think I'm crazy," she said through a nervous little giggle, "but you'll understand when I tell you that I'm widowed. I lost my husband, Danny, two years ago. His mother....I....well, you happened upon one of my weak moments."

Widowed. Marc's heart revved like a just-tuned engine. Burgeoning expectation collided with sincere sympathy for her loss. "I'm sorry," he said, wondering if changes might be made because of her pronouncement.

"Thank you. I didn't mean to make you uncomfortable...."

"No, no you didn't. It's just that when I last saw you, when Jimmy Carson asked about Rob, I naturally assumed...."

"Rob? Oh, you thought Rob was my husband?" Suddenly there was a quick step in Korey's voice. "His girlfriend wouldn't care much for that. Actually, Rob Westerfield is my brother-in-law. Danny's older brother."

"I see," he said. In the two weeks since he had met Korey Westerfield, he often found himself thinking of her but had convinced himself that the thoughts were harmless and only those of a lonely man filling idle moments. Like any man, he had an intrinsic eye for female beauty, but never before had he been tempted to covet another man's wife. Korey had called his Nashville office the week before and left a message that the sketches of the planned quilt were ready. His return call was a message to her answering machine. After a week of playing telephone tag, he had meant, when he called tonight, to ask her to mail him the sketches. He knew now he had opted to entrust the sketches to the U S Postal Service for more than one reason. Two busy people failing to make a connection was a situation easily overcome. If he had really wanted to see Korey, he would have found the time. He had not found the time because she had pushed a button inside him he hadn't even known existed. It had been safe enough to think of her now and then when he had thought her married. But she was not married.... Not thinking beyond what he had just learned, he was surprised to hear himself say, "I'll be in Chattanooga tomorrow. If this is not a good time, please say so, but I would like for you to join me for dinner tomorrow evening. I have meetings all day, but I have to eat sometime. Over dinner we can arrive at an agreement about the quilt." He extended this invitation knowing full well he had plans to dine with his business partner, Steven Aymes. Well, Steven would have to find someone else to dine with—or dine alone. To Korey, Marc belatedly added, "That is, if you have no other plans for dinner tomorrow."

It came to her mind to refuse. She had not been to dinner alone with a man, other than Rob, since Danny had died, and she hadn't much interest in doing so now. But what Marc proposed was a business dinner, she reminded herself, and she was in no position to jeopardize a fat commission check by refusing to meet at his convenience. For that reason, and no other, she accepted his invitation. "Dinner would be nice," she said. "As it happens," she added in a tone dictated by pride and intended, unconsciously, to misrepresent the fact that most evenings found her at home, "I have no plans."

Tonight, by impulsively inviting Korey to dine with him, Marc had begun a game a man and woman too often play. Tonight, by slanting her usual straight-forward manner, Korey had become a playing partner. Marc had set out the game token; Korey, in grasping the token, had made the first game move.

CHAPTER 4

▼

She would have willed it otherwise, but Marc Bradberry—if only in the form of a lingering memory—followed Korey into the walk-in closet. She had agreed to meet him at Raffaello's Restaurant at seven o'clock. At 5:15 she made her first foray into the closet. After ten minutes of fingering clothes, she set the task aside. Now, at 6:20, standing in only her underwear, a choice had to be made. Lifting a beige dress from the rack, she held it to her body and assessed the image in the mirror. Too bland. Next she tried red slacks, matching blouse and floral vest. Too loud. A short black skirt—too short and too tight. The ticking of a clock finally urged her to slip from a hanger a long broomstick skirt of shell pink silk and matching tunic sweater. A dab of her favorite fragrance, then she quickly dressed. Earrings of rose quartz beads brushed the neckline of the sweater as she hurried through the house to the garage.

She arrived at Raffaello's with time to spare. The anteroom was dim and refreshingly cool. Other than Korey, no diners waited. A maitre d' appeared immediately. On the drive to the restaurant, Korey had stared into the lemon-colored light of a late sun, and her eyes had not yet adjusted to her new surroundings. She strained to see the face that seemed to have separated from the dark suit that cloaked the man's stocky frame; his smile floated above a white shirt and wide red tie. "I'm to meet someone," she said to the white, disembodied smile.

"Are you perhaps Ms. Westerfield?" the maitre d' politely inquired from a throat that had inhaled too many cigarettes.

"Why—yes, I am," Korey answered in surprise.

"Mr. Bradberry has reserved a table for two. About five minutes ago he called to say that he's running late and asked that you be seated as soon as you arrived. If you will please follow me."

Korey was led through the candle-lit dining room to the only vacant table, an enviable location in a quiet corner set apart by a shoulder-high fountain where water burbled from the center of a copper iris and dripped from shiny copper leaves. The tanned face and black curly hair of the maitre d' were clearly visible now as he assisted her to her chair. Before she had even set the leather satchel containing the sketches on a neighboring chair, a waiter with a ready smile bent over the table and relit a snuffed candle. The young man presented a wine list, from which Korey ordered a glass of chardonnay.

Gazing at nearby tables, Korey shied from memories of the last time she and Danny had dined at Raffaello's. Sipping the chilled wine, she concentrated on the sounds in the room: ice pinging against glass, silver brushing china, water trickling through the fountain. She idly turned the stem of the wine glass, printing rings onto the starched white tablecloth. The sound of laughter circling the room above sweeping notes from a roving violin brought to mind how much she disliked sitting at this table alone. Impatiently, she checked her watch. She drank more wine, breathing in its buttery aroma to chase away a darkening mood. Her stomach growled when her eyes rested too long on mounds of pasta being delivered to a table of six. Candle flames danced a jig in the wake of a waitress carrying a tray dripping with desserts.

Why had she agreed to this dinner? With each minute of his absence, her impression of Marc Bradberry sunk ever lower. First, he asked her to an "office" which was nothing more than a hot, noisy, smelly construction site! Then, what nerve, inviting her to dinner and not even bothering to show up!

"Would you care for another glass of wine?" The voice startled her, and Korey was surprised to see that not a drop of wine was left in the glass. She looked again at her watch then stared indecisively at the waiter. Telling herself that since she was sitting in a restaurant she may as well eat, she ordered another glass of wine, threw all of her attention to the menu and prepared to dine alone.

"Am I glad to see you didn't give up on me."

Korey's eyes snapped from the menu to the man standing over her. He seemed very tall—and very contrite.

"I'm terribly sorry for being so late," Marc said as he took the opposite chair. "You must be starving, and very angry. It's 7:30." He noted the watch displayed prominently on her slim wrist and added, "But then, you probably already know that."

She smiled, the wine, or maybe his sudden appearance, draining her hostility. "I admit to checking the time once or twice, but I'm fine, really. I made myself comfortable, ordered a glass of wine." At that moment, the waiter set the second glass of wine before her. "Or two," Korey confessed. "You don't mind that I began without you?"

"Of course not. When I phoned Anthony with the message that I would be late, I never intended to keep you waiting so long...."

"Think no more of it. You look a little harried. Why not order a drink?"

The waiter, as if he had read Korey's lips, appeared at that moment, took an order for scotch and water and quickly returned with the drink. Marc relaxed against the padded back of the chair. "My partner, Steven Aymes, flew with me from Nashville," he said after a sip of his drink, "and we spent the afternoon hammering out details of our latest project. We were trapped into waiting for a couple of phone calls to be returned, and time just got away from me. And just as I was ready to leave to come here, Steven and I discovered we each had dinner dates, which created a problem since our transportation is a shared rental car. Since he had to pick up his date on Signal Mountain, we agreed he should have the car." Marc hesitated, smiled sheepishly. "Steven dropped me here. I was wondering, if it's not too much trouble, if I could bum a ride from you after dinner."

"Sure. Where are you staying?"

"At the new office. Although not finished by a long shot, my private quarters upstairs are complete enough that I can sleep there—a bed, electricity and hot water, what more does a man need?" Marc thought, as he said this, that the austere accommodations awaiting him would be infinitely more appealing if he had a woman like Korey to share them. He blanched as he realized the direction his mind was taking and hid behind a slow swallow of scotch. He had no right to be thinking this way, especially with Korey. She emitted no flirtatious signals, seemed uninterested or possibly even unaware, that some sort of chemistry existed between them. She wore her invisible grief for her dead husband as an amulet. And he, a married man, had no right....

"It will be no trouble," she was saying as he came from the world of his own musings. "Your new office isn't ten minutes from my home. If I take a less traveled route, I won't even have to go out of my way."

"I would appreciate the ride. I detest waiting for a cab."

"I wouldn't think of you taking a cab."

Marc smiled. "The least I can do, then, is feed you, as promised." The efficient waiter anticipated Marc's signal and in a matter of moments was heading for the kitchen with orders of eggplant parmesan and cannelloni with red sauce.

With dinner now in the hands of expert chefs, Korey, with genuine interest, asked Marc what project he was working on in Chattanooga. He told her of a luxury hotel his firm was designing, and Korey readily saw, in his animated gestures, how in love this man was with his work.

As she listened, his smiling green eyes, sheltered under heavy brows, seldom left hers. She wondered, as she studied him, how it could have been on the event of their first meeting that the terrible heat in that tiny room had so overcome her that she had taken little notice of a man so handsome. In a woman cognizant of her own vulnerability, such an oversight would have blown cautionary whistles. And though later she would know the danger of being pulled into a realm ruled by his devastating charm, she would admit now to seeing Marc only through the eyes of a woman objectively assessing a man. Facial features, as if formed from the hand of a sculptor, were exceedingly well placed. Korey liked his hair too; thick and dark, short but starting to curl—maybe a week beyond when he should have had it cut—combed back, parted on the side. Traces of silver at his temples bemused her; he did not appear to be a day over thirty. Tonight he wore a suit, and she pictured a tailor, worn yellow tape dangling as he measured broad shoulders and long legs for the custom fit. As he spoke, Marc rubbed beads of moisture from his glass with a thumb; each twist of his wrist sent, to the woman across the table, a wink from a black onyx cufflink inlaid with gold. For an evening of ominous beginning, Korey realized quite suddenly that she was now having a most wonderful time.

Marc paused, embarrassingly aware that table dialogue had dropped to only his monologue. "You should've stopped me, Korey," he said. "I'm afraid when it comes to my work, I can go on *ad infinitum*."

"I've enjoyed listening. Gestation isn't a word normally associated with the development of a building, but I feel as if I've followed you through the conception and birth of your newest project. I find it interesting."

For a moment he looked into her brown eyes. "You're not just saying that to be polite," he stated, somewhat amazed. "Still, you could've asked me to save something for another day."

Korey shifted under the brilliance of his smile. What did he mean, 'another day?' The words nudged a part of Korey that lay dormant. She had a suspicion, for the first time tonight, that he may consider this dinner something other than simply business. Her plans to thwart this designing architect were interrupted by the waiter delivering salad and hot crisp breadsticks.

Over a fork of lettuce and tomato, he surprised her by asking, "Do you have children, Korey?"

Suddenly not knowing what to do with her hands, she used them to shatter a breadstick, ignoring the crumbs that flew into her wineglass. "No, no children." She continued, though she did not understand why, "We had just begun to...."

"I shouldn't have asked."

"No, it was a perfectly natural question." The absence of a wedding band on his hand stopped her from asking the same of him.

"It's been a rough two years for you," he said frankly.

The sympathy plainly showing in his eyes startled Korey. She nodded, surprised to find the admission did not bring her close to tears. So unusual, but here was a man that understood. The discovery seemed to infuse her with new strength. He has suffered, she thought. Different circumstances than hers, no doubt, but he has suffered nonetheless. She barely noticed when the unsolicited waiter replaced her wineglass, crumbs settling to the bottom, with a fresh one.

Marc was confident he had not been wrong about Korey, that, in her own mind she was still married, that she was not living with, or even dating, a 'significant other.' But whatever it was inside him that had brought him this far had to be sure that Korey was not otherwise involved. He could not ask outright, of course, so he fished instead. "You're wise," he said, "having a man's voice on the outgoing message of your telephone answering machine. It's best not to advertise when a woman lives alone."

Too caught up in making Marc into someone with whom she may share a common denominator, Korey missed what lay beneath his observation. "It's Bryan's voice," she freely volunteered, "my sister Tina's husband." She did not say that the idea was initially Rob's, but that she could not bear to have Rob's voice on the machine. When recorded, he sounded too much like his dead brother. She twisted the wide sparkling band on her finger. "I agree," she said. "A woman does have to take precautions."

"Is that why you still wear your wedding ring?" Inwardly he cringed, instantly wanting to take back the words that hovered between him and the beautiful face that stared back at him. Something that he did not understand was happening to him. Normally tactful, a master of good timing, he knew when to speak and when to hold his tongue. Up until now, he had been one to usually land on his feet. But with Korey he was like a gangly teen whose mouth seemed to always be one step ahead of his brain, tripping from blunder to blunder. Tonight, before he had asked this stupid question, he had watched Korey slowly begin to open, as a flower unfolds one petal at a time. Now he sat and watched for the flower to close.

To his astonishment, Korey did not seem offended. As he was saying "I'm way out of line. You must think my mother never taught me a thing," Korey was saying, "I suppose that could be one reason." Korey smiled, knowing Marc regretted his words; it was a smile of absolution and Marc received it gratefully.

The waiter did not intrude on the ensuing conversation as he served plates of steaming pasta. The aroma of herbs escaped the smothering confines of melted cheese as Korey cut into the eggplant parmesan. "Actually," she said, "the ring isn't exactly what it appears. The gold band is Danny's wedding ring. After he died, I took it to a jeweler, had it sized to fit my finger and had the diamonds set in the band. The stones were mine; two from my own engagement ring and four from a ring belonging to my deceased mother. So you can see why the ring is, for sentimental reasons, one of my most precious possessions. And," she smiled, "as you pointed out, though not in these same words, the ring does have value as a sign that effectively states: *No Trespassing.*"

Marc choked back an impulse to ask, with a chuckle as if he were making a joke, if present company could be exempt from the warning.

Dinner continued, a progression of bites of delicious food and varied topics of conversation. Korey and Marc learned that they shared interests in jazz and more than a few country tunes—Marc stating with loyalty that he must remain true to his native Nashville. Theirs was a common love of the outdoors—Korey boasting, then, through Marc's laughter, demonstrating that she could duplicate more than one bird call.

Later, over coffee, they turned their attention to the quilted wall hanging. From among several possibilities, Marc chose a sketch of the covered bridge. Korey told how she had returned the day after her first visit and taken photos of the bridge from every angle to aid her in the design of the quilt. She laughed as she confessed to slipping on the mossy creek bank while taking the pictures, and, one foot in the shallow water, luckily catching herself before she and the camera were ruined. Wishing the evening to never end, Marc lost himself in the soft drawl that was her voice, in the glow of her smile, in the intense gaze of her wide brown eyes. He was, in fact, so lost that he was unaware that she had asked him if he preferred that the quilt depict the bridge as it was now, weathered, or as it would be when painted to match the office.

Though she did not suspect what avenues his wanderings had taken, it became obvious to Korey that Marc's attention had been diverted. This was not the first time she had noticed that he seemed to turn inward. And because she did not suspect that she was the reason, she was more than a little miffed at his sudden lack of interest in the subject at hand. "Maybe you would rather have more time to decide," she said evenly.

He knew then he had missed something and tried to call up, from the outer fringes of his hearing, what she had said. "Yes, let's use the new colors; I'll get you some paint samples," he said weakly, as if unsure the response suited the inquiry. He watched the long earrings brush her neck as she nodded. Such a lovely neck. He saw himself bending to it, placing a kiss on its soft curve.

Korey would not have him sit glassy eyed, thinking she was one who would tolerate his lapses in attention. Her time was, after all, as valuable as his. "Harking back to my days of teaching middle school," she said with a smile, "we had an understanding in my classroom that served to keep the boys alert."

Marc watched her over the rim of his coffee cup, his hopes dashed that his uncontrollable wanderings had gone unnoticed. "And what was that?" he asked.

"If I caught a boy with his eyes glazed over, I knew he was most likely thinking of one of two things: a) creative ways of enticing young Sally Jane into the back seat of big brother's car, or b) fabricating outrageous myths about his sexual prowess. The punishment for such thoughts while in class was a full report—to the whole class."

"And the boys actually *told* you?" Marc said in disbelief, thinking she would not get a straight answer from him if she dared now to ask what had been on *his* mind.

Turning away from a tray of sinfully tempting desserts, Korey giggled. "Of course not. But the embarrassment of being singled out in class was usually deterrent enough. My reputation preceded me, you see; I didn't have much trouble with daydreamers."

Marc accepted with good humor the thinly-veiled chastisement. "Okay, teach," he said, "lesson learned. I've too many things on my mind, it seems."

"Look, if I were you, this quilt would be at the bottom of my list of priorities. Why, you're up to your neck in construction. Now that I know what you want, you don't need to give it another thought. I'll take care of it." Making ready to leave, she gathered the sketches that she had scattered across the table for his perusal. "And," she added, helpfully, "I'll stay out of your way while doing it."

For her to stay away was not what he wanted but to object would be to invite trouble. As it was, he had already stepped beyond the bounds of good sense. Korey glanced at her watch, tactfully mentioned the late hour. Taking the well-aimed hint, Marc paid the tab and tried not to feel let down because this evening with Korey was nearly at an end.

*   *   *   *

They walked through the phosphorescence of the lighted parking lot in air rinsed clean of heat and humidity by yesterday's thunderstorm. A refreshing northerly breeze blew into their faces; Korey's silk skirt hugged her slender legs, a display not lost to Marc's sidelong glances as he walked beside her. She laughed at something he said, and for the space of an instant the urge to take her hand in his seemed as natural as breathing. He fought down the impulse, frightened by how close he had actually come to reaching for her.

The rattle of keys as she unlocked the car door brought Marc to his senses. He saw Korey safely behind the steering wheel, then, after running the seat as far back as it would go to accommodate his long legs, he settled himself into the passenger seat.

A motor hummed as Korey retracted the dew-covered glass of a moon roof. "Mother Nature's air conditioning," she said as she breathed the clean air. "After the early heat wave we've had, this is wonderful."

"Great sleeping weather," Marc said with a hidden meaning he would not acknowledge.

"Yes."

They rode in companionable silence as Korey negotiated heavy traffic and lane changes. Busy streets soon gave way to a quiet boulevard bordered in large trees. Friendly yellow light shown through windows in block after block of comfortable homes, reminding Korey that her own house waited for her, lonely and dark. Moonbeams flashed like strobe lights as the car passed under the leafy trees and cheered Korey away from her negative thoughts. She turned onto a less densely populated two-lane road.

As so often happens when two newly-acquainted people have endured long moments of silence, Marc and Korey each began speaking simultaneously: "I'm purchasing a new car so you shouldn't have to do this again," he said. "My family used to own a plant nursery out this way," she said.

They both laughed, each having heard only fragments of the other. "You first," Korey said.

"I have a car on order. Should be here in a couple of weeks. I'll leave it in Chattanooga, use it around town and to and from the airport. Ah, to be independent again."

"What kind of car?"

"A Mazda Miata."

"Hey, great choice." She glanced at the man beside her. It had been a long time since a man had occupied that seat…. "They say you can tell everything about a man by the car he drives. Let's see….Miata. Free-spirited, adventurous, politically moderate, casually elegant. Is that what the Miata says about you?"

It never left the tip of Marc Bradberry's tongue that the Miata was meant as a substitute, but not a replacement, for his beloved 1962 Austin-Healey roadster. He would, in the next months, relive this first omission again and again in his mind and wonder why he had not used the opening given him to tell Korey right then and there about the attack on his wife and the theft of his car. But the fragrance of a summer night mingled with Korey's perfume, the silver light flashing through the trees—such a night as this should not be spoiled by the telling of Clare's tragic tale. So he said, "You're describing a car commercial, but you might find a little of me in there somewhere."

"Five speed, 4-in-line engine?"

The sensible question about the mechanics of the car threw him off balance. He had never known a woman who had an interest beyond the prestigious label emblazoned on a car's trunk lid. He nodded.

"What color? Red, I hope," Korey said, her eyes sweeping the road ahead for familiar signs. As difficult as it was to find the turnoff to Marc's office in daylight, it would be much harder to find at night. The light of the nearly-full moon helped. "Red is the only color for a Miata."

He chuckled. "It is indeed red. Lucky for me. I don't think dealerships let you exchange cars because the color's wrong, like you would a shirt or a pair of pants."

She turned to him a face illuminated in the glow of the dash lights. Her grin was one that would be given friend to friend. The breeze ruffled her dark curls, and once again Marc's wayward mind implored him to reach out, touch her hair, but his hand instead loosened the knot in his necktie. It was reckless, insane even, to think of becoming emotionally involved with this woman. Yet, he wanted the pleasure of seeing his own image reflected in the light of her dark eyes, of hearing her sweet laughter, of one day holding her. He found himself drawn to Korey, as a parched man would be to clear, flowing water.

He said, "What was it you were going to tell me, something about your grandparents?"

"Nothing important, really. They at one time had a nursery a couple of miles east of here. As a child, I loved helping in the greenhouses. It was the only place I could get as muddy as I wanted without anyone fussing. Even now I love digging in the soil, getting dirt under my fingernails." She glanced away from the head-lights of an oncoming car. "For me it's....therapy."

"My driveway is ahead," Marc pointed. "Just beyond that NO PASSING sign."

Turning onto the lane leading to Marc's office, Korey flicked the headlights to high beam. Vegetation fed by recent rains brushed against the side of the car. Korey thought it possible to become drunk on the honeysuckle and mimosa that sweetened the cool night air. Ahead, white mist swirled like ghosts over the swiftly running creek. The passage through the covered bridge gaped, a black toothless mouth ready to devour all who entered. Korey eased the car through the bridge.

"Still don't trust my bridge, huh?"

His smile was proof that he did not take umbrage in her lack of faith. "I guess it's those clattering planks."

She avoided looking at him when he said, "You'll get used to them." Uncom-fortable in the ensuing silence, she wondered just how many trips over the bridge he expected her to make.

With the headlights now illuminating the house, Marc took these last few quiet moments to think things through. He was not a man without scruples. In his profession he worked with conscientious fervor and was therefore rewarded with a lucrative income and a sterling reputation for producing superior results. His personal life had been less successful, but he was not a philanderer, had held to his marriage vows even when his wife had not. But now he was alone; in his own mind his marriage was ended. What would it be like to have someone like Korey? Someone soft spoken, caring. Dark hair, dark eyes, olive skin—as far removed from Clare's physical and emotional traits as was possible. What would be his feelings if Korey were a part of his life in one month, two months, three? He wanted time and opportunity to find the answers to those questions.

A rabbit sprang from a bush at the side of the road, its white tail bobbing like a yo-yo as it fled the approaching car. In the brief seconds before they reached the house, Marc turned longing eyes to Korey's lovely profile. There was a warring going on inside him; he was his own enemy. Weakened by Korey's nearness—he could brush against her arm as if by accident if he chose—he was poorly equipped for the fight.

"You have company," Korey said.

"What?"

"The rabbit." She pointed as the cotton tail disappeared into the darkness at the side of the house. "With all the racket generated around here during the day, it's a wonder any animal is brave enough to come around at night."

"It is amazing. But the nights are quiet. There've even been deer at dusk, when there's barely enough light to make them out against the stand of trees behind the house."

The car stopped at the steps to the verandah. The only light in the interior of the house seemed to come from a bare bulb somewhere in the back. Marc wondered if Korey shared his opinion that this moment of silence was awkward. At last he said, "Thanks for the ride, Korey."

"You're very welcome," she said. "Thank you for a delicious dinner."

"I'm leaving Chattanooga tomorrow morning, but I'll be in town again in another week or two. Maybe, uh, we could do this again." His desire to see Korey again so overwhelmed all else, that for now Marc was numb to the misgivings this impetuous invitation would later bring. Too late he added, "That is, to discuss the wall hanging, clear up any questions that may come to you."

Surprise was unmistakable in her voice as Korey said, hesitantly, "I don't know....with all the work I have lined up...."

"Tell you what," he persisted, "I'll call you when I get back in town. We'll see then how both of our schedules look."

Keeping in mind that Marc Bradberry was a client, Korey accepted his suggestion. If he should call, she could simply tell him she had other plans. As he left the car and she waited for him to unlock the large double doors, she thought of ways she would affably discourage his future offer for dinner. But traveling the dark road home, influenced by a warmth that had everything to do with the vivid memory of his smile and the lingering scent of his aftershave, she began to doubt the harm in gazing across a cozy dinner table into the face of such an attractive man.

CHAPTER 5

▼

"What about these?" Tina Goodwin held the long earrings to her ear lobe. Hand painted melons, bananas and grapes swung from her fingertips as she peered into the jewelry counter mirror.

Korey shook her head. "I like these better." She retrieved the earrings her sister had cast aside. "Just because you're going to a Paradise Island party doesn't mean you have to go as a basket of fruit. Besides, the orchid earrings will go nicely with your sarong."

"I wish you would come with us, Korey." Tina paid for the orchid earrings. "Wendy and Jess have the greatest parties."

"Great parties for *couples*. You know how I hate being the fifth wheel."

"If that's the only thing keeping you from going, I'm sure we could find you a nice date."

The sisters merged with the crowd in the shopping mall. "No, thanks," Korey said as she slowed to look over a new display of shoes in a store window. "Anyway, I may have plans for tomorrow night."

"Oh?"

"It's nothing definite. I'm sort of on stand-by."

Tina swerved to avoid a collision with a reckless shopper then stopped, blocking Korey's path. "You're being evasive. Come on, out with it."

"Marc Bradberry said he might give me a call…."

"And you're staying home to wait for the phone to ring?"

"No. Actually his exact words were 'don't turn down any other offers, but if I can get away, I'd like to have dinner with you.' And technically, I'm not turning anything down because I wasn't planning to go to Wendy's party anyway."

"Convoluted thinking," Tina observed. "And why is it, for the past three weeks, each time you say, 'Marc Bradberry,' you say it with a smile?" She took her sister's hand. "We need to talk," she said.

Korey did not resist being led to a vacant bench under a ficus tree. Mall pedestrians passed on both sides as the sisters sat with their backs to a planter bursting with red and yellow gerbera daisies.

Looking into the depths of Korey's dark brown eyes, Tina said, "Now, is there something you want to tell me?"

Korey had known the time would come when she could no longer avoid Tina's probing gaze. She had only kept mum this long about the few evenings she had shared with Marc because Tina would receive the news of the budding relationship as something more than the friendship it was. "Okay, but before I give you the scoop, I'm asking that you not read more into it than is there."

Tina nodded, but the gleam of expectation remained in her hazel eyes.

"You'll be pleased to hear," Korey said, fingering the string on a plastic shopping bag, "that according to your wishes, I have begun to dine on occasion with someone other than the team at Channel 9 news."

"Marc?" Tina could not hold back a wide grin.

"Yes. But our times together have been casual, uneventful really. We have dinner and talk. The same things *friends* do."

"I'm happy to hear that. And now I can tell Rob that he wasn't hallucinating." Tina waited for the predictable reaction to what had seemed a nonsensical statement.

"Rob? You've lost me, Tina. I haven't seen Rob since he talked me into going with him to see that horrific disaster movie."

"Maybe you haven't seen him, but he has seen *you*."

Annoyed at having to pull the information from her sister, Korey said, "Oh, yeah? Where?"

As if this were a juicy tidbit she could not longer contain, phrases spewed from Tina in a run-on sentence. "Well, I ran into Rob at the grocery last night and he said he had seen you eating fried chicken the other night with a 'passable looking male' and he wanted to know who he was and, dumbfounded, I said you hadn't mentioned seeing anyone and asked if he could possibly be mistaken." She took a much needed breath. "He said 'no' that he had been sitting in his car at the drive-thru window and had seen you inside. He did confess to having an obstructed view, something about looking through the plastic film of one of those window display ads for extra crispy chicken, but he was certain it was you, and I said I didn't think it could have been, but," she finished emphatically, "I was certainly going to find out."

"Well." Korey hid her surprise behind a smile. "Tell Rob he was right about one thing—I was indeed eating chicken with a man. But Rob's wrong about the 'passable looking.' Marc is much more than 'passable.'"

"Hum....intriguing. And I thought your only interest in Marc Bradberry was a pay check. You're not upset, are you, that I pressed you into telling me about him?"

"Of course not. I was planning to tell you today anyway. I only kept him to myself this long because I didn't want to be teased. A woman has a male friend and before long people are jumping to the wrong conclusions."

"I'll take you at your word." Tina gave her sister a wink. "At least for now," she said.

Korey checked her watch. "Gosh, it's after four o'clock. I've got to run. Belva's closes in an hour. She called me this morning to say my fabric order is in, and I told her I would pick it up today."

"And I promised Bryan a home cooked meal tonight," Tina said as she walked with Korey to the mall exit. The smell of freshly popped corn rolled out of a movie theater and made her stomach growl. "His first in ages, poor dear. In atonement I bought a bottle of his favorite wine and a couple of thick steaks. Maybe he'll be so thrilled with the meal, he won't notice that the house hasn't been cleaned."

Korey grinned knowingly at Tina. "Hey, ply him with wine and wear that red outfit you bought last week. Take my word for it, he won't notice."

Tina laughed. "You are a schemer." She held the tall glass door open for Korey; outside air slapped them as if it were belched from the mouth of a blast furnace. "Listen, if it doesn't work out with Marc tomorrow night, please join us at the party. Wendy and Jess won't mind if you decide to pop in at the last minute. They always have enough food to feed the sixth fleet. Surely you won't be the only single woman there."

The reply was noncommittal. "We'll see," said Korey as she started off to find her car. "We'll see."

*   *   *   *

"Hey, you voted for the crook. You weren't even ashamed to admit it."

"Only," Marc interjected, holding up an index finger, "the first term."

"Well, I would never confess to being so careless." Korey's teasing smile took some of the sting from her words. "Around here Senator Peter Paulssen is known—not so affectionately—as 'In Your Pocket Paulssen.' We don't call him that for nothing, you know."

"None of the allegations have been proven." Marc wondered why he was sticking up for the s.o.b. He hated Pete Paulssen, but not so much for the reason Senator Paulssen was at this moment being grilled before his colleagues on the Senate Ethics Committee. No, Marc did not hate Senator Paulssen for being a crook; Marc hated Pete Paulssen for being, for a brief time, one of Clare's lovers.

Marc was at a loss to remember how he and Korey had come to discuss politics tonight, but now he wanted nothing more than to find another topic on which to focus. On the subject of the Senator, Korey had unwittingly fallen into murky water, and tired as he was, Marc was in no mood to wade in after her to tell about his wife and the sordid affair with Paulssen. "Korey." Marc's voice was so crisp that she searched his eyes for a spark of anger. "It's wise, I think, if we steer clear of politics for tonight. How about if we call the debate a draw?"

"I didn't mean to make you angry...."

"I'm not angry. It's just that Pete Paulssen and I used to be good friends." Why was he telling her this? "But now he's a sore point."

Slinking in her seat, Korey flushed. "Oh, my. You let me rail for thirty minutes about a friend of yours?"

"Don't worry about it." Marc drank from his coffee cup then bit into a dense piece of cheesecake.

Thus dismissed, Korey loaded her fork with blackbottom pie. She told herself that Marc was tired; he had worked at the office through dinner, on a weekend no less, but had called her to ask if he could pick her up at 9:30 for dessert and coffee. A man this overworked should be in bed, she thought sympathetically, not out smoozing with me, slurping coffee to stay awake. He seemed at a loss for words. To show him she had not been bruised by the brisk way he had cut her off, she said with a smile, "From now on, before I discuss with you the misadventures of a public figure, I promise to dig into your past before I tread too far onto someone's toes."

If his conscience had been clear, he would not have been threatened by her innocuous quip. She was only trying to neutralize a conversation turned suddenly sour. But guilt had planted its seed tonight. He had kept Clare to himself, and for that reason he could not tell Korey why the topic of Peter Paulssen was so distasteful. Clare, even in sleep, would not be ignored and peacefully serve as only a backdrop to what Marc had come to think of as his new life. To keep Korey uninformed would mean Clare would always be at the ready to rear her jeering head, as she had done tonight. Korey had to be told. But the words had to be carefully chosen; the time and place perfect. Until then…"Fair enough," he said at last. *But please*, he wanted to beg, *before we have a chance to talk, please don't dig too deep.*

*   *   *   *

Korey giggled as the legs of the slate gray slacks piled like sagging skin around Tina's shoes. "You look like a baggy elephant."

"Thanks. The people that design clothes must think we're all Amazons. Well, let's get at it."

Korey curled on the floor at her sister's feet and began folding the hem of one pants leg, measuring and pinning as she went. "So, how was the party Saturday night?" she asked around pins held in compressed lips.

"Fun. Wendy's cousin did a Tahitian dance—very provocative. The rest of us tried it—not provocative at all. Jess forgot himself and gyrated right into the pool. You really should have come. Trick Phearson was there, alone." Tina looked down at Korey.

"Stand straight or the hem will be crooked. Turn a little to the left."

"Did you hear me? I said Trick…."

"Uhm," Korey hummed through the pins. She moved to the other leg. "Trick Phearson's too old for me."

"He is not."

"He's nearly bald. Looks ridiculous when he perches his eyeglasses on top of his melon head. And his toothpick legs belong on one of those California Raisins. Turn."

"Picky, picky. Did you have dinner with Marc?"

"No."

"Korey! You stayed home Saturday night?"

"I didn't say that—turn—I said Marc and I didn't have dinner. He had to work late so we had dessert together at Crowley's. Turn….not that much."

"You still holding fast to the notion of the two of you being just friends?"

Sprawled on the floor, Korey glared up at the back of her sister's head. "Yes," she said, trying not to sound cross. She inserted the last pin, then pushed herself to her feet. "Turn around slowly." Approving the results, she watched Tina step out of the slacks and into a pair of jeans. "At least," said Korey, "I hope Marc and

I are still friends. Along with blackbottom pie Saturday night, I had plenty of room in my mouth for my foot."

"Oh, boy." Tina, with slacks and sewing box in hand, joined Korey on the sofa.

"We were talking politics." Korey paused. "I hadn't thought of this before now, but seems when I'm with Marc our conversations are always about other people or places, never anything personal." With a shake of the head the thought was gone. "Anyway, the other night we got around to discussing Peter Paulssen."

Tina squinted as she fed gray thread through the eye of a needle. "The Senator has made himself fair game, seems to me."

"Yeah, well after I yammered on and on about Paulssen being such a crook, Marc proceeds to inform me that he and the Senator had at one time been friends!"

"But no longer?" Tina looked up from her sewing. "Did Marc say what happened to the friendship?"

"No. I wanted to ask but didn't. Still, his eyes spoke volumes; there's no love lost between him and Peter Paulssen." Korey propped her socked feet on a low stool; a tiny frown marred her brow. "Later that night, I gave the evening quite a bit of thought and realized how little I really know about Marc."

"Strong, silent type, is he? Since I've yet to meet him, I have to assume what you've told me about him is accurate. Let's see, we have a guy who is nice," Tina enumerated, "modest, successful, and....oh yes, exceedingly handsome. Sound familiar?" She turned a long look to Korey. "Maybe you know him better than you think."

"Maybe."

"Oh, and one more....he's the perfect gentleman. Never made any advances."

Korey grinned. "I thought we would get around to that. Which has you most curious: has he tried, or has he made any progress?"

Tina simply smiled.

"The answer to the first part is 'no', so the second part is irrelevant."

Korey was unprepared for her sister's pointed question. "You don't think he's gay?"

"Gay?" Korey choked through bursts of laughter. "You've been standing at that cosmetic counter plastering too many facial masks on too many gay men. You think everyone is gay." Korey calmed herself. "Marc and I have a platonic relationship. We don't kiss—or fondle."

"No," Tina conceded, "I don't suppose you would."

The room was suddenly quiet; Korey dug her toes into the padded stool. Through her sister's living room window, she watched children in a neighboring yard run squealing through a water sprinkler. A dogwood tree reached out its green leaves to snag a share of hot, stingy breeze. Gripped by a strong urgency to further defend Marc, Korey said, "He's been hurt."

"A man with a past? What makes you think so?"

"I've seen signs."

With sharp scissors, Tina snipped gray thread and folded the slacks over the arm of the sofa. "What kind of signs?" she asked, giving Korey her undivided attention.

For a time, Korey was lost for an answer; observations were not always easily translated into words. "Sometimes," she began, "when he doesn't know I'm looking, I've seen sadness pass across his face like a shadow. You know as well as I that when you go through trials—first we lost Mom, then you had the miscarriage, and then….Danny—you learn to recognize pain in others, even when they wear it behind a mask. I have seen that in Marc. I've seen….uh, something else too, something I don't really care to see."

"Like what?"

Korey hid her eyes behind her hands for a self-conscious moment. "This will probably make me sound terribly vain," she said, dropping her hands, "because in all other respects he seems so in command. But at times, I would swear his eyes, as they are watching me, are," Korey actually blushed, "are smoldering."

"You have always underestimated your beauty, Korey. Surely you must know it's you who is fanning those embers?"

"I don't know that at all. You're the one men are turning to look at when they slam into sign posts and utility poles," Korey said with not a trace of envy.

"Okay, that's enough," Tina said bouncing to her feet. "I'm hungry and Bryan won't be home tonight for dinner." She took her sister's arm in an affectionate grip. "Put your shoes on. Since I am the older, wiser, and far more beautiful sister," she said giggling, "I'm going to treat you to a dinner at the eatery of your choice. But," she held up an index finger, "there is a catch. No more talking about men tonight. Only frivolous subjects—remind me to tell you about the latest letter I received from Dad." She paused, snagged by her own rule. "Okay, so anatomically, he's a man. But he doesn't count."

An evening free from talking, thinking or answering questions about Marc. Korey jumped at the offer. "You've got yourself a dinner date," she said. "And since you're buying," she puffed out her cheeks, "I'm ordering the richest dessert on the menu!"

*   *   *   *

He thought he heard the door bell ring inside the house but the music coming from within was too loud to be sure. He stepped back and leaned over the porch railing, looking in the direction of the rose garden. No one was among the bushes laden with fragrant blooms. He rang the bell again.

Korey, coming into the house through the back door, jumped as the door chime rang above her head. She went through the house and, with hands sticky from pinching spent petunia blossoms, opened the front door. Marc Bradberry, his hand resting high on the door jamb, grinned down at her from behind mirrored aviator sunglasses.

"Well, are you?" he asked.

Her perplexed stare reflected in his glasses. "Am I what?"

"A PARTY ANIMAL?" He removed his glasses; her eyes followed his to the front of her shirt.

"Oh," she laughed, tugging at the shirt hem, "I forgot I had this on. I hate to disappoint you, but I'm afraid the answer is 'no,' not lately anyway."

He eyed the shirt. It was voluminous; he could easily crawl in there with her. The mere thought sent his blood on a wild ride through his veins. "Sorry to hear it," he said absently.

"Would you like to come in?"

"I apologize for dropping by like this," he said as he glanced toward the driveway. "But I was on my way to the office from the car dealership, and….I have something to show you."

She knew then why he had come. His grin was that of a boy given a new toy. She came out onto the porch. In her driveway was the red Miata, gleaming like a sun-ripened tomato. "Marc, it's gorgeous! You just picked it up at the dealership?"

"Yep. She's only fifteen minutes old and begging to be taken for a drive. I thought maybe….that is if you could spare the time….you might go with me."

She unclasped her stained and sticky hands. "Give me a minute to clean up— I've just come in from the flower garden—and to change clothes. Come in and have some iced tea while you wait."

She smelled tangy, like petunias, as she leaned around him to close the door, and he knew then that no matter how long he lived, he would never again approach a petunia bed without thinking of her.

"The stereo is in the living room," she said over the blare of a saxophone. "Feel free to turn it off if you'd like. I'll wash up and serve the tea."

Marc located and switched off the stereo. With the music no longer playing, the house seemed eerily hushed. Water ran and ice clinked against glass. Marc ran the ear wire of his sunglasses back and forth between his fingers as his eyes scanned the living room. White walls and white-on-white furniture made the small room appear larger. A long sofa faced a picture window. Outside, like velvet spread in the sun, petunias filled the window. At the edge of the flower bed, spent blossoms were heaped in a rusty bucket. Like a person confronting a smorgasbord, a butterfly, mosaic black and gold wings aquiver, seemed unable to choose from among so many crimsons and purples. From where Marc stood in the room, brightly colored pillows scattered on the sofa and matching loveseat seemed to bring the flower garden indoors. A quilt of abstract design shouted color from one wall. Marc took note of the silver medallion hanging from a lower corner of the quilt. Without reading it, he knew Korey's initials were stamped into the silver.

He helped her when she came in from the kitchen carrying a tray, gave the sofa table a second look as he set the tray on the glass. The oval tabletop was supported by polished marble expertly sculpted into a Rubenesque nude, reposing on her side. The table lent a lusty, but incongruous air to the room. The Korey he knew just didn't seem to go with the table.

"A gift from my father-in-law," Korey said as she followed Marc's gaze. "He had it shipped to us on one of his trips to Italy. It's Carrara marble, very pricey I'm sure. It was in the bedroom suite in our....the other house. I was a bit embarrassed by it at first, but it grew on me. When I moved to this smaller house, I sold several pieces of furniture, but I couldn't seem to part with the table. My bedroom here is too small, so here it sits, in the living room." She shrugged.

"A conversation starter."

"Oh, yes." She smiled. "See how well it's working?"

Returning her smile, Marc offered her a glass of tea before stirring sugar into his own. A burst of juice momentarily clouded the tea as a wedge of squeezed lemon sank to the bottom of his glass.

Taking her tea with her, Korey backed out of the room. "Make yourself comfortable while I change clothes," she called as she hurried down the hallway.

"Thanks," he called after her, then added, "Take your time."

Downing half of the tea in one thirsty gulp, Marc wandered to the bookshelves lining a wall. His head tilted, he read the book spines. The subject of the Civil War dominated, pressed between contemporary fiction, a leather bound volume of "Ivanhoe", and some well-worn works of Shakespeare. Between pieces of Native American pottery stood several books about New Mexico. One book in particular, a pictorial guide through the state, caught his eye, but he did not bother to open it for he already knew well all of the photographs inside. A turquoise nugget, the size of a child's fist, lay among the books. Marc turned the stone in the palm of his hand.

Barefoot, carrying her sandals, Korey came silently to stand beside him. "A souvenir from New Mexico," she said. "I'm a confessed rockhound."

"I noticed some large rocks in the backyard...."

"Hauled in from hither and yon, testing the patience of all who have traveled with me. There have been occasions when rocks filled most of the space in the trunk of the car and suitcases had to be stacked in the back seat." Korey laughed. "Danny threatened once to leave me behind if I so much as picked up one more rock, even one the size of a pea. Thereafter, I behaved myself. It was a long walk home. We were in the Canadian Rockies at the time."

Marc thought he would be glad to watch her gather a boxcar load of rocks if it would make her happy. He was, dangerously, beginning to see himself as the one who would do anything to please her. He put the turquoise nugget back on the shelf. "You mentioned New Mexico," he said while wondering if he should be venturing into new territory.

"Yes. My aunt lives in Albuquerque. We used to visit her quite often, but I haven't been since....uh, it's been almost three years." Dropping her eyes, she sat to put on her shoes.

Marc ignored the obvious stumble over the subject of her husband's death. "It's a small world," he said with a smile.

"How so?" she asked, buckling a strap.

"My brother, Eric, has lived in Albuquerque for more than eight years."

She looked up, startled not merely by the coincidence but by the fact that Marc had a brother. He had never before mentioned a brother, nor any family for that matter. "How nice," was all she could think to say.

"He and his wife, Raegan—we call her Rae—are freelance photographers." His finger zeroed in on a particular book on her shelf. "One of their books, I'm proud to say."

Preoccupied with this *new* brother, she thought only to say, tepidly, "Where in the city do they live?"

"In the north valley now, but soon they will begin construction on a new home east of the city, in the foothills of the Sandia Mountains." Suspecting he understood why Korey was suddenly subdued, Marc thought it unwise to force further discussion by mentioning that he was designing the new home. He regretted even introducing Eric and Rae today. But the opportunity had seemed so right…. He said, "Well, let's be on our way. There's a blistering-red car out there just itching to show us what she can do."

*   *   *   *

Riding in the topless car, Korey did not give a thought to her wind-tangled hair. Her blue shirt, knotted at the waist, ballooned around her, saving her from roasting, as if on a spit, under the hot sun. The bottom dropped out of her stomach as the red car streaked over dips in the back road, and laughter trailed behind as she giggled like a child on a carnival ride.

Leaving Chattanooga, they had stopped at a deli and bought sandwiches and fruit for a picnic lunch before heading for Chickamauga National Military Park. Approaching the well-tended park, Marc slowed the car to the posted speed. Slipping beneath hushed oak trees, the car crept through sun-dappled light as if caught in the flickering frames of a silent movie. Civil War canon emplacements stood as memorials to the men whose blood at one time had soaked the now shaded and grass-covered ground. Low cedar fence separated woods from meadows; hiking trails crisscrossed paved roads.

Korey pointed to a lone picnic table under an old hickory tree. "Perfect," Marc said as he pulled the car near the table. A park ranger drove by and waved. "Aside from him," Marc said as he waved back, "we seem to be the only ones in the park today."

"That's why I love coming here," Korey said as she carried food to the table. "It's always so peaceful." Nearby a bobwhite called its own name and received an answer from the distance. "A fitting resting place for so many boys who died here in the war." She unwrapped the sandwiches and, after an approving nod from Marc, squeezed mustard from tiny packets onto thin slices of ham.

Marc bit hungrily into his sandwich. "I noticed," he said between bites, "several books on your bookshelf were about the war. Are you a Civil War buff?"

"Not much of one." Korey pared seeds from half an apple and set it on his paper plate. "My husband was. He had an extensive library, belonged to a group that participated in battle reenactments. I was never enthused about spending weekends playing war. Danny and I had many common interests, but that wasn't one of them. I gave most of the books to his fellow aficionados when he died, saved only the few that were signed by the author." With a napkin she intercepted a fly before it could land in her iced tea. "I'm not sure why I saved even those. You just don't know what will be important to you after….later in life."

Painful memories had come to steal some of the joy from this beautiful afternoon, and Marc was not proud of the fact that he found Danny's intrusion most unwelcome. He steered Korey's mind in another direction. "Speaking of books," he smoothly inserted, "I'm reminded, when I think of your books about New Mexico, that I rushed you out of the house before you had the chance to say more about your aunt. Tell me about her."

The faraway look disappeared from Korey's eyes. "Aunt Matty. Mom's older sister but more like a mother to us since Mom died. Matty married a man who whisked her away from Tennessee and took her to New Mexico over forty years ago. Uncle Walter died the winter before I married. He was killed when his car slid off an icy road in Tijeras Canyon. But Matty has their three children—all married, living in Arizona with families of their own. She seems to have adjusted well to life without Walter." Korey nibbled on her share of the apple. "It's interesting, isn't it, that you and I both have family in Albuquerque?"

"Yes, it is."

"Strange, though, that we didn't discover it before now." She realized how right she had been when, a few days ago, she had told Tina how Marc seemed to wear his life close to the cuff. Fingering her large hoop earring, she appeared to watch two squirrels leaping from branch to branch, but her mind was on Marc. Today he had shared with her one more morsel, another tidbit from his life. And, in fairness, she could not fault him for doling out those pieces only a little at a time. There was, after all, much in her own life story she had not told. Korey hid a smile behind another bite of apple. It seemed, she admitted to herself, as though information coming from either side was going to be hard won. But her mind stopped there; any further and she would have to admit that she and Marc seemed to have found equal pleasure in the thrill of the hunt.

After lunch they hiked one of the shorter trails. If not for the quiet as they came into a clearing, Korey could almost believe the haze that hung above a nearby hill to be smoke from a line of canons. But on the humid air came not the noise and stench of battle but a pleasing mix of damp earth, old leaves, and clover. Overhead, pushed by a gentle wind, an ethereal rainbow, like the hair of fairies, held together two gossamer clouds. Her face tilted upward, she said, "It means good luck." Squinting into a high sun, she tripped over a fat tree root.

"That's a new one," Marc said as Korey righted herself. He was thankful to be spared the necessity of reaching for her. If he were to begin seeking ways in which to touch her, even casually, it would only whet his growing appetite. "How does falling over a root bring good luck?"

"It doesn't, silly." Laughing, she pointed. "The rainbow. Quick, over there. It has already lost some of its brilliance, but if two people share it, it means good things are in store."

He thought about this. Earlier, before Korey had spotted the rainbow, he had thought of using this time to tell her about Clare. But it wasn't superstition that kept him from telling her now. This day spent with Korey would be one he would remember for its beauty; he would not say or do anything to spoil it. If Korey believed in the power of rainbows, then he only hoped when it came time to tell her about his wife, he would be hitching a ride on Korey's lucky coattails.

*   *   *   *

Marc said, as he shifted down to navigate an **S** curve on the return trip, "I'd like to show you the office now that it's finished. How about dinner tomorrow evening, then I'll give you the grand tour?"

"I have other plans." In the orange light of sunset she saw a muscle flex in his jaw. She made a snap decision. "I'm having a cookout in the backyard. Very casual—just my sister, Tina, and her husband, Bryan. Please come."

At a fork in the road he rolled the car through a yield sign and used that time to think of all the reasons he should not accept her invitation. "I don't want to impose, Korey. It's your family…."

"Exactly why I'm asking you to join us. I want you to meet Tina and Bryan." She did not think it prudent to mention how anxious Tina was to meet *him*. "Come and help me save face. My sister thinks I've become the definitive 'single woman.' Let's show her," she cajoled, "I can round up a man when I want to."

He did not want to meet Korey's family, but he hid his lack of enthusiasm behind a well-formed smile. He had tried to prepare for this day when the meter would run out of borrowed time, and he would no longer have Korey selfishly to himself. "What should I bring?" he asked of her expectant stare.

"Not a thing," she said with a pleased grin. "We're not having anything fancy, just hamburgers, potato salad, the usual backyard fare. And for dessert, home-made ice cream."

"You don't mean we men will get to display our brute strength by turning that stubborn hand crank?"

"Sorry." She shook her head laughingly. "You'll have to find some other way to show off. The only thing that cranks this freezer is electricity. But don't despair. I'm sure we ladies will be sufficiently impressed if you help Bryan lift the heavy bags of ice."

He wanted to convince himself that what he saw in her eyes was nothing more than the glow of the setting sun. It would not do for Korey to grow much closer to him. In a couple of days, he would fly back to Nashville, and the timing could not be better. Tomorrow, when he departed at the end of the evening, he would make sure Korey did not see him for awhile.

$$\ast \qquad \ast \qquad \ast \qquad \ast$$

Forty-eight hours later, jetting the short hop to Nashville, the memories of his latest evening with Korey left Marc's vow in shambles. It would take a strength he was not sure he possessed to stay away from her. In spite of himself, he had a terrific time at the cookout and developed an instant rapport with Tina and Bryan. He found them to be open, friendly, and solicitously fond of Korey. And humble. He grinned as he remembered how Tina and Bryan had refused to gloat when they soundly beat the opposition in a game of croquet.

He could not deny that the night had been a success. What he wanted to deny was what the night had done to him. At dusk they had watched fireflies: hundreds, maybe even thousands, rose from the ground and filled the pine trees with winking yellow lights. He and Korey had swung in the glider; the fragrance and magic of the warm summer night had nearly been his undoing. Oh, how he had wanted to take her in his arms and kiss her until they were both weak. He wondered now how well he had hidden his feelings from the others.

These feelings that he wished to keep hidden, what were they exactly? He was crazy about Korey, no mystery there. But was he in love with her? Marc scratched his head, unconsciously aping a student deadlocked midway into a monster math problem. There could be no future in loving her, he finally told himself. And his heart plunged along with the sudden descent of the landing plane.

CHAPTER 6

▼

"Have you heard from him?"

"Who?"

"No games, Korey. Remember it's your sister you're talking to."

"If you mean Marc, no, I haven't seen or spoken with him since the cookout." Korey, avoiding her sister's invasive gaze, bent to the task of snipping fabric around intricate patterns.

"Is it unusual for this much time to pass without him being in touch?"

"Ten days? There have been times when I haven't heard from him for weeks. He's very busy, travels a lot too." Korey straightened and swung the scissors in a lazy arc toward her inquisitive sister. "It may put your mind at ease to know I don't feel slighted by this."

Tina looked but saw no signs that Korey was being less than honest. Marc had been a delightful addition to the family gathering in Korey's back yard: helpful, charming, witty. But through the entire evening, Tina's ever-vigilant eye had failed to detect any overtures of affection between Marc and Korey. Still, that lack of affection, by its glaring absence, seemed to indicate that the evening had been lived under some carefully calculated, predetermined rules. That night, in so far as Tina saw, Marc did not touch Korey—not so much as a playful punch to her arm when he teased her for flubbing a turn at croquet nor a casual arm on her shoulder as they shared the glider under the canopy of phosphorescent fireflies. In spite of this evidence, the stolen glances Marc had given Korey throughout the evening had exposed to Tina his true feelings. Seeing inside her sister, on the other hand, was proving more difficult. Tina said, "So, how is his quilt coming along?"

"It isn't."

"This is the first of August. Marc isn't putting you under pressure to have it completed?"

"He's very patient. I told him up front that he shouldn't expect it before November. Besides, I'm sure he has more important things on his mind than what to hang on his office wall."

"Most likely," Tina said with hidden meaning.

Korey stacked colorful pieces of fabric at one end of the cutting board then diligently continued trimming new pieces. "Keep in mind that Marc is part of the reason I'm behind on my work. More than once he's enticed me away from my sewing, lured me into an impromptu picnic or a play at the Tivoli Theater. But mostly he phones; we sometimes have long conversations." She smiled. "So you see, he wouldn't dare object if he had to wait a little longer for his quilt."

"You ever call him? Hey," Tina chuckled, "don't look at me as if I asked if you had seen him naked!"

Setting down the scissors, Korey looked to where her sister shared room on the sofa among piles of fabric. "It's just that I had never thought to call him," she said. "Not since those first few times when I contacted him about the job." She tilted her head in surprise. "It just occurred to me that the only numbers I have are those of his two offices. He hasn't given me a home or cell phone number. That's not important," she said with a shrug. "I'm sure he just hasn't thought to give them to me."

To dispel an uneasy feeling, Tina stood and stretched her brown arms above her head. "I'm going to the kitchen to get some tea," she said. "You want some?"

"No, thanks. You'll find sliced lemon in a jar on the bottom shelf of the refrigerator door. Next to the pickled okra."

From the studio doorway, looking over her shoulder, Tina rolled her eyes. "Pickled okra? Since when do you eat pickled okra?"

"I don't. But Marc loves the stuff. Pops 'em like peanuts."

"Oooh," Tina drawled with wrinkled nose and puckered lips.

"They're not as bad as that," Korey giggled. "One of those things demanding an acquired taste, I suppose, like stout beer or moldy cheese." She flicked a hand as if to shoo Tina from the room. "Now go pour your tea and don't fret about the contents of my refrigerator."

The image of Korey's grin stayed with Tina as she idly stood in the cool air of the open refrigerator. Clearly Marc Bradberry was responsible for the transformation that had come over her sister in the last months. Tina likened the change in Korey to that of stepping from the black bowels of a cave into warm sunlight. At this moment Tina's tender feelings for Marc negated her need for an answer to the question brushing her mind: Why would Marc, in Korey's presence, so carefully measure the distance between them while his eyes longingly leapt the chasm he had himself created? Stirring a white cloud of sugar into her tea, Tina shook away her suspicions, convincing herself that the only games being played here were those in her imagination. After all, could there possibly be any pretense to a man so *downhome* that he eats, of all things, pickled okra?

✳   ✳   ✳   ✳

"Mint juleps?" Korey said as she joined Marc in the shade of the wrap-around verandah. She smiled up at him. "Just what the doctor ordered for the doldrums of August." Flipping the pages of a small notepad, she fanned her face. "Today certainly seems to qualify. Yes, I'd love a mint julep." A pale breeze tickled her bare ankles as it stirred the hem of her gauze dress. She glanced around the porch at the white wicker rocking chairs resting beneath baskets of lush fuchsia and decided to forgo the air-conditioned comfort of Marc's office. "Served on the verandah, if you please."

After an absence of weeks, the sight of her brown body clad in swirls of translucent yellow gauze made Marc dizzy. Struggling for equilibrium, he said, "I was hoping you would opt to bear the heat. This is the first excuse I've had to sit on the porch, and, frankly, I can't think of anyone I would rather have join me."

Korey fanned away an added flush as she watched Marc disappear through the double doors. Painted a crisp apple red, the doors no longer resembled those that had stood open to her the day she had first come to his office. Now door knockers, matching lion heads oxidized with such rich patina they could have been purloined from a sixteenth century Florentine villa, added a finishing touch. Korey wrapped her hands around a lathed post and swung side to side while remembering how her heart had pounded when Marc had phoned that morning to invite her to tour his new office. "Come late afternoon," he had said. "It's Friday and everyone will have left by three o'clock, so we will have the place to ourselves." Together alone. She had chosen to ignore what could have been implied in those words.

She had been impressed by the changes as she turned from the main road at a newly lettered sign and drove a lane cleared of weeds and underbrush. Even the covered bridge had lost its frightening shabbiness. Proudly sporting a fresh coat of dusty blue paint, its metal roof gleaming under a hot sun, the restored bridge had seemed to Korey to be exactly as Marc had described it to her.

With its brick walls painted the same dusty blue as the bridge, the house-turned-office had charmed Korey as she pulled into the wide curving driveway that bisected a well established lawn. Sashed windows trimmed in white shutters reflected circular mounds of magenta impatiens thriving in the shade of oak trees. Intricate white railing along the verandah had made Korey think of sweet cream drizzled over the blueberry house.

From the side of the house she now heard a door slam. Stepping to where the porch made a ninety-degree turn, she found Marc setting two frosted silver cups on a wicker table. With a word of thanks, Korey accepted the offered mint julep, then sat in a padded rocker while Marc took another. After so many weeks of separation, these first moments with Marc seemed awkward. Korey pushed with her sandaled foot; the chair made a rubbing sound as she rocked to and fro. With a small napkin, she wiped water droplets from the silver cup and said, "I love the house, er, office."

"I hoped you would say that," he stated, as if her approval meant a lot to him.

"Nothing looks the same as when I was here in May."

"It's amazing how much difference a few months can make."

She had no comeback to the intense look in his eyes and his mysterious smile, so she sipped the strong cold bourbon and gazed into the side yard. In the lengthening shade of the house, six foot cascades of dainty pink roses edged the clipped lawn and held back the dark woods.

"It's nice that we finally have this time together," Marc said after a pause.

"Yes, I've wanted to see the place."

He would have felt better if she had said she had wanted to see *him*, though he knew thinking such thoughts to be dangerous. Her disinterest left a void which he proceeded to fill with mint julep. What she said next, however, made him realize that he had been wrong about her. She did care.

"Now that the office is finished, maybe you'll slow down a little, have some breathing room."

Only now did he see himself as Korey saw him—worn out from weeks of late hours, business travel, obligatory but painful visits to look in on Clare. His was an unsettled life. He was as a man adrift in a vast ocean. With nothing to cling to, he must keep paddling in hopes someone would throw him a lifeline. In moments such as this, when the air was warm and sweet and Korey was at his side, he dared to dream it would be she who would someday rescue him. Wiping a hand over his face as if to clear it of weariness, he said, "Didn't know I looked so haggard."

"You don't. Most people probably wouldn't notice...."

He repressed a shiver when suddenly hit with the idea that she might see in him more than he wished her to see.

"You remind me of my dad," Korey continued. "He used to keep a pace similar to yours. Mom sometimes feared that he would fall asleep at the wheel when he traveled. Thank goodness he's retired and now has few things on his mind more taxing than his golf score. Mom didn't live to see it; we lost her to cancer five years ago. Dad remarried and moved to North Carolina."

"I know how it is to lose a parent. My dad has been gone for about that long." Splashing noises drew Marc's eyes to a birdbath. "Why did your dad move to North Carolina?"

"Stella, his wife, is from there." Korey smiled. "I'll tell you how they met, if you're interested."

Ever eager to know more about this woman who in the months he had known her had given him little in the way of anything personal, he said, "I'm interested."

"After Mom died," she said, "Dad was lost. He hadn't retired yet, and where before he had worked impossible hours, he doubled them. Tina and I were scared to death that he would keel over from a heart attack. After enduring this for two years, she and I put our collective foot down, told him we had booked passage on a ship bound for the Greek islands, and he was to be on that ship when it sailed, no excuses. We were prepared for an argument, but he was too exhausted to give us one. So we helped him pack and sent him off with a tearful 'Bon Voyage.'" Korey chuckled as she drank again from the silver cup. "As it turned out, he got much more from the cruise than any of us ever dreamed. After a month of sailing, he came home with renewed spring in his step, the tan of the proverbial Greek god, a new wardrobe, and—what a shock this was—a new wife!"

Marc shared Korey's laughter. "Oh, boy," he said. "That would be a shocker."

"When Tina and I picked him up at the airport, we had little time to wonder who the gorgeous redhead was hanging on his arm before he introduced Stella as his wife. Tina, the graceful sister, hugged Stella and welcomed her home, which gave me a badly needed pause to gather my wits enough to do the same. As we were to learn, Dad had sent us a cable explaining everything, but it had somehow gone astray and arrived after we had left for the airport."

"So, what did the cable say?"

"Let's see….something like, SHIPBOARD ROMANCE. TOO HOT NOT TO CONSUMMATE. MARRIED MARCH 19 BY CAPTAIN STANOPHO-LIS. ECSTATICALLY HAPPY. LOVE YOU BOTH. DAD AND STELLA."

Marc rocked back in his chair and let out a whoop. "Your dad sent *that*?" The chair rolled forward as Marc slapped his knees.

"Hard to believe from a man so reserved, but, yes. We saved the cable, had it mounted in a gold frame and gave it to Dad and Stella on their first anniversary. It hangs in their den among the family photos."

"Do you miss having your dad in town?"

"Yes, but I see him several times a year." Korey took the opening she was given. "What about you? Does your mom live in Nashville?"

At another time, he would have hesitated if it meant revealing more about himself than he had already. But Korey's presence had leant magic to the day and trading confidences seemed to come easier for them both. "Mom lives less than three miles from me. With my schedule I don't see her as much as I would like, but we're always together on holidays and special occasions. She travels frequently and works part-time at Kevin's office."

Korey cast Marc a bemused look. "Kevin?"

Marc's blank gaze lasted only long enough for him to realize how adept his subconscious had been in keeping Kevin hidden. Unsure of the purpose the secrecy had served, Marc said, proudly, "Kevin is my kid brother." He smiled and shook his head. "Well, not anymore. He's nearing thirty, so I should more correctly say he's my younger brother. He's a physician. Recently completed his residency at Vanderbilt Hospital and joined a group of doctors in a family practice clinic. Right now he's overworked, underpaid, and happy as a lark."

Slowly a picture was forming in Korey's mind: Marc as more than a man with only one side who, when apart from her, lived some sort of vague, even mysterious existence. After all these months, he was taking on new dimensions: the abstract becoming a real person. And like a real person, he lived in a house, had a mother and at least two brothers, and a father who was deceased. That there could be much more hidden beneath Marc's handsome facade greatly intrigued Korey. She said, with brows raised over a slanted gaze, "Well now, we have Eric who is your...."

"Older brother," Marc said freely.

"And we have Kevin, the doctor. Tell me, Marc, are there any more siblings you wish to tell me about?"

He set his empty cup on the table. "I don't think I've left anyone out." Scratching his head as if mulling it over, he added, "Nope, I'm pretty sure we three were Mom's limit. We gave her fits when we were kids. Typical stuff—the fall out of a tree, a fastball in the mouth, backing the car over her roses."

Not a leaf stirred in the yard, and Korey leaned forward to pull her damp dress away from her back. Uncrossing her legs, she rested her elbows on the arm of the rocker. Over a dry crescendo of cicadas, she said, "For all that, your mom must be proud of the way her boys turned out."

"I'd like to think so," he said. But Mom would not be proud of the way he had deliberately avoided telling Korey about Clare. Hell, he hadn't even told Mom, or anyone else, about Korey. Until he knew where his relationship with Korey was going, there could be little gained in introducing her to his family. At least that was his excuse of the moment.

"You know, this is absolutely sinful."

For a blood-pounding instant, Marc thought she had been reading his mind. "What is?" he asked.

Giggling, unaware of his alarm, she said, "The two of us. Whiling away the evening, sipping mint juleps as if neither of us has other things we should be doing."

Sinful. He slammed the door on the image that word planted in his head, but not before he saw clearly Korey's damp curls on his pillow, her liquid eyes and full lips begging him to come to her. In that frame of mind, he could not stop himself from saying, "I suppose it all depends on *what* other things, and with *whom.*"

A hiccup snatched her away from those searching green eyes; she giggled again, knew better than to take the last few sips of her drink. She glanced at the sky. The late sun had disappeared behind a cloud, and a cooling wind now blew from the north. "I'd like to see your office now," she said more abruptly than she had intended. She set aside the silver cup. "A storm may be rolling in. I'd rather be home when it hits."

Indoors it was dim and Marc flipped switches until the entire first floor glowed in soft light. Korey felt more comfortable in the illumination and was able, while she toured the rooms, to put out of her mind the suggestive remark made to her on the porch.

On entering, the place seemed more home than office and still had the new smell of fresh paint and wallpaper paste. The foyer and hallway walls were papered in pale blue with a subtle satin stripe that seemed to vanish then reappear according to the angle of light. A woven runner directed a visitor from the front door to the drafting room at the back.

A parlor, transformed into an inviting reception area, was furnished in leather, dark wood and glass. Walls were adorned with framed photographs of beautifully landscaped buildings, and without asking, Korey knew them to represent the work of Marc's company.

Rolling thunder announced the approaching storm, and Marc did not linger as he showed her the small room, stacked now floor to ceiling with supplies, where his infatuation with her had begun months before. Next to the supply room was a Spartan kitchen with a side door opening onto the verandah.

As they went together through the house, Korey quietly commented on the metamorphosis the building had undergone since she had seen it last. Marc seemed pleased, though why her approval would mean so much to a trained and talented professional such as he, only served to bewilder Korey.

The drafting room, even under a darkening sky, was filled with natural light. The ceiling swept up two stories past an entire north wall of glass. Marc explained that a section of floor in the upper story had been removed to attain the dramatic effect. Drafting tables and computers with dark screens sat about the room. A blank south wall waited patiently for the quilted work of art that would one day hang there.

Through the glass wall, a rear garden became part of the room. Marc opened a clear door and invited Korey to join him outside. The garden, the width of a narrow road, spanned the breadth of the house. A trimmed privet hedge only slightly taller than Marc bordered the garden on three sides, shielding the drafting room from the parking lot. In the rising wind, begonias hugged the edges of a curving brick walk. Tussock bluebell and tall scarlet lobelia swayed toward compact evergreens.

A black thunderhead, it's leading edge gilded with sunshine, dropped a splash of rain on the tip of Korey's nose. Marc held the door for her and they escaped inside just as a squall of fat raindrops spattered the brick walk. The shower was over as quickly as it had begun and steam boiled from wet bricks still holding the day's heat.

"You think that's it?" Korey asked as she peered through rain-streaked glass. In answer, lightning sliced the sky and thunder rattled the windows. In haste, Korey headed for the front of the house.

"Where are you going?" Marc asked as his long strides caught her at the door.

"Home," she said. "Before the bottom drops out of that cloud."

Part of him ached to have her stay, but her leaving would take from him the dilemma of whether or not to invite her upstairs to his private quarters. After a modicum of inward debate, he opened the door for her.

No rain fell but lightning popped and cracked around them. Tiny rose petals, like pink snowflakes, blew in confused circles from the side yard. Korey perched on the edge of the porch, poised for flight. "Your office is beautiful," she said. "I should have a quilt for you in a couple of months or so." She hesitated, feeling an awkwardness to this parting that before had never been there. Her eyes held his as the wind grabbed her long skirt and with it stroked Marc's thigh.

Every nerve in his body jumped to full alert. He leaned to her. Teetering backward, she stepped down with one foot, regaining her balance just as his lips, like a missile glancing off its target, grazed her cheek. Having been granted a reprieve from his own stupidity, Marc said, "Go now. Hurry, before you get soaked."

Flushed and confused, she nodded dumbly before turning for the car. Propped on a post, Marc watched her make a run for it—a yellow whirligig bouncing ahead of the storm. As she drove from sight, her scent, hovering still in his mind, mingled with the dusty smell of rain. Thinking of what he had almost done, he slapped the post, then absently rubbed the sting from his hand. Wind matted his hair, but he stayed where he was until driving rain forced him inside.

CHAPTER 7

▼

Rotten luck often prowls in packs, and in the last weeks Marc Bradberry had fallen victim to more than he cared to deal with. His cousin and dear friend, Molly, had become ill with pneumonia and had cheated death only by the skin of her teeth.

Then there was his mother's accident. Driving home from a nighttime hospital visit to see her niece, Barbara Bradberry was slammed, spun, and flipped at an intersection by a car that had failed to heed a stop sign. Bumped and bruised, Barbara and the other driver miraculously escaped serious injury. Barbara's adored car, however, came out looking like it had been dropped from an airplane.

"I don't mean to be an ingrate," she had said to Marc one day as her blackened eyes, a palette of purple and chartreuse, followed his movements as he poured coffee. "I walked away from a terrible wreck and here I am mourning a mangled hunk of metal. But as soon as I get rid of these raccoon eyes, I'm going shopping for its twin."

Since it was to be a surprise, Marc did not at that time tell his mother that he and her youngest son, Kevin, had done the legwork and the replacement car was already in his driveway, proudly awaiting its new owner.

At least the car had been in the driveway when he had left home that morning. But that night it had failed, alarmingly, to appear in the beam of his headlights as he pulled into his driveway.

"Punks," the cop had said. "Stealing 'em for joy rides mostly." He had flipped his little notebook closed. "Some we recover in one piece; some we don't." He left before Marc could ask, if by *some* he meant the punks or the cars.

Now, the crises seemed to be over. Molly was out of the hospital and growing stronger by the day. Mom was back on the streets in her recovered, and undamaged, new car. So why did he still feel at loose ends? Was it Clare, his wife who, with her endless sleep, had entrapped him? No, not this time. This time it was Korey who was the cause of his unrest.

September had come and gone, and the entire month he had been with Korey only once—with Tina and Bryan they had made a foursome for an evening of line dancing at Wild Bill's Saloon. In the weeks following, in the troubled waters that had become his life of late, Korey had been lost among the flotsam.

Marc now tossed his eyeglasses on the paper-strewn desk and massaged the bridge of his nose. From behind closed lids, Korey appeared as a beautiful vision in swirling yellow gauze. Even now, as leaves turned to crimson under cool October skies, his blood steamed with the memory of that August afternoon when he had come so close to whisking her from his verandah to his upstairs bed. With an impatient shove, Marc's chair shot away from the desk, and Korey's image vanished as if it were a bubble touched to a thorn.

Hunched, his hands clasped behind his back, Marc paced a path from wall to wall. Then he wandered to the den of his rambling one story home, only to forget his mission. And at this same moment, if someone had stepped in to ask him why, at 2:30 in the afternoon, he was working at home instead of at the office, he would not have had an answer. In the kitchen, he hunted in the refrigerator with no clear goal; coming up empty handed, he slammed the door. He picked an apple from a bowl of fruit, bruised it tossing it back into the bowl. A banana was half peeled before he rejected it also. Feeling defeated, he left the kitchen.

From the corner of his eye, he caught his reflection in a mirror. He stopped to size himself up, thinking it odd that there were no outward signs that deep inside him what could pass for a marching band had for the last hour been conducting field drills over, around, and through his vital organs. And at its head, would that be Korey, jabbing his conscience with each upward thrust of her long, gleaming baton?

He had not phoned her in weeks. Well, neither has she called you, he excused himself, shamelessly. But a day did not pass when he did not think of her. Most nights, in his dreams, she was with him, leaving him breathless in ways that would be impossible in wakeful hours. Those dreams, frightening in their astonishing intensity, were the things that stopped him the many times he had reached for the phone.

Time had become his nemesis. How much longer could he hope to have before she would no longer be there when he *did* call? She was young, beautiful and free to marry again. Each month that flew by brought her closer to the day when someone more worthy would come to offer her the life she deserved. What about Rob Westerfield, the faceless brother-in-law? Were Rob's feelings for Korey truly platonic, or was he biding his time, waiting for the right moment?

The face in the mirror touched a finger to its lips and remembered when those lips had brushed Korey's cheek. The lips were numb, as if the ill-fated kiss had just happened. Marc stared blankly at his image. So much about Korey remained a mystery. There were gaps to her life that he felt a need to have filled, though, with all the unknowns in his own life, he was at a loss to explain why the missing links in hers should even matter.

This uncertainty of purpose did not deter him, however. The guy in the mirror straightened to his full height, squared his shoulders. There was, he knew, one person who could fill in the blanks. He would go to see her at the first opportunity.

*   *   *   *

At the mall entrance to the department store, he stood tall and confident, the beau ideal in a navy pinstripe suit and conservative tie. An observer would not have guessed that beneath the cool exterior, Marc Bradberry felt neither calm nor collected. In his mind, his reason for coming was still vague, and he was unsure how to proceed if Tina Goodwin should accept his offer of lunch.

His searching eyes scanned the cosmetic counters just inside the store. The vast array of palettes used for painting female faces stupefied him; he was out of his element here. Give him paper, pen and a straight edge, and he could create a building. But here among lipsticks, rouges, and eye shadows, he was a lost frog in a strange pond.

The store was not busy; he calculated that he was outnumbered by sales women at least four-to-one. If he had not years ago stopped noticing when he was being ogled, he would have seen that a pretty blond behind the nearest counter was now doing just that. In heels, she was nearly as tall as he, her hair too near the color of the sun not to have come from a bottle.

"May I help you?" she asked, her voice a shade too eager.

Marc could not remember ever seeing redder lips. "Yes," he said. "I'm looking for Tina Goodwin."

The crimson smile became artificial. "Over there." A long painted nail pointed over his shoulder. "Third counter on your right."

No one seemed to be in attendance when he approached, and, with a sinking feeling, it occurred to Marc that Tina may have already gone to lunch. The sound of a cabinet door sliding along a metal track drew his attention. With fingers braced on the sparkling glass, he peered over the countertop. Tina, hunched on the floor with her back to him, was removing attractively boxed perfumes from a large cardboard carton and stacking them on a lower shelf. Marc cleared his throat; startled hazel eyes flew up to meet his.

"Marc!" A smile lit Tina's flawless face as she bounced to her feet. "I didn't know I had a customer." There was a pause, through which Marc made no comment. Tina looked at him quizzically. "Or maybe you were just passing through the store?"

"No, not exactly." He drummed his fingers lightly on the glass. "Tell me," he said, "what's the name of your sister's favorite perfume?"

"Ah. Well, depending on her mood, she wears one of two or three fragrances. But Samsara is her favorite." Using a tester bottle, Tina spritzed a fine mist into the air.

Marc almost expected Korey to materialize out of the scent floating around him. She was the air that he breathed, and her absence made him ache. "Make no mistake," he said in a voice Tina could only describe as dreamy. "That's the one I had in mind. I'll take the largest bottle you have."

Her hand faltered before she reached to take a box from a bottom shelf. Such a fine gift; she wondered at his largesse. What was he up to, this man who in her sister's own words was "just a friend?" Could it be something had changed, that Korey was suddenly being wooed?

"I'd like to have it gift wrapped," Marc was saying as Tina presented the box.

"I'll take it right over to the wrapping department. It should take only a few minutes. Would you want to wait?"

Marc checked his watch. "It's lunch time," he said, feigning surprise. "I think I'll grab a bite in the Tea Room upstairs and pick up the package on my way out." He paused, noting he was being watched closely. "I have an idea," he said as if a thought had just struck him, "I hate to eat alone. Would it be possible for you to join me for lunch?"

Tina suspected that the invitation for lunch, meant to appear spontaneous, had been carefully orchestrated. First, an expensive bottle of perfume; now, lunch. A puzzle—and Tina was having trouble connecting the dots. Well, it was conveniently her scheduled mealtime. And, with only a bagel and coffee for breakfast, she was starved. In the end, though, it was curiosity not hunger which made her ride with Marc up the escalator to the Tea Room.

＊   ＊   ＊   ＊

The dining room was crowded and noisy, as it was each weekday at this time. Their table, against the blue papered wall, was near the door to the kitchen. A waitress, efficient in her starched blue uniform, promptly took an order for one Cobb salad and a ham and Swiss on rye.

Tina folded her hands on the table; her enameled nails shone like jewels on the white cloth. Looking into Marc's eyes, she searched for some sign of his purpose, but, as he made the comment that they must stop meeting like this, she saw nothing beyond his teasing grin.

If he were a smoker, Marc would have filled this dead time with lighting a cigarette, reaching for an ashtray, disposing of the match. As it was, the idea of pumping Tina for information about her sister suddenly seemed sophomoric. *Hey, Tina,* he could imagine himself saying in a cracking adolescent voice, *that foxy sister of yours, does she like me or what?* When the silence at the table became uncomfortable, the man shoved the boy aside to say, "By now, I suppose you know…. that I care very much for your sister."

His hesitation told Tina that he had carefully chosen his words, and she proceeded with a caution of her own. "Yes. Your friendship has made a positive difference in her life. She's coming alive again."

Her finger traced the cool outline of a fork handle, and Marc recognized the mannerism as one he had seen Korey use in closely guarded moments. Something else about Tina brought Korey to his mind. Today, Tina's hair was piled in burnished curls atop her head—an updo he had never before seen her wear—and it startled him to note, apart from a difference in color, it was Korey's eyes that now watched him from over the rim of a water glass. He did not confront those eyes as he said, "I would like for that to be true, but, frankly, I'm a little concerned about her."

"Concerned? Why? When I spoke with her day before yesterday, she was fine. Has something happened….?"

She could not have made him feel worse. How would he know what could have happened to Korey? He couldn't remember the last time he had called her. "No, nothing has happened. Maybe I'm saying this badly, but she seems too content living in a world slightly apart."

Tina nodded, knowing full well what he meant by 'a world apart.' Though Korey had stepped one toe out of the emotional safe-haven to which she had fled when Danny died, she was a long way from fully emerging into the world. "She's terrified," Tina said, "of closeness, of losing." She let her voice die, stopping short of saying, *losing someone she loves.*

"As a means of defense, there's nothing abnormal in that," Marc returned, thoughtfully. Distracted by a loud clatter, his eyes darted to the next table where a busboy was rapidly stacking dishes into a tub. Marc seemed to speak more to the busboy than to Tina when he added, "Makes it difficult for those who care to get inside."

A phrase having something to do with the pot calling the kettle black ran through Tina's mind. From where she sat, much of the blame for Korey's reserve rested with Marc. In all fairness, a man as unreliable as Marc had been could hardly expect a woman to fall at his feet the few times he deigned to come around. Why *did* he stay away? Was it that he was every bit as frightened of closeness as Korey?

"Will there be anything else?" asked the waitress as she set the meal before them and refilled Marc's coffee cup. He dismissed her with a smile and a shake of his head.

While Marc spread mustard over the ham on his sandwich, Tina busied herself rearranging the neatly layered ingredients on her plate. Marc had not, she thought, invited her here because he knew she was hungry. He ran two offices; he was too busy to fill a lunch hour with idle chitchat. She hid a tiny smile behind a bite of salad. For months she had stood silently by, waiting for the stand-off between Korey and Marc to end. Now, though he did not seem sure-footed, it appeared that Marc was about to take the first step toward that end. And because in her mind he was so right for her sister, it was Tina's pleasure today to do anything she could to help him win Korey's heart.

There is, in the appreciation of good food, only so much which can be said for a superbly constructed ham and cheese sandwich, and after Marc had inanely said all that he could, he came around again to the subject of Korey. "Is there anything you could tell me that would help me....well, help her come out of hiding." His eyes burned with an intense sincerity. "She is hiding, you know."

No more than you. "Yes, she's hiding." Tina hedged, "But aren't you having this conversation with the wrong person? Shouldn't you be having it with Korey?"

"She hasn't said much."

"Have you come right out and asked?"

"No."

"Why not?"

"I didn't want to seem like I was prying."

"So with me, you find the prying easier?"

"With you, I think of it more as fact finding."

"Whether he comes through the front door or the back, a thief is still a thief."

He saw the glint in her eye and smiled. "And you don't want to be hauled in for aiding and abetting, is that it?"

"I only want what is best for Korey." Tina set her fork to rest on a bed of lettuce. "Korey hasn't always been….distant," she began. "It was her husband's death."

"She rarely speaks of him. Danny, isn't it?"

"Yes. In circumstances like that there is always survivor's guilt. Considering what she's been through, I think she's done an absolutely valiant job of fighting back."

"Circumstances?" Marc frowned. "Guilt?" The bread was beginning to dry out on an untouched half of his sandwich.

"She really hasn't told you anything, has she?"

He shook his head.

"Marc…." Tina hesitated, uncertain of what she was about to do. "Marc," she began again, "Danny took his own life."

"Dear God." Oddly, irrelevantly, what leapt to Marc's mind was how much he disliked bleu cheese. Someone very near was eating bleu cheese. Not only did he find the smell offensive, but he felt that today the smell could quite possibly make him sick. In a jerky motion, he poured cold water down the gaping hole in his whitened face. "I had no idea….she never."

Because she did not know him all that well, normally Tina would not have reached across the table to cover his hand with hers. But by nature she was empathetic, and the gesture of comfort was reflexive. "I'm sorry. I didn't mean to shock you."

"No, I…." The mindless question, the one he would have known better than to ask had not his senses just been jarred loose, came to his lips. "In heaven's name, why?"

Tina shook her head, blinked back a tear. "In time Korey will confide in you, I'm sure of it." Her appetite suddenly gone, she pushed away her food. "When Korey loves, she doesn't hold back. She and Danny were two people sharing one heart. But something went terribly wrong. When your very center has been snatched away, the healing can take a long time. Be patient, Marc."

He nodded.

Tina went on. "She's still in love with her husband yet struggling to find a life beyond that love. She's confused. With you she has found a fresh sense of self-worth. If you truly want to make a difference, don't coddle her but be there for her as much as you can. Take her to dinner, teach her how to fix her leaky faucet, when she wants to talk, listen."

"I understand."

"Yes, I believe you do."

There were things she was not saying; the conspiratorial tone in her voice made him doubt how well he had hidden his true feelings today. Tina had put a new slant on his relationship with Korey: As much as he needed Korey, she may need him even more. He could not think of walking away from her.

"I've given away more than I should have," Tina said, "but I did it because, frankly, I like you, and I think you're good for my sister."

Marc's already overburdened conscience stooped even lower under the weight of Tina's remark.

Leaving the Tea Room, he and Tina agreed that it would be best not to mention the luncheon to Korey, each ignoring the disquiet the conspiracy brought with it. With a beautifully wrapped package in his hand, Marc escorted Tina to her sales counter.

"Say," he said casually, "what does Korey usually do Halloween night?"

"Puts together some sort of costume, hands out treats and has as much fun as the goblins who come to the door. Why?"

"Oh, I thought it might be a good time to drop by with a gift."

"Fancy wrapping like that and she'll think it's a trick."

"No tricks." He grinned, and Tina wondered, not for the first time, how it could be that her sister seemed able to resist something so irresistible. "And remember," he said, "this is to be kept between you and me."

Before she turned to greet the customer sidling up to the counter, Tina made a motion of zipping her smiling red lips.

*   *   *   *

Six hours later, Bryan Goodwin, with very little effort, unzipped his wife's lips.

"You're pensive tonight," he observed as he popped a last cheese tortellini into his mouth. "Want to tell me what's going on in that gorgeous head of yours?" He loved the way, after nearly nine years of marriage, his wife still sweetly blushed when he reminded her of her beauty.

"I'm not supposed to tell."

"A secret, huh? Something spicy?" He stood to stack her empty plate onto his. Brushing a finger along her upturned chin, he grinned wickedly. "All the better then when I wheedle it out of you." When this did not produce a smile, he dropped back into his chair and scooted noisily across the vinyl floor. Looking closely at his wife, he said, "Hey, why so somber? I was only kidding."

She returned his gaze. "Can I trust you to not let it get back to Korey?"

"You know you can."

Tina raked together the dirty silverware and set it clattering onto the dinner plates. "You'll never guess who invited me to lunch today."

"Well, Korey would be a poor guess."

"Marc Bradberry."

"You're right, I never would have guessed. Should I be jealous?"

That brought the smile he had been looking for. "Um....jealous only of my Cobb salad. It was delicious, what I ate of it. But then you had peanut butter and grape jelly. How was your sandwich, by the way?"

"The best." Bryan made a smacking sound with his lips. "But back to this little tryst of yours."

Under her husband's fixed gaze, Tina related her conversation with Marc Bradberry. She finished with a sigh. "I admit I'm befuddled. I really can't figure what's going on between those two."

"Maybe nothing."

"Oh, there's something all right." Tina leaned forward in the chair. "When Marc speaks of her, the heat in his eyes would melt butter. And buying that perfume....acting as if it were something he would do for any friend who happens to be female. Ha! If that were the case, he would buy her a scarf to wear with her wool coat, or, if he's really daring, a brooch for the lapel of her navy suit. No, Marc's going to give Korey that perfume as much for his own pleasure as for hers."

Tina stretched her legs across Bryan's lap. Through her woolly gray socks, he began to absently massage her tired feet. "Oooh, that feels good," she moaned. "There was," she went on, "a lot left unsaid in the Tea Room today. And it doesn't seem that Marc and Korey communicate with each other any better than Marc and I did. I think their conversations go mostly like this: 'nice weather we're having,' or 'can you believe what that loon Senator Paulssen has done now?' I tell you, Bryan, they're doing the craziest mating dance I've ever seen. No sense of rhythm whatsoever." She giggled convulsively when Bryan touched a sensitive spot on her foot; he stopped tickling only after a few more tormenting strokes. "Maybe we should have," she said, wiping her eyes, "some compassion for Marc."

"Why, because he's such a poor dancer?"

Tina slanted him a look. "No, because, when he's with my sister, it must be a constant battle to keep his hands off of her. Case in point: The night of Korey's cookout, it was almost comical how far out of his way Marc went to *not* touch her. He's in love with her, yet he holds back. Like Korey, he's running from something."

"If, as you say, they're both running, then maybe they'll run into each other's arms."

"Not likely, since most of the time they are running *away* from each other. It's frustrating to watch."

Bryan kissed his wife affectionately then swung her feet to the floor. "Could it be, older sister, that you're watching too closely?"

"I am and I make no apology for it. Marc isn't around enough, yet Korey shows no interest in looking elsewhere. It's not right that she should miss out on a shot at happiness with someone else...."

"You're not by any chance thinking of Rob?"

"Not particularly. Korey loves Rob—as the brother of her husband, nothing more. Though for Rob's part, if she gave him an opening, he wouldn't hesitate to step through it."

Bryan snuffed the dinner candle; smoke rose in a fuzzy halo above his head. "If not Rob," he said, "someone could happen along to steal her right out from under Marc's less-than-vigilant nose."

"Seems to me," said Tina, pausing in the act of picking up the stacked dishes, "that is precisely what he should be most afraid of."

*   *   *   *

The door opened with a creak, exposing the hideous crone. With a startled catch in his voice, the man said, "Trick or Treat."

Only the eyes of the crone were familiar. The tangled hair, the green face, the black shawl hanging from bent shoulders, were right out of a Halloween cartoon. Her cackle, muffled slightly by the latex mask, sent a shiver along his spine. "Aren't you just a wee bit old to be trick or treating?" she rasped.

"I'll always be a kid at heart," he returned. In the eerie light from the foyer, he surveyed her from the top of her gray head to the tips of her pointy black shoes. "May I say, Madam, you've never looked lovelier."

The crone seemed to levitate as she pressed her warty green nose to his, her long hair covering the pumpkin he held in his hands. "Don't fool with me, sonny," she threatened, "or those luscious green eyes of yours 'ull be boilin' in my next potion." To end an evil prognostication with a fit of girlish giggles spoils the effect, but Marc's laughter was infectious. She glanced around the man filling her doorway to the dark and empty street beyond. "Seems you're the last of 'em. Follow me." She cackled again.

Her ragged black skirt dusted the floor as Marc followed her into the kitchen. She removed the wig, and fluffed her short damp curls. The latex mask was peeled away to expose a rosy face. "Much better," said Korey, using a tissue to blot moisture from her face. "I was about to suffocate in that thing. You are one for surprises," she said, unwinding the fringed shawl from her shoulders. "What brings you out with the ghouls and goblins on this dark and potentially stormy night?"

"What's Halloween without one of these?" he asked as he set the pumpkin on the kitchen counter.

"How nice. Thanks."

Chocolate kisses tumbled from his coat pocket as he tossed it over a chair. "And these," he said, scooping the candy from the floor and handing them to Korey.

"If I had known you were in town tonight," she said as she peeled foil from the chocolate drop, "and alone, I would have invited you to come and join me in handing out treats." With a blackened tooth, she lopped off the top half of the candy kiss.

"Sorry I missed the fun, but I had some work to do." A confessed chocoholic, he popped three kisses into his mouth.

"You want some cider to wash that down?"

"I thought I smelled hot cider. Love some, thanks."

She handed him a steaming mug and a carving knife.

"Why the knife?"

"The pumpkin needs a face."

Marc set down the cider and the knife. He unfolded a paper napkin, draped it over the pumpkin. With the clownish skill of a clumsy magician, he rotated the pumpkin. Lifting the napkin, he sang, "Ta-da!"

Smiling at Korey with toothy grin was an expertly carved jack-o'-lantern. "Oh Marc, he's adorable. Is this your handiwork?"

"He's the reason I couldn't come earlier. Had to wait to carve it until everyone left the office. I'll be returning to a real mess, left his brains piled on newspaper in the middle of the kitchen."

Korey wrinkled her nose at the thought of the stringy, slimy goo. "Let's light him," she said, turning to open a drawer.

Marc sipped cider and watched her as she rummaged in the drawer. He was amazed how beautiful she was, even in a tattered skirt and a severe, high-neck blouse. After an absence of so many weeks, it was easy to lose himself in the sight of her; the hard part was keeping his mind free of lustful thoughts. He felt as though he had truly been cast under a witch's spell.

With the stub of a candle in one hand and a matchbook in the other, she turned to find that she was the object of Marc's intense gaze. A flush suffused her already warm body. Turning aside, she emptied her hands and unbuttoned her black shirt's high, stiff collar.

Marc struck a match, touched the flame to the wick. "You light him," he said, handing her the candle.

Grasping the dried stem of the pumpkin, Korey lifted the lid. "Marc, there's something in the bottom," she said, "in a plastic bag."

Already suspicious, she became even more so when he said, too innocently, "Something in the bottom? Why, I wonder what it could be."

She blew out the candle; her dark eyes drilled into his. Plunking her hands on her hips, she said, "This is some kind of trick, isn't it? I should have known....ringing my doorbell, that silly grin on your face. What's in that plastic bag?"

"Why don't you reach in and find out?"

She saw the daring gleam in his eye and the twitch in the curve of his mouth. "You're crazy," she said. "I'm not putting my hand in there. It's something disgusting, I just know it."

Marc laughed. "You saying you don't have the guts?"

"Yuk, don't even say that word...."

"Come on, Korey, be a sport. It's harmless, really."

She took a deep breath, as though preparing to dive into a pool. Her eyes closed and her face scrunched as her hand cautiously felt its way into the moist, fragrant cavity. Her fingers found a corner of the plastic bag, lifted it slowly out of the jack-o'-lantern. When nothing wriggled in her hand and nothing exploded, she dared to open one eye. Inside the transparent bag was a box wrapped in red foil. She said, as she opened the bag and removed the box, "If something springs at me when I open this, Marc Bradberry, you're in for it." One tear of the foil paper revealed the Samsara label.

The look on Korey's face assured Marc that Tina had been true to her word. Even the blackened teeth did not spoil the radiant, surprised smile.

"Oh, Marc, this is too much," she said. "I don't know what to say; it's not even….there's no occasion." Her eyes teared. Not since Danny had there been anyone to give her a gift for no reason at all.

Seeing the shine in her luminescent eyes, Marc said lightly, "Where is it written that a friend has to wait for a special occasion to give a gift? Friends don't always need a reason, you know."

"Don't they?" Her gaze was uncomfortably steady, as if she were looking for a hidden motive.

Under the close scrutiny, to keep himself from crumbling and telling her everything that was in his heart, he chomped down a few more chocolates. It was with disbelief that he suddenly felt her arms around his neck, the touch of her lips as she bussed his cheek, her warm breath saying "thank you" in his ear. Before his stunned body could react and pull her into his arms to smother her with the kisses he had so often dreamed of, she was across the kitchen, her back to him, relighting the candle. "We'll put him in the window," she said quite breathlessly as she set the candle inside the pumpkin.

"Yes," he said in a daze, "in the window."

She offered him spice cake; he said he was too full of candy to eat another bite. She made small talk; he barely heard. Finally, saying it was late, he reached for his coat. "Is this some of your family?" he asked, picking up a snapshot from that part of the chair hidden by his coat.

"Why, yes. I received some pictures today from my aunt, the one who lives in New Mexico. This one must have fallen out of the envelope. That's three generations: Aunt Matty," she pointed with a nail painted the same grotesque shade of green as her witch's mask, "her daughter, Tate, who lives in Arizona, and on Tate's lap, twins Allie and Angie."

"Beautiful children." Marc shrugged into his coat.

"Aren't they?" Korey said as she went with Marc to the door. "Matty has been after me to come for a visit. Keeps telling me I need a change of scene. I don't know….with all the work I have to do and cold weather coming on in Albuquerque, I think I'd rather go in the spring."

Marc opened his mouth as if to say something, then closed it. Then, "Yeah, spring would be nice," he mumbled. He reached for the doorknob and felt the light touch of her hand on his arm.

"Thanks again for the wonderful gift. You really shouldn't have."

"My pleasure."

Korey asked, abruptly, "Would you by any chance be free for dinner next Wednesday night? I make a mean spaghetti sauce. I'd like for you to come to dinner."

He knew it would be best not to accept, but he was never one to turn down a spaghetti dinner—especially one prepared by the hands of this woman. "I'll be here," he said.

"Good, I'll call you next week with the time. See you then."

Walking across the porch, Marc knew his eyes were playing tricks when he saw the brightly glowing jack-o'-lantern wink at him from the window.

CHAPTER 8

▼

He no longer took much notice of the monitors. The tubes, the IV sacs were all a natural part of this unnatural world. He stared with unfocused eyes at his wife, his mind not in this room, nor in this hospital, not even in this city.

"Dr. Phil Peterson, 0215."

The announcement, clipped and atonal, detached Marc from thoughts of Korey. Clare's gaunt face sharpened into view. Vinyl creaked on the uncomfortable chair as he leaned forward, his weary head drooping nearly to his knees. Hazy morning sun, showcasing a window washer's inept handling of a squeegee, poured through streaked glass. The sun did little to warm Marc's sweatered shoulder before spilling onto the floor at the base of the hospital bed. Mindlessly, he studied the waxy swirls buffed into checkerboard tiles on the sun-glazed floor.

How, he wondered, would he tell Korey about this? Shaking his head, he snorted a derisive little laugh. This was not a case for the etiquette books; there was no proper way to state, after months of sidestepping, that one has a comatose wife. No amount of mental preparation would make such a confession easy. When he played the scene in his mind, what he saw robbed him of breath. Burdened with the weight of such a revelation, their friendship, platonic though it was, would not stand. He would lose Korey. Discovering he was a married man, she would justifiably walk out of his life.

Despite this dismal forecast, something deep within Marc urged him to keep an optimistic head. He would not let go that slender thread of hope that, if left to itself, somehow his predicament would miraculously see a less disastrous end. Normally, this philosophy of casting aimlessly about would be unacceptable to a man with a take-charge attitude. But, by his own admission, there was nothing *normal* about this life he was choosing to live. His life seemed a muddled mess; even his relationship with Korey refused to be pigeonholed. Rather than a friendship, he likened his involvement with her to that of a game. Hide and seek. He and Korey were both hiding their deepest feelings—from each other and from themselves.

What would it matter if the truth were finally flushed from its hiding place? If his love for Korey should die in the cellar of his soul, he would be saved prolonged heartache. As it was he was living in limbo, bound to a woman who had not so much as fluttered an eyelid in months. His wife, so careless in her last conscious act, had selfishly stolen from him the freedom to explore his own feelings. "I hope you're pleased," he said to the lifeless form in the white-sheeted bed.

Marc stood and massaged his lower back, the stiffness there bringing an awareness of the long moments spent hunched in the chair. In dissatisfaction, he admitted that his unprofitable thoughts had produced no clear answers. Bitterness tarnished the handsome face as he turned his back to Clare and left the room.

*   *   *   *

"Come on, Marc. Don't you think it's time you told me? Who is she?"

Shying from the question, Marc slowly sipped his beer. At last he said, "Is it that obvious?"

"Yes." Kevin Bradberry's grin became distorted when someone in the bar increased the volume on a Smashing Pumpkins rock video. Catching the eye of the bartender, Kevin rated the video two thumbs down. The volume dropped to a more tolerable level, and he again directed his attention to his brother. "I've known for a few months. Even Mom has been asking questions."

"No secrets in this family, are there?"

"Not many. Mom said she could see it in your eyes, whatever that means."

Marc wondered if his eyes had really revealed so much. "Okay," he said. "Here's the straight scoop. Her name is Korey Westerfield. She lives in Chattanooga. About six months ago, I admired one of Korey's quilts hanging in John Wexler's office. I expressed my interest and asked that he put me in touch with the artist. I commissioned her to make a wall hanging, never dreaming at the time what it would later mean to my peace of mind." He swiveled his bar stool to better see his brother. "The moment I set eyes on her I was smitten." He felt now the same flutter in his chest as when she had turned to him that first day. "But I put a lid on those feelings. Thought at the time that she was married."

"She wasn't?"

"No. widowed."

Kevin seemed surprised. "Widowed? Is she young?"

"Late twenties."

"Too young for widowhood." Kevin shook his head, thinking of the one time in his still young medical practice that he had held in his helpless arms the sobbing woman whose husband of only four months had been so wickedly struck down by cancer. He cleared his throat. "Tell me about Korey," he said.

"She's a gentle spirit, at times even shy. Soft spoken but intelligent. Her sense of humor flawless; she laughs at all of my jokes. And not the least of it, she's the beneficiary of an extremely generous gene pool—everything's in just the right place."

"Everything?"

Marc's answering scowl wiped the leer from his younger brother's lips.

"So," Kevin asked, "why have you been keeping this lovely creature all to yourself?"

Wistfully Marc gazed into the amber liquid at the bottom of his pilsner glass. If only he could go on keeping Korey to himself…. "We often have conflicting schedules. I don't see her that much. In fact, I could count on two hands the number of times we've been together since we met. Since the Chattanooga office opened I've been swamped with work, and then there's the traveling…."

Between swigs of Coors, Kevin smiled tolerantly at this evasive rambling. "Didn't realize you'd been so busy," he said to needle his brother.

"Yeah. And next week I'm off to Albuquerque. As you know Eric and Rae broke ground on their new house last month, and I'm flying out to oversee some things." The bartender filled a frosted glass, then, with a practiced flick of the wrist, slid the foaming brew the length of the bar into Marc's waiting hand. "Kevin," Marc said after testing the icy drink, "I'm thinking of asking Korey to go with me. Her aunt lives in Albuquerque."

Marc looked to the wide mirror behind the bar for a way to escape his own doubts. So shaky was his belief in the wisdom of this half-baked idea to fly Korey to New Mexico, that a disapproving frown reflected on Kevin's brow would mean death to the invitation.

Never suspecting his own conscience had been tagged to step in for that of his brother, Kevin said, supportively, "Sounds like a fun trip." After a pause in which Kevin returned Marc's gaze in the mirror, he said, "Except…."

"Except what?"

"Except you don't look particularly pleased about the prospect of taking a beautiful widow on a solitary flight to New Mexico. Not as pleased as I would be if I were in your shoes. What's the matter? Is her husband's ghost going along on the trip?"

"No. Clare's."

"Huh?"

A muscle jumped in Marc's jaw. "I saw Clare again this morning." A sharp edge cut through the soft words he had used to speak of Korey only moments before. His eyes lingered on the beer cradled in his hand. "Korey doesn't know about Clare." The sound of dishes crashing to the floor in the tavern's small kitchen effectively punctuated Marc's statement.

Wide hazel eyes turned to him. "Well," Kevin whistled, "that certainly explains why you're so subdued tonight." The disapproving frown Marc had looked for earlier on his brother's face showed itself now.

Marc stumbled over a weak defense. "I've never said I *wasn't* married. It's just…. the subject of marriage has never come up."

"How convenient for you." Kevin fingered a fat, salty pretzel. "Let me get this straight. You've been dating this other woman…."

"Don't refer to her as the *other woman*," Marc snapped. "And, technically, we're not dating."

Kevin ignored the interruption. "….since last spring. That you love her is written all over your face. Tell me, how is it you can be in love with her and not tell her you have a comatose wife? You were on the eve of divorcing Clare when she was attacked. We all know there was no love lost between the two of you." Kevin shrugged. "I must be missing some of the picture here. I just can't see why you have kept this from Korey."

A guilty flush crept up Marc's neck. In his brother's cool stare, he saw for the first time the depth of his duplicity. These past months he had sealed Clare in a tidy little box and stored her as far back in his mind as she would go. He had taken each day as it had come, not thought ahead. What he had done to Korey was unconscionable. Yet even as he accepted full responsibility for his transgression, Marc knew he would not change his course. Not yet, anyway. Some would accuse him of waiting too late. He liked to think he had not waited long enough. There would come a time, in that nebulous world known as *tomorrow*, when he would bravely say, "Korey, I have a wife; her name is Clare."

In the meantime, he would present his case to his brother. "Let's clear up some misconceptions. You've erred in assuming Korey and I are involved in something beyond friendship. As far as she's concerned, we're friends, nothing more. She seems to have no inkling that my feelings run deeper."

"Admittedly, I'm not the most perceptive guy in the romance category. But if I can see it," Kevin said dubiously, "and Mom can see it, how can you be so sure Korey can't?"

"I'm on guard when she's around. I've never even laid a hand on her."

Kevin's brows shot toward his hairline and he was not completely successful in choking back a laugh.

"Honest," Marc testified. "Hard to believe, I know, but true."

"Well, that certainly explains why you keep popping up around town with Julia Santangelo."

"Hey, Kevin, I don't like what you're implying. Julia is one hell of an architect, and I respect her as a woman. I like her. Together we've had some great times."

"I don't suppose there is any chance Julia knows you only *like* her, while you *love* Korey?"

Marc slammed his beer on the mahogany bar. Foam cascaded down the outside of the glass. "Don't be an idiot." With an inadequate napkin he swiped at the spilled beer. "I've not breathed a word about Korey to Julia. How crazy do you think I am?" The shock of his own words snapped his head up. Through a slow, lopsided grin he said, "No need to answer that."

"So while worshipping Korey from afar you're tumbling in the sheets with Julia. Some men would not find this unpleasant."

"Some men, maybe. But dammit, Kev, I'm not heartless. Just lucky. So far my juggling act is running smoothly enough."

"Well, may the day never come when those razor knives you're juggling slip and lop off a vital appendage."

Marc did not smile at the doctor's humor. "Don't you see. This way I satisfy all demands. Husband to Clare; friend to Korey. And you needn't waste any sympathy on Julia. I'm not the only man in her life. Believe me, she's not lonely when I'm not around." Hunched over the now tepid beer, Marc rested his forearms on the bar. "Best of all worlds," he said sarcastically. "I have a wife, a friend, and a lover. Same as most guys. Only difference is, most guys are lucky enough to have all three neatly packaged in one warm curvaceous body."

Fed by too much beer, the eyes Marc raised to his brother were watery. "So you see, little brother," he said, drowning in his own pity, "I'm so many different men, I'll be damned if I know which one of the bastards is sitting on this barstool tonight."

Music, laughter and smoke-filled air hung over them as the doctor searched his tired mind for a dose of medicine to administer to his brooding brother. Smiling through his own fatigue, Kevin said, "How long since you've seen Mom?"

"Um, maybe a week. Why?"

"Let's drop in on her on the way home. I called her this afternoon and she wasn't her usual chipper self. It had slipped my mind, but today would have been Mom and Dad's thirty-ninth anniversary. Her plans for an outing with the girls tonight fell through—something about everyone coming down with the flu. We'll surprise her, cheer her up."

"Sure. 'Cept she isn't going to take well to me being three sheets to the wind."

Kevin dropped several bills on the bar. "Maybe she won't notice."

"Ha! Mothers are born with a booze-sniffing gland attached to their uterus."

Laughing, Kevin shoved his arm through the sleeve of a leather jacket. "Don't remember studying about that particular part of the anatomy in med school. Must have been one of the classes I slept through."

"Yeah," Marc teased, "snoozing through lectures. That's how you graduated at the top of your class." Across a floor that suddenly had become the rolling deck of a ship, Marc wove on rubber legs through tightly packed tables. Once outside he drank in sobering air as cold mist collected like tiny glass beads on his dark head. His voice was that of the stern older brother when he said, "Listen, Kevin, not one word to Mom about this mess."

"But she's sure to ask…."

In the glow of a neon light, Marc's face was an eerie mask belching clouds of red fog as he spoke. "You'll pull it off. Hell, treat it as a doctor-patient confidence. I don't want her blaming herself. You know how mothers are. A son screws up and any mom thinks it's because she didn't breast feed the kid long enough, or because she started potty training too early. I won't worry Mom about this now. Don't lie to her, just avoid the truth."

Those last words repeated themselves in Kevin's brain as he unlocked the door on the dripping car. *I'm learning*, he said to himself, *from the master*.

✳   ✳   ✳   ✳

"I tried several times but your phone was busy," Marc said to Korey as she helped him shrug out of his coat. "I know we agreed on 8:00, but everyone had left the office and the quiet started closing in on me." He handed her a bottle of red wine. "Hope you don't mind that I arrived a little early for that spaghetti dinner.

"Of course not." He followed her into the kitchen as she read the label on the wine bottle. "Ah, Valpolicelli," she said. "Perfect." She handed him a corkscrew. "Tell me," she said as she watched him pierce the cork, "do you think I look like Dear Abby?"

He laughed and prolonged the study of her lovely face. "Can't see the resemblance myself. You been dishing out advice?"

"Not by choice. But most of my friends seem to think because I work out of my home, I'm free to listen to their woes at any given hour. That's one reason my phone is busy so much of the time. It's not that I don't want to help," she said as she lifted the lid from a large pot on the stove, "but I'm not sure I'm qualified." An aromatic blend of tomato, garlic, and herbs rose with the steam as Korey stirred the thick red sauce. A spot bubbled onto her pink sweater; she rubbed it away with a hand towel, then tapped the spoon on the side of the pot and replaced the lid.

"Qualified for what?" Marc wanted to know.

"To give advice to the lovelorn."

It was the underlying tone in her voice, the sadness, that made him take notice. A blast of heat hit him in the face as she opened the oven door and shoved a loaf of garlic bread inside. She's going through another spell, he thought. Missing Danny. Well, Marc, you have it within your power to bring her out of this funk, at least temporarily. And, by damn, Bradberry, before this night's over you're going to do it.

"Need any help?" he offered.

She looked at him over a large bowl of salad greens. "You good at telling women why some men are jerks?" she asked innocently.

To hide a flush of guilt, he took the salad bowl from her hands and turned his back to set it on the table. "Since I'm a member of that accused gender, I'm afraid my advice would not be worth much," he said over his shoulder. "Actually, what I meant was, may I help you with dinner?"

"No thanks. Everything is under control. Just have a seat and tell me what's new in the world of office buildings and custom homes."

Marc was more than happy to sink into a chair and turn the topic away from men as jerks, feeling as he did that the description hit too close to home. While Korey boiled spaghetti, he talked about work, avoiding as usual any mention of his personal life.

It was during dinner, fortified with a second glass of wine, that he asked her to fly with him to Albuquerque. In the flickering light of a half-dozen candles, she could not hide her surprise. And though she tried to say she had too much work to even think of going, he knew from the first glimpse of her twinkling eyes that it would take only a little push for her to accept. He suggested, helpfully, "If your sewing is all that's standing in your way of spending a few days with your aunt Matty, then take your work with you."

"I would have to see to a ticket. Airline rates are high right now…."

"Not to worry. You're an invited guest. I'll take care of the transportation."

"You'll do no such thing…."

"Korey." He brushed his hand lightly over the sleeve of her sweater. The yarn was soft, and for one wildly delicious moment he imagined it to be her naked skin. Distracted, he struggled to retrieve his train of thought. "Uh, it's all right. About the flight. I have my own plane."

She watched his face, any moment expecting him to laugh and say he was only teasing. Her mind scanned the months she had known him. Not once, in all the times he had commuted from Nashville to Chattanooga, had he mentioned flying in his own airplane. Neither, she realized now, had she ever heard him fret over running late for a scheduled commercial flight. "You do?" she asked in disbelief.

"Well, not entirely," he confessed. "To be precise, I own a fourth."

"Oh?" She giggled into her wine. "And may I ask in which fourth we will be flying to Albuquerque?"

"Funny. Now finish your spaghetti before it gets cold, and I'll tell you how I came to be part owner of a plane." He pushed aside his empty plate. "Some months ago, while losing miserably at poker with three buddies, I started grousing about how much I hated sitting around in airports. It came as no surprise that everyone at the table felt the same. Not being independently wealthy, none of us had any aspirations of owning an airplane, but someone came up with the idea of forming a partnership. With each beer we drank, the idea took on greater shape until, in the wee hours of the morning, the deck of cards pushed to the floor, we had a plausible plan. A few poker games later, we had ourselves a plane."

"Wow! The freedom to go anywhere, on a whim….I'm a bit envious."

"Don't be. It takes a small fortune to maintain and fly it, so it's not used frivolously, but the plane is in the air enough to warrant keeping a couple of pilots on the payroll." Marc added, confidently, "You'll meet them next week."

"*If* I go." She smiled, ignoring a vague disquiet. All these months Marc had so effectively kept this a secret…. "Tell me about your partners," she urged, twisting spaghetti onto her fork.

"We're a diverse bunch to be sure. Paul Roland is a fraternity brother. He owns a chain of women's apparel shops: Nashville, Atlanta, Birmingham, and, as of last year, one in Chattanooga."

"Hum, Roland. Name doesn't ring a bell. Where is his shop?"

"On Shallowford, near the mall. Paul operates his stores under the name Georgy's Trunk."

Korey smiled. "Oh, I love Georgy's Trunk! Beautiful clothes—pricey, but fabulous end-of-season sales. Probably half the things in my closet are from there. I've wondered about the name….does Georgy really exist?"

"She was Paul's grandmother. Paul has told the story that when he and his sister were children, Georgy would lead them up the steep creaking stairs to the attic of her stately—white columns and all—home near Natchez, Mississippi. Under a bare light bulb, Georgy let the kids have their way with the contents of her many trunks. Apparently in their day, Georgy and her husband had been members of a social set where lavish clothes were *de rigueur*. So the grandchildren spent many a rainy day in the attic strutting around in their finery: Paul in tuxedoes and morning coats; his sister dolled up in flowing satin gowns and rhinestone baubles. When Georgy died, part of her estate went to Paul. Not a vast amount, but enough to finance Paul's first dress shop in Nashville. He named it in memory of those childhood days in Natchez. The store took off and more stores followed. Now it's Paul who uses the plane most frequently. He's in every shop at least once a week, flies around the country on buying trips."

Marc leaned back in his chair, watched the candlelight play among the shadows at the edges of the room. Haunting strains of Spanish music strummed on an acoustical guitar drifted in from the living room. Wine, candles, alluring music. If he did not know better, he would think this to be the prelude to seduction. But he was learning about Korey. She would call this simply part of the "atmosphere" requisite when serving dinner to a *friend*. Damn! Call it what she will, tonight he wished she had opted to flood the room with incandescent light. Though the house was not overly warm, he felt heated in the glow of the candles. He shifted in his chair as images of Korey in various stages of undress began to tease his wayward mind.

She rescued him from this torture. "And partner number two?" she asked.

"Ah, yes." The lusty images evaporated. "Hank Steudy. A master builder of gorgeous homes, catering to people with gobs of money. His list of clients includes some very famous recording artists. The last couple of years he has shuttled back and forth from here to the U.S. Virgin Islands where he is building villas. Having use of a private jet has been a godsend for Hank."

"I'm sure. Has he built his own palatial home in paradise?"

Marc chuckled. "No, he's a simple man. Shares a modest house in Bellemeade with his wife and three teenage daughters. Lord knows with the money he's making he could live any way he chooses, but he and his family have no interest in emulating the lives of the *glitterati*."

In the company of someone with whom she could relax, Korey defied Emily Post by planting elbows firmly on the dinner table and cupping her chin in her hand. "Interesting set of friends you have," she said. "I can hardly wait to hear about partner number three."

"Chris Newely is the most....uh, I guess I should say *colorful* of the group." Marc poured the last of the wine equally between Korey's glass and his. "Nicest guy in the world, but a little left of center. Wears his long blonde hair in a pony tail, a silver arrow usually dangles from an ear lobe, and most days will find him running around in tattered jeans and a T-shirt, clean but looking as though they sat in a dryer for a week. To look at him, you'd think he didn't have two nickels to rub together, but fact is, at twenty-nine, he has tucked away a considerable nest egg."

"Saves a lot on clothes," Korey observed lightly.

"True," Marc laughed. "But it's his retail business in Nashville that accounts for most of his success. He's shrewd, has his finger on the pulse of the consumer. He sells Native American jewelry at a store he calls Newely Mined. Several times a year he takes buying trips to the Southwest. Flies into small airports, takes a rental car into remote areas, buys from Indian artisans as he goes. He visits pueblos, hogans, cabins, wherever he knows he can find the highest quality at the most competitive price." Without thinking, Marc invited, "You should see the lighted cases in his store. Silver, turquoise, jade, malachite. Some of the most beautiful stuff you've ever seen."

"I'd like that."

"Huh?"

"I'd like to visit Newely Mined....sometime."

"Oh. Yeah, quite a feast for the eyes." He made a clumsy attempt to sneak out of the corner he had backed into. "'Course, being a frequent visitor to New Mexico yourself, such sights must be old hat."

"Possibly," she shrugged and began to collect dirty dishes. "Tell me, how did you hook up with this free spirit?"

This time it was not desire for Korey that sent Marc's temperature soaring. It was panic. He had missed seeing this coming. He could not tell her he had met Chris through Clare; that Chris was the younger brother of Clare's roommate, her sophomore year at Vanderbilt. Marc absently handed Korey his plate. "Met Chris through a mutual friend," he stated, casually sidestepping the whole truth.

Korey said over her shoulder as she carried dishes to the kitchen, "Well, he sounds like a real gem." Dishes clattered into the sink. "Oh my," she giggled from behind her hand. "Forgive the terrible pun. I'm afraid it's the wine speaking."

If wine made her giddy, Marc thought, maybe it would also loosen her resistance to flying with him to New Mexico. He pressed what advantage the wine may have given him. "About Albuquerque….you're not going to pass up an opportunity to visit your aunt are you?" So there would be no misconception regarding his intention, he quickly added, "I'll be staying with my brother and sister-in-law. Matty has room for you?"

Wiping her hands on a towel, Korey faced Marc as he joined her in the kitchen. "Yes, Matty has a spare room," she said.

"Then will you fly with me?"

"Yes," she said, "I would like that very much."

Marc became lightheaded as pleasure flowed through him on a strong swift tide. But at the same time, beneath the surface of his glossy smile, a frightening undertow tugged at his battered conscience.

$$*\qquad*\qquad*\qquad*$$

Korey woke to the ratta-tat-tat of a woodpecker strafing the bark on the massive oak outside the bedroom window. Early November, yet on the warm rays of sun seeping through the curtains came the promise of another day of Indian summer. It was Saturday, and as she stretched sleep from her body, she looked forward to spending the afternoon with Tina, leisurely browsing the Autumn Street Fair at the Chattanooga Choo-Choo. As she rolled from the rumpled bed, Korey wondered what her sister would have to say about the forthcoming trip to New Mexico….

"Albuquerque!" Tina handed Korey a cone filled with chocolate frozen yogurt, picked strawberry for herself and paid the vendor. "Well, well, isn't this a surprising development? And what, may I ask, brought this on?"

"As you know," Korey answered as she swallowed a bite of yogurt, "Marc's brother and sister-in-law are building a house Marc designed. Construction began several weeks ago, and Marc wants to fly out to make sure all is going well. Eric and Rae are away from home on photo shoots much of the time and therefore can't keep a watchful eye on the builder. In fact, Marc says they may be out of town when we arrive, but he has a key to their current home."

"Ooh, how convenient for you," Tina purred.

"Sorry to toss a wet blanket over that part of your brain that's forever pushing me into a man's arms, but Marc has made it perfectly clear he will sleep at Eric's and I will sleep at Matty's. So you see," Korey smiled, "this trip is all very prim and proper."

"That *is* too bad," Tina teased. "Frankly," she said, curling strawberry yogurt onto her tongue, "I was hoping for something more exciting."

Korey pushed her sunglasses up on her nose. "You never give up, do you?"

Tina rolled her shoulders, stopped to inspect a table of crocheted purses. "Does Matty know you're coming?"

"I called her last night. She assured me she has no plans for next week. Says she can't wait to meet 'my young man.' I told her what I keep telling you, that Marc is a good friend, nothing more." Korey paused at a booth displaying stained glass suncatchers. "I must not be very convincing," she sighed, watching rows of sun-lit glass spin in the breeze. "I don't think she believed me, either."

"Well, it's things like this trip that make us disbelievers. I mean, Marc is a nice guy, fun, probably has lots of friends. How many of *them* has he invited to go on this trip to Albuquerque? None that you know of, right?"

They resumed their stroll, staying on the fringes of the crowd, giving only cursory glances at booths overflowing with hand crafted items. The clear air smelled of corn dogs and funnel cakes. "You're determined to make something of this, aren't you?" Calmly Korey explained, "Marc invited me because I had mentioned to him recently that Matty had been coaxing me to come for a visit. He'll be flying to Albuquerque. Matty lives there. He put two and two together and offered me a ride, gratis. That's all."

"Then what about that expensive bottle of perfume he gave you on Halloween?"

"What about the perfume?"

"You don't think that meant something?"

"I think," Korey said in a controlled voice, "he was only being kind."

Tina knew full well why Korey was choosing to believe Marc's motives were purely platonic: to believe otherwise would be an admission that someone was at last successfully hacking through the impenetrable vine Korey had let grow around her. Maybe it was time someone intervened before Korey became too comfortable in her insulated world. Impatiently, Tina shoved her sunglasses into her thick hair, rolled her eyes heavenward, then with a fussy little frown brought them around to pierce the dark lenses shielding Korey's innocent stare. "Kind! For heaven's sakes, Korey! *Kind* is inquiring about your health. *Kind* is holding a door, or offering an arm over an icy patch of sidewalk. Hundreds of dollars for a bottle of perfume far exceeds *kind*."

"What else could…."

"Tell me something," Tina interrupted, "has Marc ever kissed you?"

Korey answered sharply, "I don't see that's any of your business."

"It isn't. But since when has that stopped me?" Tina smiled.

Laughter drained the irritation from Korey's voice. "I see that you're not going to leave me alone until you know everything." She stepped out of the path of a rangy young man, his bushy red hair flaming in the sun and a ruby piercing his right nostril. In outstretched arms he carried a painting, dribbled squiggles of color that looked like it would be hung the wrong way no matter how it went on a wall. The two sisters tilted their heads this way and that trying to make sense of the large canvas. Their eyes met, but they held their bemused shrugs until after the man was well past.

"About that kiss," Korey said. "Marc did kiss me once. It was more than two months ago, the day I went to his new office. I was at the edge of the porch, ready to run for the car ahead of a rainstorm. And he kissed me. That is," she unconsciously touched a finger to her cheek, "if you call a skip of his lips across my face, a kiss."

"That was it? *The* kiss?"

"That was it. Disappointed?"

"The question should be—were you?"

"No….well, maybe a little. It was there, then gone; I didn't have time to think. Afterwards, I decided it hadn't meant anything." A picture of another kiss nearly forgotten flashed through her mind. But she would not titillate her sister now by revealing that Marc had in turn received a kiss on his cheek Halloween night, a comfortable and spontaneous gesture of thanks when he had unexpectedly come bearing a bottle of perfume cleverly hidden inside a pumpkin.

To Tina it was plain Korey had effectively disregarded any revealing signals Marc had chosen to give. To shake loose an awareness, she said, "So you don't think Marc is in love with you?"

Korey's head came up sharply. "In love…." She chewed the last bite of dripping cone. "Tina, really. A man that at times is practically an ice cube? Hardly. He's tough to figure. He's not moody, exactly, usually very pleasant, in fact. Quick to laugh; jokes a lot. But I'm never certain where I stand with him. Sometimes I catch him looking at me like he would pounce if I gave him any encouragement; then, in the next breath, he's treating me like I'm his kid sister."

Tina nodded, more to herself than to Korey. This assessment of Marc's behavior seemed accurately akin to her own observations.

"One day," Korey went on, "it's expensive perfume; the next, well, I can go for a week or more without hearing from him. And when we're together, his mind sometimes drifts, his eyes become vacant. I've been tempted so many times to scream into his ear: 'Hey, is anybody home?' Now he comes up with this idea to fly off with him to New Mexico." She paused. "I'm wondering, Tina, don't you think it odd that in the months I've known Marc, in all the times he has shuttled back and forth between Chattanooga and Nashville, not once did he mention he owned a small jet?"

"From someone else, perhaps it would seem strange. But Marc? No, I wouldn't say it was odd. He was being modest, I suppose, probably thought it would be too much like boasting to talk about his airplane. He's obviously a man of talent and ability, yet according to what you've told me, he seems to wear his accomplishments very close to the cuff. Not the kind to brag about jetting hither and yon."

"You're probably right. It's just, I had this feeling the other night when he told me about the plane, that it had been so easy for him to keep it from me. I kind of wondered…. I feel silly saying this, but I wondered if maybe there were other things about him that I don't know."

"My dear sister," Tina said in a soft, caring voice. "What do we women know about men, anyway? There's a lifetime of things about that man that you don't know. Yours is a relatively new friendship, after all, and a long-distance friendship most of the time. Please don't be angry with me when I say this, but since you seem unwilling to give him more than face value, it seems unreasonable that you should ask more of him."

"You have a point. It's unfair of me to want to keep my life my own, yet…" She could not finish. To do so would mean admitting there was a hidden place deep inside, hollow and craving to be filled with anything and everything having to do with Marc Bradberry. To go into that hidden place would be too risky. "Oh, never mind." Korey waved a dismissive hand through a shadow cast by Chattanooga's restored railroad station. "No more about Marc. Here we are, surrounded by all of these lovely arts and crafts, and we're being much too fiscally conservative." Korey playfully pushed her sister in the direction of a booth piled high with hand knit sweaters. "Beginning here and now," she said, "we're going to spend the remainder of this gorgeous day engaged in some serious shopping."

CHAPTER 9

▼

They fled the soggy hills of Tennessee, left the torrential rains far behind before they had flown over the panhandle of west Texas. Albuquerque awaited under a cloudless sky: A city escaping an eastern barrier of Sandia Mountains; greedily devouring land in its westward expansion; jumping a Rio Grande drunk with mud; halting, finally, at a sentry line of dead volcanoes standing on the western horizon.

Matty Cunningham had sounded disappointed on the phone when Korey told her Marc would be renting a car. Korey was therefore instructed, with a smile lining the aunt's stern voice, to "promise to come directly to my place from the plane, young lady, or else you will find me standing at the airport to greet you." Obedience guided the visiting couple straight to Matty's door.

With open arms, Matty was out of the house and rushing to them before Marc shut off the car's engine. By the time he had unlocked the trunk, Korey was outside the car and smothered in an embrace. Marc stood at the fringe and watched the affectionate display between aunt and niece.

"So good to have you here, my dear," Matty said.

"It's wonderful being here." Korey hugged the woman who had become like a mother.

"You're lovelier than ever."

"No. But you're *younger* than ever."

Matty laughed. "Who taught you to lie, child? Certainly not my sister!"

"It's true, Matty. You'll never age."

"Ump. Then what's this?" the aunt asked as she pulled on a tuft of unruly gray hair.

"The symbol of wisdom."

Matty cackled. "My favorite niece," she said as she turned a radiant beam on Marc. He was caught by surprise when, without introduction, the demonstrative little lady pulled him to her ample bosom. "Welcome, Marc," she said to his chest. "So nice of you to bring my dear Korey to me."

In stature Matty was much shorter than his own mother, but something about the aunt made him think of Barbara Bradberry and he liked Matty immediately. "My pleasure, Mrs. Cunningham. Having the company of your niece made the trip very enjoyable." He looked over Matty's head to see a blush rise on Korey's cheeks.

"Seems introductions are unnecessary." Korey grinned.

"In the house, you two," Matty instructed, prodding Korey with the edge of a small suitcase lifted from the open trunk. "The sun's going down, and it's getting too cold to stand out here and gab. Come in and have something to drink. And you, young man," she met Marc's vivid green eyes, "you're a friend of Korey's and therefore a friend of mine. My friends call me Matty."

She led the way through a high adobe arch and into a walled courtyard which hid the front entrance of the adobe house from the street. Once inside the house Marc set Korey's larger suitcase on terra-cotta tiles. An orange shaft of sunlight was extinguished when Matty closed the door, and the stucco walls of the entry-way took on the cool, earthy face of a sheltering cave. Matty fussed over her guests, hanging coats in a closet while she elicited details of the plane ride. A fire warmed them instantly as they all converged in a cozy den. Flames licked from logs in a fireplace blackened by a thousand fires like this one. Pale fingers of aro-matic smoke curled through the room like incense.

To Korey the house was an old friend: As children, she and Tina had jour-neyed here every summer in the back of the family station wagon. The den was her favorite room in the house. The same worn rugs warmed the floor, and from sepia tintypes covering tan walls, ruthless outlaws watched her with their flinty eyes. Her Uncle Walt's collection of Anasazi arrow and spear heads still hung in its rightful place above the mantel, a bittersweet reminder of how much her deceased uncle had cherished the rich and ancient history of his native state.

Matty pulled heavy drapes across the dusk, and over cups of hot toddy conver-sation flowed gently through the room. Marc was made to feel at home in this modest house as he sat with Korey on a sofa and sipped from a steaming cup. Relaxed against the sofa cushion, he was attentive while Matty listened to Korey tell a tale of her first flight on a private jet. He remembered well his own excite-ment the first time he had flown in the plane, but Korey's animated narrative placed a fresh bloom on an experience he had begun to take for granted. Her eyes smiled around the edges as she spoke, and Marc realized he was witnessing a change in Korey, one that had begun the moment the jet had entered New Mexico airspace. He saw her now as he never had, gleaming as if a polish had stripped her of a dull patina. Was it the rare mile-high air that colored her cheeks with roses and made her laughter bubble to the rhythm of a mountain brook? Once beyond the sprawl of the city, so much of this land they visited was raw and wild and seemed to draw Korey into its spell. Since their arrival, she sparkled with the fire of a faceted gem, each side reflecting a different yet no less dazzling color. His gaze fixed on her finely carved profile, and he was oblivious to the telling smile that had come to rest comfortably on his expressive mouth.

For blissful moments, his mind strolled through a world where Korey would be at his side on all of his business trips, where it would be his delight to see her smile as he showered her with small but meaningful tokens of his devotion. In that world he would pamper and dote. He would make wild and glorious love to her until she no longer remembered pain.

Marc's absent gaze drifted across the room to Matty, and her pointed stare yanked him from the Eden of his daydreams. He wondered how much of his fantasy the wily gal had seen. Had he sipped toddy while he dreamed, or had the cup simply hovered at his lips as it did now? He thought he saw a glimmer of a smile before she turned her attention once again to Korey.

Matty brought Korey up to date on the welfare of three daughters, Korey's cousins. While she did this, a part of Matty's agile mind examined the meaning of Marc's lingering gaze upon her niece. Matty was no stranger to the ways of love, having fallen madly for Walt Cunningham the first time she had set eyes on him that night forty years ago when he had grabbed her waist and swung her around the dusty floor at a barn dance. Today Marc's longing for Korey was as easily read as a billboard at ten paces, and Matty could not understand how Korey seemed to miss the sign staring her in the face.

As if she sensed the subversive path of her aunt's thoughts, Korey turned to find she was the object of Marc's fixed gaze. This was not the first time she had caught him looking too deeply, and she felt suddenly uneasy. To divert his attention, she addressed her aunt. "My goodness, Matty, how rude we must seem. Not only have we excluded Marc from this conversation, but we must be boring him silly with all this talk about our family, people he's never met."

"Bored? Never," Marc said emphatically. "But, ladies, I will use this opening to excuse myself for a while, give you time alone to catch up on family gossip and whatever else it is women talk about. I'm off to Eric's to change clothes and make a few phone calls. I doubt that he and Rae have returned from their photo shoot in southern Colorado, but I have a key and have been told to make myself at home. I'll be back here in plenty of time to take you both to dinner."

At the mention of dining out, Matty, who had cooked all week in anticipation of feeding guests, hid any expectations she may have had for entertaining Marc and Korey at home tonight. "How nice of you," she said. "Then may I suggest The High Noon Restaurant in Old Town Albuquerque? Unless, of course, you have a preference...."

"None whatsoever. The High Noon it is. I'll be back by 7:30." In high spirits, he could not refrain from playfully chucking Korey under the chin as he left.

*   *   *   *

Adventures dreamed up by the late Walter S. Cunningham and executed by Walter and his bride, Matalyn Stroker Cunningham, in times when the entire population of the state of New Mexico was no more than that of a medium-size city in the Midwest, were relived at a dark corner table in The High Noon Restaurant. Even after countless times, Korey never tired of hearing Aunt Matty tell of forays where blistering deserts were combed for Indian artifacts. Or, when nosing around ghost towns, of harrowing encounters with wild-eyed creatures, both human and otherwise. And never to be left out of Matty's repertoire were the rough and tumble rides through the high country in the Jeep dubbed 'Miss Elly.' Walt had been the proud owner of Miss Elly long before he met Matty at the dance. Matty never asked, and Walt never said, whether Miss Elly was named for an actual female. But the mystery never kept Walt's young wife from crawling into the dusty Jeep beside her husband and bouncing along barely discernible trails or blazing more than a few of their own.

Marc relaxed in a chair next to Korey and laughed in wide-eyed wonder at Matty's larger-than-life tales. With reluctance, he let the attention be turned to him when Matty stated she had dominated the evening far too long. Korey blushed to her toes when Matty insisted on learning more about "Korey's young man." Center stage, with Korey and her aunt as the audience, was Marc's idea of a hot seat. When around Korey, he was accustomed to being forever vigilant, but Matty filled him with a new terror, for she seemed skilled at looking beyond, not only into who he was but *what* he was. Propping up his courage on more than one sip of margarita, as he spoke he stayed within the reasonably safe perimeters of his work, speaking mainly of the project that brought him to Albuquerque: the new house he designed for Eric and Rae. He merely skimmed the surface of the lives of his brother and sister-in-law and was relieved nearly to the point of sagging when Matty did not make further issue of his personal life, but a fleeting thought of his comatose wife cut him to the bone.

With spicy food resting warmly in her stomach and wild honey dripping from a warm sopaipilla, Matty asked what plans the two visitors had for their short stay in New Mexico.

"For me, work mostly, I'm sorry to say." Marc's sigh left no doubt work was not his first choice. "I'll spend the better part of tomorrow with the building contractor at the site of the new house. However," he draped a lazy arm over the back of Korey's chair, "I do intend to devote the whole of tomorrow evening with your niece." He turned to Korey. "Eric called while I was at the house changing for dinner. He and Rae are still in Colorado but will be home early afternoon tomorrow. They're anxious to meet you and want us to join them for dinner." He shook his head and laid his hand on the dinner check as Matty reached for it across the table. "And Matty," he said smiling, "you may enjoy the company of your niece most of tomorrow, but count on giving her up to me on Saturday."

Since Marc had not hinted that there would be time in this weekend for anything other than his work, Korey was both surprised and pleased to hear of his plan. Though she had told herself the opportunity to see Matty was the only reason for accepting Marc's generous invitation to fly to New Mexico, Korey realized now that she had come not only because of her aunt. Even stronger was the desire to spend as much time as possible with Marc. This revelation shocked her, and she fought hard to hide her true feelings. When she finally smiled at him, she was sure her smile conveyed only mild pleasure. But to Marc, the smile seemed to say much more.

*   *   *   *

Like a plunge through ice, Eric Bradberry's enthusiasm for meeting his brother's "special friend" had cooled to sub-zero. "What do you mean, you haven't told her?" In vexation Eric plowed his fingers through sun-streaked hair. "You've been seeing Korey for six months and she still doesn't know about Clare? That's so preposterous I'd say you were kidding, but your face is such a perfect picture of guilt that I have to believe what you're telling me is true."

As if he had lost confidence in his argument, Marc said, "I'm not *seeing* her—not in the sense of *dating*. I've known her for six months, yes, but as a friend. At least that's how she sees it."

Eric had no patience for rationalizations and did not bother to hide his sarcasm. "Well, as you so eloquently stated moments ago, you have indeed found yourself in 'a bit of a fix.' Do you realize what you're asking of Rae and me?" He spoke with more disbelief than anger, but his voice still had a sharp bite. "You want us to lie for you."

"No, not lie...."

"Oh, save it, Marc! Best remember I'm not as easily manipulated as Korey apparently is. Salve your own conscience with convoluted logic if you must, but spare me the hair-splitting. You bring this woman out here and then expect me to act like some imbecile who forgets that his own brother has a wife?" Eric tossed a handful of photographs on a table. Shots of snow-capped mountains, ice-crusted waterfalls, herds of buffalo and elk slid across the polished wood. He rubbed his forehead with the heel of his hand then faced Marc head on. "Listen, I know this life with Clare must be hell, that when her life stopped, for a time yours did too. But since then you have dated a few women. You know Rae and I would not have found fault if you had brought any one of those women to Albuquerque. But you didn't. And, damn, you've never gone so far as to deceive any woman you've dated. It's not like you to do something like this. Whatever possessed you?"

Listening to Eric made it all sound so absurd that Marc was momentarily lost for an answer. He slumped lower in the chair. "To be honest, I don't know. When Korey and I met, it was strictly business, so whether or not I was married had no place in our conversations. Besides, at first I thought *she* was married."

"Oh?"

"Yeah, she still wears a wedding ring. Anyway, I admit I felt a spark the instant I saw her, and for that reason I should have applied the brakes when I found out she was widowed." He scoffed. "I thought I was in control, that I could keep everything on a professional level. But I was wrong. I invented all sorts of ways to see her. I'm the one who has applied the pressure; she has resisted my charms, commendably. I ignored what was happening until I was forced to admit that we had developed a close friendship. Even then, I somehow convinced myself that as long as we were 'just friends' it didn't matter that I was withholding vital information."

"Now it has come to matter, hasn't it?"

"Yes." Marc's voice dropped. "It has come to matter very much."

"She's got a hold on you?" Eric's brows raised in inquiry.

"All I know is, when I'm with her life is good. And when she's not at my side, I can't stop thinking about her."

"That bad, huh?"

"'Fraid so."

"And Korey? What does she feel?"

Sprawled bonelessly in the chair, feeling suddenly ungainly, Marc knocked his knees together. "We're friends. I don't think her feelings go beyond that."

"You'd better hope they don't." The warning was not without a note of compassion. "If that's the case, it's not too late to tell her about Clare. If Korey is the friend you think she is, she'll try to see your side of it."

"Maybe. I wish I shared your confidence." Marc rubbed his chafed conscience with the balm of truthful introspection. "If six months ago—the first time Korey and I dined together—I had mentioned then the circumstance of my marriage, Korey would have, as you said, 'understood.' But we would not have had these months together, and she would not be here with me now. She never would have seen me socially. She lives by a code of ethics that sometimes borders on the Puritanical." He paused. "No, that's not correct; I'm being unfair and making her sound too straight-laced, ridiculously stuffy. She's not that at all. But she has a strong sense of what is right. Believe me, she would not indulge in an affair with a married man, no matter how much I argued my own cause. But I'm not a cad playing on her sympathies, wearing her down..."

Eric interrupted. "Don't be so damn self-righteous. Isn't that exactly what you're doing now? Taking your own sweet time about it but, just the same, leading her into your arms....into your bed?"

Marc uncoiled and shot upright in the chair. "You sound just like Kevin," he nearly shouted, as if volume would fill the gaps in a weak defense. "For your information I haven't touched her!"

In the silence that followed his outburst, Marc let his head fall to the back of the chair. His eyes repeatedly traced the perimeters of the beamed ceiling as if that would help box in his runaway emotions.

"Why did you bring her here?" Eric asked.

Marc raised his head; it felt like an anvil. "That's a perfectly rational question asked of an imperfect, irrational man. The answer? I told myself I was being altruistic—bringing her here to visit with her aunt. But the truth is I asked her to come because I couldn't stop myself. This feeling I have for Korey is stronger than I am. And that scares the hell out of me. I'm a runaway train with no brakeman, Eric. The speed, the danger, are highs I've never felt before. I see what's coming—somewhere ahead I'll derail, but I'm powerless to stop the inevitable crash and burn."

Eric heretofore had credited his younger brother with having a superior intellect. Years of respect were nearly wiped out in one afternoon. "Well, if that isn't the most hair-brained, self-centered...." Eric said, fuming. "While you're waxing theatrical nonsense about trains, are you giving any thought to Korey? She's widowed. Think of the pain she's been through." Eric gulped air. "You want me to think you're nuts about her....well, what I think is, you're just plain nuts."

Marc blinked and held his fragile temper. "Hey, aren't you getting a little rough? Maybe I've had lapses in good judgment, but do I deserve that?" He returned Eric's icy glare. "It's not for you to tell me how I feel about Korey. I've created the problem; I'll find the solution."

Eric was riled, could not stop the momentum. "I wouldn't count on it." He leaned forward, elbows on his knees. "From where I sit, it looks to me like you're going to come through this the loser."

"What are you driving at?"

"Forget what I said earlier. My gut feeling is, even if you cough up the truth before the sun sets today, Korey will walk. Or let's say she finds out some other way—don't give me that savage look, I'm not going to tell her—then who would be surprised if she didn't hang around for explanations? Or what if Clare dies? Even then, I can't imagine Korey would have you."

"Why the hell not?"

"Oh, quit scratching your Neanderthal head and come out of that cave you're living in. Face it, your friendship with Korey is built on lies. Sooner or later Korey will know the truth. What woman would want any part of a man who has strung her along for months?"

"Thanks for the unsolicited assessment." Marc shifted, crossed a leg over the opposite knee then reversed the action. His brother spoke the truth, and reality had a bitter taste. Marc swallowed a second retort when he heard a car door slam in the garage. The last thing he wanted was for Rae to be caught in crossfire in her own living room. Grocery bags rattled in the kitchen. With a vigor that surprised him, Marc sprang from the chair and looked down on his brother. "All right, Eric," he said. "I'll level with Korey. But I won't have the time to do it before the four of us have dinner tonight. I'd like your word that you and Rae won't mention Clare in Korey's presence."

Absently Eric stared at a photo on the table. He wished he was still in that cold mountain air where he had stalked and captured on film the three elk posed in the fog of their own hot breath. The elk had asked nothing of him, unlike his brother, who asked so much. "Okay," Eric groaned. "For the record, I agree to this with great reluctance. Just do me a favor and don't bring Korey here. Having dinner with her tonight is going to be difficult enough. You'll understand, of course, when Rae and I plead fatigue and leave shortly after the meal is finished."

"Of course."

"Good. Then for the duration of your short stay I'll watch my tongue, and I'll ask Rae to do the same." Eric began collecting the scattered photos. "But you should know," he said, sliding a steely glance at his brother, "I don't like what we're doing, Marc. This subterfuge. I don't like it one damn bit."

∗   ∗   ∗   ∗

"All in all, the dinner went quite well, don't you think?" Rae Bradberry spoke over her shoulder as she preceded her sedate husband into the house.

"Uh, I suppose."

Hanging her coat on a hook, Rae tried to draw Eric into a conversation. "It's easy to see why Marc is infatuated. Korey's a lot of fun and very lovely." Rae kicked off her suede shoes, sank into the sofa and threw an afghan over her feet. In the shadowed room her auburn hair seemed nearly black. "And she doesn't appear to be hiding anything behind those big brown eyes."

"Um."

Ignoring her husband's pacing, Rae lifted a photo from the table. She studied it at arm's length until Eric stopped circling the room and thoughtlessly plucked it from her outstretched hand.

"You're sure," he said, his tone all business, "this is the one you want on the inside leaf of our new book?"

Rae's voice was low, unruffled. "It's the one we agreed on this afternoon. I haven't changed my mind." She watched Eric's eyes glaze over as he pretended to look at the picture. "Have you?" she asked. When the only response from her husband was a vacant stare, Rae added, "….changed your mind?"

"No. I still think he's making a dreadful mistake."

"He…. wait a minute. We're not talking about the same thing, are we, Eric?"

"What I'm talking about," Eric said, tossing aside the photograph, "is the ridiculous charade my brother is playing behind the back of that beautiful woman. Korey is a delight. I toast Marc's good taste. I refrain, however, from doing the same to his good sense."

"I'm not quite so opinionated." Rae patted the sofa, inviting Eric to join her. He placed her feet in his lap, wrapped them snugly in the afghan.

"You think I should mind my own business."

"Not altogether. Like it or not, Marc has made this our business. I agree he was wrong to hide Clare. But the consequences of his silence may not be as dire as you fear."

"They'll be bad enough. I don't mean to be heartless, but my brother isn't the one I'm so concerned with here. He is setting that girl up for a tremendous fall."

"Not necessarily. Now close your mouth, my darling, and hear me out. I watched Korey very closely this evening, and unless she's a master at hiding her feelings, Marc is the only one of that duo who is in love. Korey behaved as if she and Marc were good friends, nothing more. No longing sideways glances. A woman in love would not have passed up the chance to touch the hand of the man she loved when she asked him for the salt shaker. The signs just aren't there, Eric. And if I'm right, if Korey loves but is not *in love* with Marc, then why would she fall apart on being told Marc has a wife he was set to divorce before she became the victim of a horrible attack? Oh, I'm not saying Korey won't be miffed. Marc will have plenty of explaining to do and much of what he has done is indefensible. But Korey doesn't impress me as one to harbor a grudge."

Eric kissed his wife's forehead. He said, "I hope you're right. Maybe I've blown this whole thing out of proportion."

"I do think you're taking your big brother roll too seriously." Rae tweaked Eric on the chin. "Your younger brother has been grown for some years now. He's skilled at finding his way out of rough spots. I wish he hadn't involved us, but since he has, it's up to us to stay away from the brewing storm until it has blown past. That way maybe we all will get through this with few abrasions." She kissed away Eric's frown.

He wanted to believe what she said was true. But he found his faith could not match that of his wife. "I wonder," he said.

✳   ✳   ✳   ✳

While Eric and Rae debated Marc and Korey's fate, the objects of that intense discussion were roaming the narrow streets and festively lighted courtyards of Old Town Albuquerque, drifting in and out of cozy adobe shops. The historic village had prospered in the eighteenth century and commerce still was no stranger. Korey and Marc found themselves overwhelmed by stores chock full of sculpture, paintings, clothing, rugs, and enough silver and turquoise jewelry to satisfy the most ardent collector.

As they happily fulfilled the role of typical tourists, neither Korey nor Marc dared observe that it might be more than the thin dry air that made them lighthearted, even giddy. Strolling through inviting shops, they fingered and pawed the wares, awed by the workmanship of some items, driven to giggles by the peculiarity of others. The couple spoke of nothing of consequence, yet each phrase uttered brought the listener to a greater understanding of the speaker. This growing awareness was not acknowledged by either, as if denying the existence of a look here, a smile there would keep new feelings from rushing to the surface. Still, despite care to appear otherwise, to the eye of a passing stranger Marc and Korey could have been lovers on holiday.

One shop in particular seemed to draw Marc, and he took Korey's hand to pull her out of the chill air and into the store. Brightly lit interior walls were filled with framed photographs, mostly landscapes the size of posters, wild photogenic vistas captured yet untamed by film. Korey recognized the photos as works of art, paintings done not by hand and brush, but by a meticulous eye and a superior camera.

The shopkeeper, bohemian in his wire-rimmed glasses, earring and pony tail, greeted the browsers in the hushed tones of a librarian. Korey smiled a greeting, then, with so many sights to see, wandered away from a muted exchange between Marc and the lanky young man. His steps giving nothing away on the carpeted floor, Marc startled her several minutes later when he draped a loose arm over her shoulder.

Leaning to her ear, he said, confidently, "You like them."

His warm breath unexpectedly fanned a deeply hidden flame. She turned away to hide the heat rising to her cheeks. He dropped his arm. "Like them?" She chuckled at the understatement. "I'm awed by them."

"Excellent." He smiled and a gleam lit his eyes. "Then I'm proud to claim most of these photographs as those taken by tonight's dinner companions, Eric and Rae."

"Your grin gave you away." Korey tugged at a button on his open coat. "I knew what you were going to say before you said it. That face of yours had all the subtlety of the Cheshire cat." Her eyes swept the wall nearest them. "Imagine capturing the very essence of this magnificent country on film. The colors, the use of light and shadow—every picture jumps off the wall. With such combined talent, no wonder your brother and his lovely wife are in such demand."

"Long hours of patiently waiting for just the right shot are finally paying off. I rarely go into a bookstore these days without spotting their work. Calendars, post cards. They didn't mention it at dinner, but now they are compiling photos for their third book—coffee table variety I suppose you would say—with the first two still selling well. And they do a lot of shoots for the New Mexico Bureau of Tourism as well as those of neighboring states.

"Their business is the main reason for the new house they're building. They do their own photo processing and need more space. The new house will not be a good deal larger than their existing home but will be much better designed." Realizing that what he had just said smacked of boasting, Marc laughed. "Better designed for their needs, I should have said. Oh, what the heck, if I do say so, it's going to be a great house."

"Perfect, I'm sure," Korey said with conviction, her eyes meeting his.

Marc looked beyond the pedestal he sensed she was erecting for him and took her attention away from himself. "Allow me to brag on my family, if you will. This is not the only gallery that offers Eric and Rae's photographs. There is another on the north side of Albuquerque, one each in Santa Fe and Taos and three in Arizona."

"This comes as such a surprise. You had said so little of your family...." The thought died and Marc did not encourage its resurrection. Korey moved around the room visiting, through the photographs, mountain peaks and desert basins; limestone caverns and red rock canyons; ancient pueblos eroded to the nub and those still whole and inhabited by dark-skinned people. As she perused the gallery walls, her chest began to grow tight; it startled her to realize she was being attacked by a case of envy. There were moments of confusion before she understood that the envy was not for the skill displayed in the capturing of the photos before her. No, the envy was aimed directly at the lives of the two people behind the camera. Eric and Rae not only were privileged to live together but they worked together as well. If the warmth they had openly displayed at dinner tonight was a fair indication, theirs was a healthy marriage, flowing with mutual affection and respect. Their happiness was now Korey's sorrow; a painful reminder of a barren life. A photo of sure-footed mules descending a steep and winding trail into the Grand Canyon lost its appeal as Korey's mind took off to wander its own trail. Marc had been in her life six months now, yet she had spent much of that time withdrawing from him. Had she taken refuge in this friendship while she avoided peeking into its hidden corners for fear of what she might find? The honesty of the question demanded an affirmative answer. Glancing over her shoulder, she located Marc and studied his profile appreciatively while he flipped through a rack of unframed prints. What would happen, she wondered, if she let go her fears, gave her heart permission to go its own way? What would happen if she opened to Marc and told him the circumstances of her late husband's death? These answers would take contemplation, and this gallery was not the place in which to do it.

He watched her come to him. She brushed his arm in a offhand way, and his heart fluttered. "Should I just browse," she said teasing, "or should I mortgage my home to take a few of these back to Chattanooga?"

He laughed, glanced furtively to see that the arty young man was no where to be seen. "If we want to buy," he said in a lowered voice, "it so happens that I know two people who will see to it we get a deep discount. Frankly," he added as he swept her out the door, "these prices are a little rich for my blood."

Outside the sky seemed blacker as they passed stores closed for the night and, unhurried, made their way toward the parking lot. At one of the few store windows still brightly lit, Korey paused to admire a long skirt flowing from yards of turquoise velvet. Above the skirt hung a matching vest; in the light the crushed velvet ensemble seemed to shimmer and call Korey to trade the chill night air for the heat of the dress shop.

Marc smiled as, outside her periphery, he watched her press her nose near the glass, like a child glued to the window of a toy store. His indecision lasted only the time it took for his hand to pull hers from the warmth of her coat pocket. He nearly lifted his unsuspecting companion off her feet as he pulled her toward the store entrance.

Her hand held captive in his gentle grip, they were inside before Korey could sputter, "What….what are you doing?"

"I'm buying you that skirt."

"No. Oh, Marc, I couldn't possibly…."

"Yes, you can." The air was close, not unpleasantly, with the odor of fabric dyes. Two women customers and a matronly clerk stared at them over a clothes rack. "Please, Korey," he said. "Let me do this."

Her cheeks burned from the spectacle they were creating. For a long silent moment their eyes dueled, and the determination she saw in those green depths frightened her no small amount. It was a look new to her, and without conscious thought, she somehow knew it to be so compelling that if he should ever turn that same look on her again she would not refuse him—anything.

During the stand-off, a ripple of doubt invaded Marc's resolve. When the impulse had first struck him, he thought he simply had been hit by a generous spirit of giving. On deeper inspection, however, his largess appeared to be undermined by ulterior motive. But surely that deeper part of him was not sleazy enough to think if he invested a sizable chunk of money in some clothes, Korey would feel obliged to be less angry when the time came around for him to tell her he was married. No, he could never demean her with bribes. His sole aim tonight, he was convinced, was only to give joy.

Her voice was so low it was nearly absorbed by the clothes filling the tiny shop. "You're not going to accept 'no,' are you?"

"Might as well find your size," he said for all to hear. He caught the eye of the sales clerk, then grinned at Korey. "We're not leaving here without a purchase or two."

An hour later Korey heard a lock click behind them as, laden with boxes, they departed the dress shop. Marc had not stopped with the purchase of the velvet skirt. Over Korey's protests, he had insisted that she have the matching vest plus a long sleeve shirt in creamy silk. Boots of supple leather had come next. Even at that he had not pronounced the ensemble complete, calling it "naked," without shoulder length earrings crafted from gleaming silver and turquoise. While the fawning clerk rushed from rack to dressing room with arms full of clothes, Korey had stood patiently, tempted but not daring once to glance at a price tag. She buttoned and unbuttoned, zipped and unzipped, tied and untied. And all the while, she tried to come up with a way she could, without appearing ungrateful, return everything to the tony shop for a full refund the next day. And no matter how hard she tried, she had not thought of a gracious way of doing it.

Now, as Marc unlocked the car door, Korey was startled by his clairvoyance. "Don't even *think* about it," he said as he gingerly set two dress boxes on the rear seat then did the same with those she carried.

She detected the smile in his voice even though his darkly shadowed face appeared stern in the inadequate light of the parking lot. With a flutter of eyelashes, she peered up at him. "Think about what?" she asked too innocently.

He chuckled as he helped her into the car. "You know perfectly well what I'm talking about." Stacking his hands on the frame of the open car door, he ducked his head and grinned at her. "You were much too cooperative in that dress shop. Didn't fool me a bit, however. All the while you were indulging my whim, that frugal mind of yours was scheming to return these purchases." He leaned closer to inspect her eyes. "Am I getting warm?" he asked.

A nervous giggle escaped Korey's lips. "How did you do that?"

"What? See through that transparent mind of yours?"

She nodded.

"I don't give away trade secrets."

Though she smiled at his teasing, Korey shuddered as he closed her into the dark car. He had come to know her well.... A thought scurried across her unsettled mind: with uncanny insight, if Marc found it such a simple task to see the workings inside her head, could he as well, through those penetrating green eyes, see that which had begun to blossom inside her heart?

CHAPTER 10

▼

The day dawned gray and dim, low clouds lopping off the razorback of the Sandia Mountains. An icy wind blew a warning, bidding all fragile souls to remain indoors.

Marc and Korey, determined that the bleak weather would not steal the enjoyment of their last full day in New Mexico, allowed the weather to have its say until after they had eaten a leisurely lunch with Matty. Then, as if the young couple willed it, the temperature warmed and the arid wind seemed to absorb the lowest clouds, leaving a thinner, less ominous blanket spread over the sun.

By mutual agreement, Korey and Marc chose to spend the afternoon roaming the ruins of Gran Quivira, an ancient pueblo sleeping in the beautiful Manzano Mountains ninety minutes from Albuquerque. Korey had suggested, with conscious purpose, Gran Quivira for their outing. Having been there once before, she knew it to be off the beaten path of more popular tourist haunts and would therefore furnish the seclusion she sought.

After the excursion to Old Town Albuquerque the night before, Korey knew the time had come to open herself completely to Marc and to the eventuality that he may one day offer more than friendship. Time to tell him about Danny, to find solace in sharing with Marc the events of Danny's death.

Korey drove the rental car south on Interstate 25, Marc having graciously appointed her navigator and driver since she had plotted the route. She exited the Interstate and headed east on US 60, crossing the Rio Grande where the river flowed wide but shallow. Water lapped the shoulders of sandbars that lay like a gam of beached whales. *Mother Blue Water* the Isleta Indians call the river, but today the water ran brown, dull in the afternoon gloom. Cottonwood trees stood in great numbers along the bank, their naked branches shivering in the wind.

Terrain from the Interstate to the foothills of the Manzano Mountains was flat, featureless except for the occasional trailer home where more than a few junked cars typically stood as hulking yard ornaments.

Conversation was relaxed in the quiet car until Marc was compelled to put into words his drop in comfort level when, as they seemed to glide above the ribbon of road, he noted the needle on the speedometer hovering around 85 miles per hour. He said, only half-joking, "I wonder if you're suffering delusions of being Danica Patrick flying the oval at the Indianapolis Motor Speedway." In deference, Korey eased up on the accelerator, but the road, empty except for their car, was too straight, too tempting to keep the speed much under 70. Marc, bringing himself to trust in Korey's driving, relaxed and enjoyed the vistas.

Soon they passed through the foothills, and the landscape changed from monotonous beige to soil red as brick from which sprouted hearty green junipers which grew thicker with each rise in elevation. Breaking through the mountain pass, Korey and Marc found themselves surrounded by mesas of dark red, nearly maroon. Still gaining altitude, the car raced a train winding on tracks following the highway. The contest was a dead heat as the road became more mountainous and the car slowed for sharp twists and turns. Mesas on the far side of the train shimmered in the heat pouring from mighty diesels as the three engines of the Santa Fe Railroad strained to pull their burden of freight up the steep grade. A straight stretch of road finally handed Korey the race, and the train engineer, exhibiting true sportsmanship, amiably conceded defeat with a grin and a wave of his gloved hand. Marc in turn saluted with two fingers touched to his brow as the car shifted down to rush the steep hill, leaving the roar of the lumbering train dying away behind.

The tiny town of Mountainair was virtually asleep when Korey and Marc passed through on the way to Gran Quivira. A dusty car parked in front of the Ancient Cities Café on Main Street and two pickup trucks outside the Rose Bud Saloon were the only signs that people might be around. Korey made a turn onto state road 55 and headed the final twenty-five miles to the Anasazi ruins.

Only an occasional adobe or stone house was visible from the narrow, shoulderless road that took them along the top of a mesa. Small herds of brown cattle appeared here and there, roaming the thick stands of juniper in search of clumps of scrub grass. As the road wound past more than one collapsed windmill lying like bleached bones on the sand, and skirted small corrals with too many missing rails, abandoned ranches seemed to outnumber those that someone still called home.

From five miles away, Gran Quivira, its ancient walls crowning the pinnacle of a limestone hill, was dimly visible. The gray walls of the ruin closely matched the overcast sky and looked from a distance like a small medieval castle eroded to the nub by the ravages of wind and rain.

A park ranger's truck was the only vehicle in the paved parking lot as Korey pulled into a space. Inside the ranger station, she and Marc passed the time with a ranger starved for conversation before starting the short hike to the pueblo ruins. Cool air, thickly pungent with the scent of juniper, braced their exposed skin and gravel crunched underfoot as they climbed a gently sloping path.

At the top of the hill, finding little shelter in the pueblo's low walls, the wind put a firm hand to their backs and pushed them along. Korey snatched a knitted wool cap from her coat pocket and scrunched it over her windblown curls. Even on such a gray blustery day, the surrounding vistas added beauty to that of the village the conquering Spaniards had once called Pueblo de Las Humanas. Korey and Marc wandered at will, at times putting one foot carefully in front of the other on the tops of limestone walls where centuries of drifting sand still filled many of the six-by-ten foot rooms.

But it was neither history nor archeology that stood in the forefront of Korey's thoughts. She was on edge, a filly nervously eager to prove herself in a high-stakes race. While she mentally pranced outside the starting gate, it had not escaped her notice that Marc had sunk into a pensive mood. He had said little on their walk. She thought perhaps that was because he had been touched by the spirits of the people who, from as long ago as ten centuries, had called this village home. Korey shivered, thinking she heard rising voices coming from the mission church that stood across the village square. But glancing over her shoulder to the ancient church, she knew those lilting songs of praise were merely the wind murmuring inside the stone walls of the roofless building.

She and Marc stood only a few feet apart, each with their own thoughts. In their lengthening silence, Korey was unable to find an opening to vent that which had built up inside her; inwardly she rehearsed ways to introduce the topic of her deceased husband.

For his part, Marc too searched for a peaceful end to an inner turbulence. Without a doubt there was something spiritual about this spot on which he stood. It came to him on the whispering wind that this was a place where sins could be confessed, and if not forgiven, at least dropped among the ancient stones to be entombed with the transgressions of centuries past. With strong conviction about what he must do, he rammed his fists into the pockets of his leather bomber jacket. Loose stones crunched beneath his shoes as he pivoted to face whatever was to come. As he turned, dark eyes focused keenly on him from a wind-reddened face. Feeling that a door was now waiting to be opened, Marc started to speak, but before the first syllable was out, Korey had seized the door and swung it wide.

"It's time," she said.

"Time?" Heavy dark brows drew together in confusion.

"Time to come out of hiding."

Something jolted so hard against his ribs that Marc could have sworn he not only felt a thump but heard it as well, and in a searing moment he thought his heart had exploded. If this were to be his last moment, he would go out convinced that somehow, somewhere, Korey had stumbled upon the truth about Clare. Korey knew....but how could she? Marc's heart sputtered then settled into a rhythm of leaden beats. A deep breath fed his starving lungs. His mind ran apace with the blood shooting the rapids of his veins until abruptly everything seemed to stop, every fiber in his body slammed on the brakes. He stood draped in folds of rare serenity as his mind deluded him into believing he would be spared the torment of confession. And even better, there was none of the anticipated anger in evidence on Korey's rosy face. How odd. Unless.... Could it be perhaps that his personal life had preceded him; that she had, by whatever means, known about Clare from the outset? All these months, had he been fooling no one but himself? If he were now to be set free of the pain and guilt, he would gladly pay whatever Korey would choose to exact from him to hear her words of forgiveness.

Korey's quivering nerves did not know what to make of Marc's inscrutable face looming darkly above her, so to escape his penetrating gaze she turned away and lowered herself to sit on the edge of a stone wall. "He had the most damnable sense of honor," she said.

Belatedly, Marc realized she had spoken. The words were little more than a mutter, as if she were talking to herself, and had drifted on the wind to the cold stones below. As he lowered himself beside her, she kept her eyes on the distant mountains. While she searched for a way to continue, Marc pieced together her fractured words and struggled to identify who she was talking about.

"Such an inflated sense of pride, of responsibility. Thought he could solve all the problems; single-handedly wield the sword and slay the dragons."

Marc felt then as if he sat in the path of a crashing boulder. Clearly his wife Clare was not the topic here. He almost laughed out loud at his own idiocy. To think he had so recently freed himself from the web he had adeptly woven. What a fool to jump to the conclusion that his marriage might not have been the secret he thought it to be. How pompous to believe Korey would not hold him accountable for masquerading as a man who had no wife! With a drain to his strength, Marc diverted his attention from the doom thundering down on him and concentrated on the woman sitting on the wall beside him. He knew now why the words were coming hard for her. She was, after so many months of keeping it locked, opening that secret compartment in which she stored her memories of Danny.

As if practiced lines were at last memorized, words now rolled smoothly from Korey's tongue. "My husband took his own life," she said with an ease that surprised her. "I came home one afternoon to find him in his car, the engine running, the garage door closed. Something told me he was dead even before I jerked open the car door." She glanced at Marc, prepared to find in his eyes shock, maybe even revulsion. In place of her dreary expectations she saw instead infinite compassion and a tenderness she had never before seen him exhibit. Pulling away from those warm green eyes, she looked to the horizon where low clouds began swallowing everything into a gray abyss. Korey shifted her weight, failing to find any yield in the rock wall. Her heavy wool socks no longer kept her feet warm as her legs dangled into the empty chill of a small excavated room. She did not, however, allow her discomfort to keep her from her purpose.

"There were serious financial problems in the large chain of drug stores founded by Danny's father, Franklin. Danny blamed himself for not being able to save the business. God knows, he and Rob tried hard enough; it wasn't their fault that it couldn't be saved. It was Franklin....poor soul. Two years before, Franklin had been diagnosed with a brain tumor. Fortunately the tumor was operable, and after the successful surgery, he seemed to do so well. We were optimistic. Franklin was his jovial self again, he had resumed a near-normal work load, he and his wife, Evie, had reestablished a full social life. But then, unbeknownst to Danny, who was the manager of operations, and to Rob who was comptroller, Franklin began making irrational even inane decisions that were gravely detrimental to the health of the business. By the time his sons had discovered what their dad had done, so much money had been drained from the company that its salvation looked pretty grim.

"In the midst of this financial crunch, the doctor had to tell Evie that Franklin's tumor had reappeared. None of us were surprised, I guess. Even though we didn't dare say it to one another, we all suspected a tumor to be the cause of his erratic and irresponsible behavior. Anyway, on the discovery of the new tumor,

Franklin was taken into surgery for the second time. Though the surgeon did everything possible, Franklin died on the operating table.

"After the funeral, Danny sank deeper into an already hovering depression. He was convinced he had failed because he couldn't repair the damage his father had done. I couldn't seem to get through to Danny. Neither could Rob or Evie. He wouldn't seek professional help. Said he could take care of everything.

"Danny had an image of himself, you see, that was impossible to live up to. If he wasn't born with the world on his shoulders, he soon had it placed there by a father who was an overachiever. Failure was not in Franklin's vocabulary. So Danny thought he should be the perfect son; perfect husband and provider. He began seeing the world as smaller and smaller, as if looking at it through a spyglass, until the glass only focused on one thing—his inability to make things right. In the end, all who knew and loved him paid a terrible price for his narrowed vision."

Korey looked Marc full in the face, the wind blotting moisture from her brimming eyes. Marc sat as close to her as he dared, gladly lending his body as a buffer to the biting wind. He had listened with an anxiety borne of helplessness, and now wanted nothing more than to take her in his arms and kiss away her sorrowful memories. He rolled one hand into a fist and kept it in his warm pocket. With his free hand he reached for her left one. Her fingers were cold, stiff, and he folded them into his warmth. She thanked him with a thin smile.

He waited patiently for her to sweep her mind clean of all that she wished to tell him. Marc did not have to be told of the harsh blows despair could deal upon the human psyche; he had seen the results often enough in his own wife. Danny Westerfield had been felled by hopelessness; he was not in his right mind when he closed himself in the garage and started that car. No man in his right mind would leave Korey—if he had the right to stay. Marc did not crave the specifics of the man's demise, felt no macabre urge to hear details. All he wanted was to lend a sturdy shoulder on which Korey could put her burden to rest.

"I haven't spoken of this in so long," she began anew, "it seems surreal to say my own husband committed suicide. The words just don't ring true, as if I'm talking about someone else's husband, a man I barely knew." Her hushed voice became stronger. "When it was done, the funeral over, I was nearly insane with grief. This went on for weeks. I cried enough salt water to float a porpoise. And I discovered that I no longer wanted to be *me*. I wanted to be one half of the couples I passed in the aisles of the grocery store. I wanted to be the married teller at the bank. I saw everyone as being happy. They had someone to go home to, how could they not be happy?

"I didn't go back to teaching that next fall, couldn't face a classroom of children that would remind me everyday of Danny's children that would never be born. Besides, my own life no longer had any semblance of order, how was I then to bring order to a classroom of hormonal teens?

"Then one morning I woke perspiring from an unrecognizable dream and realized I was losing myself; I had to find a way to pull my life together. In the next instant I was out of bed, as if someone had yanked me up by the neck of my gown. When my feet hit the floor, I knew what I was meant to do. At age twenty-six I was widowed and childless. I needed to know that I could create, if not children, then something using my imagination and my hands. That very morning I began my first quilt." Korey had a far away look in her eyes when she turned her face to the man beside her. "My quilting skills up to that point were limited to simple projects," she said, "but then I began to create in my head an ambitious wall hanging. And I've been cutting and stitching ever since."

She fell silent. Marc felt her hand relax within his, but he would not yet intrude.

As the moments passed, a liberating sense of release began to spread through Korey. It was as though she had been chained to Danny's headstone and now those rusty shackles had been broken. She was free. She would forever love Danny. But he was part of a life she would never again know. He would want her to leave him here in the sun and heat, the rain and snow, to live peaceably among the ghosts of this ancient village.

Her mind erased obstructing visions of towering gravestones. For the first time since Danny's death, Korey saw clearly. Her heart opened like a new book, and she read its clean crisp pages. Marc was here for her to love. And love him she did. More than she would have thought possible. How long, she wondered, had her heart known of this love? No matter. It was enough that she was alive again. She would welcome in a wide embrace the length and breadth of this new life Marc had given her. And she would pray to see the day when she and Marc would share that new life.

The wind grabbed at a stray curl and tickled Korey's cheek. She stretched her hat away from her ear, with her right hand tucked the hair under the warm wool, then tugged the hat to her brow.

Marc noted then something his eyes had seen earlier but his brain had shoved into a bottom drawer: When he had taken her left hand and held it tightly in his, there had been no ring on her finger. That missing ring, the one Korey wore as the continuance of a marriage bond, now resided on her right hand. Until now he had not been aware of the significance he had attached to the ring. But through these months of wanting Korey, the ring had served as a psychological barrier, lulled him into the false security of thinking he would never be capable of doing the unthinkable. That false security now vanished in the cool glare of diamonds and reality knocked him soundly in the head. Korey cared for him. Today she had broken the tie to a past shared with another man. Could she at this moment be eyeing the man whom she hoped would fill that terrible void?

Marc felt his mouth go dry at the thought of what he must do. Before he and Korey departed Gran Quivira, he would tell her about Clare.

He squirmed against the hard stones, swayed his body from side to side trying to get comfortable. His legs had lost all feeling and almost failed him as he heaved himself up from the wall and tried to stand. After a bout of clumsiness, he finally gained his balance. Absently he rubbed his hands along his thighs to halt the little men who were running up and down his long legs, jabbing tiny spears into his flesh.

His abrupt departure from her side startled Korey, but she accepted his outstretched hand and was lifted to stand beside him. As he shifted his weight from one foot to the other, she worried over this sudden agitation. Had telling him about Danny disturbed him so much? She could not bear to consider that she might have revealed enough to frighten Marc away. "I haven't upset you…."

His eyes darted around the ruins, and he ignored her as if he had not heard. Then his eyes found hers. "Upset? No, of course not. I'm flattered you think enough of me to confide in me. I know how difficult it is to let go of those things we have buried within us." He shifted again. The smile he gave her had an edge to it that Korey found disconcerting. "It's just," Marc said, "my legs went to sleep while I was sitting on the wall. I'll be okay in a minute." He stomped his feet to speed circulation.

Korey idly walked away, left him to his funny little dance. Strolling nearby, seeking a diversion, she pulled from her pocket a booklet she had taken from a display shelf in the ranger station. The wind turned the pages of the small book as she passed the time reading the history of Gran Quivira.

At last the tingling in Marc's legs ebbed; he planted his feet into the wind and lost himself to the distant vistas. He watched a valley thirty miles away disappear behind the dark curtain of a snow squall and wondered what magic there could be under the heavens that would give him the courage to tell Korey about Clare. What would he do, turn to her and say, as if he had only this moment remembered: *Oh, by the way, Korey, did I happen to mention that I'm married?* Or snap his fingers and state in an offhand manner: *We've been having such a grand time together, doggone if it didn't slip my mind that I have a wife!*

"Are you all right? You look a little pale." She had come on cat's paws to stand behind him. At the sound of her voice he spun, shattering the cocky text of his imagined confession. On the hill, the wind tried to push the two people together as they stared at each other. The woman's loving concern showed plainly on her face; the man did not like what he saw there. He recognized the love he did not deserve and could not accept.

"Korey."

She raised a brow in question. Dark eyes rested on his. Eyes unsuspecting: those of a doe innocently gazing down the barrel of the gun just before the blast.

Penitent words tumbled from Marc's brain like clutter from an overstuffed closet, but try as he might he could not force the words past his lips. His jaw flexed where he clamped his teeth together, and at that moment he despised himself for the rotten coward that he was. Opportunity so ripe and he couldn't do it. Clare Bradberry would remain his burden.

In defeat, his thoughts retreated to regroup and plan where he should go from here. Korey was far too precious a gift to be enticed into the role of mistress. He had to find a way to fade into the background before his passion for her burned out of control. If not for the damned quilt, he would not again go near her after seeing her safely back to Chattanooga. As things stood, he could not avoid her entirely, but he could drastically curb their time spent together. His mind overflowed with guilt at what he must do. How had it come to this? Why had he not stayed away from her after that first restless night she had drifted through his dreams? He had brought her to the point where she would now feel the sting of abandonment. But better a sting now, he rationalized, than the pain she would suffer if he were to see his desires through to their fullest and take her as his lover.

He felt naked, suddenly very cold under her inquisitive gaze. A shiver trembled his tall frame. He stiffened, lifting the collar of his jacket to the wind. The sharp air burned his nose and made his eyes water. "Wind's picking up," he said. "Getting colder. We'd better go."

Though something told her he had meant to say more, she nodded in mute agreement and blindly followed him from the pueblo. As he led the way down the sloping gravel path, a numbness crept through Korey that had nothing to do with the weather. The icy lump that had come to rest in the pit of her stomach had formed just before Marc had turned to leave Gran Quivira. In that instant his eyes had become as dark and cold as the surrounding day. What she had glimpsed in those eyes frightened her—the newly opened pathway to a hopeful future seemed suddenly to close.

*   *   *   *

If the rain soaking Chattanooga had paused while Korey and Marc were away, there was no evidence of it as they landed in the same cold drizzle in which they had taken off three days earlier. The Miata did not warm much on the short drive from the airport to Korey's home, and both weary travelers were returning carrying a deep chill, one that seemed to transcend the hostile November day.

"Just put it over there, please," Korey said, pointing to a spot on the floor of the small foyer.

"You sure?" Marc questioned as he set the suitcase against the wall nearest the bedroom. "It's heavy. You shouldn't be lifting something this heavy."

"When you live alone," she said, shutting the door in the face of a raw wind, "you get used to it." She found his show of concern perplexing. Since leaving Gran Quivira the day before, Marc had been attentive, polite, a pleasant traveling companion. But the warmth he had earlier bestowed on her, the magic of their times together, had seemed to evaporate beneath the shiny veneer of his smile. And now, when he was about to leave her, he was worried that she might hurt herself lifting a suitcase? She brushed away his concern with a flick of her hand, and her manner seemed brusque as she attempted to hide her confusion. "Don't worry," she said as she unbuttoned her coat. "If it's too heavy to lift, I'll unpack it right here." Her coat fell open, but she did not take it off.

Her confusion mounted as Marc steadfastly remained next to the suitcase, his hand nervously taking inventory of the car keys in the pocket of his leather jacket. Not understanding the delay in his departure, she made a tentative attempt toward being hospitable. "Would you like a cup of coffee? There may even be some brownies in the freezer." She felt distinctly that she had pulled him back from someplace far away as he tore his eyes from her inquisitive stare and gave his watch a cursory check.

"Thanks, but it's late and I have an appointment in the morning at seven-thirty." He stooped to remove a tattered leaf clinging damply to the side of his shoe. Absently he rubbed the waxy surface between his thumb and forefinger, then, as if he did not know what else to do, he stuffed the leaf in a coat pocket.

Korey filled the awkward silence. "It was a great trip, Marc. I had a wonderful time. Thanks so much for letting me tag along." In the stillness, she became vaguely aware of the sound of wet leaves wickedly slapping the front of the house.

He was on her before she had time to think, so swiftly she had not seen him cross the foyer. A broad chest filled her vision as cool leather touched her nostrils.

His forefinger traced slowly down the length of her flushed cheek. "I loved having you 'tag along.'" The words were a caress, tender and unmistakable. He bent his head, and his breath brushed her mouth an instant before she felt his lips on hers. The kiss was warm and lingering, until now the kind she had not dared to dream about. A heat, like glowing coals, warmed her as her hands laced through the hair at his nape.

He knew the kiss to be an act of madness, but he had to taste her sweetness, just this once. His hand slid easily beneath her cropped jacket, and he felt through the bulk of his own coat the rows of brass buttons pressing into his chest. The knobby cables of her knitted sweater imprinted his moist palms as he held her. She stirred in his arms, fitting her slender body tightly to his, and he deepened the kiss, sadistically lengthening his own torture.

With a sudden withdrawal of his warm mouth, the kiss ended as abruptly as it had begun, leaving Korey with a bemused smile on her wet lips. She wanted to cry out for the loss of his arms as he stepped out of reach. Though his face was carefully composed, Korey had little trouble seeing the blaze burning in his eyes.

Then, as if nothing extraordinary had taken place, he said, "Well, my desk must be buried under a ton of mail and I do have that early appointment...."

Doubting her liquid knees would carry her that far, she went with him to the door and murmured a dreamy, "Goodnight." She barely heard his low parting words.

"Goodbye, Korey."

CHAPTER 11

▼

"How was the training session in New York?" Korey's words floated as clouds in the quiet air, her eyes sweeping past her sister to take in the beauty of the morning. Heavy frost glazed rooftops, sparkled as the early sun pointed fingers across wintry-brown lawns. Soft-soled walking shoes made no sound on the freshly rolled pavement as the sisters huffed up the steep hill.

"Grueling." Tina glanced sideways at Korey and managed a short chuckle. "I meant New York, but the same could be said of this hike."

Korey waited to catch her breath as they crested the hill. "Listen, you're the one who thought it a great idea to take a bracing walk before going to work. Me, I'd rather be home in a warm bed." Her thigh muscles tensed reflexively to check her speed and her arms swung freely at her sides as they started downhill. "Anyway, what about New York?"

"Fun, but hard work too. There will be a completely new line of oil-free cosmetics introduced in the spring, plus a fabulous new fragrance. Most of our time was spent in product education. Not much leisure this trip. We had only one night free. I didn't even have time to see a play. Hey, New York is old hat. Surely you must know that I'm dying to hear about your trip to Albuquerque last weekend."

"What is it you want to know?" Korey's smile was a little off-center.

"For starters, how is Matty?"

"She's fine. As much fun as always. She sends her love and said she expects you and Bryan to come as soon as the two of you get some time off."

"We'd love to. We haven't seen her since….well, since Danny's funeral."

"She's made some improvements to the house. Put in a stone patio to replace the concrete that was so badly broken. Laid the stones herself, of course."

"Amazing she didn't jackhammer the concrete too."

"Isn't it?" They opted for the safety of a sidewalk as they turned onto a street flowing with rush-hour traffic. "She also added a skylight in the guest bathroom and retiled the walls in ceramic the color of adobe. It's gorgeous. The skylight is over the shower and the effect makes you feel like you're bathing outdoors."

"I suppose the pilots at Kirtland Air Force Base must love that!"

Korey laughed. "Not unless they have bionic vision."

"What about Marc? Did you get to see much of him while you were there?" Tina rubbed her gloved hands together for warmth, but to Korey the movement seemed more of an eagerness to get down to facts.

"Yes, we had dinner together each evening." She went on to elaborate, feeling a pleasant rush as she spoke of her weekend with Marc. "The night we arrived, we dined with Matty at The High Noon. The next night we met Marc's brother and *his* wife for dinner. Saturday Marc and I went to Gran Quivira and stopped for a bowl of chili after we got back into Albuquerque. We didn't want to burst in on Matty at dinner time. She would have insisted on cooking a big meal for us."

"What else did you do?"

An easy smile curved Korey's lips as she recalled Marc's warm mouth covering hers. That kiss. All week she had found it difficult to think of anything else. But for now she wanted to hold the kiss close, keep it for her own. "We had fun roaming Old Town the same evening we had dinner with Eric and Rae. They had just returned from a five-day photo shoot and were very tired so they went home right after dinner. Marc and I wandered up and down the streets of Old Town for over two hours. You know how many shops there are." Her next words dangled like a worm on a hook. "Marc bought me something."

Tina regarded her sister. "Well? What?"

While she moved a carelessly abandoned tricycle from the sidewalk, Korey let the question hang. She then satisfied Tina's obvious curiosity. "He bought me a lovely outfit. Velvet skirt. Beautiful shade of turquoise. Matching vest. Shirt, boots, earrings—the works."

"My, he's certainly generous. And I'm sure you look positively gorgeous in it. I can't wait to see everything."

"Drop by Saturday and I'll show it off."

A school bus loaded with children rumbled past; the sisters watched a small hand clear a circle of fog from the wide rear window. An impish prankster pressed close to the glass and made a silly face.

"Brats," Tina giggled, remembering well the times she and Korey had thought it hilariously clever to do the same thing. The walkers turned another corner, making their way back to Tina's house.

"Does Marc know you're in love with him?"

The question split the momentary silence like a crack of thunder. Korey broke stride and stopped in the middle of the sidewalk. "What?" Stunned by her sister's keen perception, Korey could only think to say again, "What?"

Realizing Korey was no longer walking alongside, Tina turned. "I asked if...."

"I heard you."

Tina retraced a few steps to stand beside Korey. "Gosh, it's been so obvious for some time—a sister can see these things—and I thought, well, maybe on this trip you and Marc had become....closer."

Korey could not suppress a grin. Anyway, what was there to hide? "You know, Tina, you have a knack for hitting the target. As it happens, this time you're on the bull's eye." She hopped over a series of cracks in the sidewalk before resuming her long easy stride. "If you had asked me that same question last week, I would have vehemently denied my love for Marc." Korey sighed. "But how quickly things change. Marc seems to have no idea how I feel, but I'm finally willing to admit how much I care." She felt Tina's eyes on her as she added, "I know now that I do love him."

"What exactly happened last weekend?"

Korey answered by telling what had transpired at Gran Quivira, giving every detail as she remembered it. She kept to herself the disquiet she still felt over Marc's strange mood swing. "I haven't a clue how Marc feels." She thought again of the kiss. "Well, that's not exactly true. He likes me, I think. It's the *how much* and *in what way* that's giving me trouble."

Tina heard the wistfulness as Korey's voice dropped and was tempted to add her two cents. In her mind, expensive clothes and weekend jaunts in a private jet were proof enough, but she prudently kept these thoughts to herself.

They stopped in Tina's driveway at the end of a short cul-de-sac. Her small white house, with its dormers and picket fence, was something out of a story-book. "Would you like to come in for a while? I plan to sit down to a cup of coffee and put my feet up before heading off to work."

"Come on," Korey chuckled. "You make it sound as if we just hiked up Lookout Mountain." From her coat pocket she pulled out a set of keys and absently rolled the keys round and round the heavy ring. "I'd better not stay. I've mounds of work piled in the studio. I did some sewing on the plane but still lost a few days' work. I've been playing catch-up all week."

"So what are you going to do now?" Tina asked as Korey unlocked the car and slid behind the wheel.

"I just told you. Go home and sew."

"No....about Marc."

"What is there to do? I haven't heard from him since he dropped me off Sunday night." Suddenly too warm with a mental picture of she and Marc locked in a heated embrace, she yanked off her stocking cap. Static electricity crackled as her hair, following the cap, stood on end. She leaned to look in the rear view mirror, gave up trying to tame her hair when all it wanted to do was cling to her woolly gloves. She looked at Tina. "As you well know, it's not out of the ordinary to go four days with no word from Marc. Besides, I haven't decided in which direction I want this relationship to go."

"But if you love him...."

"Not so much yet that I can't live without him. I don't know if I'm ready for that kind of love. There are so many scars. I may never love again like I did with Danny. It's probably good that Marc is so preoccupied with his work. That way the pressure isn't there for me to make hasty choices. I miss him when he's away, but looking at it objectively, these absences are for the best."

"Yeah, I suppose you're right. But promise me one thing. If anything interesting develops," Tina shot her a sly grin, "I'll be the first to know."

*   *   *   *

Soon it had become achingly apparent there would be no *interesting developments* concerning Marc Bradberry. As one week stretched slowly into two, Korey became progressively edgy. When the phone rang, she jumped. Each time she returned from an outing, she eagerly rushed to play messages on the answering machine, her heart missing beats as she listened for the one voice she most wanted to hear. Each time her spirits sagged when the voice was not there.

By Thanksgiving Day, as she joined Tina and Bryan, and Rob and Evie Westerfield at Evie's rambling tri-level home, Korey found it nearly impossible to force turkey, cornbread dressing, and yams past the burgeoning lump in her chest.

Rob brought a date—Hillary something or other—who seemed to want no part of the dinner conversation that did not center around her tales of foraging in the choking jungles of Brazil in search of some sort of potato she was convinced would, when widely cultivated, eradicate world hunger. Midway through the meal, in the midst of a monologue riddled with scientific jargon that no one but Hillary understood, Korey was plotting ways in which to get Hillary away from

Rob. Not because Korey wanted Rob for herself but because everyone at the table, except Rob, thought the woman was a conceited, snooze-inducing bore. It occurred to Korey, while her imagination sought ways to send Hillary back to the jungle, that the woman's presence today actually had a plus side. For once, in what had seemed like an endless string of days, Korey was enjoying a respite from her preoccupation with Marc.

With the feast ended, chairs were pushed heavily away from the dining table, sated tummies were rubbed. Rob prematurely whisked Hillary away from the gathering on the suspicious pretext of viewing color slides of Hillary's most recent expedition. It was the ribald consensus, among those remaining to clean up the stacks of dishes, that it was not slides that Rob was eager to view but, more likely, certain portions of Hillary's Amazonian assets.

Tina seemed to be the only one to notice that Korey was busying herself at the kitchen sink, rinsing dishes and loading the dishwasher and was no longer joining in the speculation on Rob's love life. Tina sidled up to the sink and said, "Is something wrong?"

"Hum?" Korey lifted a questioning gaze, the scouring pad in her hand idly rubbing the inside of a pan that already reflected a mirror shine. "Oh, I was just thinking…. To my list of things to be thankful for today, I'll add one more: That I needn't lose any sleep over which direction my relationship with Marc is going."

"Good news, then?" Tina asked as she filled the soap cups on the dishwasher and snapped them shut.

"No. *No* news."

"I don't understand."

"That makes two of us."

Evie appeared to good-naturedly shoo them from the kitchen, and, without objection, the sisters joined Bryan in the den where he was feeding logs into the cavernous stone fireplace. From a bed of glowing coals, the fresh logs leapt to life, driving Bryan back with its intense heat. Satisfied that the fire would burn unattended, he dusted his hands together and announced his intention to take Claxton, Evie's golden retriever, for a long walk.

Tina flopped with Korey on the sofa the instant Bryan stepped out of the room. She snatched the television remote control and switched off a football game. In the fireplace, green wood spit and sizzled. From the kitchen came the sound of Evie putting away the last of the cooking pans.

"Now then," Tina said, kicking off her shoes and curling on the sofa. "What's up with you and Marc?"

Long moments passed as Korey watched yellow-tipped orange flames eat the bark from a log the breadth of an elephant's leg. She nervously rolled her thumbs, one over the other. At last she responded, "I'm not sure, but it appears nothing is up. He hasn't been in touch since we returned from our trip." She spoke hesitantly, her pride wounded at being coldly, unceremoniously dumped. "It's become obvious that I am no longer an important part of his life—not that I ever was."

"Of course you were."

"*Were* being the correct tense."

"I didn't mean…."

"Forget it," Korey returned, testily. "What an idiot I was to presume I could chart the direction of our relationship. As if I had ever been in control."

"You haven't followed him around like a lap dog, you know."

"I'll accept some credit for that. Still, whenever Marc and I are together, it's usually on his terms."

"That's just the natural way of things—your time is more flexible than his."

"I suppose," said Korey, sounding unconvinced.

"Korey, don't you think you may be overreacting a bit? Maybe Marc's schedule is so frantic right now that his time is not his own." Tina tried to believe her own words.

Korey squared her shoulders. "It's something I've done. I've made a dreadful mistake."

"You? What could you possibly have done?"

"After I told him about Danny's death, while we were still at Gran Quivira, I saw a change in Marc. He acted as though he wanted to tell me something and couldn't. When I was talking about Danny, Marc seemed so sympathetic. I guess, after he had time to think about it…. I never should have told him, Tina. A suicide, it's like a stigma…."

Tina could not tell her that it was not the suicide keeping Marc away, that he had already wheedled that information out of her sister over a month ago. Is that what he had come close to saying to Korey at Gran Quivira and for some reason decided against? "Listen to yourself!" Tina reproached. "You're acting as if the tragic fact that Danny took his own life has frightened Marc away. Suicide is not contagious, you know. Stop blaming yourself. Really, Korey, I'm sure Marc has a perfectly reasonable explanation for not calling." Tina smiled as if a pleasant thought had popped into her head. "I have an idea. Instead of stewing, why don't you just call him? Today would be the perfect day—wish him a happy Thanksgiving."

"I can't."

"Why not? He finally gave you his home number, didn't he?"

"Oh, yes. His many numbers—home, offices, cell—takes up a full card on my Rolodex. But I'm still not going to call him," she stated brusquely, too mulish to admit the reason: The possibility of being told that Marc had met someone new scared her to death. "In another week or two his quilt will be finished. If I haven't heard from him, then I won't have any choice but to call." She paused. "Come to think of it, these past months have been very draining. Wondering when Marc would call, *if* he would call, when I would see him again. If it's over....I won't be bothered with wondering anymore."

Wary of the look in Tina's eye, Korey was flooded with relief when Bryan chose that moment to reenter the room. Korey relaxed into the sofa cushions as Tina's attention shifted to her husband. Bryan shed his coat then rubbed his wind-nipped nose before warming his hands near the fire. Evie came bearing a tray with four steaming mugs of mulled wine, Claxton trotting at her heels.

Each of the room's occupants took up an activity typical of a family gathering. Bryan tended the fire, stoking it anew; Evie served the wine; Tina switched the television back to the football game; and Claxton thrust his large head into Korey's lap. Korey idly stroked the glossy head, the hair still cool with outside air. The petting continued until the dog closed his eyes and sank to the rug at Korey's feet.

Korey sipped the spicy wine and turned her face to the television, but her dark stare was unfocused, and she did not hear the announcer's play by play. It was not football that was on her mind this Thanksgiving night. Rather, she saw a handsome face with enigmatic green eyes, and her heart was heavy.

*   *   *   *

For ten days and nights following Thanksgiving, time progressed at a sloth's pace as Korey labored toward a singular goal: complete Marc's project then dismiss it and him from her life. His continued, inexplicable silence, an impudence even Tina no longer tried to excuse, had a friendship in tatters and each day that passed with still no word added fuel to Korey's smoldering anger.

At last the day arrived when Korey struck the final stitch in the quilt. But the atmosphere in Korey's studio upon the completion was more sad than celebratory. Carefully spreading the quilt over the sofa, Korey swiped the heel of her hand across her cheek, wiping away tears she could not stop. Stepping back to critically judge her work, she saw it as possibly her finest accomplishment, but the sour memories it stirred spoiled any accolades she might wish to heap upon herself.

Suddenly she felt exhausted, and with both hands she massaged a dull ache radiating from her shoulders. "The sewing was the easy part," she mumbled as she turned her back to the quilt. "Now comes the hard part." Taking a deep breath, she lifted the phone and punched the numbers of Marc's Chattanooga office. Relief mingled with disappointment when she was told he was out of the office; the phone seemed to weigh heavier in her hand as she next called Nashville. No luck finding him there, so she left the same crisp message she had left in Chattanooga: "*Mr.* Bradberry's quilt is completed. Please contact *Ms.* Westerfield to schedule the hanging." Those last words brought an image to Korey's mind and a perverse smile to her dry lips: Marc, stretched long and lean—dangling from the fatal end of a fat noose. Tugging at the confining turtleneck of her cotton shirt, Korey suddenly felt hot, her tongue thick; she reluctantly acknowledged that Marc continued to prey on her nerves.

An hour later, however, Korey knew it was more than Marc that was bothering her. Her throat had become so sore she had difficulty swallowing two aspirin. The ache that had begun in her shoulders had now taken over her body, and she was quaking with fever.

By nightfall she was miserably thrashing in a rumpled bed, felled by a nasty case of flu.

*   *   *   *

In an eerie, detached way, Korey's impression of the next thirty-six hours was of smelly liquids passing down her fiery throat and her sweat-soaked body wrapping its aching self around a toilet bowl. With renewed hope that she had survived the worst, she awoke now from a remarkably tranquil sleep and lay very still in the hush of the dark room. In another part of the house a phone rang, the bell chirping like an injured bird. She did not reach a weak arm for the muted phone beside the bed. Instead, she heard the murmur of Tina's voice, the words indistinguishable through the bedroom door. With motherly care, Tina had come to nurse her infirm sister.

Impatient to try her legs, Korey eased from the bed. Her swollen eyes slammed shut when she switched on a lamp. After a period of adjustment, she shuffled to where her robe lay neatly folded over the back of a chair. The robe hung like sackcloth on her sagging shoulders. Steadying herself against the chair, she slipped her cold feet into awaiting slippers. A smile cracked her scaly lips; the slippers—white long-haired bunnies with floppy pink ears—were new, a get-well wish from Tina.

Korey found her sister in the kitchen, stirring a pot on the stove, a phone to her ear. Korey leaned over the stove, breathed the savory smells rising in ribbons of steam. For the first time in days, the thought of food did not turn her stomach. She recognized the mouthwatering aroma of Evie's chicken soup with its thick egg noodles, chunks of white meat, and diced vegetables.

Tina, motioning for Korey to sit at the table, switched off the burner. She said into the phone, "No, nothing serious. She's had the flu. Had a fever that would fry an egg, but she's on the mend…. Uh, I don't know. Let me see if she's awake." Tina pressed the palm of her hand over the phone and mimed: *It's Marc. He wants to talk to you.*

In her weakened state, the vigorous shake of her head left Korey dizzy.

Nodding, Tina set the phone on the kitchen counter and stood in silence for a sufficient length of time, then coolly lied into the phone, "Marc, she's sleeping. Could she call you when she's feeling better? Oh, I see. Well, yes, I'm sure she will. Yes, I'll tell her. Okay. Bye." She looked at Korey. "Well," she said, sounding both surprised and pleased.

"So, he finally called." Disgust sharpened Korey's words.

"He was responding to your message that the quilt was finished and said he had been trying to reach you for two days and that all he had been getting was—and I quote—'that damn answering machine!' You heard me tell him you had been ill. He sounded worried, Korey."

"Yeah." Sarcasm flowed like cold syrup.

"Really. He seemed almost frantic until I assured him you were going to be all right." Tina turned her attention to the meal, setting two soup bowls on the counter and searching a utensil drawer for a ladle. "You have spread across your studio a quilt that has to be hung," she said. In payment for the unnecessary reminder, Tina received a scowl. "Marc wants you to call him to make the arrangements."

Korey raked her itching scalp; fever-ravaged hair stuck to her skull like swirled plaster. The thought of having to ever again hear Marc's voice made her head ache, and she expelled what sounded like an "ugh" as she hid her ashen face in her hands. In frustration, she ground her teeth—even *they* seemed to ache—then mumbled, "Did he say where he would be?"

"Yes. He'll be in Nashville for the next two days. Said to call him at home in the evening if you can't catch him earlier." Tina filled the bowls with hot soup and sought her sister's eye as Korey slowly raised her head. "Korey, his concern for you seemed sincere. He asked me no less than five times if I was *sure* you were going to be okay."

"When it suits him, he knows to say the right things."

"Are you being fair....?"

"Fair!" Korey bit off further retort. "Don't press Marc on me tonight. I feel lousy enough as it is. Let's have some of that delicious soup. And then I'm going to take a long hot shower, with mounds of sweet-smelling suds, and wash away this salty crust that's coating me. Now," she said with false cheer, "hand me a bowl of that soup. My stomach's like an empty cave!"

CHAPTER 12

▼

Korey struggled into the garage, a bulky bundle under her arm. Swinging wide around the open car door, she carefully fed Marc's quilt, protectively rolled in a bed sheet, into the car's rear seat. She straightened, hands on hips. Normally, delivering a quilt to its owner meant a bittersweet parting. But not this one. This time the only emotion was anger. This was one project she was happy to have out of her house. Good riddance.

Now there remained only one obstacle to her peace—the dreaded chore of getting the quilt mounted to the wall in Marc's office. She was furious with herself for succumbing to Marc's persuasive insistence that he help her hang it. He had said, over the phone only thirty minutes ago, that "there was no point in bothering Bryan and Tina with the task when I'll be at the office and have all the tools necessary to do the job."

Facing Marc today had not been part of her plan. She had been with Tina and Bryan cutting firewood, trimming family-owned acres of dying oaks and hickories. The day was raw; she had come home cold, weary, and anticipating a hot shower. A ringing phone postponed the shower. The familiar voice had set her nerves on edge and jolted her into self-conscious activity, as if Marc, through the phone line, could somehow see her state of disarray. Bent over the kitchen sink, she brushed sawdust from her hair, and shook bits of wood from the cuffs of her shirt. Marc asked about her health in a tone so warm and sincere that he almost had her believing there had been no fracture in their friendship. When he chided her for not returning his call of the week before, Korey suppressed an urge to blister his ear about *his* skills at using a telephone and mumbled something about not knowing where the time had gone. She withheld the truth: The flu had sapped her emotional strength, and she was unwilling to contact him while her defenses were down.

Her lack of enthusiasm was no deterrent. He presented again the idea that together the two of them could mount the quilt. She countered, arguing that she worked best with Tina and Bryan. Marc parried, listing reasons why only the two of them would make the most efficient team. In the end it had been the texture of his unhurried words that had drawn Korey's mind away from the fact that she had not seen or spoken to him in nearly a month. Beguiled, her thoughts glided toward the possibility that she could, this very day, feed a craving to once more gaze upon that handsome face, bask in the light of his radiant smile. Like a sapling bending to a strong wind, she had agreed finally to come to his office, alone.

Now, standing in the garage, Korey's rage at allowing herself to be manipulated bubbled to the surface. She had wished Marc out of her life. What was she doing, ready to fly to his office the moment he summoned her? Damn his golden tongue! And damn her weakness! In a rare display of temper, she gave the car tire a swift kick. Pain puckered her face. Cursing her own childish behavior, she hopped around on one foot until the throbbing eased in her injured toes. In ill humor, she threw a coat over her wood-cutting clothes—jeans and a red and black check shirt of heavy flannel that Danny had bought for an ice fishing trip he and Rob had taken to Canada. Korey did not care a whit that chainsaw oil stained the shirttail that hung to her knees, that sawdust still frosted her hair, or that she emitted the aroma of two cords of freshly cut wood.

Marc, with no outer wrap to ward off the cold, was in the circle drive when she arrived. He grinned; her return smile was cool. He effortlessly toted the rolled quilt inside while Korey held open the front door. Closing the door behind them, she followed Marc through the hall to the drafting room where he laid the bundle on the polished oak floor. The room, lit in the purple glow of the fading day, smelled fresh and new, as though the last painter had just left. Korey's pulse quickened as Marc turned to her. Not yet ready to venture closer, she fingered the drawstring on the hood of her coat and remained at the doorway to the room.

Only a blind man would miss the accusation in her unflinching stare. Why she stood silently expectant was no mystery to Marc. She awaited an explanation for his recent bizarre behavior. She deserved that, plus an apology, but those were two things he could not give.

He broke the ice by asking for her coat, and she shrugged out of the wool-lined parka, letting it fall into his ready grasp. Except to set her purse on a handy stool, Korey did not move. The room, with its high ceiling and north wall of glass, was warm. Two ceiling fans, eggshell white like the room, quietly and efficiently pushed heated air down upon Korey's head.

Laying aside her coat, Marc came to stand beside her. "Are you comfortable?" he asked.

If he meant was she comfortable with the temperature in the room, the answer would be, yes. She was not, however, otherwise comfortable in his presence. He in his neatly pressed jeans and V-neck sweater over a crisp blue shirt. She in her sloppy shirt and jeans with the filthy knees. In a snit, she had come dressed as a lumberjack, and already she had begun to regret it. Beside him, she felt like a waif. And to add to her distress, his nearness made her skin tingle. With so much going through her head, awkward seconds slid past, and she wondered if he could sense how he addled her. "Yes," she said at last. "I'm fine."

"Good, then we can get started."

Her breathing became easier when he moved away to switch on a bank of overhead lights. They worked cooperatively, exchanging words only when necessary. Avoiding Marc's frequent glances, Korey kept her head lowered to the task. They discussed location, one held the tape measure while the other stretched it along the wall. In time Marc eased into his familiar skin, his keen sense of humor overriding his own case of jittery nerves. Korey responded with a loosened tongue; the ensuing banter drained from her some of the aching tension that for weeks had entrapped both her body and her mind.

Marc brought an aluminum stepladder from the storage room, and Korey insisted she be the one to climb the ladder to where the brackets would attach to the wall. The carpenter's tape clipped to her jeans and a pencil punched through her hair, she stood high up the wall while Marc, from below, acted as spotter. Watching her, he could not help thinking that she made a fetching sight even though she looked and smelled as if she had come to him directly from a sawmill. She had offered no apology for her appearance, and he had expected none.

Meanwhile, Korey had begun to suffer for her obstinacy. Clad for working outdoors on a cold December day, the flannel shirt had become oppressive. From where she stood on her lofty perch, warm air slid down the wall to inflame her even more. For relief, she reached for the ample shirttail, lifting and tying it at her waist.

Marc gripped the ladder ever tighter, more to steady himself than to support the ladder. From his vantage point, looking up at the now unobstructed view of Korey's round bottom molded so nicely into the snug jeans, he had trouble breathing. Korey stretched her arms upward, extending the tape measure, and Marc's heart lost its rhythm. He momentarily lifted his hand from the ladder, leaving a moist print on the aluminum, and ran a lean index finger across his per-spiring forehead. A flaming torch ignited his blood: a pleasant sensation to be sure but not at all what he had in mind when he had invited, *insisted,* today that Korey come to his office. He was now both annoyed and frightened by his lack of control. The quilt had provided the perfect excuse to act on an intense longing to see her again. He had thought it would be enough to merely have her near for an hour or two. How was it possible that he could underestimate so disastrously the effect she would have on him?

Until a few days ago, he had steadfastly resolved to be as far away as possible from Chattanooga when Korey came with Tina and Bryan to hang the quilt. But his conversation with Tina, when he had learned Korey was ill, had changed his mind. True, the flu had not been life threatening. And Tina had nursed Korey. But Tina had not been there around the clock. The thought of Korey lying alone in her bed with no one to sponge her fevered skin or to spoon warm broth between her trembling lips had made him realize how gladly he would have done those things for her. These last few days, his conscience had hammered him sorely for abandoning her.

On their return from New Mexico, when his departing kiss had meant good-bye, he had preferred not to think ahead to a time when the quilt, finished and on the wall, would no longer be the glue that bound him to Korey. To block her from his mind, he had worked himself mercilessly. Fatigue became his nightly companion; with heavy steps he made his way home each evening, barely taking time to throw back the covers before falling into bed. His exhaustion had left lit-tle room for Korey to insinuate herself into his thoughts before sleep pulled him under.

Some nights he slept dreamlessly and awoke refreshed. Other nights were not so forgiving. Throughout those nights images of Korey spun and clicked as if his head were the carousel on a slide projector. Korey: the first time he saw her when her beauty had interrupted his breathing; a steamy day in August, a dress, flared like the wings of a splendid yellow bird, and expectant lips parted to receive a kiss he never gave; dark eyes brimming with love atop the stone walls at Gran Quivira and he turning his back to that love.

His epiphany had come two nights ago. He had awakened soaking wet and unable to focus his eyes, as if a black cloud had lowered onto his bed. If it had been a dream that had jolted him awake, he could not remember it. When his heart had slowed its thumping, the cloud lifted and his mind cleared. He had wronged Korey, and somehow he had to make amends. He must see her one last time to ensure that they parted as friends. He would phone her. She would give him the cold shoulder. He would find a way to melt the frost….

Now, as he looked up the ladder, no longer could he foolishly hope to banish her to an island in the nethermost regions of his mind. She would remain part of his world, though good sense told him that visits would be few. Somehow he must establish a delicate balance: spend time with Korey but teeter away from the temptation to become her lover. Difficult though it would be, his true feelings would remain camouflaged until a time when either he could offer more, or— and this possibility shook him to the soles of his shoes—he lost her to someone who was free to lavish on her the attention and affection she deserved. Marc's conscience chafed for denying Korey the opportunity to make an informed choice, an equal partner in the lopsided affair. But to bring up Clare now would surely extinguish what rekindled affection he had won from Korey. Tonight he would be on his best behavior, take what glimmer of warmth she had shown him and use it to erase from her memory his caddishly unacceptable behavior.

"Marc!"

Korey's voice sliced sharply into his thoughts. He aroused as if from sleep. "Huh?"

"Some help you are. Where have you been? This is the third time I've called your name; your mind seems to have left the building."

"Uh, I've been right here….planning….designing." He thought: If she only knew the accuracy of those words.

"Well, it's time to move the ladder and measure for the second bracket." In exasperation her mouth curved downward. "Your hand is in the way of my foot." She glared at him, one foot dangling, and the idea of lowering her weight onto his knuckles had some appeal.

He had lost ground; during his brief mental absence her mood had taken a nasty turn. He jerked his hand from the ladder. "Come on down," he invited. "I'll move the ladder for you."

Pointedly ignoring the hand he offered, her feet found the floor. She stood out of the way while the ladder's squealing rubber feet skipped over the shiny floor.

"My turn," he said, a conciliatory grin throwing his mouth off center. "You've been doing most of the work." To stake his territory, he placed a foot on the first step of the ladder.

Korey yielded without argument. Rather than hover uselessly under the ladder while Marc finished the measuring, she found her way to the storage room, returning minutes later toting a drill, a plastic case of assorted drill bits, a screwdriver, and—looped over her shoulder—an extra length of electric cord.

Marc put the tools to immediate use and in no time holes were drilled and brackets mounted. Gripped by an irrational fear that Marc might be disappointed in her work, Korey fought an attack of nerves as the time came to hang the quilt. She wiped her clammy hands on the seat of her jeans.

The quilt, still rolled in the sheet and tied at each end with narrow ribbon, made the trip from the floor to its place of prominence slung over Marc's shoulder. After securing each end of a brass rod into a bracket, he turned to Korey. "The artist," he said with a grin, "has the honor of untying the ribbons."

Braced on the ladder, arms outstretched, Korey lent a dramatic flair to the unveiling as, with a grand sweep of her hands, she gave a swift tug at the long tails of ribbon, loosing each simultaneously. The quilt unfurled, pulling taut under its own weight. The bed sheet slid in a blur of color down the wall and fluttered to a heap on the floor. The signature medallion, the familiar *KRW* stamped into the silver, hung from the lower right corner of the quilt. The medallion swung side to side, light glancing from its polished surface, slowed, then stopped.

Marc moved the ladder for an unobstructed view as Korey gathered up the large sheet. It filled her arms as she pressed the rumpled folds to her chest. Her breathing was shallow as she gazed at the quilt and awaited a pronouncement.

Over the months, Marc had seen bits and pieces of the work in progress but never enough to grasp a clear image of the whole. Staring now at the quilt, he was immensely pleased. It was there as Korey had drawn it for him months before. But the similarity between her sketch and the completed work was much the same as that of an architect's drawing to an erected building. Simplistic, like primitive folk art, intricately stitched as to defy imagination, the quilt livened the wall. The covered bridge, in dusty blue—Marc marveled at how closely the fabric matched the paint of the actual bridge—and topped by a shiny roof, spanned a mossy stream. Leaves, in variegated shades of early summer, spread over rough brown trunks. The pastoral scene lay under a silken sky, a few puffy white clouds floating on the field of blue. Marc's trained eye roamed the entire four by eight foot hanging, absorbing every detail, down to the brown rabbit perched upright on the bank of the stream, its nose to an imagined breeze. The whimsical touch, so like Korey, broadened Marc's smile. The quilt not only brought the functional room to life, but gave it a sense of élan far exceeding Marc's expectations. Turning to Korey, who had nervously remained at his side during his silent assessment, he spoke of his pleasure.

She beamed in the warmth of his glowing praise, her body nearly folding in relief. Until that moment, she had not been fully aware of how tense she had become. During the last few minutes, all the stress of the past weeks had converged to roost on her shoulders. In those frenetic last days of sewing, a fear had flourished: Marc, in his estrangement, would find fault in her labors. That worry at least was now behind her. Her obligation was fulfilled, the customer satisfied. The time had come when her association with Marc would come to an end.

In place of the euphoria she had expected, a sadness swept over her. In its finality, the moment chafed like coarse cloth worrying tender skin. Her mind locked onto the refrain: *it's ended* and turned the annoying phrase over and over in her head. She dropped her eyes, turned away to rid herself of the wadded sheet. It's ended. The words that now filled her head were suddenly the last ones she wanted to hear.

*   *   *   *

"Champagne?....Celebrate?" So unprepared for this invitation that her brain spun to catch up, Korey quietly echoed Marc's suggestion. A champagne toast to celebrate the completion of the quilt he had said. But to Korey it was more a toast to a future without Marc and for that reason the idea held little appeal.

In the space of this evening she and Marc had, however tentatively, grasped the unraveling threads of friendship. But in that same time span Korey discovered that having Marc for a friend was not what she wanted; he would have to be more than that or nothing at all. Her inner voice, the one she usually depended on to speak wisely, was now telling her to go forward, not deviate from the objective she had carried with her into Marc's office tonight: see the project expeditiously put in its place—then get out. She had arrived in blinding anger. Marc's charm had dissolved that anger. Her trust in him, however, remained severely shaken and could not be restored in one evening of his turning on the charm. To remain with Marc, drinking champagne and engaging in superfluous chit chat, as if no rift had occurred, seemed to Korey to serve no purpose.

She tried to listen to her inner voice, but Marc proved more vocal and she found herself hearing only his resonant words. "....found this in the back of the refrigerator when I was digging around today for some lunch. An 'office warm-ing' gift from the electrical contractor. Someone shoved it in the refrigerator where it was forgotten and quickly buried behind a growing collection of stale Chinese carry-out and cold pizza."

Korey was far from a wine snob, but she knew an expensive bottle of *Dom Perignon* when it was held temptingly before her. What a shame to not at least try a sampling. To relegate such a wine to a rear shelf of a neglected refrigerator, behind brittle slices of pizza—she could not bear to think of such extravagant waste. Besides, the wine's medicinal properties could work wonders to soothe her raw nerves and loosen the knot that clenched ever tighter in her stomach as the time for her departure drew nearer. What harm in having one small glass of champagne? She smiled and nodded her assent. It was then, as she said, "Okay, a toast," that she noticed in Marc's hand two long-stem glasses as though all along he had known she would stay.

He set the bottle and two glasses on the counter running atop white cabinets that hugged every available inch of wall in the tiny kitchen. An expectant smile parting her lips, Korey stood at what she considered a safe distance in the event of an explosion of bubbles. She watched as Marc peeled away the gold foil overlay from the bulbous cork and twisted loose the securing wire. As he slowly pressed upward on the cork with his thumbs, Korey tried to ignore the voice inside that said: *no matter how innocent it seems, Korey, drinking champagne with Marc probably isn't one of your smartest moves.* With her eyes fixed on the uncorking, she reached for her knotted shirttail, untied it and let the wrinkled flannel fall modestly over her thighs.

The movement drew Marc's eye, and he carefully hid his disappointment that she had draped what had been a most pleasing view of her well formed curves. Surrounded by white in the brightly lit kitchen, he thought she looked, in her red and black buffalo check, like a beautiful huntress amid drifts of blinding snow. Disoriented by the contrast of the checked pattern on the white background, his eyes swam before dropping once more to the champagne bottle.

With his attention focused elsewhere, Korey took the opportunity for a covert perusal. Painful though it was, she wanted to bathe her starved senses with the sight of him, to indelibly imprint him onto her brain, safely lock him from the ravages of time that had eroded the clear images of her beloved husband. Her eyes roamed with the same reverence they would travel the hills and valleys of an awe-inspiring landscape. His lustrous dark hair was longer than when she had last seen him, on the verge of shaggy, short uneven strands biting like sawteeth into the top of his button-down collar. Her exploration took her across his heavy brows, creased in concentration, across shadowed downcast eyes; down the straight tapered nose, lingering over lips compressed in anticipation of the cork's release; gliding along the outline of his strong, clean-shaven jaw. Her eyes came to rest on his hands: long lean fingers wrapped tightly around the slender green neck of the bottle, his thumbs, with neat square-cut nails, flexing rhythmically against the cork. These were the same hands that had so fascinated her at Raffaello's the night she had first met him for dinner. Large hands, strong, but gentle too. Talented hands, capable of dealing with the tiniest detail; hands that penned classy office buildings and elegant homes. Leaning against a cabinet, her moist palms pressed to the cool edge of the countertop, she granted herself one small concession: freedom to fall in love with those hands. But she would not allow her mind equal liberty to speculate on the power those hands would wield if they should ever caress her skin....

With a sharp POP the cork ejected from the neck of the bottle. Korey jumped, though the uncorking came as no surprise and had been so deftly executed that none of the precious liquid escaped the bottle. Giddy, as if she had already imbibed, she eagerly held out both glasses to be filled.

Marc laughed, sharing her exuberance, but shook his head. "Not just yet," he said.

"Oh." She was clearly disappointed.

"We have a matter of business to transact first."

"We do?"

A sly smile danced across his lips, but he offered no hints.

After a moment of confusion, her eyes lit as if by a switch. "Oh, yes, of course we do. How careless of me." Diamonds flashed as she extended her right hand to accept the check Marc produced from his wallet. It disturbed Korey no small amount to think she could be so infatuated that it would slip her mind that she had not been paid! Doubt crept in once more to mar the moment. What wisdom was there in remaining? But her uncertainty dissolved with the first splash of bubbles into her glass.

The toast took place at the foot of the quilt, the eyes of the two celebrants seeking not the object of the exaggerated pomp but each other. Over sipped champagne, gazes lingered and temperatures rose. It was Marc who finally broke eye contact, gallantly offering his bent arm as he invited Korey to the reception area, referring now to that room by its original, more socially intimate title of "the parlor."

A portentous verse, recalled from childhood, absurdly leapt into Korey's head. Only by pressing her lips firmly together did she keep from saying aloud, "....said the spider to the fly." But if it was Marc's intent to lure her into his web, he had done nothing, other than offer champagne, to kindle suspicion.

The parlor was invitingly illuminated by soft wedges of light from wall sconces. Korey thought if one were to replace the receptionist's desk with a grand piano of sleek ebony, the room would very well pass as a parlor. At Marc's invitation, she sank wearily into one end of a sofa. Her physical labors of the day, coupled with the evening's emotional strain, left her exhausted.

Across the room Marc lit gas logs in the black marble-faced fireplace. Flames ignited and leapt around the logs, instantly adding heat to the already warm room. Behind his back, Korey fanned her shirt against her breast and was thankful when he lowered the flames. She held the crystal champagne flute at eye level and watched, in the lambent light, the glistening bubbles nudge and bump their way to freedom at the surface. Closing her eyes, she breathed deeply, a smile touching her soft lips as the bubbles burst in a bouquet of delicious fragrance. Her eyes fluttered open, but she was so bewitched by the sensual assault of the wine she vaguely noticed or cared that she was now alone in the room. Marc's absence registered with her only when she heard what sounded like a great deal of ice rattling in the kitchen. Korey drank more champagne, leaving only a sip or two for when Marc would return and she would finish the last of it, thereby putting a gracious and timely close to the evening.

Her thoughts of leaving evaporated as Marc returned to the room, his spine ramrod straight, his outstretched hands regally bearing a plastic cleaning bucket, reasonably clean, chock full of ice from which protruded the slender neck of the champagne bottle. He set the bucket on a table within easy reach of the sofa, and she teased him for entertaining much too formally. After all, she said through a giggle, she was a common woodcutter who was his guest, not some superior of royal lineage.

He joined in the jest, defending his choice of the bucket as the only vessel he could find for holding that much ice but thinking all the while that there was nothing common about the woman who now graced his sofa, no matter how she was dressed. His angular frame settled into the far end of that same sofa, and he seemed to melt into the soft cushion as if he too welcomed a respite from something troublesome. He half turned so that much of his back rested against the padded sofa arm, presenting to Korey the full view of his face.

The room was quiet, the crackle of burning logs strangely absent in the gas-fed fireplace. Conversation was light, of little consequence, voices low as if in respect for the surrounding tranquillity. Occasional laughter rolled through the room then faded like the last strains of a melody falling over a hushed audience. One subject led to another. Marc spoke of the progress of his newest projects then turned the conversation, in a rare mention of his family, to his mother and her current tour of Africa. Korey told of Tina and Bryan's plan to put their tiny house on the market in the spring in preparation for building a new home. At no time did Korey ask about Eric and Rae, nor did Marc mention Matty, as if tacitly they had agreed that New Mexico or any related subject was taboo.

Memories of Gran Quivira, when he had turned tail and run rather than reveal the truth about Clare, only fueled Marc's urge to never stop running. Tonight Korey had asked nothing of him. Had she forgiven his neglect? Doubtful. But he admired the dignified way she had carried herself all evening. She had not pouted or shown the pitiable posture of a spurned lover.

In Korey's view, the trip to New Mexico was the wellspring from which had flowed weeks of hostility and resentment. Thanks to Marc's rejection, her pride had taken a severe beating. But the wounds were at this moment beginning to heal, and she shied away from interjecting anything into the conversation that would again lay them open.

For both Marc and Korey the past seemed temporarily forgotten; the night grew rosier with each drop in the level of champagne in the bottle. A comfortable silence fell between them. Korey set her champagne on the glass table, the crystal flute ringing musically as it touched down. She bent double to untie her ankle-high boots, the laces shedding unheeded bits of sawdust onto the floor. Stretching to the tips of her toes, she nudged the boots under the table then curled her legs on the sofa and began toying with her sock, plucking at the soft looped wool of a misshapen toe.

Marc took her fidget to mean she was not as much at ease as she appeared, and he blamed himself. No doubt in the past few weeks she had suffered much as he had. For all that he had inflicted upon them both, he felt a deep sorrow. But to mend the damage with soothing overtures would be a serious misstep. The fact was, if she remained a little wary, even slightly aloof, then all the better; his attempt to keep their relationship within legitimate boundaries would be made simpler. The daunting challenge loomed like an ogre before him, but he accepted full responsibility for seeing that he stayed true to what was right—and honorable.

Korey made a passing comment about the unseasonably cold weather, her voice husky with wine and fatigue. Through her sock, she massaged toes still tender from her earlier run-in with the tire. When conversation faltered, she began to sense a change. The air in the room was suddenly rare, and Marc, though he had not moved, seemed to be drawing nearer. He said something, but his voice was no more than a drone in the distance as Korey's mind charged between them with an announcement: *Get out of here, Korey. Think with your head not with a heart already wounded. Marc can't be trusted.* She knew that by staying she was exposing her heart to perilous risk. She willed herself to move, to flee to the safety of her car, but her legs seemed to be pressed in a locked position. She started when melting ice collapsed in the plastic bucket, setting the champagne bottle adrift. Condensation ran in lazy rivulets down the sides of the bucket and, in the firelight, formed a widening circle of liquid gold at the base. She raised her eyes to find she was the object of a covetous gaze. Alarmed, she shot off the sofa as if it were on fire, leaving Marc dumbfounded. He heard her say, "I'd better go," just before he saw her tilt, sway and start to fall.

He jumped to her side, aiding her as she regained her balance, his steadying hands pressed firmly on her shoulders. Without thought he had reached for her in a guileless act of rescue. But the moment he touched her, he knew he wanted more. Gone were his good intentions, torn asunder by this pose and the warmth of her skin escaping the heavy flannel. The resolute promises he had made to himself vanished as swiftly as dust lost to a dry breeze.

"Whoa," he said as he fought to control his breathing. "Are you all right?"

"Of course I'm all right!" she snapped. "I stepped on the floppy toe of my sock, is all, and it threw me off balance." She shrugged free of his hold, looked him full in the face as if to answer an accusation. "The champagne hasn't made me loopy, you know."

Marc stepped back and stuffed his hands in his pockets where they would be no threat. She was frightened; there was a disturbing wildness in her eyes. He had done nothing. Surely she couldn't be that frightened of him? She bent over to snug up her socks, and he spoke to the top of her head. "Relax, Korey." His voice was soft. "I never meant to suggest that you're drunk."

She reached under the table, came up slowly, her boots hooked in the curve of the first and second finger of her right hand. She smiled, shyly. "I'm sorry. I don't know why I barked at you like that." She pressed the heel of her other hand against her forehead. Through a widening smile she conceded, "Maybe I did have a little too much champagne."

She turned for the foyer. Marc followed at a carefully gauged distance. He was afraid to ask the next question, just as afraid not to. "Would you like me to drive you home?"

Stopping near the front door, she turned to find him leaning a shoulder against the doorframe to the parlor, his hands still securely in the front pockets of his jeans. She took no offense to his offer, but nonetheless declined.

"Okay, then. But before you go, how about a cup of coffee, or some hot chocolate? There's just about two cups of not-yet-curdled milk in the refrigerator." He sealed the suggestion with a crooked grin.

She remarked dryly, "Umm, you make it sound so tempting, but I'm fine, really. I won't have any trouble driving." As though she believed he needed further convincing, she added, "Honest." Dismissing a further ploy to detain her, she started for the stairway, planning to use the bottom step as a handy bench for putting on her boots.

She stopped at the sound of footsteps closing in on her. Warm breath titillated her nape. Looking over her shoulder she stared into a face so close it almost touched hers. In the thin light of the hall the green eyes were dark, dewy; they caressed her like wet grass fondling bare toes on a hot summer night. He reached for her free hand. Hers lifted effortlessly and dropped into his. With gentle strength he turned her to face him.

"If you're leaving…." He sighed as if resigned to letting her go. He bent his head. She felt soft stirrings of his breath on her mouth. He leaned closer. "If you're leaving," he repeated, "then take this with you." His lips came to rest on hers with the lightness of a new lover's touch. Strong arms captured her waist and carefully drew her to him. She was perfectly still, arms hanging at her sides, boots still dangling from the tips of her fingers. She did not return the pleasure of the kiss, she simply received. Moments later he released her, leaving behind the tingle of his mouth on hers.

She was now free to go. He would not stop her. Walking out the door was the only sane thing to do. She stood on the hall runner, her toes digging into the weave, rooted in place by the sight, the feel, the scent of him. She made no move to put on her boots, no move to fetch her purse from the drafting room or to seek out her coat. Befuddled, having no answer to his questioning gaze, she lowered her eyes.

Marc's useless hands hung from his wrists like lead weights while terrible fears threatened to rip him through the middle: Korey would turn and go, taking with her his chance to fulfill even the tamest of his many fantasies—no less daunting was the opposing fear that she would stay to see his fantasies fulfilled. Either way, his future looked bleak. Time slinked past and joined with the unnatural silence to flow through the house unheeded as Korey and Marc were each lost in a private torment.

When Korey raised dark lashes and her luminous eyes reached out to him, Marc's mind whirred with amatory visions. His temples throbbed as his blood ran hot in pursuit of those visions. His forefinger hooked her chin, lifting her face to meet his. One arm circled her waist as he crushed her against his hard chest and a hand tangled in her thick loose curls. This kiss was everything the first one was not. This was a kiss with lips eager to possess.

As his mouth tasted and explored, drawing her sweetness into his, Korey rode a tide of mindless pleasure. Yearnings long dormant surged within her, wrecking her cool facade as ruinously as a ship pounded into matchsticks upon rocks. She was unaware she had dropped her boots until, as if coming from a distant room, a dull *thump* brushed the fringes of her mind. Her slender fingers were free now to play in the feathery hair at his nape. Engulfed by him, barraged by a wondrous blend of wool and aftershave and laundry starch, of a mouth sweet and tasting deliciously of fine champagne, she deepened the kiss.

When he lifted his mouth from hers, the rush of air across her wet lips was cold—and sobering. He held her so close she barely drew the breath required to say, into his shoulder, "Marc, I really must go."

"No," he whispered hoarsely. "Stay with me. Let me hold you for awhile longer." He kissed her flushed cheek then leaned back just enough to meet her eyes.

She knew that look. It was dangerous. It was the look he had given her in Old Town Albuquerque in November. The one she would never refuse.

His voice broke into her hesitation. Cupping her face in his warm capable hands he said, "We won't do anything you don't want to do."

The words hung between them as she thought: *Oh, great, is that supposed to make me feel safe?* If so, his words failed miserably. She knew *exactly* what she wanted to do. She wanted to become lost in this man, to forget she did not fully trust him, to let him do to her whatever he would to obliterate all traces of pain and anguish that had hounded her as the widow of Kenneth Daniel Westerfield. No guilt diluted this urgent need. She wanted Marc to so satiate her senses that there would be no world beyond his arms, no thought beyond his kiss.

Marc knew she warmed to the idea of staying: Her cheeks glowed red, and a woodsy smell rose from her like steam from a forest floor after summer rain.

Trapped in the searing heat of his gaze, the flannel shirt sticking to her skin each place Marc had put his hands, Korey felt as though she were bound in a blanket. If only she could shed that blanket....feel his body against her heated skin....

Marc felt her go limp in his arms as if her skeletal framework had failed. She clung to him for support as her mouth sought his. It was long moments before his mouth left hers to travel her slender neck, the velvet tip of his tongue brushing the hollow of her throat. "Oh, Korey," he murmured into her soft flesh, "I can't begin to describe how delicious you taste."

"No need to try," she whispered, rising on her toes to trace warm kisses the full width of his parted lips. "Remember, I'm feasting at the same table."

If Marc had been holding himself behind a tremulous dam of restraint, he took her words as leave to open the floodgates. His mouth covered hers before she had uttered the last syllable. His hands were everywhere: her hair, her face, sliding over her breasts, lifting the long tail of the flannel shirt, finding her hips, pressing her tightly to him. He took a small step backward. Molded to him, Korey followed, matching him kiss for kiss, touch for touch. One step, and another, then the heel of his penny loafer struck the riser of the bottom stair. He took one step up the landing, Korey locked tightly in his arms. His hand groped along the wall until it hit a series of light switches. Flying fingers flipped switches as the slit of one eye monitored which lights came on.

Korey was vaguely aware of light seeping through closed eyelids as she went with him, slowly, across the short landing and up another step. There Marc kissed her once more, soundly, and she was abruptly released. Before she had time to think what it meant, her world tilted. Overcome with a surge of panic, she knew she was fainting. The heat that had dogged her all evening had finally succeeded in taking her under. She was lashed with the sting of embarrassment as the stairwell spun a dizzy circle around her head.

Then all was right again. She wasn't fainting. It was Marc, lifting her, carrying her in a rush up two stairs at a time, the aged wood groaning under their weight. Korey wrapped an arm around his neck and pressed close to him to save herself from bumping against the encroaching walls of the narrow stairway. She snuggled her head against his chest. His heat, seeping through his sweater, scorched her cheek. Her other hand rested over his heart, the steady thump, thump against her moist palm in rhythm with the wild, primitive beat pounding in her ear.

As they reached the second floor, he paused to look at her, a smile teasing the edges of lips swollen with kisses. He spoke softly, leaving her to momentarily wonder if it was the exertion of the climb or passionate impatience that had left him breathless. "Fair warning," he said as he inched toward the bedroom, watching her face at close range. "I'm making no promises about how long I'll last."

"It doesn't matter," she whispered against his mouth.

His dark brows shot up. "It doesn't?" Only a doorway now separated them from a bed flanked by lamps already softly burning.

"No. The second time will last."

He carried her sideways across the threshold, his foot stretching blindly for the door. "You mean....there will be a second time?" He caught the corner of the heavy oak door with the toe of his shoe and pushed. Behind them the door swung on silent hinges, clicking smoothly into the latch.

Her grin was shameless. "There will be," she said, nibbling his ear, "as many times as we like."

CHAPTER 13

▼

Starvation. It can bring on an appetite that makes you crazy. Crazy enough to willfully live the night just past. In darkness she had risen and flown with him through a world beyond dreams.

Morning light passed freely through dozens of panes of undraped glass, the cold December sun clarifying what in the dark had been a wondrous mystery. Korey pulled a corner of the bed sheet to just below her chin, shivering with the incurable chill that comes when warmth is drained from within.

The bed in which she lay brought to mind a beach after a pounding storm: pillows, like shifted dunes, strewn over bed and floor, used in ways she wished not to recall; Marc rolled to his chest in the top sheet like a fish in seaweed, the bottom sheet pulled from the mattress and curled into a wave upon his bound knees, his soft breath against her cheek the only sign of life. He lay so close that she could have easily counted each whisker that had begun to shadow the relaxed jaw.

His beauty held her captive; she watched him. He slept like a sated baby, the tiny lines around his eyes erased by the depth of his slumber. She resisted a yearning to reach out with a finger and run a feather's touch over the closed eyelids, wanting but not daring to see those green eyes flutter open and warm her with the fire she would find burning there.

An unrest stirred her, a turbulence that rivaled the bed's dishevelment. This was a new world, one that had flipped topsy-turvy, a world where she was again sharing a bed with a man. Strangely familiar, yet very different. This man she could not call husband.

She had opened and taken Marc into her body, her mind, her heart and was too close to losing herself in him. Like viewing a large Monet with a nose to the canvas, all she could see of their night together were splashes of rapturous color. She had to stand back, to view from a distance where she had been and where to go from here. The first step would be to go home. Home, where she would be free to think, where Marc's hot hands and deep kisses would not turn her mind to mush.

She would run from him, but there would be no escaping the love she felt. This love had a dark side: It brought her face to face with her fear of losing a man she loved. She defeated an irrational urge to lean over Marc and with stony fists pummel his smooth chest until he too tasted the terror this love had planted within her.

Fear, with icy arms, reached out to pull her from Marc's bed. Her back was stiff, and she was tender in places that had been long neglected. A low moan formed deep within her throat but did not rise to the surface. Instead, she bore her discomfort by wrinkling her nose and squeezing her eyes tightly shut. Carefully, she eased from the bed. More than anything she wanted to slink home and soak in a steaming bath.

A self-conscious flush traveled from her toes to her bare shoulders as she followed a trail of discarded clothing. From the bed to the door, she silently disentangled her clothes from his, resisting in the name of haste an inbred urge to collect his things and neatly fold them over a chair. Casting a wary glance toward the bed, she saw that her stirring had not disturbed his sleep. Her clothes clutched in a wad at her breast, she cautiously headed for the adjoining bathroom, praying the oak floor beneath the rich burgundy rug would not protest her passing.

Safely in the bath, she dressed quickly, tugging her lower lip between her teeth as she wriggled into her snug jeans. Realizing she was without shoes, she inched open the bathroom door, her eyes darting here and there, frantic to locate her boots. The risk of venturing forth and searching the bedroom filled her with dread. It was then, as she stepped from the bathroom to begin the search, she recalled the boots would be in the foyer near the base of the stairs, exactly where she had dropped them the night before.

Marc lay on his side just as she had left him, his arm holding captive the pillow upon which rested his tousled head. For precious moments she stood in the bathroom doorway, taking in his handsome face and the easy rise and fall of his broad bare chest.

In her quest for a silent escape, Korey tiptoed in socked feet the width of the hushed room. Holding her breath, she slowly twisted the doorknob, and the latch soundlessly disengaged. She was through the open door when she heard a lingering sigh and the soft rustle of sheets. She stopped, a hand pressed firmly to her mouth, shoulders hunched as if she had been caught with her hand in the family safe. She waited. Quiet moments passed. Her neck creaked as she finally turned to look over her shoulder. Relief flooded her; Marc, eyes closed and still packaged in the restrictive sheet, had only shifted onto his back.

The rest was easy. Closing the door behind her, her feet were a blur as they rushed down the stairs. Without wasted motion she stepped into and laced the waiting boots. As she straightened, her eyes fell on the low fire still burning in the fireplace. In Marc's impatience to carry her to his bed, the gas logs had been negligently left to heat the parlor throughout the night. Before gathering her belongings, she took time to turn off the gas but left the champagne glasses and bucket to float in a wide puddle on the table.

Frosty air cooled her flushed cheeks as she fled the wide porch to emerge in milky sunshine. Turning for final assurance that she was not being pursued, she found the double doors securely closed, the porch empty. In her chest, a rush of disappointment dominated a more recessive sense of relief. Her clean escape would not be enough, it seemed, to reduce the lump choking off her breathing.

✷   ✷   ✷   ✷

He knew she was gone even before he reached for her. His memory, a crystal recall of each awakening in their night together, was of her lying with him, skin to skin. Now he was wrapped not in the silky smoothness of warm slender limbs but in a blasted bed sheet. With eyes still closed, he ran his hand over the bed, feeling her now-familiar shape imprinted onto the sheet. Cold. She had been gone awhile.

He dared to imagine what he might confront when he would finally open his eyes to the daylight. If he should wish with enough fervor, would he find her curled in the nearby chair, clad only in that ridiculous flannel shirt, her dark eyes, still holding the glow of love, contentedly watching him sleep? He lay motionless, listening for some telltale sound—soft breathing perhaps, or water running in the bathroom—but heard nothing beyond the dry caw of crows. No, more realistically he would find that he was alone. He fretted. Had she left the house as well as his bed?

In fear of his eyes popping open as if the lids were spring loaded, forcing him to look for her, Marc covered his eyes with the flat of his hand. Within the darkness, it was easy to reflect on his night in Korey's arms. Rapturous images, nearly as sensual in memory as they had been in life, swirled through his head until he lost count of the times she had taken him to her.

Alone, the large bed held no appeal, and he rolled out, impatiently tugging the tangled sheet loose as he went. He grabbed sweat pants and a baggy shirt from a hook in the closet, hopping into the pants on his way to the window. Through the glass, sunlight warmed his bare shoulders then lit copper streaks in his hair as his head poked through the stretched neck of his shirt. His eyes shot a straight line to the empty spot in the circular drive where Korey's car had been parked. So she *had* left. No surprise, really. Until last evening she had shied away as much as he from their magnetic attraction. From here on how was this to be played? She running, and he….what? Chasing? No. Much as he longed to do just that, he could not. Aware of a hollowness in his chest that begged to be filled, he turned from the window and wondered if either he or Korey could hope to stay away from the other after their explosive night together.

The tiled floor chilled his bare feet and sleep had begun to lift its dense fog from body and mind by the time Marc fumbled around in the kitchen and got the coffee going. Leaving the coffee to drip rich amber drops into the pot, he grabbed a dishtowel and followed the soft hall runner to the reception room.

He went with purpose to the glass table, dropping the terry towel into the puddle of water that had flowed a finger's width short of the edge. Squatting for a better reach, he sopped the puddle with the towel, wringing water into the plastic bucket each time the towel became saturated. The empty champagne bottle spun in an eddy, listed, then rested its long green neck on the rim of the bucket. Drops of water splattered onto Marc's thigh, soaking cold circles through the sweat pants, but he hardly noticed. His mind was pleasantly preoccupied with reconstructing bits and pieces of conversation that had cheered the room the night before. Korey's laughter tinkled like finely-tuned chimes in his memory, and a vision of her face softened in the blush of firelight entertained him as he absently mopped. He caught himself staring into the cold fireplace, only vaguely perturbed that he had no recollection of turning off the gas before, in the white heat of his own fire, he had whisked Korey to his bed.

A smile touched his lips—one not of humor but of irony. Before last night he had ached to know every inch of her. Now that he did, the ache mushroomed and expanded against his chest wall until he thought he might explode. How would he now gather the strength to let her go? And if he should, would time take pity, and with tender strokes rub healing balm over his mind and heart, dulling the keen memory of the warm, fragrant softness that had curled in his arms through the coldest hours of a moonless December night?

His musings took a sudden, inexplicable turn, chilling him as effectively as if he had been dashed with icy water from the make-shift champagne bucket. Clare, her face translucent and as youthful as their love had once been, floated like a ghost across his vision to remind him that in the record books in the State of Tennessee she stood with him as his wife. But that was only paper, he argued. In his heart, it was Korey who now was woven into every fiber.

He shook Clare's pale countenance from his mind and that of Korey as well. Insensible, irrational, impossible—insane! Apt labels for the ingredients he had thrown into the bitter stew he cooked for himself! He grabbed the bucket, giving the water ring on the table a final swipe. His head shook as if in comic disbelief. How, he wondered, could he have in the space of a few short months and of his own doing become such a complete muddlehead?

The aroma of fresh coffee lured him to its source, and he filled an oversize mug with steaming brew. The first taste burned the tip of his tongue, but he was numb to it. For some minutes he had been anticipating that welcome flow of well being that comes when a weighty problem has lifted and been set firmly upon another's shoulders. Korey had done that for him. She had left him, thereby turning aside an awkwardness that would certainly have arisen had she taken their night together to mean more than it could. Strangely, her leaving did not relieve the ache in his chest. The temptation swelled within him to go after her, track her down and like a wild man make love to her whenever and wherever he should find her. Only then might he find an ease to his pain.

He flexed the last of the night's kinks from his back, leaned against the kitchen counter and took another sip of coffee before mentally giving himself a stern lecture. *When the torment approaches your threshold,* he scolded, *and you cry out for the deliverance you would find in Korey's arms, remember this: She ran. Perhaps in part from herself, but most likely from you and what you represent. She's afraid of being hurt again. Only a damn fool would not leave her to her choice. Remember, too,* his mind continued, bent on telling him what he did not want to hear: *You are a married man.*

His body was no more interested in being apprised of the brutal facts than was his head. It did not cease its longing for Korey but rather seemed to dwell on it until he felt like the pain would surely rip him apart. The reason for his frustration was plain enough: He wanted what he could not have. Wanted her so badly the taste of her was still on his tongue. Wanted her in his bed on early spring evenings to share a new breeze through an open window and to feel the tiny chill bumps the length of her soft body. In his bed in the blaze of summer's heat, to know the feel of her slick skin under his hand. In his bed when autumn's smoke turns the air to pewter or when wicked rains paper the windows with bronze leaves. In his bed in winter to be warmed by her through years of nights, long and cold.

With an effort that further taxed his already dismal mood, he led his mind to matters more practical. Pushing away from the counter, his eyes now red-rimmed, he made toward the promise of a warm, soothing shower. Eyes downcast and shoulders slumped, he was like a sad little boy who had dared to duel a cantankerous tree for a favorite kite—and lost. Coffee in hand, he slowly took to the stairs, bare toes scraping a lonely beat against the polished edge of each step as he climbed.

*   *   *   *

She knew it was a bounty of raw nerves that had kept her moving the last three days, a spurt of energy far removed from the condition in which she had arrived home Sunday morning after leaving Marc.

That morning muddled emotions and very little sleep had drained her, and she had soaked in a tub until her troubles seemed to dissolve in the hot water. After the bath, with assurances to herself of a cat nap only, she had given in to the tug of the soft bed. Sleep, however, had grander plans and had held her under in dreamless slumber. She awakened to a room disturbingly dim, a narrow stripe of sun slanting through the bedroom doorway from the west side of the house, and she knew she had slept away the ripest part of the winter afternoon. A wasted day, she had told herself as she shook off sleep.

But the industry she exhibited through the ensuing days more than made up for the one lost. Now, at mid-week, perched on the fat arm of a chair swamped in sunshine, she quietly surveyed the results of her work. The bright warmth of the room gave no hint of the chill that nipped at the shrubs growing just outside the window. For the past few days the weather had been of no concern to Korey. Since Sunday she had seldom poked her nose outside the house except to retrieve the newspaper, trek daily down the gravel drive to the mailbox, or step out the side door to shake dust from scatter rugs.

Before her impulsive tryst with Marc, the cleanliness of her house had been shoved aside by the urgency to finish his quilt. Her bout with the flu had only meant further neglect. In the waning days of her illness, she had practically run

Tina off at the point of a broomstick to keep her sister—who had a job, a husband, and a home of her own to look after—from cleaning the house. "Don't
worry about the house," she had said to Tina. "The dust will sit and wait for my
strength to return." And return it did. Monday morning, a full day away from
Marc's seeking grasp, Korey began to swirl through the house like a cyclone.
With brooms and buckets, sponges and dust cloths she had vacuumed, scoured,
mopped, and polished the house end to end. Now, tired dark eyes absorbed with
satisfaction the results of the domestic frenzy. The fresh tang of lemon oil hung
heavily in the room and rode to other parts of the house on warm air currents
blown from the furnace.

The pleasure of a task well performed was short lived, however. The housework, which had served so well as a numbing tonic to blunt her thinking, was finished, and the flurry of the past days settled coldly around her. Now that she was
no longer able to stuff images of Marc into the shadowy corners of her mind,
vivid memories of the sights and sounds of the night spent in his arms tumbled
through her head.

Korey swallowed nervously. Rubbing against her conscience was the way she
had left him—sneaking away much like a hooker who had a john's fat wallet
pinched between her ample breasts. For a glancing moment she felt a twinge of
guilt for staying with Marc in the first place, but she pushed the guilt aside. She
had, after all, stayed with him of her own will. She loved him. The throbbing
ache in her chest was a measure of how much. And even though what had been
might never be again, she knew if somehow the clock were turned back and the
choosing, to go or to stay, were yet to be done, the choice would be the same. No,
there would be no regrets.

Still, something not clearly defined needled her mind. Disappointment,
maybe. Not in the way Marc had treated her, surely. In what had been one of the
most beautiful nights of her life, he had—at times, quickly; other times, slowly;
at all times, tenderly—spun her starving senses through a vortex of pleasures. But
out of it had come an unfulfilled expectation. Marc had not, even while showing
it in countless ways, said the one word that she yearned to hear.

Korey slid from the arm of the chair to the soft cushion. Through the window
she watched a squirrel store an acorn in the loose soil of the rose garden. The furnace switched on, fluttering the hem of the floor-length drapes. Her dark blue
jeans soaked the sunshine through to her legs. She leaned her head against the
chair and closed her eyes to the brilliance in the room.

Love. Such a tiny word, structurally simple. Yet it intimidated. It made strong
men cower and their throats constrict, so that the word would often not travel

the path from the heart to the lips. Marc loved her. She knew love between a man and a woman. Through Danny she had seen it in too many ways to not recognize that she was seeing it again. Three nights ago Marc had shown a tenderness and a selfless giving that could only be a mirror of his feelings.

Still, there were other times when he seemed so remote, holding a piece of himself in reserve, guarded, fading in and out of her life as if on a whim. But in all fairness, had she not done the same? Could it be, she wondered with new revelation, that he too had fears? Fears that rode sidecar with hers? What a pair they made! Each drawn to the other. Each erecting detours along love's roadway.

Facing down a rising desire to abandon all common sense and run to him, Korey forced herself to look coldly at the facts. Sunday afternoon she had half expected Marc to show up on her doorstep. He had not. She thought surely he would phone. He had not. Now, with nearly four days gone, maybe he would not. She tapped her toe in vexation. It was like the aftermath of the Albuquerque trip all over again. Both times she had given more of herself than she thought wise; both times he had taken what she offered, then turned aside.

"Hey, Korey," she said aloud as if to bring her scattered thoughts sternly into focus. "Don't be stupidly swept into a sea of dreams by one night of carnal madness." He had given her a sweet taste of what it could mean if he freed himself to love her fully. Perhaps one day he would offer her another glimpse. She shifted in the chair and let out an unconscious little sigh. To resist his tug….ah, what a thing to ask. Simply thinking of it made her whole body ache.

*   *   *   *

The tree was beautiful, standing on a trunk straight and sturdy, peaking just above her head. She had first noticed it the week before when she had been cutting firewood with Tina and Bryan. A cedar, deep green and bushy, its aroma filling her head when she had stopped to pinch a sprig of soft needles. It stood now in her living room, in a metal stand filled with water, wrapped in strings of freshly popped corn and ripe red cranberries. Hundreds of densely-strung red lights cast a glow like a rosy sunset across the otherwise unlit room. Crystal icicles swayed in the current of warm air flowing through the house.

She was extraordinarily proud of this tree she had cut. She had awakened early that very morning, well rested, the house cleaning accomplished, restless for yet more physical labor to keep her mind from straying to thoughts of Marc. It had occurred to her then, not without some panic, that in her recent state of agitation not a step had been taken to prepare for the Christmas fast approaching. The spirit for holiday decorating had deserted her the two Christmases since Danny had been gone. But this year, well this year would be different. She would have a tree. Not one from a sales lot. She would cut her own. And she knew exactly where to find the perfect one!

She had dressed in the same warm clothes she wore the last time she saw Marc, had taken with her a thermos of hot cocoa and arrived at the spot on Dad's land where the tree waited just as the sun was burning frost from the tips of the feathery branches. She cut the tree by hand, working a sharp pruning saw back and forth across the small trunk. The felling of the tree lengthened her confidence, but she found the task of fitting the tree into the trunk of the car more formidable than the cutting. Nonetheless, the foray had been a pleasant one.

Tina had come that afternoon to help string cranberries and popcorn. The sisters had poured mugs of warm mulled wine, gossiped and giggled. Thankfully, Tina had been tactful and had not marred the day by asking about Marc. Korey, only to appease her sister's tacit curiosity, offered a crisp and concise descriptive of the hanging of his quilt. At no time was she moved to reveal to Tina the treasured secrets of the night spent with Marc.

Nor did Korey feel compelled to discuss the two messages he had left on her answering machine while she was out cutting the tree. He wanted to "touch base," he had said. Just wanted to talk. Nothing that couldn't wait. He would try again. Korey had come close to erasing the messages as soon as she heard his greeting, had told herself that what he had to say was of no interest. Instead, she heard him out. Caring little about the content of the message, she replayed it time and again simply to hear the sound of his voice. There had been as much distress as comfort in the listening, but she had not stopped the machine. He had sounded tired, or maybe distracted. Congenial beyond his usual way, as though he was trying too hard. But how was she to tell anything from a few words spoken into a machine? Wasn't it difficult enough to read him when he was so close she could feel his breath on her skin, those damnable green eyes drawing her in while at the same time withholding so much?

Now it was dark. Tina was gone, home to a husband and a cozy fire. Korey hung the last crystal icicle on the tree. *White Christmas* played on the radio while, in Chattanooga, not snow but buckets of rain streamed down the window and turned the lights on the tree into thousands of glittering red stars. The tree was everything she had pictured it to be. The house smelled strong of cedar and popcorn and cinnamon candles. Christmas was just around the corner. But her earlier festive mood had vanished. She gripped tightly a mug of cocoa in hands stained red from stringing cranberries. A sudden mist formed over her eyes, and the tiny lights trickled around and over each other as they blurred and ran down the lacy branches of the tree.

*   *   *   *

The messages had lost all tolerance and escalated to thinly controlled anger. Marc had been calling for three days. She finally turned the volume down on the machine so she could not hear incoming messages. She played them back at night, the sharp edge in Marc's voice biting deeply into her solitude. She returned calls from everyone but Marc. His latest message left her to wonder what would happen next.

"Dammit, Korey! I've had just about enough of your hiding behind that answering machine. I know you have to be home *sometime*. If I weren't in Nashville right now, I'd be tempted to come over there and yank that damn machine out of the wall." Here he paused, then, in a calmer voice said, "Call…." But apparently his contrition only went so far. "….Dammit!"

She had *never* known him to swear like that. He *was* angry. Her mind saw him sitting at a desk, the skin stretched white over his knuckles, the large vein on his hand throbbing as he tightened his grip on the phone. Through his anger, she thought she heard a trace of pleading. She must have played the message a dozen times.

But still she did not call.

CHAPTER 14

▼

One shapeless rainy day melted into the next as if the clouds would scrape their fat bellies to the earth until free of every last drop of water. The air was weighted with a soggy chill, but the wind had ceased its howling, and the rain now fell vertically as though flowing along fine threads.

Korey sat on the porch swing, glad for her failure to store the swing in the garage for the winter as she should have. A zipped windbreaker held two thick sweaters close to the warmth of her body, but the cool air still left its pink print on her cheeks. Dampness set her lovely face in an ornate frame as her hair, open to the weather, curled across her forehead and over her ears.

The day before, hunched over the desk in her studio, rain spattering a crackled glaze on the window, she had signed, addressed, and stamped a teetering stack of Christmas cards. Now the cards were tied in bundles awaiting pick up, the red flag raised on the mailbox as a signal to Kenny, who would, even on a day such as this, call hello from his mail truck and flash a friendly smile.

Tending to the task of writing a Christmas shopping list, she swung to and fro to the squeak of a rusting chain. With only a week remaining until Christmas, the list was nearly complete. For Tina nothing would do but the slinky turtleneck dress spotted last week on a visit to Georgy's Trunk. Bryan had said something about needing a new lens for his camera....Tina would know which one. Dad and Stella should be ready for a fresh supply of personalized golf balls, tees and markers. Rob's favorite sweater was showing its age, and he might not be so stubborn about giving it up if it could be replaced by a nearly identical tweed. Evie— well, buying for her was never difficult. Anything that had a place in a kitchen would be put to frequent use. A few choice gifts for friends would round out the list. And, not to be forgotten, a large box of biscuits for Evie's golden retriever, Claxton. Not even below that of the dog did the name Marc Bradberry appear on the list.

Korey looked up as a low black shape rose out of the mist and trotted down the street, hard nails scrapping the pavement, wet matted hair sticking to muscle and bone. Korey strained to see. It was Rubin, the neighborhood hound. Crazy mutt seemed to thrive in nasty weather. Now that evening was near, he was heading home to Emmett. Emmett, who was as old as God, would have supper waiting in the warm little house on the corner that he and Rubin shared.

Korey closed her eyes to absorb the peaceful sound of rain. Swollen drops fell from slick branches to a saturated ground—plop, plop, plop—like notes dripping from a sheet of music. Water rushed across the roof and gurgled into the gutter, chuckling as it plunged through the dark ride in the downspout. A breath of wind pushed the rain sideways just enough for a fine mist to brush her face and settle on hands she had quickly fanned to protect the open notebook in her lap.

She would have known the familiar hum of the car engine even if she had not seen a flash of red as she opened her eyes to the dusky light. Wet gravel crunched beneath wide tires, then the slam of a car door cut through the hypnotic pulse of the rainfall. He appeared out of the drizzle, standing before her outside the cover of the porch as if mistrusting the consequences of getting too close. Rain rolled from his dark hair to his nose, dripping from there to the shirtfront left exposed by an open trench coat. A wide belt hung loose from the coat, its square buckle dripping water onto a soggy shoe. His baggy khakis were dark along the thighs and cuffs as if he had walked for some time in the rain.

They studied each other, green eyes locked onto unflinching brown ones. Korey stopped the swing. Marc stood in the pelting rain. Words seemed to elude them. Marc so resembled the lingering image of a drenched Rubin loping along the rain-swept street that Korey could not keep her eyes from dancing as she squelched a grin.

Had Marc any inkling that the softness he spotted in those expressive brown eyes had to do with her likening him to the waterlogged mutt he had nearly hit as he turned a fast corner onto Korey's street, he would have taken it as a cue to leave. Instead, in his innocence he instantly gained heart that she would invite him into the shelter of the porch, or, daring more, ask him to join her on the swing.

"You're wet." The first words she had spoken to him in six days, and they sounded inane to her own ears.

Not what he had hoped for. He glanced down, then raised a brow. "So I am." The statement was flat, revealing nothing of his feelings for his miserable condition.

"Well, don't just stand there. Get out of the rain before you catch your death."

"Would you care?"

She stood beside the swing waiting for him to gain the steps. "Maybe." Then, "Come on in the house." It was more an order than an invitation. But after brushing droplets of rain from his coat, he obediently followed her inside and closed the door behind him. The house was warm and dry and smelled so much like a childhood Christmas he was shot through with waves of nostalgia.

Without another word or backward glance, Korey left him to stand alone in the foyer. She reappeared, unfolding a fluffy bath towel as she came. He accepted it from her outstretched hand, smiling in gratitude, and wiped the worst of the rain from his face and hair. Korey watched him, her arms crossed over her chest, as he daubed the shoulders of his coat and dried the metal belt buckle. She showed no inclination to play gracious hostess and relieve him of his coat so he left it on. When he appeared sufficiently dry, she took the damp towel and mutely watched him.

"You can guess why I'm here."

"Yes."

"You are, I presume, aware I've been calling you for days."

"Yes."

"So, if you got my messages, why didn't you call?"

Here was the question that begged a thoughtful answer, something other than the sheepish shrug she gave him. But she could not bring herself to air her darkest fears. "Look, Marc, I appreciate your interest, but...."

Damn if she was not as stubborn as she was beautiful! After having spent days shutting him out she was not giving an inch, her stony face a picture of determination. Well, he was in no mood for games. He had not come storming over here to be so easily dismissed. "Appreciate my *interest*? You make it sound as though this is a business call. We're not talking business anymore, Korey. Not after what happened in my bedroom last Saturday night!" There was a keen edge to his voice that commanded her full attention. "Now, I ask you again. Why didn't you call?"

She dropped her eyes and nodded. "Okay." He deserved the truth. It was she, after all, who had left him without so much as a peck on the cheek. She held tightly to the damp towel. The cuckoo clock in the kitchen chirped the time but neither Marc nor Korey bothered to count the hours. Only Marc was absently aware that the house was growing dim in the gray, thinning light.

She told him that she had run because her feelings for him sapped her of the strength she desperately needed to think rationally. She told him that she was terrified of caring too much.

Marc pried her left hand from within folds of towel, her slender fingers laying cool across his warm palm. When he smiled, it was as if the rain had stopped and the sun had broken through to cast a golden radiance upon her world. The smile broadened and grew brighter as his doubts about her feelings evaporated. It was as he had suspected: She had run from the love she felt for him. He knew it was within his power to wrap her in passion so consuming there would be no time nor space for fear.

But this awesome power, if abused, would it destroy them? All week, while Korey had been safely in hiding, he, in every spare moment, had worked his mind to numbness trying to answer that question. He had flipped through a long list of reasons why he should not let himself go to her. But only one had stood up to an intense scrutiny—Clare. And Clare was no longer reason enough.

The past was out of reach; mistakes could not be undone. With the future, however, he had a semblance of control. But there would be no future without Korey. So now he would do what he had come to do. He would offer only what was in his power to give. And if she accepted….they would share each day in love—and the devil take the tomorrows.

"Korey."

"Yes?" Her eyes, large as an expectant child's on Christmas morning, studied his face.

"I love you, Korey." There. It was said. Not by a sane man perhaps, but Marc Bradberry had not been sane since the first moment he set eyes on Korey Reynolds Westerfield.

Those magic words she had longed to hear. Now that they were spoken, she was not at all sure what she would do with them. She had not thought ahead and planned for a moment such as this. Was she ready for a commitment of this kind? Marc's fluid words had run rich with conviction. This was no namby-pamby declaration simply to get her back in his bed. He meant what he said. He had finally stopped straddling the fence and was now looking to her to do the same.

Marc waited long moments for a response, his nerves dangling somewhere between euphoria and terror as he tried to guess Korey's string of thoughts. When she appeared to vacillate, he went about giving her a little nudge. Releasing her hand, he ran a lean finger the length of her arm, a touch of explicit purpose but yet so light that through her layered clothing she thought if she should close her eyes to its progress, she would miss the pleasure of it.

"What are you doing to me?" she asked.

"I'm trying to love you, Korey. Let me."

He leaned to her and satisfied a tiny bit of his craving with a small taste of her lips.

She worked the damp towel in her hands, pulling and twisting until it resembled a licorice whip.

Stepping back, he asked, "Won't you let me love you?"

Without another thought, she draped the towel around his neck and, ignoring his soggy clothes, pulled him to her, covering his mouth with hers.

He had his answer. And it was ever so much sweeter than words.

*   *   *   *

"Do you know how long I've dreamed of this?"

She felt his warmth spooning with hers, his breath tickling the back of her neck as he spoke into the darkness. The cold drizzle patting the roof was background music to their lovemaking. "No." She turned in his arms and traced a drunken line from his navel to the hollow of his throat. "How long?"

"Since I gazed across the desk at you in that hot box I so generously called an office."

She chuckled low in her throat. So sensitive were his nerve ends he could feel the vibration running through his fingertips. "That room was rather uncomfortable," she said. "Not much to look at, either. As I recall, I spent a good deal of time, while you were taking those interminable phone calls, trying to think of a graceful way to make a swift exit."

He was smiling. She could hear it in his voice. "And at the same time, *I* was plotting ways to keep you there. I felt like such a sleaze."

"Why? You had no control over the weather. Or the phone calls, for that matter."

He arrested her wandering hand, pressing it to his warm chest. "It wasn't the heat, the tiny room, even the phone that aggravated me so much as my lack of control. I had always been too savvy to become infatuated with a married woman."

"Married?"

"The ring." He circled his thumb around it now, slowly, as if counting the stones.

"Oh, yes. The ring."

A hush fell between them, and they both became aware of the rain pounding the roof with renewed force. Marc said, "The time I called and invited you to dinner….the dinner was not my purpose for calling." He released her hand and curved his beneath his head. "I called for another reason entirely. To ask you to mail your drawings. You see, I had already decided the less I saw of you, the better. Temptation, given enough opportunities, has a way of winning." He sighed then, a sigh that could have meant his defeat.

She traced smooth crescents on the delicate skin beneath his eyes. "And what made you change your mind? Ask me to dinner?"

"You said early in the conversation that you were widowed." He kissed her damp forehead.

"I'm not sure when I first knew….that I loved you. It sort of sneaked up and snagged me, I guess. Even then, I didn't want to admit it to anyone. Not Tina. Not even to myself. I was so frightened of loving again."

He found her hand, took it in his and gave it a gentle squeeze. If she only knew….in any given moment, any time day or night, he was probably more frightened than she. He squeezed her hand again, this time drawing from her the strength necessary to keep from shaking, thankful for the favor of darkness shielding his eyes of the chance to give him away. "None of that is relevant anymore, my love. Let's not," he said, as much for his own benefit as for hers, "think of anything but what matters most. And that is *us*, now, in the moment."

He kissed her fully on the mouth. And for the space of that kiss, even he believed in the truth of what he had just said.

*   *   *   *

His trench coat lay crumpled on the floor beside the chair from where it had slipped sometime during the long night. Smiling, Korey picked it up and hugged it to her, not caring that its dampness seeped a chill through her robe. Scents filled her head as she pressed her cheek to the cool fabric: the wet wool of the lining; a slight chemical odor of water repellent; spicy aftershave clinging to the collar. She stood at the foot of the bed listening to him breathe. Then silently leaving him to finish his peaceful sleep, she took the coat to the bathroom and hung it to dry on the shower head.

The ringing of a phone close to his ear jarred Marc awake. Bleary eyed, he groped for the phone, feeling around objects unfamiliar, knocking things over. After three rings, the phone was silent. It was not until he had set upright the first toppled picture frame that he came fully awake and realized he, most assuredly, was not in his own bed. Staring at him from the ivy-embossed silver frame was none other than Danny Westerfield. Terrific. Nothing like having a dead man watch another man gamboling in bed with the dead man's wife! A second, larger frame lay face up on the bedside table. Marc rolled himself up on an elbow, lifted the picture and set it in front of Danny, effectively hiding the piercing blue eyes from view. But upon inspection, Marc found the second photo no less disconcerting. It was immediately obvious that the handsome pair gazing at him were Korey's parents. The woman's heart-shaped face and dark round eyes were the very image of Korey.

Marc pulled the sheet over his face, laughing into tiny woven rosebuds, seeing the humor in being spooked by a couple of harmless photographs. It was no wonder the pictures had escaped his notice the evening before. He hadn't an eye then for anything but Korey. The rest of the world could have sheered off into an abyss and he would not have noticed. What a night! If his heart would cease its beat this very instant….well, he would die a happy man. But if he was to be lucky enough to have more of life, then last night was just the beginning….

*   *   *   *

She heard his progress as the hardwood floor awakened under his feet, the boards creaking and popping.

He stopped at the living room window overlooking the backyard, and her phone conversation drifted easily to him from the kitchen. Thin winter sun glowed white through moisture-soaked air, and water dripped prisms from the tips of bare branches or shimmered atop drooping brown chrysanthemums. An eclectic collection of crystal candlesticks stood tall on a small table in the corner of the room nearest the window, the flawless glass gathering light from the weak sun then projecting rainbows onto the walls.

It took him only a few minutes of listening to Korey's soft voice to ascertain the subject of the conversation—weather—and to know that Tina was at the other end of the phone line. He came up behind Korey, his hands stuffed deeply into empty pockets of badly wrinkled khakis, and stood at the back of her chair, bending low to plant a kiss on the top of her head.

"Surely it's not going to be *that* bad," she said into the phone. Reaching behind, her fingertips felt their way up his smooth bare belly. "Twelve inches? Oh, come on. When was the last time we had twelve inches of snow?"

Marc pulled a hand from a pocket and laced it through hers. Coming to stand beside her, he was content just to touch her and hear the sound of her voice. He watched the wind begin to whip the dripping needles of a pine tree growing near a kitchen window.

"But the rain was coming from the Gulf......Oh, I see....No, I haven't had the radio or TV on since yesterday." Korey squeezed his hand, looked up at Marc and grinned wickedly. "Uh, uh...I hadn't noticed a shift in the wind.... Nashville? Gosh, that much already?.... Don't worry. If I'm snowed in, I'll be fine. I've got something to keep me busy." She winked at Marc. "And, yes, enough food.... No, I'm not coming over there......Yes, I know, but.... No! Whatever you do, *don't* call Evie! I mean, she would go crazy stuck in my house in a snowstorm.... But....listen, Tina....Tina, I'm *not* alone." There was a long pause. Korey held the phone away from her ear, and Marc clearly heard as Tina drew out the word, "Ohhh?"

"Marc is here with me."

"Oh. Well....uh, well, I'm glad you have someone with you. I uh....Marc, huh? At 8:45 in the morning?"

"Yes. Marc. At 8:45 in the morning." Korey pressed her lips together, trying her best not to laugh.

"Well, Korey." Tina giggled softly. "Then let it snow." Another giggle. "Just call me soon, okay?"

"Sure. And don't worry. I'm in good hands."

"So it seems."

Giving Korey just enough time to say her goodbyes, Marc pulled her into his arms. "Do you think she was scandalized?"

"Hardly. Surprised, is all."

"And the weather report? Does she always get so frantic over a little snow?"

"Hey, you know very well that snow is not an everyday winter event around here, so when a storm is brewing, it causes some excitement. Especially a storm this size. Nashville has eight inches on the ground and still falling, and Tina says we're next. Something about cold air from Canada.... Anyway, as much as I'll miss you, I guess you had better go."

"Why?"

"You know you won't be going anywhere in that Miata if we have a heavy snowfall."

"Yes, I'm aware of that."

She watched his eyes tap a mischievous dance. What delirious joy it would mean to be snowbound in the house with Marc. But he could not be thinking of playing hooky from work, staying with her through the storm?

"Think maybe," his lips brushed lightly over hers, "we could find enough to do if we were forced to remain indoors through the snow?"

She put on a face that was pure innocence. "Oh, I have several jigsaw puzzles—each a thousand pieces—great fun in foul weather."

"Um." He kissed her again. "Not exactly what I had in mind."

The kiss ran long and deep and made jelly of her knees. Her hands roamed his bare back before clasping around his neck. "Oh, my," she sighed. "Forget the puzzles. But shouldn't you at least put your car in my garage?"

"Plenty of time for that." He gazed out the window. "The sun's weak but still shining. It's not going to snow for awhile yet." He turned to look into Korey's upturned face and missed the first snowflakes as they fell past the window, sparkling in the last rays of sun. "We need to keep our priorities in order, here. I believe," he whispered to her parted lips, tightly cinching her waist and drawing her closer, "in taking first things first, don't you?"

CHAPTER 15

▼

The weather forecast was half right; by nightfall Chattanooga lay silently blanketed in six inches of snow. For a city unaccustomed to heavy snowfall, six inches was enough. As the snow had piled up through the day, nonessential businesses closed their doors, employees and customers setting off on harrowing rides home. School buses, teeming with children incapable of harnessing their excitement over falling snow and the resultant half-day head start on Christmas vacation, braved clogged streets and hilly, slippery roads to deposit the rapscallions safely at their doorsteps.

For Korey it was a day custom made for love. In the warmth of Marc's arms she sat on the floor and watched lacy snowflakes land on the window ledge. Later, when tree limbs were piled high with snow, she roasted marshmallows in the fireplace over red hot coals and fed them to Marc when his marshmallows erupted in flames—a consequence of his nuzzling her neck instead of watching the bubbling glob on the tip of his barbecue fork. Laughing, she kissed the sticky sweetness from his mouth until the laughter became moans and her own fork was abandoned to drip sugary goo on the slate hearth.

When Marc could no longer ignore his pressing responsibilities, he reluctantly picked up the telephone and spent some portion of the afternoon handling the business matters that allowed no exceptions for snow storms—or passionate interludes.

But with the early darkness, business was guiltlessly cast aside. Snowfall tapered to fitful flurries; a half moon blinked through racing clouds and spattered sharp purple shadows over the unspoiled landscape. The young hours of the evening found Korey and Marc eating buttered popcorn and watching old movies on TV. And much later, the moon, now high and free of clouds, illuminated through a bare window the frenzied play of the new and eager lovers.

*   *   *   *

In the beginning, when the snow was a mere dusting on the ground, Marc had thought to spend one day with Korey. He stayed three. Having no change of clothes, he daily put the washer and dryer to use laundering the clothes in which he had arrived. While his own clothes sloshed through the wash cycle, he wore a faded plaid robe, one he was left to assume had belonged to Danny, finding it slightly small but warm.

With Saturday morning came full sunshine, and the sun soon cleared the street, reducing the snow to no more than gray slush melting in the gutter. From everywhere—trees, lampposts, downspouts—came the sound of water dripping. Wedges of snow slid from roofs to land, *shloop*, on the mushy ground below.

Marc, with high humor and no stab to his conscience, gave up blaming the weather for his prolonged stay and sat with Korey in the breakfast room at a table ablaze with sunshine, eating French toast and drinking coffee laced with drops of rich cream. The hour was so late that the meal could be quite properly termed brunch. When the lovers spoke, it was with voices still husky with sleep, their conversation blending harmoniously with the sounds of the melting snow. There was discussion about what to do with the remainder of the day. It took very little debate; they would build a snowman with what was left of the snow. Korey cleared the kitchen of dirty dishes while Marc showered; she showered while he shaved. The morning before, she had produced from her linen closet a new disposable razor and toothbrush that she always kept in reserve for forgetful house guests. She had chided him then for being so absent minded that he would come for a stay without so much as an overnight case.

His smile now was one of contentment as he shrugged into clothes still warm from the dryer. When he had come to Korey on Thursday evening, it was to talk. He had no thought of spending even one night. And now here he was staying the weekend, dressing in her bedroom, listening to her sing in the shower. He could hardly believe his luck.

She came from the bathroom dressed in clinging silk long johns. At the sight of her his mind swerved recklessly, roaring off in a direction that had everything to do with finely molded body parts but nothing to do with those of a snowman. He kept all of this to himself. He would, for a time, play with Korey in the snow.

They named him Rusty. It was a fitting name for a snowman blemished with slimy brown leaves and wads of dead grass. A carrot, shriveled and limp, found beneath a questionable package of celery in the crisper drawer of the refrigerator, served as the nose. Pearlescent blue buttons became large gleaming eyes, and Rusty's unblinking gaze seemed to follow the two humans as they played in the yard.

Marc, working in a pair of Danny's gardening gloves plucked from a dusty flower pot in the garage, fashioned Rusty's jolly grin out of a length of red yarn. He was just pressing the last corner of the upturned mouth into the softening face when a snowball, packed round and firm, punched him squarely in the back. His return missile, hastily made and awkwardly thrown in the too-tight gloves, sailed over Korey and flew on to slap the mailbox, bending the raised flag.

Bodily harm she could take; damage to her property meant war! Turning a laughing face to his, Korey scooped up snow and charged, her armed fist raised and ready to fire. Retreating from the impending onslaught, Marc slipped, his wet shoes skating across the slush before he fell face down like a tree in a bog.

Korey granted no quarter. She was on him before he could roll over, her knee planted in the snow at his side. She pulled his collar away from his neck, her gloves shedding ice crystals down his back. He shivered and groaned but would not concede defeat. Mercilessly she rubbed snow along the bare skin at the back of his neck.

"Ahhhh," he gasped. "Korey! Too cold!" One side of his face was buried in snow. "I surrender! I surrender!" he choked, laughing in spite of his misery.

"Do I win?"

"Yes." He squirmed. "Yes. Now let me up."

"Not without," she said as she pressed a heavy hand to his back, "the promise of the spoils of war."

His face was freezing. He spit a leaf stem from the side of his mouth. "Name your price," he wheezed.

The pressure on his back was gone suddenly. He sat up and brushed snow from his sleeves as Korey stood wordlessly beside him. She bent almost double, her mouth close to his. "It's really going to cost you," she said. His cold lips tingled with the warming as her mouth covered his. She grabbed his arms and helped him up, their lips never losing touch even as he struggled for footing in the snow. His blood ran hot at the prospect of spending the rest of the afternoon with Korey negotiating a truce. He was certain plumes of steam were rising from the back of his neck....

The kitchen was warm; their shoes left slushy prints on the tile floor. They barely made it inside before he had her down to her long silk underwear.

*   *   *   *

Fire popped and hissed as boiling pockets of sap exploded, shooting bits of flaming wood against the fireplace screen. Korey sat snuggled into a corner of the sofa, holding in one hand a glass of wine, red as rubies. Marc's legs stretched the length of the sofa, his head nestled in her lap. His dark hair lay in closely cultivated rows where her slender fingers had run through it from forehead to crown.

By the soft light of a table lamp, they read from a book of poetry. It was a game of sorts. Like cutting a deck of cards, they took turns opening the book at random, then reading what appeared on the page. They had read love sonnets, verses of whimsy and of sorrow.

Now it had fallen to Marc to read Lord Byron's 'Fare Thee Well!' The last four stanzas hit Marc like a fist to the throat. He hesitated, his breathing restricted as if the leather-bound book resting upright on his chest had suddenly become too heavy. He saw himself in Byron's words. They leapt off the page and spoke clearly of a time when Korey would discover his duplicity.

> All my faults perchance thou knowest
>   All my madness none can know;
> All my hopes, where'er thou goest,
>   Wither, yet with *thee* they go.
>
> Every feeling hath been shaken:
>   Pride, which not a world can bow,
> Bows to thee,—by thee forsaken,
>   Even my soul forsakes me now:
>
> But 'tis done: all words are idle,
>   Words from me are vainer still;
> But the thoughts we cannot bridle
>   Force their way without the will.
>
> Fare thee well!—thus disunited,
>   Torn from every nearer tie,
> Seared in heart, and lone, and blighted,
>   More than this I scarce can die.

Rather than handing the book to Korey, Marc quietly closed it and placed it on a table, effectively ending the game. Thinking of the untimely end of her own marriage, suffocating in stagnant memories, Korey did not question the swelling silence. Then Marc's warm hands cupped her face and parted lips invited her kiss. Once again rising passion erased for them both those things which they did not wish to remember.

*   *   *   *

For those driven by ambition, some things in life cannot be ignored. So it was that the necessity of tending to professional obligations forced apart Korey and Marc on Sunday. By the following Thursday, however, two days before Christmas, they reunited. Before going their separate ways to celebrate the holidays with family, they would remain in seclusion, nested in Korey's home to claim lovers' rights to the next twenty-four hours.

They opened gifts on the floor by the tree, the strings of red lights chasing away the gloom of an overcast sky. At Marc's request, Korey opened the largest of his three gifts first. She pushed aside the shredded wrapping paper, exposing a cardboard box nearly a yard square. On one side a strip of clear tape secured a flap, and she slit it open with a short thumbnail. Unassisted, she pulled from the box a framed photograph. Even through a layer of plastic bubble wrap, she saw that it was a picture of the pueblo ruins at Gran Quivira. Marc saw a glistening along the rims of her dark eyes just before she bent down to peel away the protective plastic.

He had brought it home from Albuquerque in November, hidden on the plane. It was meant as a gift for Korey, but even when he bought it he was not sure when, or if, he would give it to her. This seemed the perfect time.

Since he had not spoken of Gran Quivira, Korey had feared that he did not want to be reminded of the afternoon spent there. But the gift banished her fear and relief flowed through her. Rising to her knees, she leaned across the photo to kiss him, then held up the picture so they both could see.

The size and clarity of the photograph brought the scene to life in her hands. So much so that the scent of juniper touched her nostrils and cold air attacked her face. Gran Quivira at dawn: Under thin clouds set afire and fleeing a rising sun, the pueblo's limestone walls, scarred and broken, were transformed like a chameleon from cold gray to warm shades of red. Growing at the base of a crumbling wall, a tall cane cactus hammed it up, waving its long spiny arms at the camera. At the bottom right corner, in bold black strokes preserved behind a sheet of glass, was written:

Korey,

Best wishes from the Land of Enchantment,

Eric and Rae

If this were to be her only Christmas gift, she would have been content. But there was more. The photograph was set safely aside, secure in its packaging until just the right spot was chosen for its display. Marc handed Korey a second present, this one wrapped in paper striped like a candy cane. Inside, in a gold box embossed with the words **Georgy's Trunk**, was a tunic sweater knitted in apricot angora. The sweater was beautiful and after another lingering kiss Korey would have donned it over her silk shirt if she were not already overly warm with excitement.

From under the tree, Marc produced a third gift. Korey untied the lacy silver ribbon from a gray velvet box. She opened the lid, revealing a gleaming silver necklace. From Newley Mined, Marc said. Only last week shipped in from Santa Fe. He clasped it around her neck, stealing a kiss on the soft flesh beneath her ear as he did so. Fifty strands of silver heishi beads sparkled on her teal shirt like sun-drenched water spilling over moss-covered stones.

It was sometime later, after he had been the willing recipient of a luscious string of kisses, that Marc began to demonstrate an interest in an activity far more enticing than a gift exchange. But Korey, her body still pleasantly tingling from his amorous attentions earlier in the day, had other ideas. With a playful giggle she broke from his heated embrace and pushed a large box across the hardwood floor. She moved with the impatience of an excited child as he pulled the box to him.

"Is this all?" he asked in mock disappointment, his hand resting atop his only gift.

"Yes." She raised her brows in an effort to look stern. "Why? Do you think you deserve more?"

In response to her teasing he grinned, but it felt shallow. From her he deserved nothing. Simply being in her presence was more than he deserved. He must have hesitated too long, for she shifted a hip on the floor and asked, "Aren't you going to open it?"

Torn paper soon lay around the base of the box, Santa Clauses and reindeer crumpled on the floor like contortionists. Marc lifted the lid. Just under the flaps, nestled in red tissue paper, sat a pair of forest green slippers. "Very nice," he said, his smiling eyes holding hers. "Great for keeping my feet warm on cold evenings. That is," he added with a knowing wink, "when you're not around."

She felt heat rise along her neck. She shifted again on the floor and pointed to the box, an invitation for him to return his attention to the gift.

Tossing aside the tissue paper, he found a towel folded neatly into a square. Lifting it from the box, he shook out the folds. Exclaiming, "They don't make them larger than this," he stretched his arms ceilingward so the towel would not drag the floor. Thick and fluffy, the towel was woven of Egyptian cotton terry to match the slippers. A simple *M* stitched in white satin thread adorned one corner. Marc stood, wrapped himself in the towel, toga style, and took on a pose.

Hugging her knees to her chest, Korey laughed. She looked up at him. "Dig deeper," she urged. "There's more."

He dropped the towel over the back of a chair and discarded another layer of red tissue paper. From the bottom of the box he pulled a robe, yards of plush terry in matching green, a white *M* expertly stitched on the breast pocket. With a lazy smile, he wordlessly pulled the robe over his shirt and slacks, tied the belt at his waist and shoved his hands into deep pockets. Korey studied him lovingly. The robe fit perfectly and the color deepened by several shades the green of his eyes.

From a pocket Marc produced a slender box sealed in clear cellophane and tied with curly green ribbon. A sly smile lit his eyes. "Humm," he mused. "A toothbrush—green handle, naturally. Let's see....robe, towel, slippers, and a toothbrush. You're not very subtle, are you?"

She came to her feet, stepping within his reach, her eyes locked to his. "Not when it comes to something I really want."

The house was hushed; Christmas carols played low on a radio. Heavy clouds invited an early dusk. He untied the robe, holding out the sides like great wings. She slipped into his warmth. "And what is it you really want?" He knew the answer. Just the same, he wanted to hear it from her own lips.

"For you to stay here," she said, her arms wrapped snugly around his waist. The robe became a cocoon as he folded it around them. "As often....whenever you can." She heard the soft rush of his breathing, felt the steady beat of his heart.

He rested his chin in her hair and stared at the Christmas tree. Through an unfocused gaze, the tiny lights were a blur and twirling icicles mere slashes of light along the edge of his vision. He touched his lips to her forehead. "Are you sure," he said, giving her an out he did not want her to take, "this is what you want?"

Basking in the pleasure of the moment, she looked deeply into his eyes and said, "I've never been more sure of anything in my life."

*   *   *   *

Mere seconds remaining until the countdown.

Champagne in hand, she stood in the glow of the lighted tree, only marginally aware of the good cheer flowing around her. *Strange,* she thought, *how the mind ticks through the monotony of everyday life but marks notable events with the same reliability that chimes on a clock announce the hour.* She could recall very little of the first four months of the year now speeding to a close but remembered clearly the first time Marc Bradberry's voice came over her answering machine. Only a voice, a lead for another job, no particular reason to commit it to memory. But her mind had preserved that golden moment and stored it away as if immediately recognizing its value.

The countdown had begun behind her, "nine, eight, seven…." and she turned toward the crowded room. Her dad and Stella eyed her from a spot not far away. Korey smiled and raised her champagne glass in a silent toast. "….four, three, two, one…." Suddenly she was in a three-way embrace. Boyce Reynolds called, "Happy New Year" above the cheers of the crowd while Stella kissed her cheek and whispered, "May you find love in this new year." Then Boyce and Stella moved away, leaving Korey to wonder if Tina had been telling tales.

Rob Westerfield surprised her, encircling her waist with one arm while lifting his other to drain what was plainly not his first glass of champagne. He spun her around, the sequins on her dress bouncing stars off his laughing face, then leaned into her as if for support and kissed her full on the mouth. The kiss was chaste, but still it was the only time in her widowhood that he had indulged in such a bold maneuver. Rob's lips still covering hers, Korey stared through wide eyes into the fiery glare of his date, Hillary. Having emerged from the jungle for the holidays, Hillary was now at a range so close she was like a hawk perched on Rob's shoulder. Korey fought back the temptation to transform the dry kiss into one wet and wild, solely to needle Hillary. Instead she broke the embrace and, wishing her brother-in-law a successful new year, left him in the hawk's clutches.

Korey scouted the room to see if she and Rob had been a spectacle, but no one seemed to have noticed. As much as she cared for those now pressing around her to toast the new year, theirs was not the company her heart desired. If only Marc were here…. Her time with him before Christmas had passed too swiftly. She missed him with an ache that rested just below her breastbone. But, from a year just seconds old, she looked ahead. Because of Marc, the future seemed like a new penny—freshly minted and shining.

CHAPTER 16

▼

It was the fifth day of the new year: cold, gray, spitting snow. Tina's tiny kitchen was warm as toast and smelled of baked cookies. From behind the rim of a coffee cup, Tina studied her sister's high color.

Korey knew her own face gave her away, that her smile alone said it all. "Oh, Tina. I feel like I've been reborn."

"And this rebirth wouldn't have anything to do with Marc, would it?"

The smile became a radiant grin. "It has *everything* to do with Marc, and you know it."

"Actually, it would be hard to miss. Anyone who's been within eye-shot of you the past week or so could see the change. Except maybe Rob." Tina flashed a sly grin.

"Now don't start teasing about that kiss. I was hoping no one saw it."

"Oh, I saw it, all right."

"It meant nothing. Rob had too much to drink. And besides, not long before that he and Hillary were in a corner obviously having a few *words*. Rob used me to make her jealous."

"That he did. I felt the heat of her glare from across the room."

"Believe me, it was worse from where I stood." Korey shook her head. "I don't think this would be a good time to take her up on the offer to join her on an Amazon expedition. Not that I was considering it. Slogging through a steambath, tripping over snakes....not my idea of a fun time."

Tina arched a shapely brow. "Haven't we drifted a bit from the subject?"

"Subject?" asked Korey.

"Don't be coy."

Words came easily as Korey told Tina of the night spent in Marc's private quarters above his office, then of the week following when she miserably tried to purge him from her system; of his appearance at her doorstep, dripping rain; of their time together after he declared his love. She omitted the most private moments, those would remain his and hers alone.

As Tina listened, part of her mind sought an answer to a niggling question. Still to be explained was Marc's strange behavior following the flight to Albuquerque. The glow now on Korey's face plainly stated that she no longer remembered her own loneliness and self-doubt during those bewildering weeks. Love, after all, holds no grudge. Unlike Korey, Tina was not blind to Marc's flaws. But from what Korey was now relating, Marc seemed, in the last few weeks, to be making up for the unkindness he delivered in November. His loving attention had given Korey a new stability. Recent events prompted Tina to make a silent wish on her sister's behalf: that Korey's love affair with Marc be only the beginning of what would become a life-long partnership.

*   *   *   *

The year turned; Korey and Marc snatched whatever scraps of time they could to be together. They became like squirrels stashing nuts for the winter, grabbing enough golden moments to nurture them through days of separation. They put in few public appearances: a movie or two; dinner out occasionally; a handful of evenings spent in the harmonious company of Tina and Bryan.

Marc's clothes began showing up in Korey's closet. One day she found two of his three-piece suits and several sets of casual clothes mixed with hers. Without asking he had intruded on her closet space, had been bold in his presumption that she would not object. He had also been correct. When alone, on spontaneous trips to the closet, she loved to run her hand slowly down the sleeve of his suit. On occasion she would surreptitiously don one of his silk ties, smile into the mirror and admire her skill at tying a flawless Windsor knot.

On long winter evenings, she frequently wrapped herself in Marc's green robe, then curled into a chair to quench her loneliness with a fat novel. It was in his robe—soft, warm, and infused with his scent—that Korey endured many cold winter nights with Marc absent from her bed.

Spring came at last, windy and warm. Leaf buds pushed through winter casings; daffodils, dancing heads yellow as the sun, formed brilliant borders in greening lawns.

One fine day Korey asked Tina to help hang wallpaper in the guest bathroom. Korey had never been fond of the existing paper—too many fish in colors too bright—and now that Marc used the bath during his stayovers, she had an incentive to change it.

"We're thinking of putting our house up for sale," Tina was saying as she watched Korey measure and cut a long strip of wallpaper. "Spring is a good time. The market is hot right now, and interest rates won't stay this low forever."

Korey reversed the paper, rolled it to eliminate the curl. "What if you sell it right away? You haven't even cleared your new lot yet."

"It's been awhile since you've been out there. We cut most of the bigger trees this winter. There's really not much more to clear for the driveway and house. The rest we will leave in dense woods." Tina popped a doughnut hole into her mouth and chewed slowly, savoring the only one she would allow herself. She licked sugar from her thumb. "We can always lease an apartment if we have to give up the house before the new one is finished."

Korey set the rolled paper in a soaking pan. "I know you were having problems finding a builder you liked. Did you finally settle on one?"

"Yes, just last week. Marc asked around and found him for us. Cecil Cooke is his name. Bryan and I looked at several of Cecil's houses in various stages of completion. He does beautiful work." Tina inhaled deeply as a breeze came through the open window and stirred the air in the small room. "Um, I love that smell of wet paper and paste. Smells like a new house." She grabbed a damp sponge as Korey lifted the dripping paper from the water and carefully slid it onto the wall. With the sponge, Tina began smoothing the dainty floral paper. "As excited as I am about a new home," she said, "I'm not looking forward to moving. All that packing and unpacking. Ugh."

"Yeah," Korey agreed. "Moving isn't one of my favorite things. I'll probably stay in this house forever." She pressed the paper tightly to the wall with a plastic trowel. Milky paste oozed along the edges and ran down the wall.

Tina wiped away the paste. "Forever, huh? I've been thinking that before long I may lose you to Nashville."

"Nashville?" Korey's hand ceased its motion. Paste dripped from the trowel and puddled negligently onto a cloth spread on the floor.

Tina looked into Korey's unreadable eyes. "Uh, you know….you and Marc. I thought maybe…."

"Maybe what, Tina?"

"Marriage. I thought maybe you two were talking about marriage."

"Oh." Korey squatted, neatly creasing the paper against the baseboard. With the flick of a sharp blade, she cut away the excess paper and dropped the gooey strip into a wastebasket. So here it was, she said to herself. What she had come to dread. The doubts had begun in February. Valentine's Day to be exact. It had been a day anyone in love would have envied. But that night Marc had said something in passing, and it had rattled around inside her head for weeks....

Korey rinsed the sponge, wiped paste from the baseboard. "No, Tina," she said, tossing the sponge into the sink, "the subject of marriage has never come up." Now that she was exposed, it would be nice to confide in someone. Who better than her sister, her dearest friend? "Let's take a break. The hardest part is behind us. I'm hungry. I'll make lunch," she offered, heading for the kitchen at the opposite end of the house, "and we'll talk."

Later Korey lingered over the last bite of chicken salad sandwich. "Marc said something, uh, peculiar a few weeks ago."

"Peculiar?"

"Yes, he said, 'when we can make some plans....'"

"What kind of plans?"

"That was it. Just 'when we can make some plans.' I can't remember what we were talking about at the time, but after he said it he looked as if he hadn't meant to. When I opened my mouth to ask what he was talking about, he....well, I became distracted." Korey grinned.

"Distracted." Tina chuckled. "Say no more." With an unpainted nail, she pushed bread crumbs around her plate. "And he hasn't said anything like that since?"

"No."

"You've known him almost a year. Doesn't his lack of commitment bother you?"

How easy it would be to reply "No," and cut short this cheerless subject. But a denial would be a lie. Marc appeared satisfied with the status quo, but Korey was losing patience. Her retort was spiced with sarcasm. "It doesn't bother me enough that I would ask for *his* hand in marriage."

Unfazed by her sister's tone, Tina pressed on. "You would marry him if he asked?"

Korey nodded, and her eyes took on a dreamy quality. "Yes," she said, "I would tomorrow, if he asked."

"How often do you see him?"

"As much as possible." Korey paused and tilted her head, as if this were the first she had taken time to think about it. "But not much more than I ever have."

It was true. And hearing it, spoken in her own tentative voice, made the—Love affair? Courtship?—seem like something so vague it defied naming. Shoving these disquieting thoughts aside, Korey went about setting up a line of defense. "Marc stays so busy. He's been in Nashville a lot lately, working on an office complex to be built on Old Hickory Boulevard. It's taking most of his time." She sighed, aware that her voice lacked the proper conviction. "But," she offered brightly, "I hear from him most evenings." She looked forward to those calls: to discuss the day's events; to speak of love. "I suppose," she continued, "it's just as well he is otherwise absorbed. I have so many projects lined up, I really can't afford the distraction."

Tina took her empty dishes to the sink. "Why don't you go to Nashville with Marc the next time he asks. Seems like it's time you went home to meet Mama."

In surprise, Korey twisted in her chair, fixing a stare on Tina's back. "What do you mean, next time?"

Tina said, over the sound of running water, "Well, he has asked you, hasn't he?"

"No."

Tina shut off the faucet. "I assumed you hadn't gone to Nashville with Marc because you didn't want to take time away from your work. You're telling me," she continued in disbelief, "he has that plane yet he's never even *invited* you to Nashville?"

Korey shrugged, feeling, through her cotton shirt, her shoulder blades brush the slatted back of the chair. "I know it seems a little strange…." She was embarrassed. The absence of an invitation to meet Marc's family had begun to glare at her long before now, and she was in no mood to be grilled about it, even by Tina. "What is this, anyhow, an inquisition?" she snapped, sharper than she had intended.

A pulsating siren howled on a nearby street. Tina waited for the siren to ebb before she said, "Of course not. I'm concerned, is all."

"I know and I'm sorry. I guess I'm a bit on edge. It's just that lately I've been doing some thinking. Danny and I had a….a synergy. At times I feel the same thing with Marc, but he keeps me off balance. He can be a mystery. Sometimes I have an almost uncontrollable urge to ask him, 'Who are you, really?' He carries something inside that he won't let me touch." She sighed, frustrated. "I can't explain it very well, but I can *feel* it."

Tina again sat at the table and reached for Korey's hand. "Listen, honey," she said in a soothing voice. "You know all I want for you is happiness. Marc seems to be a wonderful guy. Bryan and I like him a lot. But if you have doubts, if there is a mystery that begs to be answered, please make it your business to solve it."

*   *   *   *

He was delivering a rose bush. He would hand her the bush, exchange a few pleasantries then leave. Safe enough.

It had not been in his plans to buy her the plant. Last week, when he had spoken to her on the phone from a hotel room in Dallas, she was mourning the loss of her favorite rose. On impulse he had wheeled into a nursery on his return to Nashville and asked the young girl behind the counter if she had a rose called Double Delight. She said he was in luck; a new shipment had arrived the day before. He bought the bush, stored it in his garage, remembered only at the last minute to bring it with him to Chattanooga.

He had not seen Korey for three weeks, during which time his booming business filled his days and nights. There had been pauses in the frenetic pace when his head stopped long enough to potently remind him that the life he lived in reality was not the same idyllic life he lived in his mind. He had split in two. It was easy to ignore who he really was when he was with Korey. But he was fearful that one day, in confusion, he would forget his role: The beast he had created was poised to devour its master.

So why was he now standing at Korey's door, tempting the beast when only yesterday he had vowed to appease it at the first opportunity by telling Korey about Clare? The timing, the place seemed wrong for a serious declaration. Maybe he should invite Korey to Albuquerque on the flight he had scheduled. Maybe there she would better withstand the shock. Maybe he....

Unaware that he had pressed the doorbell, he raised his head to see Korey smiling in the open doorway. His throat went dry; he wondered if she might read fear in his eyes.

Her gaze fell to the potted rose he clutched in his hands. To Marc the rose had become a symbol, something of himself to go on living near her if he could not. He hoped that after learning about Clare, Korey would not yank it out of the ground and toss it into the compost pile. Nearly losing his nerve, he thought to reach out, wordlessly shove the bush into her hands, and run.

He managed a scratchy, "Hi."

"Say, stranger, this is a pleasant surprise."

A thrill surged through his chest. God, she was beautiful. How could he have convinced himself, on the drive to her house today, that during the past three weeks he had not missed her all that much? Liar.

"What have you got there?" she asked.

"Oh....a rose bush. For you. Double Delight. You haven't already replaced the one that died?"

"No, I haven't. I was waiting until the weekend." She could hardly believe what she saw. He could have been a young lad, painfully shy, nervously presenting a nosegay to the object of his schoolboy crush. This was a new face. Endearing. Adorable. She wanted to reach up and playfully pinch that boyish cheek. Placing her hand on the sleeve of his dark suit, she said, "Oh, Marc. How thoughtful." A cool breeze blew through the doorway. She stood on one side of the threshold, he on the other. "Come in," she invited.

"No, uh, I just stopped by to give you this. I shouldn't bring it into the house. The pot's dirty."

"Okay. Just leave it on the porch. I'll plant it later this afternoon." Without a scratch, she found her way around the thorny branches and gave him a kiss. "Thanks. You're a sweetheart. And I insist you come in for a little while at least. We haven't talked on the phone for days. And need I remind you I haven't seen you in three weeks?"

All right. He had some time to spare. After all, what harm could come from a few minutes of just being sociable? He set the plant on the porch, brushed his hands free of loose soil.

*   *   *   *

He was checking his watch again! He sat too rigidly on the sofa while she stared at him from the loveseat. It had not gone unnoted that he had taken to the sofa after she was already seated. He had kissed her in the foyer, a lingering kiss, but after three weeks it had not the fire she expected.

"Tight schedule today?" Pointedly, she glanced at his wrist.

Marc, caught with his anxiety showing, took a last swallow of iced tea. A lemon wedge slid down the tall glass; juicy bits of pulp clung to the sides. "I have an appointment soon," he said. He cleared his throat.

"Well then...." Korey stood. A stray hair teased the corner of her eye; she brushed it away with fingertips smelling of fresh lemon. Marc also stood, but not before Korey saw a look of surprise pass across his face. She nearly said aloud: *Surely you didn't expect me to beg you to stay.* She would not be toyed with, yet she harbored no anger or resentment. Instead she felt challenged. This time he had underestimated her. She would not play mouse to his cat as she had when, in November, he had ignored her for weeks. Though she had no taste for manipulation, when pushed she could play the game.

He startled her from her thoughts by reaching for her hand as they walked to the foyer. "I'll see you soon," he said. Still clutching her hand, he brushed her lips with a kiss.

"I'll look forward to it." She smiled warmly, as if the scant kiss were not taken as a sign of diminished affection. Rising on her toes, she laced her hands behind his neck. "But I wouldn't think of letting you leave," she purred, "without properly thanking you for the rose bush." She kissed him then, a pleasing kiss but lacking, just as he had given her upon his arrival. Her heels lowered to the floor. He looked deeply into her eyes and did not move against the pressure of her hands on his neck.

"I don't suppose," she said through pouty lips, "you could spare a few minutes more out of your busy schedule…." She trailed off into a soft sigh, slender fingers of one hand now stroking the knot in his tie. A gentle tug and the knot slipped an inch or two; she freed the top button on his crisp blue shirt. Korey had become a she-cat. What had come over her he could not imagine, but her timing could not have been worse.

Warm lips nibbled his flesh at the V of his collar, and an aggressive knee massaged his inner thigh. Even as he became pliable beneath her touch, his mind screamed for mercy: N*ot now, Korey, oh, please, not now.* Not knowing when his hands had reached for her, he dropped them from her waist. "Korey, I don't th…."

The words fell uselessly into her open mouth as she kissed him. She freed the knot in his tie, the loose ends framing a long row of buttons on his shirt. "What time did you say that appointment was?"

"Uh….three; three-thirty…." His brain was sluggish. "Something like that."

"Umm, plenty of time." Her fingers worked down the shirtfront, her lips sizzling a path behind each loose button.

With sapped strength, Marc captured her arms. He held her away from him, but, in his surrender, his grip was light. "Ms. Westerfield!" he said with a teasing grin, "just what is it you intend to do to a gentleman such as myself on this fine spring afternoon?"

She giggled; her eyes gleamed like a cat's in a headlight. "Why, Mista Bradburrry," she drawled in her best southern belle, "y'all mean afta awl these munths, you haf ta aysk?"

He shook with laughter and ignored the warning in his head. She played the *femme fatale* well. Too well. But he didn't ever want her to stop.

She wove both hands through his hair, sifting the thick strands through her long fingers. "I wus hopin', suh, y'all would agree on this luvely spring aftanoon to let me have mah way with you."

"My appointment...."

"Oh, shush!" She kissed him, long and deep, and he shared this kiss to its fullest.

Her heart racing, she leaned back in his arms. Very soberly she looked up at him. "I love you, you know."

"Yes. I know."

The gleam returned to her dark eyes. "So, three o'clock...." She touched her lips to his chin, to the corner of his receptive mouth. "Or three-thirty?"

"Huh?....Oh, yeah.... Like you said." His moist breath moved a lock of her fragrant hair. "....Plenty of time."

*   *   *   *

"I hadn't planned on this."

That was obvious, but she did not say so. "Why not?"

"Didn't want you to think this is the only reason I hang around." He smiled, slow and lazy.

"Hey, in the first place, showing up every three weeks," she rose up on an elbow to look him full in the face, "is hardly 'hanging around.'" Underscoring her message, she pressed her thumb to the flesh in the middle of his hard chest. The pressure left a white thumb print on his skin. The print faded an instant later, but not before she had wished it to be permanent, like a brand naming him hers, eliminating altogether the further need to probe and follow through on Tina's advice to "solve the mystery."

"And secondly," she continued, dismissing that unpleasant thought, "we can't really hold you responsible for this, now can we?" She breathed a throaty chuckle into his ear.

"Good, so I'm absolved. That was quite an assault you put forth, lady. Would have taken some pretty heavy artillery to fight you off." Truth was, after the second kiss, he had ceased to have any interest in repelling her attack. He acknowledged his weakness with no small degree of regret. His jaw took on a firm line as he vowed to avoid future temptations. He would not again compromise his determination to come clean about his wife.

Korey's voice, suddenly exuberant, broke into his thoughts. "Do you know what today is?"

"Wednesday."

"Besides that."

"Uh." He suddenly realized the significance of the date. "Why, it's our third month anniversary." The most beautiful, and most painful, three months of his life.

"You had forgotten." Her lower lip protruded in an exaggerated pout.

He smiled, stroking her lip with his finger. "Only temporarily." Reaching for her hair, he wound a lock around the finger, giving the curl a coaxing tug. His soft lips brushed back and forth over hers.

"Forgiven," she said. "But I won't let you off so easily if you forget next month." Laughing, she snatched a pillow and playfully rubbed it in his face.

His eyes closed to the assault. Three glorious months, he thought. Stolen from the clutches of a life that otherwise held little meaning. The third month anniversary. And only he suspected, in this moment of searing pain, that odds were he and Korey would not be together to celebrate a fourth.

CHAPTER 17

▼

"*Next* Wednesday?" The slender needle paused in mid air, then pierced the fabric, marking the spot. Korey took the phone from where it had been wedged between her shoulder and ear and now held it in her free hand. "I don't know....that's just four days. The Spinnaker quilt is due in two weeks. I'd love to go, but I'm not sure I can spare the time." She hesitated, trying to decide. "Do you have to go next week?"

"Yes," Marc said. "That's the only time I can string a few days together for the next two months." To Korey he sounded mildly annoyed at having to explain. "Also, Eric and Rae have some free time next week. And Eric wants me to meet someone, a business acquaintance who is planning a move from California to Taos and wants to talk to me about designing a house. This fellow—can't think of his name right off—will be in Albuquerque next week."

So there you have it, she thought. Go next week or not at all. His take-it-or-leave-it tone left her a little cold. There was a pregnant pause while she mentally went through a schedule of things to be accomplished.

Marc broke in. "I thought you would be prime for another visit with Matty. You could take your sewing, work on the plane like you did in November." As though to preempt a refusal, his voice switched to a note of urgency. "Besides, lately we haven't had much time together to talk."

Talk. She wondered what it was he wanted to *talk* about. She glanced at the fabric stretched on a quilting frame. There would be hours on the plane in which to work. "Okay. Count me in. But," she smiled into the phone, "I want it to be duly noted that you, sir, where my work is concerned, are a dangerous distraction."

If she expected him to laughingly echo her remark, she was disappointed. His familiar, easy wit seemed to have deserted him.

"Good," he said.

Good what? she wondered. *Good*, nice to have you along? Or *good*, it feeds my ego to be considered a dangerous distraction?

"I'll pick you up Wednesday morning, should be around ten-thirty. I have a meeting that morning at eight. If I get held up, I'll be no later than eleven."

The next four days promised to be busy ones but not so tightly packed with work that she could not indulge in a phone conversation or two. Yet here he was talking as if he assumed they would not speak again until he came for her Wednesday morning. Forced now to face what she had avoided for weeks, she admitted that Marc's phone calls were less frequent, had fallen off sharply from the nightly calls he had made during the winter months. He was on the down side of another of his mood swings, emitting confusing signals, and she was feeling the wear of the emotional roller coaster ride. If not for the prospect of seeing her aunt, Korey had a mind to bow out and leave him to go the trip alone. Therefore, it was with Matty in mind that she said, "I'll be ready on Wednesday. I'll phone Matty so she'll be prepared for a house guest." Not really expecting the sleeping arrangements to be otherwise, Korey was nonetheless disappointed when, considering their intimacy, Marc did not suggest that this trip they share a nice hotel room.

Their plans made, the phone conversation ended. Korey, with an unsteady hand, hung up the phone. Marc was again pulling back from their love. He carried with him a fear; at times she had glimpsed it in his eyes, felt it in his touch, heard it in his voice. This knowledge had led her to be tolerant of his moods. What was it, she asked herself as her clever fingers returned to her stitching, that could be so terrible in his life that would cause a tall, strong-shouldered man to be so frightened?

*   *   *   *

April in New Mexico: cool nights; warm days; no Tennessee humidity to make skin sticky or a house musty. Under a clear Thursday sky, with sharp afternoon sun glaring off the hood of the rented Jeep Cherokee, Marc and Korey traveled west on I-40, the Acoma Indian Reservation their destination.

Neither had slept well the night before. In houses separated by miles, each tossed fitfully in a roomy bed and ached to be in the arms of the other. Thursday morning, as well, had been spent apart. Korey and Matty had lazed in their sleep wear, chatting non-stop over scrambled eggs and thick slices of whole wheat toast dripping with sorghum.

For Marc, breakfast on this sun-washed morning had not passed so pleasantly. Midway into Rae's delectable omelets, Marc had brought eating to a halt with the casual but shocking statement: "Korey flew out with me."

Eric's grip on his fork had been so tight it should have bent the fork. "So," he frowned, "this is still going on?" The answer obvious, Eric went on. "In November, when Rae and I met Korey, we both liked her, instantly. Since that time, in my phone conversations with you, I haven't once asked about her. Surely you were aware of this omission."

A blank stare was Marc's answer.

"You never mentioned her, and I didn't ask about her because I didn't want to hear that you were still seeing her. Doubtless we both had the same reason for staying away from the subject of Korey." Eric set the fork on his plate, a cold bite of omelet on the tines. "I suppose it's too optimistic to say you've told her you're married, and now she justifiably uses you only as a free ride to her aunt?"

Using his empty fork, Marc sparred with the diced green pepper that littered his plate. Though deserved, he could have done without Eric's sarcasm. Eric could still, with few words, easily reduce his younger brother to the stereotypical bumbler. "I have not," he said, meeting Eric's solemn stare, "told her. But we will not be returning home without her knowing. I brought her here to tell her. I thought it might be easier."

"Easier for you, you mean."

"No, dammit!" Marc glanced at Rae, sorry she was at the table to witness this; he was surprised to see she had calmly resumed eating. Well, with four brothers of her own, she had probably been in the middle of more than a few family arguments. Marc's eyes went back to Eric. "I want this to be as painless as possible for Korey."

"Aw, come off it! If it were Korey you wanted to spare, you would've told her about Clare long ago." Eric calmed a bit. "Look, I don't like playing the moralist, but, by god, someone should. You've run fast and loose with Korey long enough. This....this moral elasticity has been stretched to the limit and any time now will come around to zap you right in the balls."

Marc gave up all interest in food. Dropping his fork, he pushed away his plate. Vulgar phrasing aside, his brother was absolutely on target. In a great whoosh of emotion, Marc exhaled and planted his elbows squarely on the table. Staring past Eric to a featureless window, he wrapped a free hand around a tight fist, rested his mouth against the knuckled lump, oblivious to the teeth digging into the soft flesh of his lower lip. No one spoke. The refrigerator rumbled briefly as the ice-maker dumped frozen cubes into a tray.

"Listen to me, man." Eric's voice was suddenly softer. "I know you're a tormented soul. But don't you see Korey *has* to hear this from you? The damage will be far worse if this bomb is dropped by someone else." Eric closed his mouth before his next thought could be aired: If Marc should shirk this responsibility, the guilt would be so corrosive it would eat him alive.

Giving no hint he had heard, Marc sat as though he had died in the chair.

"You've perched us all on a powder keg," Eric said, frustrated by the lack of response. "Well, Rae and I are getting off *now* before some fool strikes a match!" He sought his wife's eyes and went on speaking for her too. "We're not trying to be petty. We won't introduce the subject of your wife. But if something comes up, we won't cover for you."

Marc raised his head. His lower lip throbbed. He focused on his brother's clear stare. "I'll tell Korey…." He hardly recognized his own voice as his words cracked. He cleared his throat and began again. "I'll tell her on the flight home."

"Why wait?"

"I'll have a captive audience. She'll have to listen; she can't walk out on me."

"More likely she will throw *you* out."

"That's a possibility I've considered." Marc expelled a morbid little laugh, "I trust you've not misplaced the combination to the safe where I keep my Last Will and Testament."

Eric did not so much as smile.

✳   ✳   ✳   ✳

Four hours later the morning's table conversation still sat, along with half an omelet, as a lump in Marc's stomach. Traffic on the interstate highway was light, but he drove with the precision of someone surrounded by the congestion of a big city: hands tightly wrapping the steering wheel; eyes in motion, sweeping the road ahead, checking mirrors. Eric's harsh words rolled through his head like sharp sounds echoing off canyon walls. In Nashville, creeping along Briley Parkway in lanes clogged with rush hour traffic, how many times had he wished for an open road such as this? Yet today, exhaust fumes, horns, and lane-weavers would be a welcome diversion. His troubled mind would accept almost anything that would bar the memory of his brother's voice.

This afternoon he had left the house under a fragile truce. Rae had smiled and wished him a *fun day*. It was because of her suggestion that he now drove with

Korey to Acoma. Beautiful country, Rae had said. An inhabited pueblo atop a mesa, only an hour from Albuquerque. When he had phoned Korey, she had shared his enthusiasm for the outing.

It wasn't until Eric had walked with him to the Jeep waiting in the driveway that the spirit of adventure soured. Eric's parting words, obviously meant as a joke, had nevertheless stung. "The Indians," Eric had said, "call their pueblo Sky City. You'll see why. Just don't get gutsy and pick that spot to tell Korey about Clare. She will shove you right off the edge of the mesa—splat—367 feet to the valley below."

"Marc?"

"Um?" He turned his head, emerging slowly from his woeful thoughts.

Korey glimpsed in his sunglasses a sharp image of herself before he again turned to the highway. "Did you see the sign? The next exit is the road to Acoma."

No way was he about to tell her he had not read a road sign in the last twenty miles. He nodded. "Gotcha," he said. "Next exit."

When a teenager, Korey had visited Acoma with her family. Acoma held no memories of Danny, no pain to cloud the fine, clear day. She remembered from years ago only impressions of beauty, silence, peace. Acoma would be the same today, for she and Marc had entered a timeless country.

Her memory had not done it justice. It was an isolated world of clear air and wild dry wind; of vivid hues—buff cliffs overlapping blue sky, red sandstone trimmed in green sage; of a people living with one foot in a new millennium, the other foot still in centuries past. Korey and Marc stood hand in hand at the edge of the mesa, slightly apart from the small tour group. Their guide, a petite woman named Sarah, brown skinned with a white smile, was talking, but to the couple the soft voice was only a drone in the background. A car door slammed in the valley below—more tourists gathering for the next bus run to the top of the mesa. The sound, though muted by distance, lifted easily on the wind.

"What is that?" Marc asked, looking east. "Over there?"

Korey followed his gaze across a few miles of scrub-carpeted valley to another mesa, its nearly perpendicular walls rising more than four hundred feet from the valley floor. "Isn't it beautiful? Like an impregnable fortress. It's called Enchanted Mesa. At least that's the romantic translation. The Indians call it Katzimo, which some say means 'accursed.'"

"Accursed? I wonder why?"

"There's a legend. Would you like to hear it?" She looked into his eyes as he watched the afternoon sun brush ever-changing strokes of color onto the face of the mesa.

"How is it that you know the legend?"

"I remember it from a visit here, years ago."

It crossed Marc's mind that this was the first he had heard of a previous visit, but he made no comment. Ignorance of any details was preferable to learning that she had been to Acoma with Danny.

"For some reason," he heard her say, "the mesa, the legend, has always fascinated me. The story goes that many centuries ago the ancestors of the Acoma lived on top of Katzimo, safe from all enemies. There was only one place on the sheer walls that could be scaled, where the people had carved toe and finger holds for climbing. Everything used for building had to be hauled to the summit. Just as was everything needed to build this pueblo at Acoma." Korey looked over her shoulder to the adobe dwellings and the mission church. She paused long enough to try to imagine the labor it must have taken to accomplish such a stupendous task, then turned her attention back to Enchanted Mesa. "The people grew crops in the valley below. One spring day everyone in the village, except a young girl and her grandmother, had descended to the valley to farm. There came a great storm and violent rain pounded the mesa, sheering off the mass of rock that held the only way to the top. The people in the valley could not rescue the old woman and her granddaughter."

Korey looked at Marc. "I've heard a couple of endings to the tale. Do you want the tragic version?" She smiled. "Or the romantic one?"

He tucked a wind-tossed curl behind her ear, let his fingers caress the lock before dropping his hand. "I can guess which you most *want* to tell, but go ahead and give me both versions."

"All right. Tragic first. Since there was no way down, rather than face the horror of starvation, the two leapt to their deaths."

"Tragic is right."

"My favorite ending says the two turned into majestic eagles and flew west, guiding the rest of the people here to Acoma, where they have lived since 1150 AD." Korey glanced around, realizing self-consciously that the rest of the group was moving away, following Sarah. Korey said to Marc, "If we had been more attentive, I'm sure Sarah must have just told the same story—only better."

Marc firmly clasped Korey's hand as they fell in behind the ten other members of the group. "I would," he said, donning sunglasses against the horizontal glare of a low sun, "much rather hear it from you."

Still lagging behind, they strolled through a dusty street in the village. Dwellings were quaint but primitive: no electricity; water only in the form of rain captured in cisterns. Stucco had crumbled raggedly from walls of many of the homes, exposing naked patches of adobe brick. Tall thick-runged ladders leaned against outside walls, leading to second floor apartments off limits to the tramping feet and curious eyes of tourists.

Korey's attention suddenly swayed, and she abruptly pulled away from Marc, leaving his arm reaching for her. She approached a boy who looked to be about six, timidly standing guard at a table of beautiful hand-painted pottery. Bending to the child's eye level she asked kindly, "Did your mother make these?" Shyly glancing away from her smile, the child nodded, a fringe of straight dark hair falling across his brow.

Others from the group gathered around similar tables, fingering the distinctive pottery, chattering about price, but Korey had no interest in shopping elsewhere. The boy's sweet brown face and large dark eyes entreated her to buy.

And buy she did as Marc stood beside her observing her prowess at driving a hard bargain. For Tina and Bryan, she chose a large wedding vase with the traditional dual spouts; a thimble, intricately painted with flawless black strokes, would make an extraordinary addition to Evie's collection; deftly decorated clay pots for Matty, Stella. Each item, as chosen, was wrapped in layers of yellowed newspaper, the boy's small mahogany hands working with practiced care. He placed the padded bundles in two brown bags, set the bags in Marc's ready arms, and accepted from Korey, with a shy "thank you," a fist of folded bills.

Sarah then urged everyone toward the point of departure. The bus would come soon, dump another load of oglers and return their group to the tourist center. Leaving the packages in Korey's care, Marc made one last stop. He bought fresh Indian fry bread from an old woman with a face weathered as the rock on which they stood. The bread, smelling delicious enough to make his mouth water, was flat and round, larger than his awaiting hands put side to side, and generously dusted with powdered sugar. He knew how Eric and Rae loved the doughy confection; he would give it as a peace offering.

The approaching bus could easily be heard rattling loudly as it bumped over the washboard road. The engine strained through steep turns. Marc, the fry bread dangling from his fingers in a clear plastic bag, took one of Korey's bulky packages as the bus came into view and halted in a cloud of dust. As the bus emptied, Sarah surprised the departees by offering a choice for leaving the top of the mesa: ride the bus to the valley, or, for the more adventurous, climb down the mesa using the ancient stone steps and hand holds the Indians themselves had used for centuries.

"Let's do it," Marc challenged with a crooked grin.

Korey's eyes were wide and her mouth agape. "You don't mean it."

"Somehow it seems safer to descend by our own wits than to trust our fate to that rickety bus."

She knew he was only half joking. Truly, the yellow bus was none too new; still she thought it preferable. Marc grabbed her free hand, started pulling her toward the sandstone steps that lead off the edge of the mesa. "Wait," she said with some alarm. Like a mule, she stubbornly dug in her heels. "You're crazy. We can't climb with these packages."

"Oh," he said as if he had completely disregarded the sacks of pottery. "No problem. Here, give me yours. I'll take care of everything."

Korey hesitated. Her fragile purchases, snugly tucked in the protective crook of her arm, were her only sure ticket to a ride to the valley. She hadn't much time to ponder. Already people were filing onto the bus. It seemed she and Marc were the only two in the group daring to consider the alternate route. Reluctantly, she parted with the brown paper sack. "Okay," she said. She watched with misgiving as Marc walked away.

He approached four white-haired ladies moving in line toward the bus. Korey could not hear his words, but her intense gaze did not miss the gentle smiles and eager nods of the ladies as Marc trustingly placed his arm load of packages in their care. Astonished, Korey opened her mouth to protest. But, over their shoulders, the ladies gave her such cheery smiles she did not move to stop them. With her precious pottery added to their own, they hiked fragile legs and boarded the bus.

Marc returned to reassuringly squeeze her hand. "Come on," he coaxed, grinning. "An adventure to someday tell your grandchildren." The response was a deep frown. "Hey, it couldn't be that dangerous, or we wouldn't be invited to do it."

"Marc," Korey said under her breath, not giving even an inch to the pull of his hand. "You gave my pottery to those strangers!"

Realizing she was now more upset about the pottery than the climb, Marc tried to pacify her. "Would I chance losing your purchases? Korey, those gals are as honest as my Grammy Harriet."

The bus ground into gear and was off, leaving behind an oily blue cloud. "Well, I don't *know* your Grammy Harriet," Korey snapped, her eyes searching the dust-clotted windows as the bus rolled past. "Is she honest?"

"She was incorruptible."

"What do you mean *was?*"

"She died some years ago."

"Oh." Korey felt a little foolish. They were alone. The second tourist group, with Sarah as guide, had gone into the adobe village. Marc stood close; she wished for a kiss but none came.

"Relax," he said soothingly. "The ladies—and your pottery—will be waiting when we walk into the visitor's center. Now, let's go. Just pretend you're a mountain goat."

Korey's apprehension eased as they started down. The first third of the way was by steps carved into the sandstone wall—safe enough as long as she watched her footing. The rest of the descent was by hand and foot holds, but wide ledges allowed room to perch and eliminated the danger of a long fall. With a steadying hand or a strong arm at her waist, Marc was with her at every turn. By the time she set foot on the valley floor, she was laughing. Hand in hand she and Marc walked the dusty trail that lead to the visitor's center.

As promised, the four ladies waited patiently on a wooden bench in the shade of the one-story building, mounds of paper sacks clustered at their feet. Quietly they speculated. Were they married, that handsome young couple who had kept to themselves on the tour and whose laughter now reached to the shaded bench?

"Honeymooners," said one.

"No," stated another. "No wedding rings."

Four white heads swiveled toward the approaching pair. Someone breathed a long sigh. In unison, as if from a well rehearsed choir, came four voices. "Ahhh," they said with envy. "Lovers, then."

∗   ∗   ∗   ∗

Headlamps tunneled through a dense blackness that seemed to open just enough for the Jeep to pass then fold behind. Korey, lulled by the hum of deep-tread tires on the pavement, let her head fall back to the headrest.

After leaving Acoma, they had found a cafe in Grants that served sandwiches—only so, so—but the coffee, surprisingly, was hot and delicious. From the chrome edge of a gray Formica table, they had watched the setting of a giant orange sun, hazy through the grimy glass that passed as a window. The cool air of a mountain dusk had followed them from the cafe across the cracked and pitted parking lot to the Jeep.

She was toasty now, the car's heater blowing a warm stream of air around the hem of her jeans. She rolled her head on the headrest to peer out the side window. A picture of Marc, faint in the low lights of the dash, shown in the flawless glass. Beyond his reflection, bright stars were visible. Korey leaned forward, seat belt tugging at her shoulder, and, through the windshield, studied the clear night sky. Stars. Everywhere.

"Marc," she said, her eyes still to the heavens, "pull off at the first exit we come to where there is no town, no house lights."

He looked at her sidelong. Her fit of yawns a few minutes before had been contagious. Now she had this impulse to exit the interstate and, very specifically, to do it in the middle of nowhere?

Korey did not return his bemused stare but had a peripheral sense of his quizzical expression. A slender finger pointed skyward. "The stars," she explained. "They're too beautiful to miss."

Soon a spot presented itself: a flat two-lane highway with no cars in sight, and, once away from the vapor lamps at the exit ramp, no lights. Marc steered the Jeep to the gravel shoulder of the road, switched off the engine and headlights.

Korey had both feet on the gravel and the door closed by the time Marc came to stand beside her. She turned a full 360°, her head tilted far back, her delicate chin nearly skyward. She had never seen a more spectacular display of stars. From horizon to horizon nothing broke the view. It was as though an immense star-encrusted bowl had been inverted over their heads. "Beats anything I've ever seen," she said in awe.

"I'll say."

In star-soaked darkness, they leaned against the Jeep, Korey's arms crossed over her chest for warmth. For long moments they silently watched the sky. A few cars traveled the interstate to the north, barely a whisper across the desert. Korey shivered and pulled her oversize sweater down to hide her hips from the cool night air. Wordlessly, Marc set his warm hands on her shoulders, smoothly guided her to him, and molded his warmth to her back. He wrapped his sweatered arms around her waist and rested his chin in her soft hair.

"Umm. Thanks." Her hands ran up and down the soft knit on his forearms. "You feel good," she said. A breeze touched her face, and she snuggled closer to his heat. Dry grass rattled in the wind. "All those billions of stars." Her voice was low. "Maybe countless other life forms out there. We're specks on a teeny planet. Makes you wonder what it's all about. What our purpose is."

"Yeah." His response was intentionally colorless to discourage her further introspection. He knew all too well *his* purpose: to hold Korey, as he did now; to keep her from life's chill, always. His heart wept for the imminent loss of that purpose. A thought stabbed his mind, the pain of it nearly making him sick: *This could be the last time I hold her.*

The schedule of his two remaining days in New Mexico thrust itself into his aching head. He would spend most of tomorrow in conference with Huey Lake, Eric's friend from California. Marc wished now he had never agreed to take on the task of designing Huey's new home. His own time with Korey was more than ever at a premium. He would prefer to spend those costly hours with her. Tomorrow night he, Korey, Eric and Rae would make a foursome at High Finance, the restaurant at the summit of Sandia Peak. Saturday morning another meeting with Huey; late afternoon, a cookout at Eric's. Korey would be there, of course, but he would not have her alone. Then….Sunday and the flight home. That dreaded plane ride. Marc could hardly draw a breath for thinking of it. He raised his chin from Korey's hair, forced a healthy draft of cool air into his lungs. He would not think about Sunday. It would come soon enough. *Don't spoil what little time you have left….*

"Tired?" She had heard him breathe deeply, had felt his broad chest expand against her back.

"A little." He hugged her tighter. "This high plateau air….makes me sleepy." A semi swept under the yellow lamps at the interchange, heading east, making good time. The cab was only an outline of dozens of amber running lights. Marc watched until the lights blurred and diminished to a dim string.

"Maybe we should hit the road?" It was a tentative question, as if she had not wanted to ask it.

"Matty must be wondering what I've done with her niece."

"She knows I'm in good hands." Korey turned in Marc's arms. With chilled fingers she framed his face and kissed him. "It's been a beautiful day. Wish it didn't have to end."

It was not so much the feel of her body against his, but her voice, a mellow flexible drawl, that tipped him off. He looked down into her lovely face, upturned in the starshine. She would be his, willingly, on this dark highway, even leaning against the Jeep, if he wanted. Never in his life had he wanted anything more. Just the mere thought of it—a quickie under the stars—made him wild. But he fought back the lust, held it down until he felt he would explode.

He would forever remember the hollow feeling in his veins, the emptiness of the instant he finally made himself drop his arms away from the slender waist. He kissed her sweetly on the forehead, as if he were too dense to catch her meaning. "We'd better get you back to civilization," he said, stoically assuming the role of surrogate brother, a role he had once, months ago, naively pretended for himself.

Korey accepted the rebuff without hostility, ceding to his better judgment, recognizing immediately the risk of making whoopee in the chill night air. No matter the isolation, they stood at the edge of a public thoroughfare where at any time someone could drive past. But why did she feel such an urgency, as if their time together was drawing to a close? She told herself it was only because the trip was nearing an end. *Be patient,* she said inwardly as Marc closed her into the lingering warmth of the Jeep. *If things go as you dare to hope, you will have a lifetime of places in which to make love to Marc. The luxury of all the time in the world.*

Marc was pensive the final thirty minutes into Albuquerque. Long stretches of quiet filled the car, giving Korey much time to wonder at Marc's silence. If he had been so anxious to use this trip as an opportunity to *talk,* why had he not introduced whatever it was he wanted to talk about? When they had stopped to watch the stars, why had he not used that time, those minutes when they could have been the only two people on earth, to say whatever was on his mind? For the entire trip most of the verbal exchanges with Marc had been a little too flavorless for her taste. He had said nothing in New Mexico that could not have been said in Tennessee. No earthshaking pronouncements. No proposal of marriage.

Korey felt her heart sink. This night could be the last alone with Marc before leaving for home. Reality called to her; she made herself listen. It was *she* who had envisioned, in some nebulous cloud, this dream of marriage. She had let it rule her imagination. How foolish to trust in dreams. They so seldom come true.

The Jeep skimmed a rise in the interstate. Out of darkness, Albuquerque suddenly flowed across the valley in a blaze of winking lights, sparkling as if a lid had opened on a chest of matchless jewels. To Korey, the glittering display was like magic dust. Her sober mood disappeared in the multicolored lights, and she thought of nothing beyond the spectacle of the immediate horizon. Blessedly, she could not know that this night would be the last for some time when she would look upon the world and see beauty.

*   *   *   *

Seated at a table of four, Eric and Rae had their backs to the large window, giving over the panorama of city lights (the view being much the same as from their own den) to Korey and Marc. High Finance Restaurant, perched at the summit of Sandia Peak, was a full house this Friday night. Patrons by the dozens had hung from a giant cable and ridden the aerial tram up the side of the mountain, high over conifer-dotted crags and gullies to dine at the apex ten thousand feet above sea level.

The foursome at the cozy square table contributed, with frequent bursts of laughter, to the lively conversational din in the restaurant. Between bites of food, Marc and Eric entertained with mischievous tales. The phrase, "remember when", prefaced nearly every sentence as the brothers spilled hilarious childhood exploits. Happily Korey listened, for the first time feeling like she could be a member of the family.

"And there Marc was," Eric was saying, his knife slicing cleanly through a slab of rare prime rib, "hanging upside down in the tree, yelling his fool head off, his best dress shirt snagged on a limb, and Mom running...."

A booming voice interrupted Eric's chuckling narrative.

"Eric! Eric Bradberry!"

Eric looked past his brother's broad shoulder, and the smile already on his face widened to a grin. He pushed back his chair, stood, extended his hand. Marc, turning in his own chair, caught sight of the familiar face just as the older man came to stand beside the table and clasp Eric's hand in a firm shake.

"Why, Mason," Eric said with surprise. "What a small world! So glad to see you."

The backs of his legs hugging his chair as he stood, Marc felt his hand gripped tightly as the man pumped a vigorous handshake. "It's been a long time, Mason. What in the world brings you to Albuquerque?"

Mason's spirited answer rang proudly from his round flushed face. "Richard, my stepson, is stationed here at Kirtland Air Force Base. Flies a C-130."

Stepping into the exchange, Eric said, "Mason, you remember my wife, Rae-gan."

"Yes, of course." He gave an eager nod, putting in motion his multiple soft chins. There was a moment of polite inquiries after which Marc introduced Korey. "This is Mason Wills, a dear family friend from Nashville. Mason, please meet Korey Westerfield."

A pause ensued, through which Mason seemed to be waiting for more. The pause lasted only the length of time it took for Marc to draw a painful breath. Gracefully, Mason greeted Korey, swiveling his round thick-lidded eyes only once to Marc before devoting Korey his full attention. Her home was in Chatta-nooga she said; she was in Albuquerque visiting an aunt.

"And are you enjoying your stay in Albuquerque? Seeing all the sights, I hope," Mason added kindly.

"As many as time will allow."

"Good, good," he said a little absently. His large graying head turned to Eric. "I see your mother from time to time. We mull over what's wrong with the world, exchange some harmless gossip." A chuckle shook the shirtfront at his spreading middle. "She's always up on everyone's doin's."

At the mention of his mother, Marc lost the tune of the conversation, a solitary thought boiling over in his mind: Mason will go home and tell Mom that he met Korey....

"Well." Mason's voice brought Marc back into focus. "It's time I let y'all get back to your meal. I see my party is being seated." His eyes went to a round table in the corner. "I'm having dinner with a few army buddies, sort of a mini reunion of our old unit. We had just arrived when I spotted you."

Mutterings of "great seeing you...., nice to have met you...." mingled with "my best to the family." Then after handshakes all around, Mason Wills set off to join his comrades.

Two tables away he stopped, turned as if struck by an afterthought. "Oh, Marc," he said, meeting Marc's cautious gaze. "Give Clare a kiss for me."

Clare? Clare? Korey missed the scorching glance Eric and Rae simultaneously gave Marc. She was herself watching him, staring resolutely at the back of his dark head. She saw his head tilt in an almost imperceptible nod in answer to Mason Wills' request, saw his left hand squeeze the life from a brown linen napkin. A small wedge of Steak Dianne, balanced on her stilled fork, waited at her parted lips. Rich brown sauce rolled off the tender meat, dribbling with delicious bouquet onto her plate.

Eric took to his chair, seated himself with an unsteady jerk, like a panicked man popping into a life preserver, leaving Marc to save himself as best he could.

Time arranged itself in two very different ways: It passed in breezy, unwavering conversation for the rest of the room, but sputtered then stalled for Marc and his table companions. It seemed an eternity before Marc deflected the shock of Mason's parting words. He stole a glance at Korey, his mouth unable to stretch beyond a thin smile, and read in her face precisely the confusion he had expected to see. He tucked his lean frame into his awaiting chair, trying his best not to droop, to look as limp as he felt. Like a dog circling, readying his bed, Marc made unnecessary work of the seating—scooting the chair around, straightening it against the carpeted floor, fitting it to some arbitrary ideal distance from the table. He had no cognizance of the comical chair-wrestling act he performed for his audience of three. His mind, having left the table, was churning in its own froth: If only he had Korey to himself, he would put the truthful answer to the question so clearly etched upon her face. But here? In a crowded restaurant, high above the city with a tram car the only way down? If there could be a worse time or place to discuss the fact that he was married, he could not imagine it.

Meanwhile, Korey had begun chewing her slice of steak, the meat suddenly cold and flavorless. The Tiffany lamp suspended over the table draped Marc's paling face in a sickly yellow. Korey surveyed his profile, studiously, as if his face were a page from a just-opened anthology of legends—more myth than truth.

Eric shattered the island of silence, his words like waves pounding on rocks. "Well, that was certainly a surprise, wasn't it?" He took a long drink of wine.

"Sure was," Marc said, the answer encompassing a range of implied meanings. As he replaced the wrinkled napkin to his lap, he flashed a smile around the table. A smile a little too bright, thought Korey—as if he would have been happier cloaked in darkness but had turned on a light to blind her probing gaze.

With a voracity of ravenous wolves on a downed deer, they resumed the meal. Knives scraped bone; forks chased odd bits of food across plates. Conversation, stilted at first, eased as the minutes passed, becoming more fluid relative to the consumption of wine. Still, Korey could not help but wonder if it was only her imagination that through the entree and into dessert Marc, when he turned to her at all, shied from looking her in the eye. Rae and Eric, too, seemed to be less than direct when her eyes sought theirs.

She struggled to interpret the night's events. What was going on? Why did she feel she had just been tossed out of a friendly home and *Clare* had been the one to do the ousting? Was Clare a family skeleton, an embarrassment? Perhaps a loon hidden away in a mental hospital; or a jailbird convicted of taking to her husband's lover with an ax? If so, why had Mason Wills addressed his behest only to Marc? Korey's questions went begging; Clare was taboo, a ghostly fog floating above the table. Despite the warmth of the room and the glow of candles on the table, Korey felt a chill sweep over her shoulders and down her spine.

After dinner, with Eric and Rae in tow, Marc escorted Korey to Matty's living room. Declining an invitation to stay for coffee, the three Bradberrys, all pleading fatigue, made their departure in controlled haste. If Matty noticed that their leaving seemed too carefully orchestrated, she made no mention of it.

For her part, Korey refused to let venomous thoughts poison her mind. Before falling to sleep, after long minutes of debate, she had convinced herself that Clare was no one to fret over. Simply, if Marc felt there was something to be told, he would tell it. Otherwise....well, for godsakes he was her lover. She had known him for nearly a year. Never in that year had he uttered the name Clare. Therefore, as logic goes, of what consequence could Clare be?

CHAPTER 18

▼

Eric Bradberry leaned with his back against the kitchen counter, watching his wife wash fresh vegetables. Large beads of clear water jiggled on heads of broccoli and cauliflower. Eric rubbed the lower half of his face across the shoulder of his dingy shirt, wiping sweat from his chin. "Thank goodness that job's done," he said between gulps of ice water. "I may never again lift another rock."

Rae peered out the window over the sink, admiring the new rock garden. Flecks of mica winked at her as she stretched forward for a better look. "It's beautiful," she said, leaning over carrots and cucumbers to plant a kiss on her husband's lips. She smiled. "Maybe we should have guests for a cookout more often. Seems great motivation for finishing your do-it-yourself projects."

Softly he slapped a familiar hand to her backside. "Hey, you know a tinkerer's work is never done." He pushed off from the counter, taking his water glass with him. "I'll take a shower and be back shortly to help." One finger pushed aside Rae's thick French braid, clearing the way for him to tickle her slender neck with a kiss. She was still giggling when he left the kitchen.

Smelling of soap, his damp hair darker than its usual sandy brown, he was back in fifteen minutes to find Rae with her head bent to the cutting board, slicing cucumbers with more vigor than finesse. "We're going to have fingertip salad if you don't slow down," he warned lightly as he put his glass in the dishwasher. "We've plenty of time before Marc and Korey arrive." He padded across the floor to be nearer his wife, his bare feet resting on brown tiles warm with strong afternoon sun.

Rae released the large knife, set one hand on a hip and glared grimly at her husband. "We may not have as much time as you think."

A feeling of dread gripped Eric. This was not the same woman he had left giggling in the kitchen a few minutes ago. "What's up?"

"Maybe everything."

The crease between his brows grew deeper. "Care to elaborate?"

"Korey called while you were showering. She wants to talk to us. She'll be here in about half an hour."

Eric sagged against the pantry door and closed his eyes. His face, healthy pink from a day working in the sun, darkened a shade. "Terrific."

"Exactly." Rae picked up the knife, resumed chopping. "I can think of only one reason why Korey would want to talk to us without Marc around."

Eric opened his eyes, spoke over the rhythmic click of the knife. "Must be that episode with Mason Wills last night. About Clare. It has to be."

"Eric, I don't understand. Why doesn't she go to Marc with this? Why come to us?"

"For one thing we're available right now and Marc isn't. Korey knows he's tied up until mid-afternoon with Huey Lake. But how's this for an even better reason? Marc really screwed up last night, didn't play it cool. He was rattled when Mason said Clare's name. Hell, we all were. I watched Korey through those first critical seconds. She didn't take her eyes off Marc. She's no dummy. She knew something was going on. She didn't get the explanation she was obviously waiting for. Now she's had a night to think about it. Maybe she thinks we'll be more forthcoming."

The knife stopped. Like fallen dominoes, thin circles of cucumber overlapped across the cutting board. "And will we?"

"You know we will. It's not like Marc wasn't warned."

"We've never really done anything to mislead her, Eric."

He thought about this for a moment. "No, I don't suppose we have—directly anyway." He crossed his sun-browned arms over his chest. "But," he sighed, suddenly sounding very tired, "we're about to experience first hand how it feels to be found guilty by association."

*   *   *   *

She was at this instant a knot of tangled nerves. Korey jabbed her finger at the doorbell. Now there would be no turning back.

Last night, before sleep had drugged her mind, the goal had seemed so clear: banish all thought of Clare. But the night had been far from restful. A mysterious woman with an unformed face had starred in a night of fitful dreams. Daylight and a drowsy consciousness had brought a new plan. Eric. She would go to him. Put to him the question of Clare so Clare could be put to rest.

Indeed this morning the idea had seemed so reasonable that, while she dressed, calmness had replaced the agitation of not having slept well. Earlier, when she had phoned and spoken to Rae, Korey had been master of her own emotions. Even setting out in the car borrowed from Matty, Korey felt relaxed, as if her nervous system had been fooled into thinking it was out merely for a joy ride. But the jitters had met her somewhere along Tramway Boulevard, and now she depressed the round button on the doorbell a second time to occupy her trembling hand.

Eric opened the tall carved door, his face lit by a smile much the same as that of his brother. The edges of his eyes crinkled in the reflected glare of the high sun. "Korey. Come on in! So glad you could come early."

She stepped into the cool shade of the entry hall. "Thanks. I hadn't seen your new home, and...."

Taking long graceful strides, Rae came from the back of the house. "My, you look lovely today," she said, embracing Korey in a sisterly hug. "What an adorable outfit."

As though she had forgotten what she wore, Korey glanced down at her roomy floral slacks and matching shirt. "Thanks. Matty and I went to Old Town yesterday, and, well, I couldn't resist." She shrugged, knowing the woman in Rae would understand the weakness.

Eric said to his wife, optimistically, "Korey's come to see the house."

Rae had no time to expel a sigh of relief before Korey amended, "Oh, I *do* want to see the house. But I had one other reason for coming...."

Rae took Korey's hand. "Fine. But first we must have something cool to drink."

Korey's flats squeaked against flagstone as she pivoted to follow Rae. Behind her she heard the front door close.

The living room was average size but, with three sky lights set in the high sloping ceiling, had an airy feel of spaciousness. The east wall was glass, bringing the base of the Sandia Mountains into the room. Woven Navajo rugs scattered patches of color across the tiled floor.

At Rae's urging, Korey sat on a curved sofa facing the mountain. Rae sat opposite, rigidly, in a padded straight backed chair with low arms. The women engaged in limping chit-chat while Eric left the room to prepare drinks. Korey had asked for ice water, Rae for white wine.

Returning in short order, Eric served drinks and set a square wooden bowl heaped with mixed nuts on the table nearest Korey. Then, a glass of scotch in hand, he took a chair beside his wife. His intrusion created a lull, as if by entering the room he had severed the slender thread that held the conversation together. To fill the awkward void, all three went to their drinks.

Korey, in her anxiety, took a long swallow of water to slake a desert thirst. Come on, Korey, she told herself. Quit stalling! Get to the point. She spoke to the bottom of Eric's glass as he took a second sip of scotch. "You're wondering about my other reason for coming early." A short fingernail picked nervously at the nubby fabric of the sofa. Eric set down his glass, met her eyes with an openness that compelled her to add, "but then, maybe you already know."

Rae, hopes fading that this had nothing to do with Clare, slipped in with a calm voice. "What is it, Korey?"

Korey sipped more water, then squeezed the glass in the fist of her hand. "I'm not sure what I'm about to ask is any of my business." She paused. "I don't know any way to do this other than to just come right out with it."

Simultaneously, Rae and Eric drew in and held a conscious breath.

Korey focused on Eric, stared deeply into his hazel eyes. Without blinking she asked, "Eric, who is Clare?"

He had thought himself prepared. But hearing Clare's name on Korey's lips stunned him. His face drew taut like canvas stretched between stakes; his mind shed thought as a tent sheds rain.

Korey held his blank stare, not distracted by the swiveling of Rae's head first to Eric, then to the sofa, back to Eric. Korey twisted a corner of a paper napkin between thumb and forefinger. From Eric, she read no recognition of the name. Optimism blossomed anew. She had blown this out of proportion. Clare had been a threat only in a night of deranged dreams. In daylight she was harmless.

To control trembling from within, Eric squared his jaw. "You should be hearing this from Marc," he said. Weighted air hung close in the room, charged as air before a storm. His mouth felt as if it were working in slow motion. "Korey, Clare is Marc's wife."

The world stopped. For moments she sat in a vacuum. Then the silence became a living thing, feeding on air meant for her lungs. She gulped. A buzz began in the back of her brain, pulsating like the busy circuits of a phone line. The buzz grew until it filled her head with throbbing pain. Korey never identified the noise for what it was: the striving engine of a small airplane flying low over the house. She was aware only that the noise faded, leaving the pain behind. Her mind was rubble; a bomb had gone off in her head and ripped apart the circuits.

Eric and Rae sat miserably glued to their chairs. They watched....waited. Across the sun washed room, Korey's eyes were dark, cold. Looking into them was like looking into the windows of a vacant house.

From a dark cellar of the vacant house came a croak. "His wife? I....I don't understand. Marcus....Marcus is married?"

Rae gripped the arms on her chair and fought back tears.

Eric nodded. "I'm so sorry...."

"Sorry?!" The import of what was happening—Marc's betrayal, the family conspiracy—crashed head on with the latent anger and sorrow of Danny's death. Korey was overcome with a fury beyond any she had ever known. Red hot words spewed forth. "Sorry! I find it impossible to fathom the depth of your regret!" Shaking uncontrollably, she slammed the near-empty water glass to the table, rose on legs that felt like sponge and wrapped her arms around her middle to hold herself together. Stinging tears sliced into her eyes; the bright designs of the Navajo rugs ran in watercolors on the floor. Married! God, how she had loved him! Now all her dreams....

She heard a voice, that of a shrew, and was horrified to find it was her own. "How could he do this? How could he be so...so...?" Odious slurs and vile accusations tumbled through her head vying to be first out of her mouth. But the words could not withstand the searing heat of her anger and melted away, unsaid. The shrew was gone. "Oh, Marcus, why didn't you tell me?" she sobbed.

Eric came to her and gently placed his hand on her arm. Regaining control, Korey jerked her arm free. "Don't touch me," she barked. "I don't want to be touched by a Bradberry." It occurred to her then, with Eric a close and fitting stand-in for his weasel of a brother, how satisfying it would be to leave behind her hand print on his sun-flushed cheek. For one tempting moment she fantasized about this but decided instead of satisfaction what she needed most was to be alone—to scream or cry, or to be sick. Maybe all three.

"I'm leaving now," she stated with a quiver in her voice. "Belated though it was," she added, "I suppose I should thank you for finally letting me in on the family secret."

Turning on her heel, she was almost to the door before Eric overtook her.

"Don't leave, Korey. Please wait for Marc, give him a chance to explain."

If she had not been so wretched, she would have laughed. "Would an explanation change anything? Marc's married. He belongs to someone else. He and I have been lovers. I suppose that makes me an adulteress. Or maybe not. I'm not the one who is married. I'm not quite sure how that works. Maybe your brother can explain *that* to me!"

"If you won't wait for Marc," Eric pleaded, "at least let me tell you a little about Marc and Clare. Hear me out, please."

Why she allowed herself to be guided back to the sofa she would never know. She stared beyond Eric; a shadow of a cloud flew like a gigantic bird across the scarred cliffs of the Sandia Mountains. In a low steady voice, Eric spoke of the brutal attack on Clare and the resultant coma. Korey watched the lone cloud, its edges tattered by the wind, sail over the crest of the mountain. Eric talked; the cloud disappeared. Korey thought there was something torturously incongruous about a sky so blue on a day her world had plunged into gloom.

In the background she heard Eric say, "Clare is from a wealthy Nashville family. Lots of money made in the music business. She and Marc met while students at Vanderbilt. She was spoiled, wild but fun, and beautiful. Marc, himself frisky, was very attracted to her. But marriage and a promising career settled him down. Clare remained the party girl. She couldn't give up the drinking, the playing around. She had affairs—God knows how many."

Korey felt her attention slip, her mind taking refuge in a realm of unreality. Thinking of Marc as belonging to another was too exhausting. To Korey he had been a comforting friend, a caring but passionate lover. She could not think of him as husband to a wild, spoiled woman named Clare Bradberry.

Bewildering scenes from the past began to gel in Korey's head: Marc's mood swings, his disinclination to reveal much about his family, the periods when he was incommunicado. Things that had been confusing began to drop into place like labeled and sorted files into a drawer. What a fool she had been.

She saw that Eric's mouth moved, but she did not hear his words. Her eyes went to the bowl of mixed nuts. The thought of the salty, oily nuts made her stomach turn. A sharp pain began forming deep in her chest, growing stronger, as though a large hand had taken hold of her heart and slowly started to squeeze....

"....was planning a divorce when Clare was attacked and left for dead." It was Rae's voice that Korey now heard. "His love for her died a long time ago, Korey. Long before he met you." If Rae had let it go at that, she may have seen a note of empathy in Korey's sad eyes. But Rae went on. "He's caught in a trap. Korey, he loves you very much."

The part about the trap, though it was of his own making, she could take. But love her? Ha! Korey bounced to her feet. "No," she said, her voice quaking with rage. There were no tears—just the same, her eyes ached. "No, if he loved me, he never would have done this."

This time only Eric's words followed her as she went for the door. "He wanted to tell you, Korey, really he did. It's been tearing at him for months. I hope you'll change your mind about hearing his side."

The plea was so ludicrous it spun Korey around. "His side? He's had a year....and opportunities without number to tell me 'his side.' Now this is *my* side. Tell him I don't want to see him again, ever. Tell him the fun's over; he'll have to find himself another tart." Her hands were white fists at her sides. "Tell him I think he's a....a heartless, unscrupulous....bastard!"

She groped for the doorknob. The door flew open, banged against the stop. Korey was no more than a blur as she shot through the opening. Standing, Eric and Rae could do nothing but stare. Then the door slammed shut with a force that rattled the windows.

CHAPTER 19

▼

He stood at the tall window, looking out, seeing the world not as a splendid April day but through a frosty gloom more befitting winter. A desert sun burst on the valley below, blanching the city to shades of pale but doing little to warm Marc with its rays. He shivered.

Something was terribly wrong. He knew it the instant he had stepped into the house, returning from the meeting with Huey Lake. One look at Eric and Rae had been clue enough. Eric had put off any questioning by insisting on drinks. "Let me pour us some scotch. I'll join you in the den."

Marc had protested. "No, I'm going to change then pick up Korey for the cookout."

"Not just yet. First we need to talk," Eric had said, almost shoving Marc in the direction of the den where Marc had since waited through long, suspenseful minutes.

Now, reaching a hand to the back of his neck, Marc massaged cords of taut muscle. His lungs felt heavy, unable to expand under their own weight. Only one thing would account for the long faces that had greeted him on his arrival.

Ice cubes popping, cracking, tinkling against glass, told Marc he was no longer alone in the room. Without turning, he said, in a lifeless voice, "She knows, doesn't she?"

The answer took heart-thumping seconds to come. "Yes, she knows." A scotch and soda appeared at his elbow, offered by a lean brown hand. He took it, warily, as though accepting a token last request from his own executioner. Still facing the window, he asked, "How...? Who told her?"

"I did,"

Clubbed into a daze, Marc shook his head, then nearly spilling the scotch, spun on his brother. "You! *You* told her?" Broad white knuckles squeezed the bulge of his glass. "Dammit, Eric..."

Eric was in no mood to tolerate a tongue lashing, especially one he considered undeserved. "I felt very strongly," he said crisply, "that you should be the one to tell her. However, she came here this afternoon and asked point blank about Clare. You were not available. I had no choice but to tell her." He set a cold eye on his brother.

There was no need to ask what Korey's response had been. The brutal reality of his failure weighted Marc's eyelids closed. He should have been the one to tell her; he had meant to be....the messenger had dawdled, arrived a day late with the message. Opening his eyes, he said through a tight throat, "Where is she?"

"I don't know."

"You mean you just let her walk out of here?"

"*Let* her? Hell. As if I could have stopped her! What should I have done? Chased her down, roped her, tied her off like a maverick?"

Marc's voice rose. "Yeah, something like that." In frustrated anger, he flung an arm in the direction of the window. "She's probably out there in a car, screaming down some long stretch of road. Even under saner conditions, she drives the deserted highways much too fast. God only knows what she'll do now." Slamming his untried drink on a table, he took a long stride past Eric.

"Where are you going?"

"To find her."

"Oh? Where? Just how many hundreds of square miles can you cover at once?"

"Don't get sarcastic with me!" Marc turned to glare at his brother, his eyes flaming with anger and fear. He hesitated, grasping for a methodical plan for his search. "I'll start with Matty. If Korey isn't there, Matty will most likely know where she is."

"Fat chance she'll tell you." The words sounded more combative than Eric had intended. He softened his tone but not his resolve. "Let her go, Marc. Korey doesn't want to see you. Don't make things worse." When Marc seemed to waver, Eric pushed. "You say you love her."

"Of course I love her."

"Then prove it. If you truly do love her, you *will*," Eric prophesied, "let her go."

*   *   *   *

Mindlessly flowing in a traffic tide, Korey took the ramp from Paseo del Norte Drive onto I-25, southbound, not caring where the tide was taking her nor thinking that she was stealing away in Matty's only car. Guided by a sixth sense, she drove with her eyes fixed on the car ahead, not even glancing onto the waters when the highway, at the southern tip of the city, spanned a wide breadth of the Rio Grande River.

Her mind was its own rushing river where memories bobbed to the surface like corks in a whirlpool. Marc was before her, beyond the windshield, just out of reach. She remembered his face exactly as it had been the first time she had seen it, amidst the dust and noise of his new office. A sharp pain pierced her breast as she relived the incandescent wonder in his eyes the night he first made love to her. She saw his rain-spattered hair, the determined line of his firm mouth the day he braved the foul weather, and her frigidity, to say: *I love you.* Endearments whispered across candlelit tables or in quiet bedrooms brushed her ears as if his deep sultry voice were now coming to her from the rear seat.

Traffic thinning to a trickle, the car continued heading south, its driver not seeing the oasis of Sabinal Vineyards pass to her right, the grapevines a patchwork of bright green lace among the dust and sage. Soon the pastel hills of pink sandstone followed the highway and for a time were her only traveling companions.

Over the miles, Korey's head gradually began to comprehend what her heart already understood: Marc would not be, indeed had never been, hers to love. Married! How could she have been so blind?

To escape two roaring semis that seemed to be making a game of sandwiching her car between them, Korey left the interstate highway at the nearest exit. She had already bounced over a set of railroad tracks and crossed the Rio Grande for the second time that afternoon before the road began to look familiar. She was on US60, traveling the same route she and Marc had taken in November to the pueblo ruins at Gran Quivira.

Conceived in a flare of recall, that visit to the ruins lit her mind like the sudden illumination of a motion picture screen. Of course! At Gran Quivira Marc had seemed on the brink of telling her something, had opened his mouth as if to speak, but there had been no words. That's how close he must have come to confessing his duplicity! Korey ground her teeth. That lying, cheating....

She drove east now, her back to a lowering sun. Weary of staring through dark lenses spotted with salt from dried tears, she yanked off her sunglasses and, in a fearsome snit, flung them to the passenger seat. Pain seeped to her very roots. She was living a nightmare. Like the road, a lonely and barren life uncurled before her. Scenes from a drab future floated dully across her mind: the humiliation of acknowledging her stupidity to Matty, then Tina, then a host of others; the struggle of returning to places she had enjoyed with Marc; the days, months clawing her way up from the same pit of despair she had scaled after Danny's death. Already weakened by widowhood, battered from being so cruelly used, this time the pit loomed deeper. She could not imagine where she would find the strength for the climb. A plunging dread pressed her lower into the velour seat.

The car skimmed the two-lane highway, Korey's right foot heavy on the accelerator. The sparse landscape, the absence of people or animals, the silence, all became suddenly frightening, as if she were the only thing living after a holocaust. Switching on the radio, heedless of the station and grateful for the noise, she turned up the volume. The car ate up the miles yet there was no sensation of speed. The arid land produced no trees to flicker past as the speedometer climbed. Scrub grass growing to the edge of the pavement bent to the ground in the rushing wind of the passing car.

From several miles away a shard of reflected sunlight leaped from the windshield of an approaching car, catching Korey squarely in the eyes, effectively waking her from a grief-induced trance. She was shaken to see the speedometer reading above ninety, while at the same time amazed the four cylinder engine in Matty's little white car could generate such power. Korey lifted her foot from the accelerator. How suicidal it was to fly from her woes at such reckless speed. She would not kill herself over Marc, the s.o.b. The car coasted along the level roadbed, slowing to a saner speed. Korey gripped the steering wheel, braked, and, through wheel-high grass on the wide shoulder, brought the car to a stop. She set the gear to park, left the engine running and radio playing.

Her hands, still tightly wrapping the top of the steering wheel, cushioned her forehead as her head fell forward in despair. Time for a few unsullied moments of self pity. Marc had given her new life then snatched it away. Twice loved; twice lost. Now what was to become of her? A tear stood on the tip of her nose. She wiped it with the back of her hand.

A sharp rap against glass brought Korey's head up. Broad shoulders and a weathered, frowning face filled her side window. She stared wide-eyed at the face for a moment, her heart beating double-time. Then as if by reflex, to hide her watery eyes, she reached for her sunglasses and slipped them over the tip of her red nose.

The man called through the glass, "I didn't mean to startle you."

Far from being in her right mind, the danger in yielding to a stranger on a little-traveled road did not occur to her, and, at his beckoning, Korey fumbled blindly for the button that would roll down the window. The glass dropped several inches. Korey switched off the radio.

The man spoke over the hum of the car's engine. "I was coming from up the road a ways." He gestured with a large thumb, pointing east, toward the Manzano Mountains. "I saw you swerve off the road. Thought you might have a flat tire or something. Might need some help."

His eyes, under the wide brim of a dusty cowboy hat, were level with hers. She saw them clearly—black to their depths—through the narrow slit of open window. They made her think of the slick planes of a fine obsidian nugget she had once held in her hand in a university geology class.

"Hey, are you all right?" His frown grew deeper.

She realized then that her lack of response alarmed him. "Yes, I'm…I'm okay." She smiled tentatively. "The car's fine too. It's just that I suddenly became aware the speed had gotten away from me. Shook me a little, so I thought I'd better pull off the road and calm down a bit."

He flashed a knowing grin, his teeth white on his dark face. "Easy enough to do on these roads. I'd be tempted myself, but Ole Wilbur doesn't seem to be up to it." He glanced behind him, then turned back just as Korey caught sight of a battered, dusty pickup parked on the opposite shoulder of the road. The man paused, as if unsure how well his jest had been received. "Well," he said, "take it easy out here, ma'am."

"I will. And thank you for stopping. It was very kind."

He smiled and in farewell touched a forefinger to the brim of his dark hat. He waited for a car to pass, then the tall heels of his scuffed boots clicked on the hard pavement as he crossed the road to his truck. Korey saw then the heavy black hair gathered at his nape, wrapped in red yarn and falling to just below his shirt collar. She returned his departing wave as he drove away in a smelly cloud of smoke.

Korey turned off the car engine. For some minutes she sat in silence watching a train five miles distant wiggle along the base of the Manzano Mountains. Its silver skin, slick as an eel's, flared orange in the setting sun. Then, with the train gone and dusk settling thick around her, she started the car, made a U turn on the empty road and drove for Albuquerque.

*   *   *   *

A table lamp hung a veil of copper light in the earth-tone room and projected onto a far wall a lengthened shadow of kokopelli. With each tick of the wall clock, the spring inside Marc's constricted chest wound ever tighter. Korey had fled more than four hours ago. If Matty was to be believed—and he would not think otherwise—Korey had not returned. Outside it was dark, black as pitch beyond the reaching fingers of city lights. Where would she have gone? Absently, he tapped the expansive window with a knuckle. What could she be doing, alone, in that vastness beyond the glass?

On the neighboring street below a car turned a corner, its headlights sweeping the glass and in that moment lighting a face so sunken in worry it resembled a skull. Marc watched the car drive into a garage then his bloodshot eyes went to the distance where thousands of other cars, in glittering red and white ribbons, threaded through the valley. He imagined Korey being among them driving in circles—much as his own mind traveled—hurt, confused, unable to find her way to Matty's. Anxiety welled inside him. He yanked his clammy hands from the pockets of his pants. For the fourth time in as many hours, he reached for the phone.

It was answered on the first ring. "Matty," he asked, sounding breathless, "is she back yet?"

"No."

"You haven't heard…"

Matty cut him off. "Listen here, young man." She barked in a voice so stern Marc had a clear mental picture of her wagging a stubby finger at him. "Are you finally prepared to tell me what's going on, or am I to continue to sit over here and gnaw my fingernails to the nub?"

"Matty, don't make me refuse you again. I'm sorry. I can't tell you."

"Won't, you mean."

"There's been a misunderstanding. No. No, it's not that at all." His sigh was laden with sadness. "Let's just say I've been less than honorable. Indeed, there is much more to tell, but Korey should be the one to do the telling."

"I see."

He knew, of course, that Matty did not see. She could have no understanding of why her niece would suddenly run from the man she loved. He said, a bit desperately, "You will call me, won't you, the second she returns? Let me know she's safe?"

"You will be notified," she briskly answered.

Marc opened his mouth to express his thanks but a sharp click then a dial tone became a piercing signal that his exchange with Matty was over. Cheerlessly, he set down the phone.

From the kitchen drifted sounds of water running and dishes clanging. After a solemn meal where he had only picked at his grilled steak, he had helped with the cleanup until, his mind reeling, an empty earthenware pitcher had slipped through clumsy fingers. It landed with a hollow crash on the tile floor, but Rae assured him the pitcher could be easily and inexpensively replaced and would not let him sweep up the shattered mess. With compassion, he was instructed to find a comfortable chair far away from the kitchen in which to rest his jangled nerves.

Left to roam the house alone—preferring it, really—he paused in the living room to watch the lighted Sandia Crest tram glide up the dark mountain face to hover like a UFO at the summit. Then he was off again, restlessly wandering room to room, until he settled at last at the window wall in the den. There he stared vacantly into the sparkling bowl that was the valley. And awaited news of Korey.

The noise in the kitchen now suddenly ceased. Impatient with the suspense of waiting, he shoved both hands through his hair, grasping in each a fistful of the thick dark mass as if he would in a moment of insanity yank the hair out by the roots.

"Any word?"

Marc dropped his hands, turned in surprise at the sound of Eric's voice. "No. Nothing. I spoke with Matty less than five minutes ago. Korey isn't there. Matty's not heard from her."

The sight of his brother shocked Eric. Marc looked demented: face ghostly pale; hair standing out at the sides as if his head had grown wings. Eric came to stand beside him, pressed his shoulder in a consoling grip. "She's all right, Marc."

"I'd like to believe that."

"You *must* believe it. True, she's hurting. But that gal has spunk. She won't do anything crazy. She'll get through this."

Marc stared mutely at his brother. Those green eyes, devoid of life, seemed to say: *Yes, perhaps she will. But will I?*

Eric found himself suddenly very tired. It had been one hell of a day, and he did not care to contemplate the ramifications of the day's events. Taking his hand from Marc's shoulder, he crossed the room to sink into the folds of a chair near the empty stone fireplace. For a moment he sat wrestling with his own mix of emotions. Then he asked, "Want to talk?"

Marc shrugged. In the reflection of the window his drooping shoulders were those of an ancient, stooped man. Finally he sat opposite Eric, raggedly settling into a cowhide loveseat, his long legs reaching into the room. "You know," he said, looking up with glazed eyes, "I'm still not sure exactly what happened here today. You haven't given me all the gory details." As if to shield an already wounded heart from further drubbing, he crossed his arms over his chest. "Let's hear it."

Eric knew that his brother wanted to punish himself by living out the whole horrible scene. He only hoped the experience would prove cathartic. "You sure you're up to this?"

"No….but let me have it anyway."

So it was told, in a play by play so close to actuality that Eric passed the ensuing minutes reliving the scene where, as the bearer of bad news, he was cast as the ogre, a role he had accepted reluctantly and not without some bitterness. Now, however, in pity he took the sting from the episode's end, omitting the part where Korey had blown from the house like a gale-force wind. No need, he reminded himself, to have it sound as acrimonious as it was.

At the finish no response came from the direction of the loveseat. Though his insides had quivered, Marc had slouched through the entire narrative and listened impassively, as someone might upon hearing a story for the second time and for whom the climactic ending holds no surprise. Through the hush Marc sat unmoving, his eyes locked absently on a cluster of framed photographs hanging on the wall behind Eric.

"One other thing," Eric said, uncomfortable with the lengthening silence. "She did call you a name, uh…."

Marc broke in, "…a lot of them, I'm sure. None complimentary." He was startled to hear, through the sadness in his voice, a spark of self-effacing humor.

Eric heard it too. A tiny smile curved his mouth. "Well, there were a few choice ones, some casting doubt on the validity of your birth." In deliberation, he ran a brown hand back and forth across his lean jaw. "There was another name, though. One I haven't heard for awhile, and then only from Mom when you're in for a good scolding."

Marc straightened, looking more alert than he had all evening.

"Odd," Eric said, thoughtfully, "but this afternoon Korey called you Marcus."

An iron fist to the gut could not have hurt more. He had never had a fondness for his full name, had ever since he could remember discouraged anyone from using it. Until, that is, Korey used it their first night together. She had taken him to her and in a moment of ecstasy had called his name, *Marcus, Marcus,* again and again. Thereafter for him *Marcus* had spelled magic. Exclusively, only in their most intimate, rapturous moments did Korey call him Marcus. Yet today, swamped in shock, anger, and sorrow she had spoken the name before Eric and Rae. Only now did he truly feel the depth of Korey's pain. "Oh, that," he said. In a gesture of nonchalance, he flicked a hand, brushing the name aside as though it meant nothing. "Korey does....uh did....call me Marcus....occasionally." His face erupted in a heated flush.

"Not for the same reason Mom does, I trust."

"No, not for the same reason...." As his voice faded, all was quiet. In the silence Marc thought he heard his heart shatter, like fragile crystal, into a million tiny pieces.

✳   ✴   ✴   ✴

"My dear child!"

Korey found herself snatched into a snug embrace the instant she stepped through the door.

"What a sight you are for these nearsighted eyes. I've been so worried."

"Oh, Auntie"—she had not called her *Auntie* in years—"of course you've been worried. I borrow the car for the afternoon then disappear with no consideration for your plans. I'm so sorry. I should have called you....I....it's just that I wasn't thinking too clearly...."

"Never mind my plans or the car. I have plenty of friends who have cars if I need one, goodness knows. I was worried about *you*." Matty kept a possessive arm around her niece as she led Korey into the living room. "And my concern grew with each phone call I received from Marc." As soon as Marc's name flew from her lips Matty felt, against her arm, Korey's back stiffen. For her careless words, Matty wanted to bite her own tongue.

They both dropped to the sofa: Korey from exhaustion; Matty in relief. From late afternoon, when Marc's first call had alarmed her, on into an ominous darkness, Matty's fluid imagination had run through terrible car crashes, carjackings, abductions and rapes. But Korey was back. Safe and sound. No, not sound, judging from the tears suddenly lining her niece's eyes. But at least safe.

"I don't mean to pry, dear," Matty said after some moments, "but something dreadful has happened between you and Marc." She said it not as conjecture but as fact. Her voice was that of a mother concerned for her child. "Sometimes it helps to talk...."

The sofa, clad in a slipcover Korey had always thought too flowery for her earthy aunt, felt nonetheless comforting, like sitting in the ample lap of a doting grandmother. Determined to do no more sobbing, Korey made a hasty swipe at the tears. She said with only a small quiver, "Oh, Matty. It's the worst possible thing."

A veined hand with its short fingers and blunt nails came to rest softly on Korey's arm. "Could it really be that bad?" Another glaze of tears.

"He's married, Matty."

Stunned silence followed, as if the house itself were holding a long breath. *I've been less than honorable,* Marc had said over the phone. *Less than honorable.* Indeed. "Married," Matty echoed slowly. She cleared a sudden obstruction from her throat. "Oh my."

Korey sniffed. She dug in a pocket of her slacks, withdrew a limp tissue and dabbed her nose. "Kind of like a bomb going off on your doorstep, isn't it?"

"Yes…I should say. What the devil is this all about?"

Korey's face was a picture of confusion. Exasperated, she threw up her hands then with a slap let them fall to her knees. "Oh, I don't know….something about a wife in a coma. She was beaten, robbed, left for dead. Last spring some-time….I'm not sure. This all came from Eric, and, well truthfully, I don't think I heard half of what he said."

"I don't wonder."

"Anyway, according to Eric, the marriage had been in serious decline for some time. Marc was preparing to divorce Clare—that's the wife," added Korey unnec-essarily, "—when she was attacked." Korey wearily shook her head, an unruly mass of curls framing an ashen face. "This all seems unreal, a terrifying dream…."

Matty took in a soft breath, as if she might say something.

Korey appeared not to notice. Her eyes were looking into the past, far beyond the hands they seemed to study in her lap. "You remember last night I made note of the small world we live in. I told you that Marc and Eric had run into a family friend from Nashville while we were dining at High Finance. Mason some-body….Wills, I believe. Anyway, as he was leaving our table, Mason's parting words to Marc were, 'kiss Clare for me.' The name brought a palpable change to our table. Naturally, that piqued my curiosity. Since no one said another word about Clare, I tried to dismiss her.

"But through the night the name tested my imagination with all sorts of possi-bilities. So today, knowing Marc was tied up with a client, I decided to ask Eric about Clare. I thought I was prepared to hear one of any number of identities: Clare, the eccentric relative; Clare, an old flame; Clare, one half of a broken engagement. Even Clare, the ex-wife. Conceivably Marc could have been on such friendly terms with an ex that he would think nothing of greeting her with a kiss. Not once did it occur to me that Clare could be a present wife. Now, graced with hindsight, it appears so obvious." Korey raised her eyes to her aunt. "How could I have been so gullible?"

"Listen, dear, don't be so hard on yourself. At times we all look without seeing. He had us all fooled."

Korey suddenly pressed a hand to the top of her head. "I have a lulu of a headache." She rose from the sofa, stiffly, as though her joints were rusty. "I'm going to swallow a few aspirin then have a little something to eat. I'm not the least bit hungry, but I haven't had a thing since breakfast, and I refuse to starve myself into illness over that man."

Feeling that the world had flipped upside down, Matty remained on the sofa. For that charming, clever young man to take part in such roguery was almost beyond belief. She was furious with Marc, but despite his shortcomings, in her benevolence she was saddened for him. Marc's love for Korey showed plainly. To be sure, he had been self-serving, yet the pain he had inflicted on Korey was perhaps no less than that inflicted upon himself. Matty shook her head. Tonight she would waste no more sympathy on Marc. Right now her loyalty was to her niece.

A rattling came from the bathroom.

"How about some roast beef?" Matty called.

The rattling stopped. "Did you say roast beef?"

"Yes. I'll make you a sandwich. Lots of mayo."

"That would be nice. But let me help."

"Nonsense. Pamper yourself. Get out of those clothes, wrap up in a soft robe, lie on the sofa to await your food."

Korey showed her head, a shadow of a smile on her lips. "You're spoiling me. Are you going to feed me too?"

"Nope. That you must do yourself."

Her appetite surprised her by returning the moment Korey sank her teeth into the first bite. Thin slices of rare beef were stacked high between two slices of dark Russian bread. The sandwich tasted delicious. She balanced a plate on her robe, over legs curled on the sofa.

Matty sat near in a rump-sprung chair with worn arms, her hands cradling a steaming mug of coffee. "Feeling better?"

"Much." With two fingers Korey plucked a dangling sliver of tender pink meat from beneath the bread and popped it into her mouth. "You're a godsend. I think you saved my life." She licked her fingers. "The headache is gone and I...."

"Oh damn!" Matty said in response to a shrill buzz coming from the kitchen. "Not that telephone again." She sprang nimbly to her feet. "Three guesses," she said with irony as she left the room.

Korey did not need three guesses. She bit heavily into the crusty dark bread and chewed without tasting the sandwich. For a time Matty's words drifted from the kitchen as no more than mumbling. Then a change of tone startled Korey.

"No!" Matty sounded more alarmed than angry. "Coming here would *not* be a good idea....yes....yes, well I'll see what I can do." Click.

Korey let the last bite of sandwich fall to the plate, her appetite gone. She set the plate away from her. "What did *he* want?"

Matty sank into the chair. "Wanted to know if you were back. When I said you were, he let out a sigh of relief that would have inflated a balloon."

"I'll just bet."

"He sounded sincere."

"The nerve. Calling here with such an act."

"Is it an act?"

"Oh, yes. And he's marvelous at it—the phony. Who does he think he is?"

Matty said, as cool as could be, "Your ride home, for one."

Korey slapped her forehead with a palm as if to jiggle her brain. "Damn!" Like a cornered dog, she growled through bared teeth. "How could I have forgotten?"

"Seems natural. Your mind, after all, has been taken up with other things."

With a jerk, Korey swung her feet to the floor. "I'll have to get a seat on a commercial flight. Flying with....with that *snake* is, of course, out of the question." She stood, wriggling her feet into velvet slippers. "I'll get on the phone right now. It's going to take persistence and more than a little luck to get a ticket in less than twenty-four hours." With one bare heel still fighting for room in the slipper, she made for the nearest phone.

Twenty-five minutes later Korey was huddled in a wad on the sofa, her mood nearing a new low. "....Nothing. Getting out of Albuquerque is no problem, but all flights into Chattanooga are booked." Her face sagged like softened wax.

"Stay here for a few days. I would love to have you. Go home later in the week."

"You're sweet. But what kind of company would I be, moping around? Besides, I have an appointment with a new client Monday at two-thirty. She has already rescheduled twice. I don't dare cancel. I must go home tomorrow."

"Then it seems you have no choice."

Korey's stare was blank, as though she could not see the obvious. "I can't face him. Don't you see why that's impossible?"

"No, Korey, I don't see. You act as if you're the guilty party. Don't lose sight of the fact that it's the other way around. I know you're hurt, embarrassed. But in spite of his acting like a jackass, in my heart I feel Marc never meant to play you for a fool."

Something flashed to life in those sad dark eyes. "I can't believe you're taking his side."

Matty straightened her spine. "I most assuredly am not. For the pain he has caused you, I would gladly wring his neck if he would be so careless as to present it to me. But did he act with malicious intent? I don't think so. He made a grave error in judgment. He was thoughtless, selfish even, but..."

"Whatever." Korey waved a hand, dismissing the aunt's argument. "I don't want to see him. I think I'll be sick if I see him."

"Korey, listen to yourself. You've faced enough of life's rough edges to know you can't ignore them, wait for them to smooth themselves out. You have to get in there and work, grind them down. That's not to say you won't suffer a few scrapes in the process, but they'll heal over time. Begin the healing tomorrow. Fly home with Marc. Now before you object, let me finish. Give him a chance to have his say. He owes you that much, and you owe it to yourself to listen. Don't live your future under noxious clouds filled with unanswered questions. Clear the air. Vent your anger. In the end you'll feel better for not having run away."

The lecture was over, yet the words captured the room in a heavy silence. Inside Korey's head the wisdom of Matty's words clashed with stubborn pride. After long moments, wisdom won. Korey said in a tiny voice, "Do me a favor, please. Find out from Marc what time I should be at the airport tomorrow. Tell him...." She hated swallowing her defeat. "....tell him I'll be there."

*   *   *   *

Heart thumping behind her breast, she awoke with a jolt, surprised that she had been asleep. She knew she had been dreaming, but the dream was lost in soupy fog. Her head lay like lead on the downy pillow. Through open curtains a distant street lamp drew eerie shadows onto the walls. A car rolled along the street, the hoarse engine wheezing. Korey heard the slap of rolled newspapers hitting sidewalks.

She pushed off warm covers, went to the open window and breathed the pre-dawn air. A breeze ran icy fingers up her bare legs and caught her gown, flapping the long folds like a sail. She shivered, wrapped herself in her arms. Her eyes felt hot, dry and scratchy. She leaned into the breeze, closed her eyes and let the cool air stroke her burning lids.

Tomorrow—no today, in a handful of hours—she would be flying home with him. An entire afternoon of sailing through the skies with only the two of them in the small cabin of the airplane. Those eyes of his, set like emeralds under his dark brows; his full warm mouth; the long lean fingers—they all at one time or another had touched her, everywhere. And with no way to elude him, today they all would touch her again, if only in her own mind. The strength that she would need to endure such a day ebbed from her limbs. Opening her eyes, she reached out and grasped a fistful of curtain for support.

She had never felt colder—or more alone.

She scanned the sky for a hint of dawn but there was none. Attracting her gaze, a crescent moon hung in a slash of silver above the treetops. The night before she had spotted in the black sky the same moon, seeing it then as a silly lopsided grin. But tonight the grin was different somehow. Fatter perhaps. For some time she and the moon eyed each other across the cool morning. In her exhausted sight the grin transformed into a sneer. And the moon mocked her.

CHAPTER 20

▼

The sight of the airplane made her queasy. There had been a time when she had thought the plane sleek and beautiful. But that was another lifetime.

A huge jet raced down the runway to her right, lifted off and vanished through a ceiling of gray clouds. The roar of the engines overlay all other sound long after the plane disappeared. The smell of jet fuel was strong in the damp wind.

Across the wide expanse of tarmac, Korey spotted Marc standing on the far side of the nose of his plane, his back to her. He was in deep conversation with the pilot, Tim Penny, their gazes intent on the lowest clouds somersaulting over the Sandia Mountains. Skirting puddles, not caring to be seen, Korey walked briskly, wheeling her suitcase behind her to the plane, any sound of her approach sufficiently drowned by the landing of a fat orange Southwest Airlines jet. A cluster of suitcases and briefcases sat at the base of the steps. She left her travel bag among the others, choosing the only drying spot on an otherwise wet pavement. Carrying her bag of quilting, her fingers skimmed the cold metal handrail as she climbed the stairs then ducked into the plane.

As if programmed, she settled into the same seat she had always used. Outside the small oval window a movement caught her eye. Tim stepped away from the plane; Marc followed. In a wind-rippled puddle, Marc's tall reflection danced on the tarmac. His strong profile was turned to her. The wind lifted his hair and whipped it around his forehead, flapped the pointed collar of his jacket against his cheek. It tore at her heart to watch him, but Korey could not look away. He pushed up the cuff of his jacket to check his watch then turned to scan the tarmac. Obviously he had not seen her slip aboard. Fine. Let him think she wasn't coming.

Tim, pointing northeast, touched Marc's arm to bring him around. Korey leaned forward, her nose to the window, following the line of Tim's outstretched arm to where a large patch of cerulean sky split the clouds. The storm that had pelted the city with rain most of the morning appeared to be breaking up. Korey wondered if the trip home might be in jeopardy because of the weather. "Please, no delays," she whispered to the window. Her warm breath fogged a circle on the glass. It had taken sheer will and much prodding from Matty to come this far. Now that she was here, all she wanted was to take to the air and have done with the flight—and Marc. The spot of blue sky was growing rapidly, the clouds chased and scattered by the wind. Through ragged holes in the clouds, shafts of sun shone golden spotlights on the mountains. Korey watched as Tim Penny's freckled face smiled up at Marc, then the men disappeared from view. She fastened her seat belt.

There were footsteps on the stairs, the flexing of metal. Korey's pulse quickened. She grabbed the first thing she could get her hands on, a copy of *Architectural Digest* and put it to her face. It would not have mattered if the magazine had been a special edition of *Field and Stream* devoted exclusively to the art of tying one's own fishing flies. Anything would do to serve as a handy hiding place.

"How long have you been on board?" Marc did not conceal his surprise.

The child in her took no small amount of pleasure in having sneaked onto the plane undetected. It was a tiny victory in a war of defeats. She kept her nose to the magazine. "Long enough," she said coldly.

Without another word Marc took the seat facing hers. She heard him sink into the soft leather, and from under the heavy slick pages of her magazine she saw his polished brown loafers stretch out to her, nearly touching her feet. Reflexively she drew her feet under her seat. Why had she not taken a seat nearer the back where there was no seat to face her? Now, of course, it was too late to change. She would stay put, would not have him know that his presence made her want to skitter away.

She felt some bumping, heard the chatting pilots enter the plane, heard the door latch. Marc's seat belt clicked into place. Korey turned pages in the magazine without seeing a picture or reading a word. The engines whined to life, impatient to be away. She felt a vibration through the flat soles of her shoes. Anxiety lodged in her breast; she breathed deeply. Normally flying did not frighten her, but this flight did. She would be trapped for the next few hours, locked in a noisy metal tube with Marc Bradberry, despoiler of dreams. The whine of the engines grew louder until it seemed to Korey like a mournful wail coming from within her.

Once in the air she sat with a stiff back against the seat, ready to endure the trip. From behind the safety of her pages she heard the rustling of paper—Marc most likely reading the Wall Street Journal. She glanced out the window. Nothing to see but an endless shelf of clouds, fluffy white cotton against a blue sky. Her brittle posture was beginning to stiffen her neck and make her arms ache. The magazine cover felt soggy under her finger tips. She yawned and her ears popped.

The newspaper rattled again, much longer this time. Then silence. Korey saw Marc's feet cross at the ankles, the toe of his right shoe nervously bobbing up and down.

"Finding that magazine interesting, are you?"

She said nothing.

"It's a long flight, Korey. Made even longer if we go out of our way to *not* talk to each other."

She pressed a button; the seat reclined a few degrees. She gave up the magazine, letting it fall open to her lap. He tossed aside the newspaper.

She met his eyes, stared at him for long seconds. As bad as she knew she must look, he looked worse. His eyes were hollow, presumably from lack of sleep; his hair wind-tattered. There was a small cut just under his nose where he must have nicked himself shaving. The small dark mole on his right cheek rode the ripples of his flexing jaw. She dropped her eyes. They were drawn to his dark socks showing beneath the cuffs of his khakis. The socks did not match: one navy, one brown. She almost smiled. Apparently his morning had been as trying as hers. There was some justice in the world, after all.

"All right," she said, surprised by the control in her voice. "You want to talk. Then go ahead. Talk."

He had hoped for this chance. But now that the time to tell his side had been handed him he thought it a useless exercise. Nothing he could say would justify what he had done. She looked gray, as if any moment she might cloud up and rain. The whole of her feelings for him seemed to show in her eyes. Through puffy lids, the eyes watched him as if he had just come slithering from under a rock.

Over his thoughts she said, "You amaze me. I thought you would leap to your own defense." Bitterly baiting him, she said, "What's the matter, your twisted rope of lies choking off your breath?"

Her cold stare was no less than he expected, but still it unnerved him. He offered a thin truth. "I've never lied to you, Korey."

As she thought about this, she reached up and adjusted a cloisonné comb that held her hair away from her face. The small light overhead painted purple shadows, like bruises, in the hollows of her cheeks. "From one point of view I suppose that's true. No surprise you would see it that way. Well, never mind about the fine print," she said impatiently. "Tell me about Clare. I want to hear every-thing—from your lips."

His mind dug into the past, beginning when he had met Clare at a party at Vanderbilt. The memories came in a rush of pleasure and pain. He spoke of Clare's alcoholism; his own long hours of working to build a business successful enough to satisfy Clare's extravagant tastes; his shock at finding out about the abortion when he hadn't even known Clare was pregnant; his decision to seek a divorce; his wife's tragic beating. He even took Korey step by step through the afternoon when he had chosen to put aside his wedding ring. He held nothing back, told her things about his life with Clare he had never shared with anyone.

Korey listened, stunned to silence by his frankness, her eyes seldom wavering from his. The pain of having failed to save his wife and his marriage showed plainly on his face. Korey wondered how it was she had missed seeing it before. Anger still occupied the largest portion of her breaking heart, but as he spoke, his voice firm and pitiless, she felt her most bitter feelings give way to a tiny bit of compassion.

The telling took an hour or more. "The attack was front-page news. People came forward to say they had seen Clare in four other bars in as many nights. The police followed hundreds of leads. All dead ends. Nothing. No witnesses. No weapon. No trace of my car. After a year, what slim trail there was is now as cold as Fairbanks in February." He shook his head. "I'll never know why she trolled the bars, flaunting her jewels. She was sick enough to invite a violent death as punishment for sins—hers and mine. And what better way to inflict pain on an estranged husband? Set yourself up for a street crime so your husband could for-ever carry guilt for not being there to save you. And if the crime were never solved? All the better! No closure for the husband. But even Clare, at her most twisted, could not have foreseen what has become her ultimate revenge. She sleeps….while I walk a treadmill and watch life pass me by." He paused for a much needed breath. "So there you have it. Ugly, yes. But an end to the secrets and half truths." And though the truth had been delivered posthumously over the ashes of their dead love affair, it was the best he could do. For better or worse, it was a cleansing.

It took a while for Marc's words to percolate through Korey's benumbed brain. When she finally spoke, it was to ask the obvious. "Why didn't you tell me all of this…before?" She let the thought hang, not wanting to say what was on her mind: *before I so willingly fell into your bed.*

"When we met, my marriage was of little consequence. Frankly, I had ceased *feeling* married long before you first came to my office. Ours was a business association, yours and mine. I never discuss my private life with business acquaintances. Even though at the time of Clare's attack the story appeared in the Chattanooga newspaper, few people in Chattanooga knew me as her husband or if they did, they usually had the good manners to not mention the sordid affair.

"I still visit Clare. Out of guilt, duty…. Unless I'm traveling, I see her about once a week. I never stay more than a few minutes. I sit. I pace. I pray—the petition varies: that she doesn't suffer; that our lives won't go on like this forever; that there will, one day soon, be an end."

Frightened by his last words, Korey almost flinched. She wondered how often, in moments flooded with despair, he had wished his wife dead. Korey suddenly felt detached, as if she did not know the man sitting across from her. He was a stranger with whom she was sharing a plane ride. And somehow this stranger had found his way into her heart. She trained her eyes on his face to bring her wandering mind back to what he was saying.

"….then you and I took a step closer, into something we mutually, but tacitly, defined as *friendship.* Friendship was good. I could be reasonably content with that. Through some mental gymnastics, I conditioned myself into believing I could live within the boundary of a platonic relationship. You see, I loved you from very early on. But I was certain you cared for me only as a friend, and I contented myself with that because it forced me to uphold that image. It kept me straight." He paused, shifted in his seat, rested his chin on steepled fingers. "Then, abruptly, it changed."

"Last November, at Gran Quivira."

"Yes, at Gran Quivira. You let me see inside you then, farther than ever before, to the very depths of your feelings for me. I don't mind telling you, what I saw scared me to death. I tried at that moment to confess, to stop what was happening to both of us. But I couldn't do it. I was terrified of losing you. I loved you too much."

"Or not enough."

Marc dropped his hands. "That's not true." His voice was firm in his own defense. "You had become the center of my life.…"

"Oh?" she interrupted. "The center, you say? So much the center, that after the flight home, you turned away without conscience, without the courtesy of even a slim excuse? You left me not knowing what to think, yet just the same thinking all sorts of things. Not the least of which was that I had scared you off by telling you my dearest husband, the center of *my* world, had killed himself!"

A look of genuine shock passed over his lined face. "No. For godsakes, Korey, it was never that!" He could not, even now, tell her that he had already known about the suicide. He would not have Korey thinking her own sister had had any part in his subterfuge. "I wanted to spare us both. I'll admit I took the coward's way. But I simply could not tell you about Clare."

"Really, Marc." She said it as if convinced he had misplaced a vast supply of brain cells. "You must've known there'd come a time when I'd find out."

He barked a dry humorless laugh. "I wouldn't let myself think about it. Too busy dream spinning, creating a fantasy world in which only you and I lived. Helluva thing, but I thought if I wanted something as badly as I wanted you, that it couldn't be wrong. Ill-timed maybe but not wrong. I fooled myself into believing that what we had was too special to not go on forever. It seems insane now, I know. It must have seemed insane then too, but we humans have an endless capacity to deceive ourselves if we work at it with diligence. Which it seems I did."

"Plead insanity if you will but don't expect me to buy it. Your behavior has been more infantile than insane."

"The thought of you walking away...."

"Damn you!" she flared, her simmering self control at last exploding in his face. "Oh, you're maddening! You in your elevated wisdom, so cocksure that's what I would've done!"

Her outrage did not surprise Marc. He had been waiting for it, deserved it, wanted to flog himself with it. What did catch him off guard were her words. He sat straight up in the seat. "You don't mean you would have let me hang around, not after you knew...."

"I didn't say that!" she snapped, stoking her anger. She looked him square in the face, her chin steady. "I don't know. However, I *do* know you should have been honest with me, left it to *me* to choose what was best for *my* life. I thought you knew me. You seem not to know me at all. I'm not some pleasure-driven bimbo you picked up in a saloon. You insulted my intelligence. You assumed I was incapable of comprehending the unthinkable strain you tote from day to day. In your arrogance, you treated me as if I were incapable of loving wisely enough to stay with a kind, wonderful man simply because he was unfairly chained to a wife known to be unrepentantly drunk, sadistically cruel, and indefinitely asleep!"

He was stunned. How could he have been so myopic? Korey was right. He had not given her the credit she deserved. From the beginning he had looked at this embroilment through the window of his own stupidity, never through Korey's more objective vision. Clearly that oversight had been the fatal mistake, an error perhaps more grave than keeping secret his marriage. To think, if he had been upfront about Clare, Korey may have had the goodness to open herself and take him, burdens and all, into her life. Misery blocked his throat like a bitter pill. He swallowed but found it impossible to speak.

Korey was not finished with her dressing down. "So you chose for me, damn you. And then stood back and watched me make an abysmal fool of myself."

His voice, when he found it, was filled with remorse. "I'm the fool. Not you."

She did not refute this. It was in her mind to have him stew in his own pot. A silence of minutes came between them. The roar of the jet's engines pulsated in Korey's ears, urging to new life the headache of the night before. She stared out the window seeing patchwork of farmland through gaps in the clouds. Her eyelids felt heavy; she longed to close them and drift into endless sleep.

But one question remained to be answered. It had niggled at her for the better part of twenty-four hours. She hesitated in asking, part of her afraid to open herself to further humiliation. Concluding at last that another blow to her wilted pride would be less painful than the unknown, she risked the question. "Tell me." She paused to clear her throat. Marc's eyes slid from his window to her face. "If you had not been….if it had been possible, would you have asked me to marry you?"

"In a heartbeat. Months ago."

"Oh." It came out in a sigh of surprise. What had she expected? Certainly not the love playing softly in his voice or showing on his face as though chiseled there. Why had she asked this of him? If he had sneered at her, said, "No, I was just using you, chump," it would have been somehow easier. After the sting of his callousness had worn off, she could have hated him. The hatred would have spread, filled her to overflowing, squeezed out the pain. But he loved her, and he was married to someone else. He loved her; she could never again trust him. He loved her; his love was of no use now. She wanted to look away from the sadness in his gaze, but his pain joined with hers to forge a bond that held her captive.

He saw clearly that she was fighting tears. "Korey, I'm sor…."

"No," she said, shaking her head. "Don't say it." A hammer was smashing against her skull from temple to temple and from the top of her head to a spot between her burning eyes. As she reached to massage the temples, the plane lurched, dropping the bottom out of her stomach. "Ohhh…."

Marc was beside her before she could think what had happened. "You okay? We hit a little turbulence, is all."

The ride was again smooth. She did not look up at him but stared blindly at the lap wrinkles on his slacks. "Yes, I'm all right," she lied. He was leaning over her, the scent of him filling her pounding head. She began to rub her temples.

"You sure?"

The head would not be ignored. In understatement she said, "I have a headache." She heard the squeak of leather when his hand gripped the high back of her seat as he reached beyond her to switch off the reading light, felt the seat move as he reclined it a little more.

He said, "I'll get you something for your head."

He came back with two white capsules and water in a disposable cup. Korey swallowed the pills as cool water soothed her dry throat. She thanked him, handed him the empty cup, sank back into the supple leather and closed her eyes.

Marc pulled a shade over the window to close out a ray of sun. He left her again to shortly return carrying a damp washcloth. He found her breathing softly, easily. A thick fringe of dark lashes rested against her flushed cheek. He folded the cloth and placed it carefully across her forehead. At the touch of the cool cloth she stirred but then settled again into an apparent slumber.

His lips brushed her warm cheek. "I love you," he whispered. "I would give you the world, Korey, if only it were mine to give." She felt the soft touch of his breath on her hair.

Weariness running to his bones, he took his seat and pulled his own window shade. His head fell back as his eyes closed. He did not see the tears of the woman facing him seep through her long silky lashes.

*   *   *   *

She had said, brusquely, that she would call for a cab. He had said, incontestably, that he would not hear of it. The drive from the airport to her home was made in suffocating silence. Korey felt every bump in the road; counted every click of the turn signal; read each sign that rushed toward the headlights; was conscious of every pitch change when Marc shifted gears. It had been the longest fifteen minutes of her life.

Now he crossed the porch and set her travel bag at the door. His back was to the only source of light—a coach lamp at the juncture of the walkway and drive—his face in shadow so deep she could see only the dark sockets that were his eyes. Her mind, in its current morbidity, saw a man on his way to the gallows, stooped under the weight of his guilt, a black cloth with two eye holes cloaking his head. She looked away from the grotesque figure.

Time became a terrifying symbol of doom as Marc and Korey each waited awkwardly for the other to take the first step toward their final parting. She knew he was watching her. She felt a tingling where his eyes touched her face. In the enduring silence, he reached with empty arms and gently coaxed her to him. She let herself be pulled close without actually touching. His hands felt light on her shoulders, yet his fingertips pressed her flesh through her clothing, as if he were torn between clinging to her or setting her free. She laid her forehead against his hard chest.

From a nearby tree, a mockingbird, refusing to join other birds in sleep, twittered a string of mimics. The calls were shrill, sometimes harsh. Marc interpreted the calls as a bitter scolding.

Something warm dripped on Marc's shirtfront just above his belted waist. Another drop. There were no sobs. Only a silent stream trickling from her eyes to the tip of her perfect nose. He crushed her to him, her wet cheek pressing his chest. She was limp, boneless, a rag doll in his arms. In the night air his shirt was a soggy chill against his skin.

He held her tightly, the longing to kiss her growing in him until he could almost feel her tears wetting his cheek, her mouth on his. But the perpetrator could not also be the consoler. He would not kiss her. For him to do so would mean no stopping. He set her away from him. She looked up with round startled eyes. He softened his abrupt move by tenderly running the pad of his thumb beneath those dark glistening pools.

He said, "May I unlock your door? Set your suitcase inside?"

She pressed her quivering lips together and shook her head.

Leaning to her, he barely grazed her cheek with his lips. Her thought was how much this last kiss was like the first. So many months ago….in the sticky heat of August as she had fled his office to race the rainstorm.

"Goodbye, my darling," he said now in a weak distant voice.

He felt himself move away from her, but his legs were lethargic, wobbly, as if they had not been used in a long time. The few yards from the house to the driveway walked like miles. He opened the car door and dropped into the low-slung seat. A quaking began in his depths, spreading rapidly to his arms and legs. Shaking even to his teeth, he gripped the steering wheel and held on for dear life.

She did not watch him go. His footsteps scuffed on the walk as she fumbled in her pocket for the house key. A car door clicked open then slammed shut as she pushed the key into the lock. The house opened its warmth to her. She slipped inside, pressed her back to the closed door and in darkness listened to the sound of wheels throwing gravel as the man she loved sped out of her driveway—and out of her life.

✳   ✳   ✳   ✳

Tears still flowed as Korey dropped the small suitcase on the floor of her bedroom. For the moment she was beyond caring whether the tears ever stopped. Tomorrow she would see it differently, she knew, but tonight there was something darkly romantic in being the mistress played false, bathing her bleeding heart in a river of warm tears. In the style of Old Hollywood, she itched to grab a priceless vase overflowing with flowers and hurl it, in grand drama, across the room. But this was not Hollywood of yesteryear where life played in the simplicity of black or white. This room held no fresh flowers, no vase conveniently available for shattering against a wall. This was reality in vivid, tormenting color.

Sleep. Suddenly sleep was all she could think of. If she could just close her eyes….escape for tonight the events of this dreadful weekend. Temptation loomed large to sprawl fully clothed on the bed. But her mouth—tasting like the inside of a moldy cardboard box—sent her dutifully seeking a toothbrush.

A bottle of Xanax tucked in a corner of the medicine cabinet caught her eye as she brushed her teeth. The pills had been prescribed to help her through Danny's funeral. Since that time she had used them rarely and only as a sleeping aid after a string of fitful nights had taken her to the brink of exhaustion. But if ever she needed something to help her sleep, tonight was the night. She rinsed her teeth, splashed cold water over her tear-streaked face, patted it dry with a soft towel. Because the prescription pills were three years old and likely had lost some potency, she shook out more than prescribed. The tiny white tablets slid easily into her empty stomach.

Quickly she undressed, donning an ankle length nightgown, her favorite cotton knit, soft as down and embroidered in daisies yellow as lemons.

It was when she reached to turn down the covers on the bed that she was slapped by a wave of emotion so electrifying she almost sank to her knees. She couldn't sleep in *this* bed! Not the bed she had shared with Marc. The very thought of sliding between those sheets made her stomach churn. Abruptly she turned an about-face and fled down the hall. The heels of her slippers raised carpet nap like fur on the back of a hissing cat.

Pulling a set of clean sheets from a drawer, she yanked the cover off the guest bed and tossed it on a chair. "A fine thing," she fumed, stomping from one side of the bed to the other, her face and neck rosy with fresh rage. "Chased out of my own bed." Grumble, grumble. High over the bed, crisp sheets snapped the air then floated onto the mattress like the silk of a downed parachute. "Damn you, Marc Bradberry," she said into a fat pillow as she wriggled it into its case, "I'll remember you for the weasel you are!" Letting the pillow land where it may, she flopped onto the bed and threw a loose blanket over her sagging body. As the mattress cradled her aching bones, she curled into a fetal position. The sheets smelled sweet and made a lazy crinkling sound as her limp wrist reached for the bedside lamp. Then a numbing blackness seduced her.

CHAPTER 21

▼

Korey lay in a gray haze somewhere in that final peace before the day's sorrows greet the open eye. A dream fractured and fragmented into kaleidoscopic chips. A shrill sound—a referee's whistle?—pierced the disconnected dream. She flipped onto her stomach, tossed a pillow over her head. The noise continued. Who, in the middle of the night, would be blowing a damn whistle?

Her face pressed into the mattress, she awoke gasping for air. It took some time before she realized the whistle was actually a ringing telephone. Finally disentangling her sluggish limbs from the grip of the blanket, she stumbled from the guest room to the adjoining studio, nearly knocking the telephone to the floor in her haste to answer it.

"Hello?" A frog could not have bested this croak.

"Korey? Korey, is that you?"

As if stuck for an answer, Korey voluntarily blinked twice. Her eye lids felt as though they were sliding over marbles. From her throat she cleared what could have been a fur ball. "Yes."

"Gosh, did I get you up? It's after eleven o'clock."

"In the morning?"

Tina said, "Of course, morning. That yellow glow outside is the sun."

"Kind of late," Korey mumbled, rubbing her eyes of thirteen hours sleep.

"Marc wear you out, did he?"

Korey ignored Tina's innuendo. "Imagine, almost half the day gone, and I'm still in my gown." She yawned.

"Korey, what's the matter with you? If I didn't know better, I'd say you were drunk."

Korey spied her own reflection in the smoked glass doors of a storage cabinet. She did look drunk: Hair sprouted from her head in unbecoming curls. If not for a petrifying fear of snakes, she would have admitted to being Medusa's twin. She expelled what was meant as a derisive laugh, but was more a labored wheeze. "Must be the Xanax. I took a handful last night. Well, not literally. Three....I think."

"Three Xanax. Why on earth...."

"It's a long, dreary story. One I'd rather not go into now."

Tina seemed nonplussed. After a pause she said, "How about meeting me for lunch?"

"I don't know...."

"Listen, obviously something's not right. Surely you're not going to keep yourself locked inside the house all day. Take a shower. Wake up. Meet me at Sonya's Garden at one o'clock. The lunch crowd should be thinning by then. I'll call Sonya and reserve the table by the corner window. The dogwoods and azaleas in the garden will be splendid today."

Korey knew that today *nothing* would be splendid. But lunch with Tina would be a way of getting her bearings before meeting with the new client at two-thirty. "All right," she said, with little enthusiasm. "One o'clock. See you at Sonya's." Without saying goodbye, she hung up the phone.

*   *   *   *

"You look better than I imagined you would."

Korey made a quick hand motion over her face and hair. "It took some work to look *this* good. But we both know I still look like hell."

"Oh, pooh." Tina absently overstirred her iced tea. "You're a bit flushed is all and maybe a little puffy around the eyes."

"Nice. Puffy and flushed. What a grand impression I'll make walking in on a new client looking as though my face is about to burst."

"Believe me, only your sister, who knows you so well, would even notice. And speaking of knowing you well, you're not the picture of happiness I expected to see returning from New Mexico. What happened this weekend that caused you to knock yourself out with pills?"

There was no avoiding the inevitable, but the thought of reliving the weekend gave Korey heart palpitations. She said, hesitantly, "Prepare yourself for a shock."

"Korey, what has happened?"

"Marc is married."

The teaspoon clattered into the ice filled glass. Tina's cheeks paled to the color of the dogwood blossoms fluttering beyond the window. "My hearing must be going. I thought I heard you say Marc is married." She began to smile at the absurdity but stopped on studying Korey's face.

"Nothing wrong with your hearing. Marriage to Marc is out. Seems Mr. Bradberry already has a Mrs."

"You don't mean it?" Tina was breathless, as though she had just completed a ten mile run. She stared into Korey's glistening eyes. "But of course you do. What a stupid thing for me to say. It's just….I'm so stunned. All these months….how could he…. Oh, shut me up, Korey. I'm babbling and being absolutely no help." Unstrung, she slumped into silence.

Korey turned her head to the window and gazed introspectively at clusters of azalea bushes glowing red, like flames, in the sunshine. "Amazing, isn't it," she said, "how easily a man living in another city can have such a secret? And not until I fly halfway across the continent do I find out about his wife. I shutter to think how long he may have kept me on the end of his string if I hadn't gone on this trip."

Tina ventured to ask. "You never suspected?"

"No. Incredible, huh? I could pass for the village idiot. There were so many holes….you already know some of the things I questioned. But those holes were like trifling pieces missing from a jigsaw puzzle—an irritant maybe, but not reason enough to altogether give up the fun of working the puzzle. I *assumed*—how irresponsible that word seems now—he wasn't married, and, because he never mentioned an ex-wife or children, that he had never been married." Gazing beyond her sister's shoulder, she looked into the past. "I don't even recall when I first noticed that he wasn't wearing a wedding ring. At the time it must not have been noteworthy. Anyway," she said, bringing her focus back to Tina, "we were close friends for a sufficient length of time for him to confide his marriage to me before….well, you know. The past two days I've been pretty hard on myself for not having seen what in hindsight I shouldn't have missed. But I've begun to understand that only someone more jaded would have suspected that he was married. In other words, I've begun to forgive myself for my blindness."

For the sake of her sister, Tina checked her rising anger. "How did you discover….the marriage?"

"In the most freakish way imaginable." Cognizant of the time constraint—Tina would return to work in thirty-five minutes—and her own emptiness of spirit, Korey concisely related the events of the weekend. Her voice was bland, as though dead to all emotion.

Too thunderstruck to do otherwise, Tina listened in silence, her delectably arranged fruit salad still untouched on its chilled bed of greens. She heard it all, from the chance encounter with Mason Wills through Korey's flight home. During Korey's recitation on Clare Bradberry's injury, an unsettling thought scratched at a closed door in Tina's mind. Something about this was strangely familiar.... From a remnant of memory came a vivid scene: Spring, a year ago in John Wexler's law office; a tall dark-haired man exiting through the rear door; the receptionist saying the man's wife had been attacked.... Was it possible Marc had been that faceless man? When Korey had finished, Tina could only mutter, "Sweetie, no wonder you're shell shocked."

Korey shrugged. "Well, today I performed a counter attack. I boxed the clothes he left in my closet and dropped them on his office porch on my way here. Spiteful, I suppose, but exhilarating."

Tina tried her salad but seemed not to have the stomach for it. She said, "In a way I share some responsibility for what has happened."

"For godsakes why?"

"I feel as if I encouraged the romance."

A small bemused smile curved Korey's mouth. "To my memory Marc and I didn't need much encouragement. Our feelings grew without outside influences." She nibbled a corner from her chicken salad sandwich.

"Last fall I had an opportunity to steer him away from you. But I didn't. If only he had dropped a clue...."

Korey stopped chewing. "What are you talking about?"

"Marc took me to lunch in early October."

"Lunch?" A frown marred Korey's brow.

"He came to me to buy the Samsara he gave you on Halloween. He asked me to have lunch with him. It was time for my lunch break, I was curious about his motive, so I accepted. It was quite innocent. In fact, we spoke almost exclusively of *you*."

"Me? But why?"

"Even then it was clearly apparent that he was very much in love with you. He seemed to have a....it's difficult to describe....a craving to know everything about you. You were as much a mystery to him at that time as he was to you. Oh, he tried to be nonchalant about it, but I saw through him right away." Tina shook her head in disbelief. "There he was, wanting to practically get inside your skin when he was, of all things, hiding a wife...."

"I still don't understand what he wanted from you."

Tina realized she was on the verge of saying too much. Nothing good could come from the revelation that it was she who had first told Marc of Danny's suicide. So now she carefully worked around the subject. "I'm not sure he knew exactly what he wanted. At lunch he wasn't wholly comfortable as if his purpose wasn't clear. He seemed to be groping for ways to satisfy a hunger."

"And you're not talking about food, are you?"

"No, not food. His hunger was for you. I saw it plainly in his eyes when he spoke of you. Knowing now that he's married, I can see that he must have been fighting a furious inner battle, pitting his sense of decency against a raging desire. He wanted to make you part of his life but was at the same time frightened of what he might do if you were. I suppose he felt safer in coming to know you through me, your sister and confidante."

"What you're saying makes sense to a point. But it loses plausibility when you think of it in terms of happening six months ago. Marc was a friend...."

"Honey, that's where you're wrong. At the time, I know that's what you *believed*. But if the two of you had faced the truth, you would've seen your love for what it was. And I thought he was the catch of the decade: gentle yet self assured, handsome, successful. Perfect for your second chance at happiness."

"Yeah....I had been thinking along those same lines," said Korey wistfully.

"I hope you're not angry with me for keeping the lunch with Marc to myself. It seemed important to him that you not know."

"No, I'm not angry. Confused, is all." Korey waved a dismissive hand. "Just another tidbit to add to a long list of strange things that Marc has done. At least now we know the reason behind his behavior."

Tina checked her wristwatch. Sun glanced off the dial face and danced across Korey's ecru blouse. "I've got to get back to work. Alice fumes if I'm even two minutes late. You going to be okay?"

"Talking to you has helped. My condition has been upgraded from absolutely horrible to simply awful."

Tina smiled. "Then there's hope for you."

"Actually, I feel numb. Like a fist is holding tight the anger, frustration, embarrassment—all the things I should feel—ready to sock me with a killer punch as soon as my defenses are down." Setting her napkin beside the nearly full plate, Korey began to push her chair away from the table.

Tina did the same then suddenly stopped. A burst of laughter from the kitchen echoed among empty tables draped in clean yellow linen. The sisters perched as if something had them on the edge of their seats. Tina said, "Forgive me, Korey, but I can't seem to stop myself from suggesting....would it be so terrible for you and Marc to continue the way you were? Good grief, stop gaping at me as though I'd suggested you peel to the waist and dance topless on this table."

"Migod!" Korey's words seemed to vibrate with shock waves. "I do believe you actually mean it!"

"I do mean it," stated Tina reasonably. "Look, Korey, he's been your lover."

"Thanks for the unnecessary reminder."

Tina ignored her. "It's a new millennium; no one's going to think the worst if you remain Marc's uh…."

"Mistress?" Korey was surprised by how easily the title had come. "I almost wish I could. It was different before…." She shook her head. "But now I know about the wife. I don't have whatever it takes to carry on an affair with a married man. There's no permanence in it; I can't live that way. Marc didn't even hint at such a possibility, thank goodness. I'd like to think it's because he has a few scruples left. Don't hold out any hope, Tina. There isn't any. You've seen the last of Marc Bradberry. You'll do me the greatest favor if you never again mention his name."

Tina opened her mouth then closed it.

In a firm, steady voice Korey said, "I know you'll be there for me. If I need to talk, I'll come to you. Try not to worry about me." As though it had been her sister, not herself, who had taken a severe blow to the heart, Korey reached across the littered table and rested her slender fingers on Tina's hand. "Patience," she said. "This will take time. Just let me handle it in my own way."

*   *   *   *

Through clouds of memories came a vision of a life lost. With index fingers hooked at the small of his back, the man prowled the length and breadth of the house. The clock read 2:36 a.m.; full moonlight illuminated the rooms. Dressed only in pajama bottoms, oblivious to the morning chill, he paced: around the sofa in the living room; circling a mahogany table in the dining room, aligning a chair; switching on the television in the den, staring blankly, switching it off; scraping his hip on a sharp corner of the island in the center of the kitchen; stubbing a bare toe on the copper leg of a plant stand; pausing in the bedroom to stare at the bed with its covers undisturbed. Repeated hour after hour. Night after night.

*   *   *   *

Korey worked in her studio, her life measured by daylight, darkness and the chiming of a grandfather clock. Daily, through the window, she counted new rose blooms uncurling their petals in the warm sun, but she seldom went outside to inhale their sweet perfume. At the slightest nudge of wind, the older blossoms, unpruned and fading, spilled their sad, neglected petals to the ground.

For weeks hers was an abysmal existence. Cloistered much of the time, she sewed until her hands ached and her fingers stung with needle pricks. Preferring her own bleak company, she saw Tina infrequently, Bryan less, and others not at all. Phone messages left on her answering machine were rarely returned.

Alarmed by a spreading rumor that she was unwell, those closest to her voiced mounting concern into her machine:

"Korey, my dear, you're not deserting your mother-in-law, are you? I haven't seen you in weeks. Please call to let me know you are all right." *Beep*

"Korey. It's Rob. What's going on over there? No one has seen you. Bryan says you're okay, but I have my doubts. I'll grant you another week of solitude. Then I'm coming over to see for myself." *Beep*

"Korey, Tina tells me my youngest child has suffered a setback. What's so terrible that you can't talk to your dad?" *Beep*

"Korey, I know you're going through a rough time. But is this—letting yourself go, closing yourself off from those who love you—is this what you meant when you said to me, 'I'll handle this my own way?' Dad is worried about you. Please call him." *Beep*

Not until late May did Korey find the will to turn her life around. It was a warm day, heavy with moisture, when Korey recounted to Tina an event of the night before—a seemingly mundane trip to the grocery store had become something quite different and had jolted her from weeks of apathy.

The sisters were on the private balcony of a second floor apartment, deep in the first true conversation they had enjoyed in weeks. Only three days before, the apartment had become Tina and Bryan's place of residence. In April the couple had listed their house for sale; a buyer had appeared almost immediately, stunning the owners with an offer that matched the slightly inflated asking price. Only one problem arose out of this good fortune: The buyer wanted possession of the house before the end of May. Not to throw any obstacles in the way of such a quick sale, Tina and Bryan had left behind their home of seven years, put much of their furniture in storage and moved into the small apartment they would call home for the time it would take to finalize plans and build their new house.

Today was Korey's first visit to the apartment, a Wednesday, and the last of three days Tina had taken off from work to unpack boxes and hang curtains. Tina set her iced tea on the deck of the balcony, the glass instantly making a wet ring on the concrete. "You're going away?" she said, surprised by her sister's announcement. "But where?"

"I wish I could say, 'To the dark side of the moon,' but as it is, I'm sticking closer to home. I'm going to North Carolina to see Dad and Stella."

"When did you decide this?"

"Last night. Late. After something happened to snap me out of my destructive stupor. I phoned Dad early this morning. Caught him just as he was leaving for the golf course. He said I was welcome to come and stay as long as I like. I'm going to deliver a finished quilt next Monday, pack a suitcase on Tuesday, toss another project in the car and leave a week from today."

Tina was encouraged to hear some of the old strength returning to Korey's voice. A stay with Dad would not be a panacea, of course, but it was bound to help. "Good. Go. Don't think about anything but being with Dad and Stella among those beautiful pine trees. I'll watch after things at your house; water the roses if we don't have rain and take care of the house plants."

"Thanks." Korey massaged a sore joint on her right hand. "It feels good to finally be taking a small step forward."

"Yes, you've begun to crack that shell you've built around yourself. Things will get better. You'll see."

There was a pause during which Korey showed no sign of corroborating Tina's apparent optimism. She was instead studying the acres of rooftops that shimmered in the sun.

Tina said, "So, are you going to let me in on what happened to you last night?"

"Huh?"

"You said something happened last night that made you decide to take this trip."

Korey took a long drink of tea. Ice cubes slid forward in the glass, bumping her lip. "Yes," she said slowly, remembering. "It was around nine-thirty. I was in the studio sewing, one eye on the TV—an old John Wayne western—when my stomach reminded me that I hadn't eaten since breakfast. You know how lax I am about keeping enough food in the house, so you'll not be surprised to learn that when I checked the refrigerator, there wasn't much there beyond a heel of bread and the light bulb. Without so much as a glance in the mirror, I grabbed my purse and took off for Red Food.

"There I was, at ten o'clock, scooting up and down the aisles, the shopper from hell: cut-off jeans, no makeup, hair uncombed. In record time I had enough food to last several days so I made for the checkout counter. Only one lane was open at that late hour and there were three or four people ahead of me. So I'm standing in line, my growling stomach serenading those around me. I'm reading the cover of one of those silly tabloids. By the way,"—she grinned with little cheer, as if smiling were an effort—"thought you would like to know, Elvis *is* alive, disguised as a bag lady and living on the streets of Cleveland."

Tina chuckled. "Figures."

"Then," Korey continued, "I….I heard this laugh…."

Korey looked away, toward a row of tall trees beyond a parking lot, but not before Tina saw tears soften those sad brown eyes. Giving her sister time to sort out her feelings, Tina scanned the courtyard and swimming pool below. Afternoon shade had not yet slanted across the vacant pool, and the sun's sharp rays danced on the glassy water. Tina's eyes darted away from the painful glare. From behind a glowing green spot floating across her line of vision, she found Korey again turned to her.

Regaining control, Korey said, "It was Marc, of course. At the head of the line, joking with the cashier, laughing as if he hadn't a care in the world. And there was….," Korey paused to clear her throat, "….there was a gal standing near him taking part in the fun, a small sack of groceries in her arms. She was very pretty, extremely well put together and had a rage of strawberry blonde hair.

"So I wouldn't be caught staring, I hid behind the woman ahead of me who was, thankfully, of abundant circumference. When I heard the cashier thank him, I stole another look. He was walking toward the door, his companion saying something to him over her shoulder. I couldn't take my eyes off his receding back. He wore that Ralph Lauren shirt I gave him for St. Patrick's Day. You remember—the emerald green plaid."

Tina nodded.

"All I could think was how well he filled out the shirt, how those shoulders had felt under my touch…. I was so lost in the sight of him, I didn't notice right away that he stopped just before reaching the door and stood there, looking at the window. I thought he was trying to find his car in the parking lot. Then I realized he had seen my reflection in the glass. Everything slowed—Marc's motion of turning, the voices around me—like the world was running on dying batteries."

"What did you do?"

"Nothing. Just stood there, flummoxed, my heart pounding out of my chest. Suddenly it was just the two of us in that store, with no space separating us. I could read in his eyes a terrible stirring of surprise and longing and pain. He must have seen something similar in mine because his mouth curved into a tiny smile that seemed to say: 'I know, I understand, I feel.'" Korey's voiced ebbed as she took a moment to savor the memory. "Then, shyly, he dipped his head, and I was snapped out of my trance by a gruff voice from behind calling to my attention, none too politely"—she dropped her voice to a coarse mimic—"'Lady, you're holding up the line.' Sure enough, it was my turn to check out. The cashier's good humor had vanished, and she fixed me with an awful scowl for being the cause of a lengthening string of restless customers. I'm sure my face turned every possible shade of red. Thank goodness, when I glanced to the front of the store, Marc was gone and so was the blonde with the wasp waist and painted-on jeans."

A warm breeze skimmed the pool and lifted a whiff of chlorine to the balcony. Korey absently rubbed her nose. "On the drive home last night I realized I had been living in dread of running into him. With his office and my place being in the same area of town, it was bound to happen eventually. But at the grocery, at such a late hour....who would have thought?" With an impatient hand she brushed at a gnat that had been annoying her ear. "Seeing him....the shock of it tore me apart. I didn't sleep a wink last night. If I'm ever to have a moment's peace, I have to put time and space between us. I couldn't bear to run into him again, seeing him with someone else. Silly of me, but I never thought of him dating....this soon."

On impulse Tina reached for Korey's hand. The hand felt thin and too cold on such a warm day. "Hey, you don't know that he's dating. Just because there was a woman hovering around him last night....well, that doesn't mean much. There are bushels of single women who are not at all bashful about making the first move. Marc probably attracts women wherever he goes, without provocation." Even as she said it, Tina wondered what had compelled her to speak up for Marc. After all, to speculate on his dating activities was pointless.

Korey put Tina's thoughts into words. "Well," she said dismissively, "whether they were together or they weren't, or she was one blonde or twenty, it doesn't matter anymore."

"No, I don't suppose it does. You're doing a wise thing, honey, going to Dad's." A silence came between them. Tina sipped tea and tried to stop her mind from going back to the past weekend. She could not. In her head it was once again Saturday night. She and Bryan, attending a dinner party on Signal Mountain at the home of Todd and Ulla Swafford, had come upon a scene for which they were unprepared. She had not told Korey about it, nor would she. Of all people to be at the Swafford's…. She and Bryan had spied Marc immediately, his dark head nodding above a small circle of guests on the crowded patio. Furtively, she had watched him as he moved from one cluster of guests to another as if bored—or restless. He was alone; no showy blonde hanging on his arm that night. He spotted Bryan first, then his eyes fell to her where she stood at her husband's side. His smile was trimmed at the edges, as if he were unsure of how he would be greeted. He made no move to join them across the flagstone patio. But Bryan, gregarious sometimes to a fault, smiled and raised his hand in a friendly wave. She, for appearances, did the same, but her smile felt stiff as she turned her back to Marc and rejoined the lively chatter among a cluster of their friends.

She had not seen him again. His place at the lavishly set dinner table was conspicuously vacant. After dinner, with the party spreading through the spacious house, she found a moment to coax the hostess into a quiet corner. "Ulla," she had said, "Marc Bradberry….he was here but left before dinner. May I ask why?"

Ulla Swafford's smiling face had suddenly closed. "Ump. Something about pressing business in Nashville. Told me not ten minutes before I summoned everyone to dinner. Business indeed! On Saturday evening?" Ulla had cocked her small coiffed head and, with heavily painted, close-set eyes, searched Tina's face. "You know him, obviously. How well?"

"Only casually," Tina had lied.

"I had never met the man. Invited him out of kindness. His wife, poor dear, was—goodness me, I shouldn't speak of her as if she were dead—*is* a close friend of my sister-in-law. Well, Mr. Bradberry's first appearance in this house was also his last. How rude to not tell me early on that he could not stay. The very idea…."

Korey's soft voice broke into Tina's reflection. The image of Ulla, in layers of periwinkle silk, fluttered away like a butterfly.

"It will be such a relief," Korey said.

Tina turned to her. "What will?"

"Getting away from here for a while. Knowing there will be no possibility Marc will be picking out a can of peas in the next grocery aisle, or lurking near the hammers at Ben's Hardware, or pulling into the lane beside mine at the next stop light. For weeks I've feared all those things and more. I'm letting that fear drive me away. But I don't care."

"Hey, you're practically apologizing for going to visit your own father. Nothing wrong in wanting to get away, nothing cowardly in the desire to take a break from your troubles. Don't second-guess the motive. Just go. Eat Stella's fabulous southern cooking; rub a coat of wax on that old thing Dad calls his *errand* car; make a huge pine cone wreath for the porch of my new home; float off to sleep each night in that monstrous waterbed in the guest room. Do all those things," she said, "and you will come home renewed."

Korey asked, with a sly sidewise glance, "I'm wondering, does this recommended *therapy* come with any sort of guarantee?"

"Nope." Tina stood, stretched her brown arms over her head, then picked up the two tea glasses.

"I thought not." An impish smile lighted Korey's eyes. "Free advice....worth every penny you pay for it." She too stood, plucking her clinging blouse away from the moist small of her back. She sighed. "Wouldn't it be nice if we could somehow rub away the terrible stuff of our lives? You know, like erasing rude remarks from a chalkboard."

Tina paused, her hand on the door to the apartment. "Yeah," she said, "if only it were that simple...."

*   *   *   *

As he leaned back, the tilting coil flexed, and the chair yielded easily to his heft. He massaged his eyes with the heel of a hand then stared with blurred vision at the ceiling. The sun had been down for half an hour, and the room was somber with imminent darkness. On the desk a computer sat unused along with a pair of cast-off eye glasses. A halogen lamp threw white light onto papers scattered in disorganized stacks. In the strong reflected light, his face was whitewashed. All day he had been nursing a sour stomach, had downed a half bottle of Tums. He still felt sick.

Last night....next to no sleep. Today....punishing meetings and deadlines....hours of work yet to do.

Korey's startling reappearance into his world had shot through him like a bolt of lightning, searing her picture into his brain. He could not stop thinking of her. Last night she had looked spent and what little color there was to her face had drained the instant her eyes met his. Yet, pale and drawn, unkempt as he had ever seen her, she was still his beautiful Korey.

Her vulnerability had tugged at his instinct to protect; his willful arms had wanted to sacrifice the sack of groceries for her. In those few precious seconds when she had held his gaze, he was visited by a rapturous fantasy: His gleeful arms carelessly dropping the groceries, he rushed to her; she did not rebuff his touch but welcomed it; oblivious to the stares, the piercing bleep-bleep of the cash register, he heard only the blending of two beating hearts as he crushed her to him, coddled her, stroked her hair.

Of course, he had not tortured them both by acting on the fantasy. Those dark eyes, wide with shock and unrepressed pain, leapt at him from her pale face and stopped him cold. He had done nothing. Even though his tongue had burned to speak, he found he could not utter as much as hello.

Figuratively, he had run from her. The instant Korey had looked away, he left the store, brushing aside the advances of the transparently clingy woman who had latched onto him in frozen foods. Now, nearly twenty-four hours later, he did not recall how abrasively he had discouraged the chatty pest when she began trailing him to his car.

He rocked forward. The chair pitched him against the littered desk. His chin came to rest in his hands; lamplight bleached his rolled shirt sleeves. Deep contemplation severely creased his brow. He must, he thought, change his way of doing things, find a way to spend far less time in Chattanooga. The city had become poison to his already ill system. First, the Swafford party on Signal Mountain, the rotten luck of seeing Tina and Bryan Goodwin. Then, only three days later, running into Korey at Red Food. It was too much; he was wound so tight another jarring like last night would send him flying apart.

Starting now, unless his presence in Chattanooga was critical, he would stay away. In his stead he would send Steven Aymes. Steven was capable of handling anything. A fun-loving bachelor, he should have no objection to spending several nights a month in the Chattanooga office, especially if the pot were sweetened with a travel bonus and use of Marc's own private upstairs living quarters.

An important decision made, Marc turned off the desk lamp. He was alone, the downstairs office emptied for the night. Hit by a strong gust of wind, the old house groaned. A squirrel dropped to the roof from the overhanging oak tree and scampered from one eave to another. Marc rocked to and fro in the chair, as an ancient man might do on a porch. Images of better times, when Korey had been the sunrise on the horizon of his days, drifted across the darkness.

To have set eyes on her, possibly for the last time, had been heaven—and hell. For him, she could no longer be real, but she would become an ethereal vision, one he would carry for....how long? He wanted to believe that she would be in his heart, in his soul, until the end of his days.

CHAPTER 22

▼

The fairways and putting greens at day's end were empty, all golfers gone—either home or to the clubhouse where liquor flowed and put a florid shine on noses already sun-reddened. With grass sheared like velvet, the golf course spread in long green fingers over rolling hills. Nothing disturbed the serenity: no ball cracking off the head of a club; no talk of hooks, slices, three under or two over; no temper tantrums or expletives. Birds singing soprano heralded the beautiful evening. In scattered blue ponds, boastful bullfrogs vibrated the windless air with their resonant bass.

But while no golfers remained, the course was not entirely deserted. Two people—a man past middle age and a young woman looking too thin in baggy plaid shorts—walked briskly up and down gentle hills on the meandering cart path. From time to time they would vanish into a stand of pine trees, then could again be seen following the edge of a fairway, green and flawless as emeralds. To anyone glancing through a window in one of the many houses fringing the course, the walkers would seem to be chatting lightheartedly, each head turning now and again to meet the other. But a close observer would see something quite different. Neither Korey nor her father was lighthearted. And theirs was not idle chat about the fresh cooling air, or the intimacy of their solitude, nor the golden radiance of a lowering sun.

Boyce Reynolds had a frown set between his thick graying brows. "So, this Marc fella, he's not only an obstruction in the way of your happiness, but he's created another full scale mountain for you to climb." Oh, the anger he felt toward this man he had never met! What had Marc Bradberry done to this daughter who had, at the suicide of her beloved husband, been left brittle to the point of breaking?

"Another mountain to climb," she said, as if the very thought robbed her of all confidence. "No, this time it's more like I'm tunneling through, using a spoon."

"I know, honey. I felt that way when we lost your mom. Just getting through the day....putting one foot in front of the other was a chore. Terribly unfair for Marc to put you through this. Helluva thing...." He had not wanted his anger to show but knew he was not hiding it well. Damn the boy! What had he been thinking, toying with Korey's affections, and—perish the thought—no doubt her body, as well.

They had been walking together for nearly an hour. And, though neither was consciously aware, the experience—sharing confidences; probing feelings—was a resurrection of a father-daughter bond that had, because of a separation of miles and lifestyle, lost some tensile strength. Today was reminiscent of days of childhood when Korey had carried to Dad the task of disentangling a messy math problem; repairing a greasy bicycle chain; or, when Mom wasn't available, advising a love-struck teen on the best way to reel in that *hunk* who sat third row center in history class. Now once again she had come to Dad, this time bringing with her an ache far beyond anything imagined in her younger years and one for which Boyce Reynolds had no easy fix. No math computation, sophomoric advice to the lovelorn, or slight of hand with a wrench would work magic here. But Boyce was doing his best to console his youngest, this child grown to a fine, beautiful, yet star-crossed, woman.

"This is a thorny business, Marc having an office in Chattanooga," Boyce said. "You running into him....well, unpleasant, to say the least." Thinking of what he would like to do to Marc Bradberry, he kicked from the path a nine-inch pine cone fallen from a stand of longleaf pines. The cone tumbled end over end, then rolled into a rough of knee-high ornamental grass. "Tell me," he said, "have you thought about getting away from Chattanooga?"

She smiled. "Um. And I thought I *was* away."

As her hand swung to the beat of her stride he grabbed it, squeezed gently and swung with her a few paces before letting go. "I was thinking of much longer than the three days you've been here. Why, you're already talking about going home."

"Oh, that's just talk. But I don't want to wear out my welcome."

"Impossible. Stella and I meant every word yesterday when we said you're welcome to stay as long as you like."

"You're sweet, and I love you both for your generosity...."

"But…."

"I'm harboring some guilt. I can't just walk away, abandon my obligations indefinitely. My business won't run itself. I have a house to look after, a yard to tend. And, not the least of it, my behavior lately with people I love has been dreadful. I left home without telling anyone but Tina where I was going. I must go back to the real world." She added vaguely, as if shying from any kind of dead-line, "Soon."

"Yes, you do have to go back to the *real* world, but you needn't be in such an all-fired hurry to do it." His eyes teased. "Without you, the world won't wobble off its axis. At least, not right away. Now, may I bring up something I've been mulling over?"

Korey slowed her pace. "I'm almost afraid to hear it. You're wearing your 'I've come up with something revolutionary' look."

Boyce laughed; the deep sound carried far over the deserted course. "Nothing so profound. Just an idea I had."

A sweet smell touched her nose then was gone. She found the fragrance famil-iar, but her mind took no time for identification. "Okay," she said. "Out with it."

"How would you feel about staying away from Chattanooga for….well, let's just say an extended period?"

In astonishment, she gaped at him. "Surely you're not suggesting I give up my home, allow Marc to run me out of town!"

"Certainly not. What I'm proposing is that you give yourself the gift of new surroundings. Perhaps for a year or so."

Korey opened her mouth to object. But Boyce's suggestion appealed to her subconscious—that less courageous person living deep within her who, given the chance, would run from life, pausing only long enough to locate the nearest exit.

From the corner of his eye, Boyce watched a mix of emotions contort Korey's face. Was he detecting a weak link in his willful daughter's armor? "No need," he said, "to remind you of how mean spirited life has been to you lately. So do your-self a favor and leave behind the reminders. How do you expect your wounds to heal when they're constantly being reopened?"

"Laying it on pretty thick, aren't you, Dad?" She looked along a fairway to where white sand traps sat like bowls of sugar. The pristine air, still ringing with birdsong, was minus the fumes from anything motorized. She thought of this place as one that could nourish a human spirit, especially one so near starvation as hers. "Are you suggesting I come to North Carolina, to be near you and Stella? I don't know if…."

Boyce shook his head. The sun, sinking behind tall pines, tinted his smooth white hair to a salmon hue as delicate as the chamber of a conch shell. "Much as I—we—would love to have you close, it's not here that I have in mind."

"Oh. And just where is it you want to pack me off to?"

He hoped the hurt, the rejection he now heard in her voice would vanish once she understood his reasoning. "New Mexico," he said.

"New Mexico! You're not serious? Good grief, as if I don't have terrifying memories waiting for me there!"

"Memories, yes. But terrifying? Only if you let them. They're not unconquerable, Korey."

She weighed the truth of what he said. "What would I *do* in New Mexico?"

"Same thing you're doing at home. Make beautiful quilts. Or teach school on an Indian Reservation. Learn to make pottery, weave rugs, work on a dude ranch."

She laughed at that one. "A dude ranch? Why, I've never been on a horse. Dad, have you lost your...."

"No." He patted the top of his head. "The hair on this head may have grayed prematurely, but I assure you, my darling daughter, there is nothing wrong with what's inside."

Korey suppressed a grin. True enough. And he was, after all, thinking only of her welfare.

"So, what do you say?"

"What can I say, Dad? Part of me finds the idea irresistible."

"And the rest of you?"

"Points an accusing finger and calls me 'yellow' for wanting to run."

"Nonsense. Tell you what. To soothe your pride we'll call it a sabbatical."

"Sabbaticals are for people like Bryan, teachers and...."

"You're a teacher."

"Dad, really. Seventh grade? That's a bit of a stretch."

"Dammit, girl, why are you being so mule headed about this? What do you have to lose?"

She had no logical answer. "But why New Mexico?"

"Why *not* New Mexico? That part of the country brings out a spirituality in you that I've not seen anywhere else. Something almost mystical. With the limitless horizons you'll have space to convalesce, to heal."

Korey saw it all in her mind's eye: mountains, desert, red mesas. She had last seen New Mexico from the window of Marc's plane. The words *New Mexico* seemed synonymous with pain. Could she forgive the land for the wounds inflicted upon her while on its soil? "Oh, Dad," she said. "I don't know...."

At the eighth green, a water sprinkler halted their stroll. A plume of water, like that thrown by a regatta, swung across the cart path. In the light of a red sun, rubies of water dripped from the tips of long needles as the mighty plume fired into pine trees edging the green. Korey wiped a fine mist from her face.

Boyce patted her arm as they stepped around puddles and resumed their walk. "It's all right," he said. "No more fatherly advice."

"I'll think it over. A sabbatical, huh?" She plucked playfully at the sleeve of his knit shirt. "I kind of like the sound of it."

*   *   *   *

While Boyce and Stella spent the afternoon in blistering sun whacking a hard, white ball around a golf course, Korey was grateful for the solitude. She sat alone on the patio in the sheltering shade of the house, her hands working a needle. A troublesome germ inflamed her mind. New Mexico. After three ponderous days, she had made no decision whether or not to act on her father's suggestion. One minute she was titillated by the romance of it; the next, all temptations vanished in a stream of practicalities. She ran her thumb over the nubs of a thimble as if hoping the answer to her quandary were written there in Braille.

A humid breeze flapped at a corner of the fabric in her lap. In swaying tops of pine trees sixty feet above, three crows squawked like a bee of old deaf women. On lower tree trunks, black-capped chickadees scritch-scratched along the thick layered bark, ferreting insects. Sunburned pine needles formed a thick mat around the recently swept patio. Their smell, deliciously sweet, made Korey think of melting caramel just beginning to scorch. On a gardenia bush, the first creamy-white blooms of the season released an exquisite perfume that mixed splendidly with the aroma of the pine needles. Korey abandoned her sewing as the fragrance, stirred by the wind, exploded around her. She breathed deeply as if the sweet air were an elixir. In response, tension drained from her body. A smile touched her full, unpainted lips. Ahh, if only this magic potion could be bottled....

Though her eyes were closed, Korey's vision was suddenly clearer than it had been in weeks. She saw the road to New Mexico as uncluttered, free from the 'hows' and 'what ifs' that had stood in her way. She would take that open road. She would phone Aunt Matty and solicit Matty's help in seeking employment and a place to live. Matty seemed acquainted with half the people in the state; she would sniff out something suitable.

For two days following Korey's initial call to her aunt, the telephone lines between North Carolina and New Mexico buzzed with energetic conversation. Matty Cunningham had first received Korey's unexpected news with a startled sputter, followed by a joyous whoop. And Matty had not laid a moment to waste. She contacted friends and quickly put together a list of opportunities for her niece's consideration. By the evening of the second day the long list of possibilities had been narrowed to one interesting probability.

"....I've known the Sanchez family for thirty years, Korey." Matty's voice was enthusiastic. "They're good people. It's Maria Sanchez who needs live-in help. She lives south of Albuquerque, a drive of well under two hours. Her husband died four years ago—lingering cancer, poor soul. Maria herself is not well. Nearly crippled with arthritis. Her daughter, Marcelina Encho, lives in my neighborhood. Marcelina's daughter—Maria's nineteen year old granddaughter—has been living with Maria the past year. But this fall, about three months from now, the granddaughter will be coming back to Albuquerque to attend the University. Marcelina has tried to talk her mother into moving to the city but to no avail. Maria remains adamant about not leaving her home. Frankly, I'm on Maria's side. It's not easy, as we get older, to think of giving up our homes. Anyway, Marcelina has seen the futility of trying to persuade her mother to move and is in search of someone trustworthy to live with Maria. On my recommendation alone, Marcelina is willing for you to be that someone."

"Gee, Matty, I don't know....this is not the kind of thing I had in mind."

"I know. But you must understand you'll not be taking on the job of nursemaid. Maria's not an invalid. Far from it. She's a fighter, but she's slowing down. I see it each time I visit her. Mostly, she needs companionship, and someone to help with the heavier housework. She lives in an isolated area—nothing rare about that out here, as you know. She dislikes driving so you would drive her to town for supplies, doctors appointments, things like that. She's a kind, gentle woman, Korey, easy-going but fiercely loyal to those she loves. It would not take her any time to count you among those she loves. I've no doubt of that."

"Flattery."

"Not at all. You and Maria would get along famously."

"Because she's a friend of yours, I'm fond of her already."

"Well, what do you think?"

"I think I'm tempted."

"Good."

"When would Maria want me to come?"

"We've not discussed dates, but I would guess around the second week in August."

"The timing seems perfect. That would give me the summer to finish some projects and make arrangements about my house. I don't have to decide tonight, do I?"

"Heavens, no. The urgency you hear in my voice is my excitement at the prospect of having you so near. But Marcelina, understandably, would like an answer soon."

"I never would have thought of it myself, but this offer may just be the perfect thing for me right now. Please tell Marcelina that I'll have an answer for her within two days."

"Splendid. I'll relay the message. By the way, if you should choose to come, what would you do about leaving your house?"

"Funny you should ask. Today I discussed that very thing with Dad and Stella. We've come up with what seems an ideal solution. I'd like to convince Tina and Bryan that they would be doing me a great favor by living there while I'm gone."

"But didn't they just move into an apartment?"

"Yes, but they have a short-term lease. And last week they had a setback on the start of construction on their house. The contractor had an emergency triple heart bypass, so the house probably won't be completed until next spring. Something tells me Tina would rather spend the winter in the comforts of my home than in that tiny apartment."

"An arrangement too attractive to refuse."

"Hopefully. To have the house occupied by two people I love and trust would save me a lot of worry."

"Well, good luck, my dear, in putting together your plans. We will be talking again soon."

"I'll call the minute I know my own mind. And, Matty, thanks for all your help."

"Happy to do it. That's what aunties are for. Besides, I would go to any lengths to have you near me for however long you might stay. For now, I'll free the air waves by signing off with, 'hope to see you the middle of August.'"

"That's my wish too, Matty. Truly it is."

*   *   *   *

The decision to live with Maria Sanchez was easily made. Now all that remained was to break the news to Tina. Not by first choice did Korey do it over the telephone, but she would not wait until arriving home to tell her.

"Gosh, Korey, what a surprise! But I must congratulate you on your wisdom. Going to New Mexico sounds like a wonderful idea!"

"I take no credit. Dad put the bug in my ear, where it buzzed around for a week."

"And you said nothing when we talked three days ago."

"I didn't want to say anything before I'd made a decision. If word had spread throughout the family, everyone would've wanted to have their say. I was in enough of a dither without having to juggle a half dozen conflicting opinions."

"No argument there. This is coming at a good time, Korey. But you're my best friend. I'll miss you so. We all will."

"And I'll miss you. For that very reason I almost chose not to go. But hey, this isn't a move, just an extended stay. In a few days I'll be back in Chattanooga, and we'll have a summer of fun before I leave for New Mexico. And while I'm out there, we'll phone and write."

"Ha! I haven't written a letter in years. *You'll* write. *I'll* phone."

"Fair enough. Say, Tina, I wonder if you might do me a favor?"

"Name it and it's done."

"Someone should be in the house to look after things while I'm gone. Would you and Bryan please stay there?"

"Careful! Remember, you're talking to a gal who only a short while ago lugged dozens of boxes up two flights of stairs. Um….this will take some thought."

"Well, while you're thinking, picture this: comfortable house with plenty of room; all the modern conveniences; lovely yard; lots of privacy. A perfect love nest to share with that handsome and affectionate husband of yours."

"You are a born saleswoman."

"Then I'll count on the house being left in good hands."

"I'll talk it over with Bryan tonight, but I'm sure he'll agree."

"Great. Then it's all but settled, and it'll be a load off my mind. I'll be home soon. I'll call you the minute I finish unpacking the car."

CHAPTER 23

▼

Dearest Tina,

Is it possible the third week in September could come so soon after my arrival in New Mexico on August 17? My first weeks here have been a blur of new faces, names, and places.

Now, to fill you in on some things not covered in our brief phone conversation last week. I continue to meet more of Maria's immense extended family. From an ancient grandfather to the smallest child, everyone has welcomed me with open smiles and warm hugs. Theirs is a close-knit, loving and very social family. Most weekends find us at one home or another, gathering for a party of festival proportions. Music and dancing are the very heartbeat of the parties and never in my life have I danced as much! I suspect Maria's grandson, Peter—Marcelina's seventeen year old son— has developed a crush on his grandmother's new companion for he has taken it upon himself to teach me every raucous dance he knows. I leave the parties with barely enough energy to drive home!

We meet at homes in locations that branch out from Maria's like spokes on a wheel. From Socorro to Albuquerque to Santa Rosa to Roswell. Sometimes that means a round trip of over two hundred miles, but I'm seeing some gorgeous country and loving every minute of it. Maria and I both look forward to the weekend outings since during the week we are quite isolated and if not for the companionship we give one another, we would be very lonely.

Matty had told me, of course, that Maria lived in the Manzano Mountains, but not until I arrived did I understand the loneliness one can feel at being so far removed from a large city. With Mountainair the nearest town and a population of only 1170, although picturesque, it is a town sleeping high in the mountain sun and not what we would call a hot bed of activity.

Maria's house is small but comfortably inviting, made of adobe and looking as if it simply sprang from the ground. It's within hiking distance of the pueblo ruins of Gran Quivira, and if not for the windbreak of thick juniper trees surrounding the house, we would see from the window in the kitchen that ancient ruin crowning its hill.

Beyond the house, over much of Maria's one hundred acres, is blooming sage, short clumps of chartreuse springing from the dry brown earth. Sometimes I go alone past the rear of the house, past the tall stand of junipers so I have an unobstructed view, and I stand so still my only movement is my breathing. Here I see the sky of shining blue come down to touch the yellow sage, and I breathe the sweet dry air and there is no sound other than what my mind speaks, and in a fleeting fancy I think this is what heaven must be like. But in the next moment I'm homesick for green Tennessee hills, trembling blue lakes, and chuckling waterfalls. As I become more at home in these new surroundings, I'm sure my longing for Tennessee will become less keen, but still I'll continue to miss my home state, my dear family and friends.

I've grown very fond of Maria and find much enjoyment in time spent with her. She is infinitely kind, her smile and smooth brown skin reflecting a sunny disposition—this despite the nearly constant presence of pain. She weaves the most beautiful rugs I've ever seen (count on receiving one as a housewarming gift for your new home!) and works tirelessly at her loom. Her arthritis is localized mostly in her hips and knees, restricting her ambulatory movements, but, thank goodness, thus far her nimble fingers remain pain-free.

She is teaching me to cook in the traditions of her family in Old Mexico and those of her late husband's Native American family. Slowly I am developing a taste for the spicy foods, but I fear I may never match the enthusiasm I see Maria and Matty show for the really hot stuff. On my return home, if you and Bryan are feeling adventurous, I'll prepare for your enjoyment a meal guaranteed to have tears rolling from your eyes and steam from your ears!

As I mentioned on the phone, Maria has a horse called Sundancer. A beautiful golden animal—of which breed I know nothing—gentle, but to yours truly, who barely knows a mane from a tail, I find the large animal very intimidating. Sundancer is the only horse Maria kept out of a herd of eight. The rest were sold after her husband, Mike, died. Also sold with the horses, to a neighboring rancher, was a small herd of cattle. The empty corrals have now fallen into disrepair, but Maria rebuffed the family's suggestion of having them torn down. A part of her life with Mike that she will not let go. I sympathize and understand those feelings only too well, so from time to time I grab a hammer and a fist full of nails and set right a few boards that hang askew. With my patchwork, maybe the corrals will be presentable, if not functional, for the years Maria remains in her home she shared with her husband of forty-two years.

I've learned that Pooler Jones, Underwood Tack, and Jayne Hill are not neighbors but types of barbed wire. Before you begin to form a false picture of your little sister as a tried and true ranch hand, let me set the record straight. Most of what I do involves helping Maria with household chores and being her willing chauffeur. (Even when her health was good, apparently she never did like to drive and left most of it to Mike). I have no aspirations to become a wrangler! This does not, however, mean that I will shirk from doing that of which I'm capable.

Fortunately there is someone else Maria can call upon for help with heavier work and repairs exceeding my skills. He owns the adjoining ranch and is, at three miles away, the nearest neighbor. I have yet to meet the man (he's either very elusive or extremely busy), but as time goes on Maria seems to bring up his name more and more frequently. Repeated stories abound, and I believe, since the subject of this man seems the only area in which Maria's memory is failing, she fancies herself a matchmaker and is convinced she is being sly about it. Out of the blue she will say, as if for the first time: "You know, Jim Yellowhawk is a bachelor. Never been married. Can't imagine why." Or, "After all those years of struggle, Jim Yellowhawk's ranch is now paying its own way, handsomely." And, "Jim Yellowhawk, he's like my Mike, he can trace his people to several tribes. He's big and strong and all the ladies like him, though he's not as good looking as my Mike." She has even gone so far as to say he will teach me to ride Sundancer. Poor man! I suspect Mr. Yellowhawk has not even been consulted about these proposed lessons nor could he be prepared for the challenge he would face in teaching me, the greenest of the greenhorns.

What is to come of all this strategy and intrigue? Nothing, I'm sure. I've said nothing to Maria to dampen her fun and won't for a while. But as you well know an involvement with anyone of the male gender is at this time the very last thing on my mind.

And speaking of men....I will surprise you—and myself—by writing here of Marc; a short, final paragraph. Through a slow leak, my anger has drained, but there's still a private place inside me where Marc makes unwanted appearances. Even though I expect to never again hear from him, it has become very liberating to be in a place where he could never find me if he should try. Finally I have freedom from the fear that each time the phone rings it could be Marc, and the terrible collapse afterwards when it is not. Now I barely give a second thought to the ringing of a phone or a tap at the door. I know so few people here beyond those in Maria's family. Here, there is great comfort in anonymity.

Love and hugs,

Korey

*   *   *   *

He had begun to make her nervous, this strange, taciturn man. For well over an hour he had labored on the broken water pump at the windmill near the corral. And for the better part of that time he had been stealing glances in her direction. Each time her eyes sought to confront his, his would dart away, feigning a myopic focus on mending the pump.

The furtive looks were not the only reason Korey was uneasy in this man's presence. From the moment she had answered his rap on Maria's rough plank door, Korey felt, strangely, that this was not the first time she had laid eyes on Jim Yellowhawk. A memory had flickered, then died. Now he watched her as if he might feel the same. Impossible. Before this morning, when he had responded promptly to Maria's plea for help with the broken water pump, Korey had never seen Jim Yellowhawk. But Maria had spoken of him so often, Korey had carried a picture of him in her mind, one that no more resembled the real Jim Yellowhawk than DeVito resembled Swartzenegger. The Jim of her imagination had been much shorter than this giant of a man. Much older too. Not quite Maria's sixty-seven years, but perhaps nearing fifty, his short dark hair salted with gray. The man now squatting beside the disassembled water pump was nearer thirty than fifty, and, from under a wide-brimmed hat, his jet black hair fell to halfway down his broad back.

Even though a dearth of words had passed between them, as the morning opened its arms to her Korey had chosen to stay near the windmill, careful to keep out of Jim's way. She told herself she remained because she thought she should become initiated to the mechanical workings of a water pump. Living on a ranch, she should know these things. But more than that, the real reason she stayed near Jim Yellowhawk was to discover why he touched a familiar cord in her. Korey squinted, her eyes following Jim as he stood against a climbing sun. He wiped his beefy hands on a oily rag.

"'Bout does it, I think. Now just to hook it up. She oughta work." He spoke not to Korey but to the pump, his warm breath clouding the air on this crystal morning at September's close.

"Mind if I watch?"

"Nope." His black eyes blinked at her before he bent to the pump. Where had he seen this woman? When she had opened Maria's door to him earlier this morning, her simple beauty had stunned him. But his mind had soon been taken up with other things. He had assessed the problem with the pump, knew he had the necessary replacement parts at his place and had rushed off the get them. He made the return trip in record time, trading his aging pickup truck for the more rugged Jeep Wrangler with a roll bar and abandoning the paved highway for the rougher but shorter overland road. Not until he began work on the pump, when Korey had joined him beneath the windmill, did he see in the rising light a face he had seen before. This woman was less haggard than the one in his memory, but there was no doubt she was the same woman. But how could it be? Maria's new companion had been in New Mexico only a few weeks. He could not have seen her in town; he would remember a new, pretty face. Korey Westerfield was from Tennessee, Maria had said. He had never been east of Tucumcari. Where could their paths have crossed? A two hour mind search had found no answer.

Korey shooed a horsefly from her hatless head. She told herself she should be in the house, helping Maria with the cleaning. And she should get away from Jim Yellowhawk—never mind that Maria thought the world of him. The way he looked at her was downright creepy. But curiosity made her want to stay just long enough to see the pump running. To block the expanding sunlight, she reached into a vest pocket for her dark glasses and slipped them on.

When her movement proved a distraction, Jim glanced out of the corner of his eye. In the next instant, his head swung full around to stare at Korey. That was it! He straightened to his lofty height. Like a slash of white light, a wide smile lit his rugged brown face. With an oily thumb, he tilted his dusty hat from his eyes. "Well, I'll be doggone," he said.

"What."

"It's you."

"Of course, it's *me*!"

"Glad to see they don't have you locked up at the Socorro County jail." As though he thought this a wonderful joke, he roared with laughter. He almost told her how much prettier she was now than when he had seen her last, but the storm gathering on her face was warning enough.

Korey's fists landed on her hips. This bumbling ox certainly had a funny way of ingratiating himself. Words slid from her acid tongue as she demanded, "You will be kind enough to explain that remark."

"Speeding. I'm talking about the way you drive. On our last encounter, you were flying toward me like a bat out of....uh, like you were out to set a land speed record at the Bonneville Salt Flats." His voice, free of ridicule, made it plain he was only teasing her. The dark glasses shielded from his view the confusion in her eyes. But he imagined he could hear files flipping inside her head, searching....

A slender finger flew to her parted lips. She said, as if in awe of the potent power of incredible coincidence, "Last April! On the highway! It was you who stopped to see if I needed help."

"Yeah. I *knew* I had seen you someplace."

"Me too."

"But for the life of me, I couldn't remember where."

"Yes, exactly."

"Then you put on those sunglasses, and I knew. You seemed distressed that day. I hesitated to leave you there."

"It was nice of you to stop."

"You got to where you were going all right?"

"Yes, to my aunt's home in Albuquerque. I was visiting."

"I see." He did not ask why he had found her heading east when Albuquerque was north. "I'm sorry about the joke just now about your driving. But I thought, if you made a habit of going those speeds...."

"Not anymore, I don't."

The rapid exchange ended suddenly. Even Jim, by his own admission not the most perceptive of men, could see that Korey did not want to talk about the circumstances surrounding their chance encounter. "Well," he said awkwardly, "let's see if we can get some water flowing through these pipes."

Sometime later, after Maria filled Jim with her spicy fried chicken and full-bodied coffee, Korey walked with him to the Wrangler. "I don't know what Maria would do without you, Jim. She adores you like a son."

"My mom died when I was seventeen. I guess Maria has taken her place. And Mike, well he was a second dad to me. I miss him." He heaved a tool box to the rear floor of the Jeep.

Korey surveyed the vehicle. "What happened to Wilhelm?"

"Wil...? Oh, you mean my truck, Wilbur."

She giggled. "Yes, of course. Wilbur."

"Wilbur's been ailing. Lately I've had to nurse him along, patching here, patching there." He lifted his hat, wiped his broad brow with his shirt sleeve. "'Fraid he may not be around much longer. Suffering from old age. Hate to give him up, though. He's been a good friend."

"You sound as if it were a horse, not a truck."

"When you've been over as many rough roads together as Wilbur and I have, you form a bond. But you can't drive everywhere. Some places you just gotta have a horse." He set his hat over the cascade of shining black hair. "Maria says you don't ride."

"Horses, you mean? No. That's what comes of being raised in the city. Only horses I'm acquainted with are under the hood of my car." With the toe of her boot, she absently flaked dried mud from a caked tire. She admitted, "A horse frightens me a little. I've been perfectly content all these years to view a horse from the side, or head-on even. But looking *down* on a horse, now that view is another matter entirely."

"You'll be staying with Maria for a time?"

Korey nodded. "How long, I don't really know, but probably close to a year anyway."

"You should learn your way around a horse."

"Is that an offer to teach me to ride?"

He smiled. "Yeah. And to shoot too."

Her head snapped up. "Wait a minute. Are you talking guns? Because if you are, my fear of horses pales in comparison to my fear of guns." Her alert eyes swept the landscape. "I don't see anything around here I'd need to shoot."

"Fact is, you're a heck of a lot safer here than in the city. Up here, we're short on muggers, rapists, and purse snatchers." He hooked a thumb into a pocket of his oil-streaked jeans. "'Course, there are critters you need to be aware of. Coyotes, a few rattlers."

At the mention of snakes Korey paled, put her palm to her forehead and groaned. "Oh, God." This was turning out to be far more than she had counted on when she had accepted this job for room, board and a small stipend.

"Now, don't let 'em worry you. Chances are you won't see hide nor hair of either one. They don't much like people. Just the same, it's good to know how to protect yourself—and Maria."

Korey felt as though she had stepped back in time into a culture for which she was ill prepared. She looked into Jim Yellowhawk's open face. He was right. Unaccustomed as she was, to make the most of her time in this land she would have to live by its unyielding rules. And here, filling her vision, stood someone obviously very capable and willing to teach the skills she needed.

She had never much believed in destiny, but now it was difficult to ignore the probability that there was a purpose for Jim Yellowhawk stepping into her life. Even for friendship, it would take courage to again trust a man, courage she was not sure she possessed. But opening to her was a chance for new companionship. Someone other than Maria to talk to, someone with whom she could share sunshine and clean air, maybe even an occasional sunset and moonrise. With Jim as a buffer, maybe the task of living day to day without Marc would be less painful. Should she take the risk?

Fleeting seconds passed before there was an answer, and it was in Jim's voice that it came. "I'll tell you, there's not another spot on Mother Earth where I would rather live. We're spread out up here and that's most of what I love about it. But if you need help, it can take awhile in coming. I would sleep better at night knowing you could take care of yourself."

Korey was startled by the tenderness she saw openly displayed in his deep-set eyes. He seemed a changed man from the stoic one she had met only that morning. Her smile was one of relief after a prickly problem had been resolved. "In that case, Jim Yellowhawk," she said, reaching to shake his callused hand, "if you're willing to teach, I'm willing to learn."

✻   ✻   ✻   ✻

"How is it you've been here almost two months, and you still don't have a hat?"

"I *do* have a hat." For emphasis, Korey touched a finger to the hat bill.

"That cap you're wearing isn't a hat." Jim Yellowhawk tugged at his wide brim. "*This* is a hat."

This was to be the day Korey first rode Sundancer, but at the moment Jim seemed more interested in her attire than her horsemanship. They were at the stable, Korey leaning on a corral fence post. Jim's wide hands filled the back pockets of his faded jeans; his long boot was hooked over a rail.

Suffering from jittery nerves, Korey was anxious to get on with the business at hand. "Look, at this point fashion isn't uppermost in my mind, so if we could just…."

"Fashion?"

He was laughing at her again. To her chagrin, each of the few times she had been with Jim, she had unwittingly supplied him ample ammunition for teasing.

"Is that what you think this is…." He brushed his hat with his palm, disturbing the red dust on the high crown. "….a fashion statement?"

"I only know cowboy hats are the *in* thing, even in the South."

"I don't know why people wear them back east…."

"South," she stated with regional pride.

"Wherever. But out here they're very functional. We wear them for protection: sun, rain, sleet, snow, wind, sandstorms. Why, I'd as soon go out without my pants as my hat."

Korey turned a little pink.

"Besides," Jim said, "you should quit hiding behind those dark glasses. Your eyes would show better in the shade of a wide brim."

Korey felt her face grow warm as her blush deepened. She was not at all sure how to take his remark about her eyes. Jim Yellowhawk was not a charmer like some men who toss flattery about like cheap trinkets. "Okay." Her hands rose and fell. "Where do I go to get an honest-to-goodness *hat*?"

"I may know just the place." He pushed off from the fence. "Come with me."

Korey heard Sundancer whinny and looked toward the stable, greeting with mixed feelings the delay of her inaugural ride. Jim, oblivious to her turmoil and without a backward glance, started the quarter mile to the house. Korey ran to catch up and stretched to match his long easy strides. Near the house Wilbur sat waiting; the wide chrome grill seemed to grin as they approached. Korey laughed to herself: why, that old truck *was* almost human.

Blocking Korey's view, Jim grabbed a door handle, reached into the truck and removed something from the seat. When he turned, he held in his large hands a Stetson hat the color of brown sugar, the low crown banded in silver conchos the size of nickels. He said, hesitantly, "Hope it fits. I don't have much experience buying hats….for women."

Behind her sunglasses, Korey felt tears sting her eyes. That this man, whom she knew only slightly, would be so thoughtful…. "Oh, Jim, it's beautiful. I…." Words failed her.

He held it out to her. "Here, try it on."

She took it. The felt was cashmere-soft against her hand. She yanked the frayed ball cap from her head and dropped it in the dust. The new hat settled on her head as if it had been specially blocked for her. Vanity drew her to the large square mirror bolted to the truck door. The mirror had a small crack, like a star, in the upper corner where a stone had hit, but it did not mar the grinning image staring back at her. "Oh, Jim," she said again. "Thank you." With her hands, she lovingly caressed the brim, then traced a finger over the silver conchos. The silver was warm with sun; as she bobbed her head, tiny beams of light pierced the mirror.

Jim came to stand beside her. His hair, as it was the first time she had seen him, was pulled back and neatly bound at the nape. For the first time, as she looked up into his shaded face, she saw him as handsome. Fluidly, as if he were accustomed to being this close to her, he reached with both hands and gently removed her glasses, carefully folding and dropping them into the breast pocket of her denim shirt.

"There," he said, looking into her eyes. "Now the hat is a perfect fit."

She grew uneasy in the gleaming light of his gaze and would have moved away, but with her back to the truck, she found her exit blocked. He sensed her timidity. Nearly losing his balance on a clump of scrub grass, he moved backward three steps, reeling in the evidence of his infatuation as he went. He said, in a very different voice, "Sundancer's ready and waiting for you. And," he added, his mouth curving into a smile a teacher would use to encourage a student, "you are ready for Sundancer."

*   *   *   *

Dearest Tina,

Gone from home over five months and this only my second letter—what would we do without telephones? Which is the only reason I'm writing today. We're in the midst of a blizzard and our phone is dead. You may, however, still hear my voice before receiving this letter since the half mile trip to the main road and a mailbox could be days away. By my guess, there's a foot of snow on the ground and still coming down hard. The junipers surrounding the house are barely visible in their white coats, like sailing ships moored in dense fog. And the wind! It blows across the mountaintop and heaps the falling flakes into drifts as tall as two men.

By deliberate design, Maria's little adobe house has a minimum of windows and is reasonably airtight—except for under the front door where we have rolled a large rug to keep out wind and snow. Everything we need we have in the way of food and fuel for heat. Maria lives prepared, accustomed as she is to winters here. At this moment I'm sitting near a roaring fire of piñon logs. Um, the smell is heavenly. This home, dim and snug and warm, makes me feel as if I've returned to the loving security of the womb.

This winter's above average snowfall has had its plus side (except when this southern gal finds herself struggling to drive in the stuff!) With nothing much else to do, I have attacked my needlework with great industry. As you know, a wonderful little boutique in Old Town Albuquerque has sold one of my quilts and is awaiting delivery on another, which I'll have finished by early spring.

Maria weaves her beautiful rugs while I stitch, and we engage in wonderfully endless conversations. Why, the topic of her family alone—courtships, engagements, marriages, births, divorces and deaths—has us talking for hours. We have found great comfort in each of us telling of the lives we shared with our dear deceased husbands. I have even told her about Marc, of how much I loved him and how he hurt me. Talking it out has helped, and it is with new lightness of heart that I report I can now look up the hill to Gran Quivira, even go there and stand on those cold gray stones, and not think at all of the raw November day I stood there with Marc.

One down side of the cold winter, a serious one, is that it has been hard on Maria's health. Her arthritis has worsened over the past couple of months, and I seem to be rubbing her joints with warm liniment more and more often. Marcelina is urging her mother to have the hips, and possibly even the knees, replaced. Maria is understandably resisting surgery. It will be a long process, each joint done at different times, with recovery and rehabilitation time between. She would be living in Albuquerque with Marcelina through it all, and she does not want to leave her home. I don't think I'm imagining that her hair is becoming grayer with worry. But in spite of her poor health, she has the most youthful, unflagging spirit, and our hours together are spent happily. She has even taught me a few of her favorite childhood songs—in Spanish, no less!

We have not seen Jim Yellowhawk for a while. I miss his companionship, especially our horseback rides together. He isn't one to chat on the phone, only calling regularly to ask how Maria and I are doing and if he can bring us anything from town. Ranch work keeps him very busy, and on long winter nights he does silversmithing, carves alabaster, and even does some sandpainting. I've never before known anyone so diversely accomplished yet at the same time so modest. It has taken me months to learn, by bits and pieces, of his achievements. Maria says he has won awards for his alabaster sculptures, but he has made no mention to me of awards. His larger sculptures command a high price. Little wonder. I have seen a few in his workshop, and they are beautiful. He's nearing completion on an alabaster buffalo that I would almost give an arm to have.

Jim is the rough and tumble sort (no three-piece suits in his closet), but in his way he is kind and gentle. Coming to know him has been like turning the pages in a book and finding a surprise on every page. Why, only two weeks ago I learned he has a small herd of buffalo! They roam the acres of his ranch farthest from Maria's. He took me out there once, and I glimpsed the herd from a distance. Nevertheless, I was close enough to appreciate what magnificent beasts they are. My brain cannot imagine a landscape black with herds, as they appeared in the days before "civilized" man slaughtered them for sport. Unlike his cattle, Jim does not sell the buffalo for meat but keeps them, as he says laughingly, "as pets."

I am delighted by your news that your house is coming along so well. Framed and under roof. With the mild winter weather you have been reporting, you and Bryan will be mounting drapes and hanging pictures before you know it!

Love and hugs,

Korey

*   *   *   *

Always an early riser, Matty Cunningham was up drinking coffee when the phone rang at 7:15am. She asked herself, as she picked up the phone, who would be calling at this hour.

"Hello….Hello?" Such a long pause ensued she thought it a wrong number and was about to hang up.

"Matty?"

"Yes. Who is it?"

"Marc. Marc Bradberry, calling from Nashville."

"Hello, Marc," she answered civilly after a moment of stunned silence. "I didn't recognize your voice." His tongue seemed slippery, and Matty knew it could only be her imagination that had her smelling alcohol fumes.

"You'd rather not hear from me." The statement was piteous.

"If that's what you think, why did you call?"

"To ask a question."

"Well, I won't promise you an answer," she said, "but go ahead, ask."

"It came over the grapevine that Korey's no longer in Chattanooga. Understand, I'm not trying to locate her. But it's been eight months…." Matty knew a sigh of desperation when she heard one. "I just need to hear that she's okay, Matty. That's all."

Through the clear phone line Matty heard bursts of ragged breathing. The man on the phone this morning was far removed from the calm, self-assured, sober Marc Bradberry she had known. This man was disintegrating. Matty hoped what few words she could offer would be of some comfort. "Korey is all right, Marc."

"That's what I had hoped to hear. Uh, when you talk to her, please don't tell her I called."

Matty did not tell him she had been instructed by her niece to never speak his name. Instead she said, not unkindly, "Don't worry, I won't say a word."

"Thanks. And Matty, thanks for talking to me, not cutting me off. Take care of yourself."

Before Matty could suggest he do the same, the line went dead.

*   *   *   *

Doctor Kevin Bradberry pressed the line of phone numbers that would connect him to his brother in Albuquerque. "Eric, it's Kevin."

"Hey, what's up kid?"

"Quite a bit. Listen, I can't talk but a minute. I'm at the office, between patients. Flu season, you know. The waiting room is SRO. I'm calling about Marc."

"What about Marc?"

"He's headed for trouble."

"What kind of trouble?"

"Lately his mood has been vile. Thinking he needed time and space to sort things out, I've given him a wide berth. That may have been a mistake. Unless I'm mistaken, the last few days he's been on a real bender."

"Drinking? Doesn't sound like Marc. What makes you think so?"

"Neither office has seen or heard from him in a week. Two days ago, after endless calls, I finally reached him at home. He seemed surprised that there were those who had begun to worry about him. My impression was that he had lost all track of time and wasn't aware of how long he had been away from the office. He insisted he was all right, just working at home for a while. He had been drinking. He didn't sound drunk, but his words were too deliberate, like it was an effort for him to concentrate on our conversation. I think the only work he is doing is that of draining a bottle."

"Sounds serious. Frankly, Kevin, I'm surprised Clare's death hit him this hard. He wasn't exactly prostrate with grief at the funeral."

"You're looking at this from only one angle. There is another. Korey."

"Korey? Why, he seemed to hardly miss a beat after the initial shock of their breakup wore off."

"And that was exactly why I became wary. He took it *too* well. He was crazy for Korey, yet within weeks after returning from New Mexico, he and Julia Santangelo were spied in every dim, smoke-filled nook in town. Every time I turned around I heard: 'Hey, Kevin, saw your brother with Julia last night at So and So's—man, does that woman ever have a great pair of legs.' I can tell you, Eric, I'm damn sick of hearing stuff like that."

"I thought you liked Julia."

"I *do* like Julia. That isn't the point. She's just not the right woman for Marc."

"And Korey is?"

"She may be the only one who has what it'll take to heal him. He's ill, eaten up with guilt and anger."

"But Korey's no longer in the picture."

"Not at the moment, anyway."

"Kevin, surely you don't think Korey would...."

"No. Wishful thinking. We don't even know where she is. Marc made such a mess of things with Korey then buried his emotions in a shallow grave. With Korey gone, and now Clare, the skeletons of his failures are washing to the surface."

"What do you propose we do?"

"I thought I'd drop by his place unannounced, see what kind of condition I find him in. I was hoping you'd go with me."

"I don't know....It's just been a month since I was there for Clare's funeral and I'm running behind. The Manzano Mountains south of here had a huge snowfall yesterday, and Rae and I have been hired to go there for a shoot."

"Eric, we're talking about Marc. He needs us—now."

"Okay, count me in. I have a photographer friend who may be willing to help Rae with the job."

"I don't have a second free 'til Thursday afternoon. That gives you a couple of days."

"I'll call the airline. I'll do my best to be in Nashville by noon Thursday."

*   *   *   *

Kevin Bradberry parked the car in the driveway of the sprawling stone and glass house. In silence the brothers traveled the stone walk, towering leafless trees stenciling black shadows upon their backs. Eric Bradberry rang the doorbell then scooped up three rolled newspapers, yellowed and soggy.

The two men waited. Kevin reached across his oldest brother and impatiently depressed the bell. When there was no response, Kevin said, "You wait here. I'll check the garage." He returned, moist dead grass clinging to the soles of his shoes, a frown pinching his round face. "I looked through the window. His Lexus is in the garage. Every drape in the house is closed."

"You'll have to use your key," Eric stated with controlled urgency.

Kevin sorted through a ring weighted with keys. He selected one and shoved it into the lock.

They found him in the den, lying face up on the sofa: eyes closed; mouth a gaping maw in a mess of black whiskers.

"Sweet Jesus," Eric breathed. In the ailing light, he studied the slovenly figure stretched the length of the long sofa. "Passed out cold." His flinty eyes joined Kevin's in sweeping what resembled a landfill. "Just look at this place."

"Worse than I expected," said Kevin, his senses stunned to disbelief by what he saw—and smelled.

The draped room had the look of twilight though it was mid-day. It reeked of liquor, cigarettes and food. Within a lazy arm's reach of the sofa, a glass, empty and knocked to its side, teetered on the edge of a low table. A dark stain circled the beige rug beneath it. Pretzel boxes and potato chip bags littered the floor; crumbs were ground into the rug at the sofa. Kevin's eyes traced along the hardwood floor and followed a trail of greasy crumbs that led into the room from the direction of the kitchen. On a mammoth desk, three whiskey bottles stood empty. Next to the bottles, in a microwave dish, was partially eaten lasagna, the noodles curled, a fork protruding from the cemented center like Excalibur from the stone. The coffee table was buried: tattered matchbooks; ashtrays overflowing with crumpled cigarettes, some looking as though they had barely been lit before being crushed; ashes everywhere. This from a man who, as far as Kevin knew, had never touched a cigarette. In an open armoire a television was tuned to George Strait warbling something about love gone wrong. Startling color leapt off the screen into the gloomy den.

Eric stepped over discarded shoes and socks to switch off the television. He looked to the doctor for guidance and sounded exhausted when he said, "Where do we start?"

"With Marc. We'll have to get him up and sober enough to eat some decent food." Kevin took Marc's limp wrist and held it while Eric opened a wall of draperies. Winter sunlight nearly blinded the two brothers as it rushed into the room. "His pulse is good," said Kevin.

"God, he looks terrible." Eric's gaze would not linger on Marc, as if he found the sight too ghastly.

"He's going to *feel* terrible too."

"I had no idea how much he was hurting."

"Probably been unraveling since April, but so slowly we didn't notice until recently." Kevin prodded his drunken brother. "Marc," he said three times into an ear. Sleep went undisturbed. With quick snapping motions, Kevin patted Marc's bristled cheeks. "Marc!" he barked, this time giving the shoulders of the snoring hulk a hard shake.

After a sputter and cough, the snoring ceased. Marc's eyes rolled wildly under closed lids, punching their way to freedom. Moments later two slits peered at the ceiling. Heavy eyelids opened as if slowly cranked by a winch, and swollen, blood-red eyes stood naked in the white winter light. One long blink later the eyes began to focus through an alcohol haze. A tongue, thick and sticky, dislodged from the roof of his mouth. Marc swallowed, and a mangy wet animal slid down his throat. He prayed for a merciful death and closed his eyes in preparation of deliverance.

Laid out in his casket, his eyes reopened to find his brothers Eric and Kevin leaning over him. Even in death his head throbbed—clearly a disappointment. Troubling too were his brother's faces: Absent were the expected signs of grief at his passing. They did not care that he was gone! Eric, that opportunist, had probably already stuffed the keys to the Lexus in his own pocket! And where was Mom? Surely she would have flown back from Aunt Helen's to bury her middle son—wouldn't she? This was no time to be a pessimist, but so far death had been a real let-down.

Kevin's voice intruded, loud as a church bell. "Welcome back, buddy, to the world of the living."

The bewildered corpse reluctantly scanned the wreckage in the part of the room it could see without moving its bloated head. No funeral parlor, this. A long deep groan rose from its sagging chest. In a voice washed in gravel, it spoke: "Oh, damn, I'm not dead."

Opening the mouth was a huge mistake. A greenish pallor surged up Marc's neck and into the black bush on his face. He clamped both hands over his mouth and darted from the sofa as though propelled from a slingshot.

"I hope he makes it," Eric said as Marc sped past, bare feet pedaling to the nearest bathroom.

From somewhere within earshot, a toilet lid slammed against a porcelain tank, instantly followed by sounds of horrible retching.

Kevin gave Eric a thin smile. "Well, at least he'll feel better afterwards." He pushed aside clutter on a chair and sat. Eric propped himself on a door frame, folded his arms to wait.

The toilet flushed, followed by more coughing and gagging. Another flush, then silence.

Someone was crushing his head in a vise. When his brothers came with plans to remove his wrinkled clothes, Marc snarled, "I'm not an infant. I know how to take a shower. Now get the hell out of my bathroom, both of you!"

Kevin and Eric were motivated to leave as clouds of steam filled the room, and a bar of soap sailed past their heads. From the hallway they moved in opposite directions: Eric, to the kitchen to prepare Marc a palatable meal; Kevin, to Marc's bedroom.

Drapes closed out all daylight. Kevin, expecting the worst, switched on a table lamp. The bed was a mess. At the foot, the bedspread flowed onto the carpet. Two blankets, knotted as one, hugged the carved headboard. In the center of the bed, a long shirt sleeve paired with a pants leg to twine into a top sheet. This room Kevin could handle; he would have the bed clad in fresh linens in no time. As for the rest of the house—he could only imagine in what condition Eric had found the kitchen—Mrs. Grayson, the housekeeper, would have to be summoned. Later, he would phone her, describe the task at hand, promise Marc would pay double the usual fee, plus a generous tip. Even at that, Kevin mused, Marc would be damn lucky if she didn't spin on a heel and flee the moment she saw the place.

Not until the close of the winter day was Kevin persuaded to leave his recuperating brother. Eric had unpacked his suitcase and had taken over Marc's spare bedroom. He would stay in Nashville for as many days as Rae and the photography business could manage without him. After a hot shower and adequate nourishment, Marc was left curled in a clean bed to sleep off an extraordinary hangover.

Eric walked to the car with Kevin. In the crisp evening air, light from a quarter moon became tiny stars in frost on the roof of the car.

Eric warmed his hands in the pockets of his jacket. "Where do we go from here?"

Kevin shook his head. "I'm not sure. So much depends on Marc's frame of mind when he sobers. Right now he's the sickest I've ever seen him. Maybe that will be incentive enough for him to stop this sudden love affair with the bottle."

"Hopefully. But staying away from the booze isn't the real cure."

Kevin gave in to weariness as his body sagged against the car door. "No. But you know as well as I that the medicine he needs for the cure is out of reach. She's gone, Eric. Korcy won't be the one to save him. And without her," his sigh was one of sorrow, "who can say when—or if—Marc will have his life back?"

CHAPTER 24

▼

Marking distinct depressions in the fine red dust, one set of shod hooves moved to join another along the fence line. Panicked by the approach of the second horse, a covey of quail, flapping and squawking, fled a haven of sagebrush. With a gloved hand, Korey leaned forward in the saddle and patted Sundancer's glossy neck.

Jim Yellowhawk, his weathered face cheered by a gleaming smile, brought his horse to a halt. "Morning," he said as he cupped his brown hands over the saddle horn. "Spotted you some distance off. Knew it was you. Recognized the hat."

Korey watched his grin widen. Was he so happy to see her after these many weeks, or was his ego showing because he had chosen the classy hat?

"With the sun glinting off the hat band," Jim said, "you're like a beacon in the desert."

Korey self-consciously reached up to touch the silver conchos. She smiled. "Since these were crafted by your hand, was that your intent?"

"No," he chuckled, "no premeditation. Serves that purpose, though."

Under his warm scrutiny Korey glanced away. The morning wind was cool on her face and rich with the scent of juniper.

Jim said, "You're out early."

"I'm checking the fence for winter damage. Wanted to get it done before going to Albuquerque on Friday, in case I need to buy anything for repairs." She looked along the fence line. "I haven't been out this far since the snows stopped." The early sun lighted her dark eyes as she turned her face to his. "And you?"

"I rode over to see about the buffalo cows. Some will be mothers real soon now. I was on my way back to the house when you caught my eye." He paused, then said, abruptly, "Wilbur died last week."

"What...Wilbur? What happened?"

"Engine threw a rod. He's beyond saving. He was a good one, but it's time to buy another truck." Jim gnawed his lower lip. "You said you're going to Albuquerque on Friday?"

Korey nodded. "Maria has an appointment with the doctor, and I have a finished quilt to deliver to a shop in Old Town. We'll spend the weekend in town. Maria will stay at Marcelina's, and I'll be at Matty's."

"I'm going in Friday to look at trucks." He took a deep breath. "I'll be at a dealership on Lomas. How about joining me in Old Town for dinner? We'll celebrate the first day of spring."

The invitation took Korey by surprise. Jim had never before suggested dining out. He had generously given his time to teach her to ride Sundancer and to fire the rifle that was now holstered on the horse's flank. So much of what she had learned about life in this land, she had learned from Jim. He was more than a friend; he had become an extension of herself. Having him around was like having an extra pair of senses through which she could come to know her surroundings. In her mind, Jim *was* this wild country. Until this moment, she had not thought of him outside the context of the ranch. But beyond the ruggedly handsome rancher there was a *man*. With a ripple of excitement, she heard herself say, "I'd love to, Jim."

"Great." Dancing sideways, his horse began to move away, but Jim turned in the saddle, his eyes not leaving hers. "The High Noon Restaurant, then. Say, around five-thirty?"

"Yes," she called over the spreading distance. "Friday, five-thirty at The High Noon."

*   *   *   *

"Well, I'll be...." Too stunned to finish, Eric Bradberry dropped his voice.

From across the narrow table, Rae watched her husband's lips twitter while he stared wide-eyed at something beyond her left shoulder. Prodded by curiosity, Rae began to turn.

"Don't," Eric said, halting Rae's movement. "Don't turn around." He raised the restaurant menu to where only his eyes were visible.

"Eric...."

"Study your menu," he ordered.

"But I already know what I want."

"Rae, please keep your head down and do as I ask."

Defiantly, she looked him square in the eye. "This is nonsense. What on earth is the matter with you? What's going on back there," she threw a thumb over her shoulder, "that you don't want me to see?"

"Not *what* but *who*. And I don't mind if you see *her*, but I don't think she should see *you*."

"Her?" The gauge climbed on Rae's temper. "Her? Who are you talking about?"

"Korey."

"What?"

"You heard me. Korey Westerfield."

"Oh, Eric, you've had one margarita too many. Someone who resembles Korey perhaps...."

For the first time since he had become distracted, Eric looked at his wife. "I'm telling you, it's Korey. No doubt about it. She's waiting to be seated. She's talking to someone. They appear to be together."

"Probably her aunt."

From behind the High Noon menu, Eric's eyes smiled. "Definitely *not* her aunt. Male. Very tall. Good looking. Indian....and vaguely familiar."

"Can't I just sneak a peek?"

From his hiding place, Eric chuckled. "Sorry, honey, not now."

"Eric, you're being silly. Why hide from Korey?"

His eyes went blank. "I really hadn't given that a thought. I reacted to the shock of seeing her. But something tells me she would not want Marc's brother and sister-in-law to know she's in Albuquerque. Oops! Here they come...." He ducked so only his sandy hair protruded from the crease in the menu.

Cooperating now to the fullest, Rae leaned an elbow on the table, cupped her chin in her hand and averted her face. As the couple passed near her table, Rae recognized Korey's voice before the smooth drawl was lost in the buzz of other diners.

Eric dared a look; Korey and her companion were nowhere to be seen. "Good," he said, "the hostess seated them in the patio room." He closed his menu, folded his hand over it. "As long as we leave first, Korey will never know we've seen her." With an impatient lift of his arm, he summoned the waiter.

After the dinner order was given, and they were once again alone, Rae said, "Korey must be visiting her aunt. But the man…. You said he seemed familiar. You've seen him someplace?"

In puzzlement, Eric's brows drew together. "More than that, I've met him. But for the life of me I can't think where. Too bad you didn't get a look. You remember faces much better than I."

Rae smiled. "So you finally admit it! Well, as it is, if you're to ever identify him, I suppose you're on your own." She sipped her margarita and languidly licked coarse salt crystals from her upper lip. "Are you going to tell Marc that Korey's in Albuquerque?"

Eric said reflectively, "Now that's a tough one. As you know, he's only recently begun to pull out of a long winter funk. True, Korey's in Albuquerque. But does her presence here tonight mean she'll be here tomorrow? And if so, I don't know that I'd tell him. Both Mom and Kevin report that Marc and Julia Santangelo are like this." Eric raised a hand and twined his first and second fingers. "Maybe I shouldn't muddy the waters by telling him we've seen Korey….and on the arm of another man, at that."

"Not *we*, Eric," Rae reminded him. "*You*. You have seen Korey."

"Okay, *I* have seen Korey."

Rae asked, "And *was* she on the arm of this other man?"

"Just a figure of speech, honey. But come to think of it, I didn't see any hand holding or anything. Korey certainly didn't look at him like a lover."

"No stars in her eyes?"

"Not that I could see from here."

Rae refused to accept that all was lost between Marc and Korey. Thinking aloud, Rae said, "If somehow we could find where Korey is living….then if you told Marc…." Eric raised a dubious brow, but Rae would not be deterred. "….would he go to her, do you think?"

"Do you mean, now that he's getting his head on straight, would he risk setting himself back a year to go on what easily could be a wild goose chase? I wouldn't presume to answer that, but there's one thing on which I *will* speculate."

"Go on," urged Rae.

"Marc may have come to terms with living without Korey. Some day he may even marry Julia Santangelo and be happy enough. But Korey will forever be the only true love of his life."

*   *   *   *

"Uv gud ut!" Eric sputtered through a mouthful of toothpaste.

Rae halted in the act of turning down bedcovers and cocked an ear to the adjoining bathroom. "Did you say something?"

Clad only in stripped pajama bottoms, Eric came out of the bathroom wiping a ring of white foam from his mouth. "I said, I've got it!"

"Got what, heartburn?" Rae smiled in pointed reference to the haste in which they had devoured the spicy meal at The High Noon. It was not, as it turned out, the leisurely dining they had planned for this Friday evening.

Eric reached to help Rae with the bed. "That too," he said with a grin. "But indigestion isn't the only thing that's been bothering me."

"I know. You haven't heard anything I've said since we got home."

He kissed her cheek. "I'm sorry, babe, but I've been running Korey's escort through my memory bank."

"And you found him."

"Yep. Jim Yellowhawk."

"Jim Yellowhawk." Recognition came as Rae rolled the name over her tongue. "Why, he's the guy whose buffalo herd we photographed last year for the savings and loan calendar." Not until she had finished the thought did the incredulous look come over her freckled face. "*He* was the one with Korey tonight? *That* Jim Yellowhawk?" Eric nodded. Rae plopped on the edge of the wide bed, a mile of bare leg dangling from her nightshirt. "But why would he be with Korey?"

"Beats me."

Criss-crossing her legs, Rae propped herself against the pillows at the headboard and began unwinding her French braid. "How strange," she said. "Where would Korey meet a man who ranches near Mountainair? Matty must figure in this somehow."

Eric sat beside Rae and absently ran a hand up and down her silky leg. "Jim Yellowhawk has to be the key," he mused. "When Marc told us that Korey had left Chattanooga, we all assumed she was in North Carolina, near her dad. But seeing her tonight with Jim…." Eric's wandering hand suddenly stilled.

"What are you thinking?"

He answered her query with one of his own. "Is it possible Korey has been practically under our noses all of this time?"

"I suppose." She ran her fingers through the last plaits in her heavy hair; the mane spilled across her shoulders in mahogany waves. "Not that it mattered as long as poor Clare was alive."

"True." Eric played with a lock of his wife's hair. "But Korey's whereabouts may matter now. Clare is gone, and Marc is free." Thinking of Julia Santangelo, he added, "At least for the time being." An instant later, he reached for the bed-side telephone.

The abrupt movement alarmed Rae. "What are you doing?"

The dial tone droned from the lifted phone as Eric turned gray eyes to hers. "On the way home, you said Marc has a right to know that I saw Korey tonight. I've come to agree with you. I'm calling Marc."

Confidence in her earlier opinion waning, Rae asked, "Are you sure you want to call him now? You may be stumbling into a hornets' nest. Wouldn't it be wise to sleep on it?"

Despite the logic of his wife's words, an inexplicable urgency impelled Eric to make the call; the phone played a discordant tune as he pressed buttons. "I have to do this," he said out of the side of his mouth. "There's such a distasteful dishonesty in withholding the truth. You saw what happened when the Korey/Marc/Clare debacle was shoved into my arms."

"Yes, and now you're putting yourself in the middle again."

"Look, how can it get any worse? Insane as it seems, Marc still blames me in part for his break-up with Korey. Let's say I don't tell him: He marries someone else and discovers down the road that she's the wrong one. I'd never forgive myself for knowing that Korey may, perhaps for a last time, be within his reach." Eric paused before pushing the last button to connect the call. He looked steadily into his wife's eyes, then drove his point home. "Rae, don't you know if situations were reversed and this was about you and me, I'd pursue you into the most treacherous terrain on earth if it meant the slimmest chance of having you back?" He pressed the last digit. With the ringing phone to his ear, he said, "My brother, vexing though he is at times, should have no less than that chance."

Touched by her dear husband's gallant, convincing argument, Rae drew her legs to her chest and settled back in the pillows to listen to his part of the imminent conversation.

The sultry, unmistakably feminine voice that answered the phone momentarily startled the caller. Eric glanced at a clock. 11:30pm Nashville time. Given the late hour, should he assume the voice to be Julia's? *Just play it safe, Eric.* "Uh, hi, this is Eric...."

"Hi, Eric. Julia here. Hold on just a second, I'll put your brother on."

Eric pressed his palm to the phone and whispered to Rae. "Julia"

"Your brother having a sleep-over?"

"So it seems. I wonder...."

"Hi, Eric." Marc's voice was husky and a little edgy.

Eric had the feeling his call had been made at a most indiscreet moment. The temptation to chide his brother caused a delay in his getting down to the reason for the call. "Not interrupting anything important am I?" he asked. Without pause he went on to say, "Seems you're not working your usual late hour tonight."

"No, something came up," said Marc through a yawn.

"I have only to imagine...."

The edge to Marc's voice grew keener. "What is it you want, Eric?"

Eric's sense of purpose slipped a notch. Would another time be better to tell Marc about Korey? *No, tell him now, you fool, or forget it.* "Uh, this is rather personal, Marc. I'm not sure you would want Julia...."

"We have no secrets. Anyway, she just stepped into the shower."

"Do you believe in kismet?"

"What the hell are you talking about?"

"Rae and I had dinner this evening at The High Noon Restaurant in Old Town. I saw an old friend of yours."

"Uh huh," Marc interjected, sounding disinterested.

"Korey." The name vibrated over the phone line. Eric laced his fingers with those Rae offered and sat to wait out the ensuing silence.

In a barely audible voice, as though the wind had been knocked from his lungs, Marc asked, "What was she doing there?"

"She was having dinner," came the obvious answer. "And she was not alone."

"She was with Matty?" Marc sounded hopeful.

"No." Eric laid it on thick. "A handsome, towering man by the name of Jim Yellowhawk."

Marc seemed to not have heard the answer. "How is she, Eric? Did....did she ask about me?"

"We didn't speak. Rae and I had a table in a far corner of another room, and Korey didn't see us. From the glimpse I had of her, she appeared to be fine. Beautiful as ever." Eric accepted without qualm his own subtle attempts to prod his brother into action. Usually debunking superstition, he had, within the last few hours, come to think of tonight's sighting as some kind of sign, one that said Marc and Korey were destined to be together.

Marc broke the long pause. "And just who is this,,,,this Jim Yellowfeather?"

"Yellowhawk"

"Who *is* he?"

Eric readily detected a jealous excitability in the asking of the question. He thought to answer truthfully and without embellishment. On the other hand, he saw no need to diminish the image of Jim Yellowhawk as a possible candidate for Korey's affections. "Jim owns a ranch south of here, near the town of Mountainair. Runs some cattle and has a small herd of buffalo. Rae and I did a camera shoot at his ranch last year. He's also quite an artisan, locally renown. Does silversmithing and sculpts in alabaster. Rae and I don't know him well, mind you, but he seems to be a fine, upstanding man."

"Oh, I see. So now Korey is being escorted about town by a man of many talents who is also *upstanding*. Meaning, of course, that I am not."

Eric had an urge to retort: *If the shoe fits....* But he held his tongue and said, "That's not what I meant at all, I...."

"Eric, why are you telling me all this?"

"Because you asked."

"*You* called *me*, remember? Why?"

"Fact: Korey is in Albuquerque, tonight at least. Fact: My brother—and don't dispute this—is in love with her. Conclusion: Brother should be apprised. Period. This information is to do with what you will."

The fight was gone from Marc's tired voice. "Okay. I'm sorry for being such a shit. Listen Eric, I really don't care to talk about this right now."

"I understand. Anyway, I've told you all I know. If we discuss this again, it will be by your initiative."

"Suits me. Goodbye, Eric."

Rae wrapped her arms around her husband's neck. Disappointment clearly showed in her eyes. "I take it Marc will not be flying here as soon as tomorrow."

Eric forced a smile. "Hardly. He's in shock, I think. Korey resurrected was the last thing he expected. He may just let it pass. Only time will tell." He lovingly took his wife's face in his hands and studied every fine detail while thinking how lucky he was to have her. His heart was heavy with the possibility that Marc and Korey could miss the happiness he shared with Rae. He said to her, speaking words of encouragement for her benefit and his own, as well, "But be assured, my love, if Marc chooses to find her, he will let absolutely nothing dissuade him from that goal."

*   *   *   *

From his side of the large bed, Marc stared at rays of yellow lamplight on the high ceiling. With hands behind his tousled head, he stretched the tension from his long lean frame.

Damn Eric's meddling hide! Just when memories of Korey—the silky feel of her; the sweet taste; the heady fragrance—were beginning to dull only a little.... Just when the wound was only now beginning to close.... Along comes this lightning bolt to sear his unsuspecting soul. Marc's hard chest expanded in a sigh. What to do now? A beautiful, willing woman this moment using his shower. Another woman a thousand miles away, even more beautiful but surely unwilling, and for all he knew, unavailable.

Like rubber balls skipping off a wall, questions bounced in all directions in Marc's befuddled head. Was Korey in New Mexico for reasons other than to visit Matty? Would she be there long? How did this Jim Yellowfea....Yellowhawk fit into her life? Could a seeker, with a map drawn from guesses, half-baked ideas and wild conjecture, hope to find the trail of this elusive woman? And if by luck she was found, would love or damnation be the finder's reward? Should he, shouldn't he? These unknowns and more led to a heap of tangled emotions and finally to a benumbed brain. For now he would have to put Korey out of his mind. Later, when he could think more clearly, he might find an answer....

The water stopped in the shower. Marc rolled over, deliberately turning his back to the empty side of the bed. A door opened. Whiffs of femininely fragrant steam rolled to his nose. The lamp clicked off. He felt the mattress give slightly under Julia's weight. There was none of the familiar electricity when her soft, warm body touched his. Her hair draped his face as in the darkness she whispered a torrid invitation into his ear. Presenting to her the broad barrier of his unyielding back, Marc kept his eyes firmly closed and feigned sleep.

*   *   *   *

Rolling easily in the saddle, Korey tilted her head skyward; the April sun, red through her closed lids, warmed her face. Giving Sundancer his head, she rode this way for a space. With her eyes closed, the late morning air was sharp with amplified sounds. Bees, industriously digging pollen from the bowls of newly opened flowers, wove buzzing notes around the clomp, clomp of hoof beats and the horse's breathing. At the intrusion of horse and rider, crickets ceased chirping; birds twittered and ruffled their feathers.

Sundancer whinnied, and Korey's eyes popped open. She cautiously surveyed the surrounding brush. Seeing nothing out of the ordinary, her gaze, from an unobstructed vantage point atop the mountain, wandered lovingly over neighboring red mesas, then far beyond to hazy blue mountains. Today the sight of beautiful vistas was bittersweet. With spring upon her, the remaining stay in her adopted land might be counted in weeks, or a few months at most.

Maria had suffered a painful winter. Though warmer days had brought some improvement, the inevitable still loomed large: Maria had finally accepted as the only course the sensible joint-replacement surgery. Now the surgery was only a matter of scheduling. And once the date was set, Korey would then plan her own trip home.

Tennessee meant lush green hills, summer air dripping with moisture and sweet honeysuckle. New Mexico was red mesas, rugged mountains, and dust. Two worlds, each with an intrinsic beauty. For the rest of her life, she would belong to both.

Again Sundancer's whinny sent Korey's eyes searching, but horse and rider seemed to be alone. When Korey realized she had ridden farther from the house than she had ever gone without Jim, the thought to turn back seemed a good one. It was then, as she guided Sundancer around to retrace their steps, that she spotted the buffalo. Less than two hundred yards away, on the far side of the fence separating the Sanchez and Yellowhawk ranches, stood a mother and her calf. Having little fear of predators, they had confidently wandered from the herd, no doubt in search of a private feeding ground. Shadowing its mother, the calf ignored Korey, but the cow stopped munching on scrub grass, raised a massive head and eyed the approaching horse. Korey tightened the reins and brought Sundancer to a halt, giving the mother time to assess for danger and make her move. After several minutes, plainly sensing no threat, the beast comfortably resumed feeding.

Stroking his neck, speaking softly, Korey eased Sundancer forward to a cluster of short juniper trees within the last fifty yards of the fence. The creak of saddle leather sounded loud to her as she dismounted. The day was warming; she removed her denim vest, slung the sleeve hole over the horn of the saddle and tethered the reins to a sturdy juniper branch. In a slow fluid motion, she went to the fence and claimed the only clear spot on a fence line clogged with wind-stacked tumbleweed.

She looked on in heightened excitement as the calf nudged its mother and began nursing at the cow's udder. Aware of her audience of one, the mother stared with eyes black as jet into the eyes of the interloper. Like children holding a contest, Korey and the bison locked onto each other: the woman, hands hanging at her sides, perfectly still; the beast motionless except for the slapping of a short tail—its bristled end splayed like an old paintbrush. Then, as though bored, the cow shook her shaggy head and moved nearby to graze, leaving the youngster to either follow or fend for itself.

Korey set a relaxed pose. Careful not to snag her flannel shirtsleeve on the barbed wire, she cupped her hands over a fence post and rested her chin on her hands. As she contentedly watched the pair, her hat shielded her eyes from the sun as it reached its apex and started a lazy descent across the deep blue sky.

She tried to imagine the spectacle created when millions of these creatures had roamed the plains in migrating herds at times twenty-five miles wide. How the earth must have trembled as a herd of sinewed bulldozers rushed headlong through tall plains grasses and laid waste to anything in its path.

The objects of Korey's fascinated gaze were mere remnants of that vanished scene. These two animals seemed almost docile as they browsed the sparse grass. They were moving away from her now, slowly munching their way over a low hill. Korey watched so intently that she did not see, at the corner of her eye, a movement along the ground at the edge of the tumbleweeds on her side of the fence. Mother and offspring topped the hill. Silhouetted against the sky, they stood for long moments, their heads turned to the woman as if in farewell. Korey smiled, dismissed as silly an urge to raise her arm and wave. Then the cow turned and disappeared from view, the calf gamboling after her.

With the show over, Korey turned to leave. In the next instant, a terrifying sound, foreign yet instinctively recognized, halted her booted feet as if they were suddenly plunged into setting cement. The jolt to her momentum nearly pitched her forward. As she brought herself up rigid, a dry horrified sob flew from her throat. From somewhere close behind her came a rattle and hiss, sounds out of the worst nightmare. Immersed in fright, every cell in Korey's body screamed. Icy rivers ran in her veins. Because she could not see the snake, she had no way to judge its distance or her chance of escape. Panic smothered her. Her eyes bulged when she could not draw a breath. The air was filled with the deathly rattle. Her mind, driven to senselessness, went blank.

Then, as if through a miracle, Jim Yellowhawk's words of caution, spoken months before, reached out to her: *Rattlers strike when threatened; don't startle them; above all stay calm.*

Don't startle....stay calm.... Jim's teachings took control of Korey's mind, for the moment nearly drowning out the awful hiss. She could almost feel Jim's presence as the voice in her head coached her: *Don't move, Korey, don't move.*

Korey felt the hysteria ebb. She took a shallow breath, followed by a deeper one. For the first time since the appearance of the snake—had it been minutes that had passed, or mere seconds?—her attention was diverted to Sundancer. Only her eyes, as if moving in the sockets of a marble bust, swiveled to the horse. Sundancer pawed the ground, moved forward and back, testing his tether. Korey's frantic eyes locked onto the horse's flank. Too distracted by what she saw there, she did not think of the danger Sundancer's prancing could pose. Hope surged as the polished stock of the rifle Jim had so patiently taught her to fire gleamed at her from its slim leather scabbard. But, as quickly as it had risen, hope sank like a stone. For all the good it would do her, the fifty yards between her and the gun might as well be fifty miles. The rifle she always so obediently kept on Sundancer's flank would be of no use to her now.

Korey swallowed, nearly gagging on a throat dry and coarse as sandpaper. In the blink of an eye her whole world had become a game of nerves—hers versus those of a venomous snake. With a heart thudding against her chest wall, frightened beyond anything she would have thought possible, she ceded to the only option open to her. She would not move; she would wait for the snake to lose interest. And she would pray.

Steeling herself to mentally endure the deadly stand-off, Korey fought the sour swell that churned in her stomach. The roar of her own blood in her ears was not enough to drown out the awful hiss behind her. A tingling inched up her spine and erupted in a thousand tiny needles pricking her scalp. The urge to scratch under her hat nearly drove her wild. Cold sweat popped out on her forehead, ran in a slow tormenting trickle between her shoulder blades. Her clenched hands throbbed where her short nails dug deep crescents into tender palms. As moments passed, a full awareness of her grim plight began to erode her will. *Dear God! I can't stand much more of this! Please, God, do something!*

Be careful what you ask for.

Sundancer, spooked and causing an awful stir, reared on his hind legs and with a jerk of his corded neck, snapped the branch that had held him. Injected with fresh fear, Korey watched in horror as the horse, snorting and pawing, backed farther from her. The sound of the rattle grew louder. She awaited an imminent strike and wondered, morbidly, if she would feel pain when the fangs pierced her skin. Hot tears rushed down her white face.

No! She would not stand by, hopelessly, helplessly waiting. If the snake was to get her, it would have to get her on the run! Her right foot was poised to dart forward. But she never took that first step. The crack of a rifle shattered the air. Violent spasms shook her as the sound reverberated across the low hills. Then— silence. The strong smell of gunpowder drifted to her nose.

A frantic voice broke the stillness. "Korey! Korey! Are you all right?"

She spun on her heel, hand flying to her mouth. Jim! Dear Jim! His long legs vaulting a sagging section of fence, now dashing toward her! Through a blur of tears, her eyes darted to the headless snake writhing on the parched ground. Korey's lips trembled as a flood of fresh tears ran down her face.

Then Jim was there, dropping the gun at his feet, offering his strong, protective arms. "You're all right?" he asked again.

She managed a stiff nod before collapsing against him. Her arms wrapped his waist as her weakened legs threatened to fold. He let her sob, saying only, "It's okay, it's okay, you're safe now." Pushing back her hat, he stroked damp hair away from her face. Through her clothes, the wind chilled her wet skin; she shivered. He hugged her tighter and felt her fingers dig into his waist at the back.

Finding her voice at last, she blurted into his rough denim shirt, "Oh, Jim, I've never been so scared. I....I didn't know what to do. I didn't know where the snake was, how close I mean, or where it had come from, but I remembered you said not to move and then Sundancer went wild and I was afraid I was going to be sick and...." She hiccuped; fear's metallic taste still coated her tongue. "....and I nearly lost my mind."

Her cheek pressed to his broad chest, she felt Jim's resonant words before she heard them. "You did exactly the right thing," he soothed. "You probably had that snake outwitted, but I wasn't about to take a chance. I've never been," he observed dryly, "much of a snake mind reader."

The absurdity of his remark tore a laugh from Korey, but Jim wondered if the laugh held more hysteria than mirth.

Mopping her tears with her shirt sleeve, she pulled away from his arms, sensing his reluctance to let her go. Clearing her throat, she said, "Thank you seems so inadequate....you came in the nick of time." Jim's large body charitably blocked her view of the now limp snake. She set her hat aright. Drawing her dark brows together, she said, "Where did you come from, anyway?"

"I was out checking on the buffalo herd and counted a missing cow and calf. The pair was coming down the side of the hill when I saw them and urged them back to the herd. I can't say what made me turn and ride on up the hill. Just as I topped it, I saw you turning from the fence. I opened my mouth to call to you, but then I saw you stop dead and I knew something bad was going on down here."

"I'd been watching your roving pair. I even think we became friends. But when I started to leave….the fence was a mess of tumbleweed….I didn't see…."

Jim plucked the rifle from the ground, took her cold hand in his warm one. His spurs chinked as he led her in the direction of Sundancer, away from the gruesome spectacle of the dead snake. "As soon as I got close enough to see the fix you were in," he said, "I left my horse, came the rest of the way on foot. I had a chance for only one shot, so I got as close as I dared before I fired."

Still holding tightly to Jim with one hand, Korey picked up her vest that, in his frenzy, Sundancer had thrown from the saddle horn. Shaking dust from the vest, she slung it over her shoulder.

Jim made a clicking sound with his tongue, calling Sundancer. "Sorry the gunshot frightened you," he said. Warily, the horse ambled toward them, dragging along behind the tethered juniper branch.

Unable to conquer her chill, Korey freed her hand and slipped into her vest. She coaxed the horse to her and, as much to calm her own trembling as that of the horse, stroked the long thick neck. One hand still on Sundancer, Korey turned to her savior and said, unnecessarily, "I'm telling you, Jim, when it comes down to feeling the fangs of a rattlesnake, or jumping out of my skin at the report of a rifle, believe me, I'll take the latter any day." She stood in Jim's shadow and smiled up at his handsome, wind-burned face. Her eyes, still red and sensitive, squinted as the sun peeked from behind his hat. "I owe you one. Or should I say 'one more?' Seems you have been watching over me since….well, before I came to Maria's."

They both knew she referred to the day—one year ago on this very date, as it happened—Jim stopped on the highway and tapped on her car window. Only within the last month had Korey brought herself to tell him why she had been on that lonely stretch of road. It occurred to her now that this was the first time in many days that she had thought of Marc.

Jim said, "You don't owe me a thing. You would've done the same for me."

"Not with such life-saving accuracy, I'm afraid." She squatted to disentangle the leather strap from the juniper limb. Over her shoulder she said, "How would you like to come to dinner tomorrow night?" She rose, slapped the reins on her thigh, watched the dust dissipate in the wind. "Maria would love for you to come. And so would I." Idly she rubbed at the dust streaks on her jeans as she watched Jim's ebony eyes. Something indecipherable lurked there in the shade of his wide brim. He dropped his head as if suddenly having a need to study the gun he held. Sand, like raw sugar in a spoon, sat in a dimple in the crown of his black hat. His face came up in a wide white grin.

"I'm always happy to get out of my own kitchen," he said.

He nodded toward Sundancer. "You want me to ride home with you?"

"No, once I stop shaking, I'll be okay." She mounted Sundancer then leaned down to squeeze Jim's firm shoulder. "Thanks, Jim, for….you may have saved…."

He stood with the rifle pointing to the ground. "Heck, anybody could've done it."

She knew that was not true, but it was obvious her repeated expressions of gratitude made him uncomfortable. "Maria and I will be looking for you around six-thirty tomorrow night."

He waved as the horse moved away, the rider standing in the stirrups for a final farewell. He watched until she was lost among the thick junipers, listened until he could no longer hear the sound of galloping hooves. Retracing his steps, Jim rolled the lifeless snake around with the toe of his dust-covered boot, picked it up, held it at arm's length. At seven feet, its tail touched the ground. He knew then that Korey had been within easy range had the snake chosen to strike.

"Make a nice belt," he said aloud while carrying his trophy to his horse. "But I must never tell Korey."

＊   ＊   ＊   ＊

They had a grand time at dinner. Maria's high spirits were equal to those of Korey and Jim. Bursts of laughter rang within the thick adobe walls as a history of range life—how wildly fictionalized, Korey could but guess—flew between Jim and Maria. Then Jim brought the subject around to present-day adventures. He made Korey out as a heroine for standing up to a seven foot rattlesnake. She blanched when he mentioned the length. Korey insisted Jim was the hero for killing it. *He* paled when she confessed to being only a step away from making a run for it when he had fired the gun. And through the whole recounting of the dreadful incident, Maria's bronze face seemed a little ashen.

After dinner Korey and Jim cleared the table and cleaned the kitchen—he washed the dishes; she dried. Meanwhile, Maria nodded off by a crackling fire.

Leaving Maria comfortably snoring in her rocking chair, Korey strolled at Jim's side toward his truck, their way across the hard ground lit only by starshine.

"I could eat my weight in Maria's Corn-Green-Chili Chowder." Jim chuckled as he patted his rounded belly. "Fact is, I nearly did."

"It's a favorite of mine too. But tonight it was the second serving of warm raisin pudding that did me in." Korey groaned in exaggerated agony. Flushed from the effects of a warm house, laughter, and too much good eating, she welcomed the touch of the night air on her face. She turned her head to the tall man walking beside her. "Maria especially enjoys cooking for you."

"And I thoroughly enjoy eating what she cooks. Tonight's meal was a far cry from the ones I'm accustomed to pulling from my microwave. Maria spoils me." They came to the truck. Jim's deep voice suddenly lost all levity. "She's leaving for Albuquerque before long, isn't she?"

"Yes. We don't speak of it much, but she has accepted that she must have surgery. Her spirits are good. You know how she always tries to look at the bright side."

"Will you stay, take care of the place while she's gone?" He sounded hopeful.

This was a moment she had long dreaded. "You might as well know, Jim. Maria may not be returning. This isn't a simple undertaking. She will have several surgeries, months apart. Marcelina, with the support of most of the family, has been trying to talk Maria into selling the ranch."

Jim ran a big hand over his head. Tonight his black hair was smoothly pulled back, tied at the nape, and left to fall down his back. Even in the darkness, Korey could see by his expression that the possibility of Maria's moving was one he had not considered, or one he had chosen to deny. She said, unable to hide her own melancholy, "Nothing can stay the same forever, Jim. When Maria leaves, I'll be heading back home."

"Back to what? An empty house, living alone?" He was surprised to hear the edge in his voice; part of him wanted to take back the words.

She retaliated: "You've known my arrangement with Maria wasn't permanent."

In atonement he tried to smile. "Guess I was hoping we could convert you, turn you into a native. Great strides have been made toward that end in the last eight months."

"Tennessee is my home."

Stubborn woman. "Enough of this," Jim mumbled under his breath as he set out to move the mountain. In what seemed to Korey as one movement, he took a long stride, placed his hands on her waist and bent his head to brush her lips with his.

This unprecedented demonstration of affection at first stunned Korey. Then, as his lips amorously tasted hers, she admitted she would have seen this coming had she allowed herself to recognize his growing infatuation. But she had ignored the little signs, hoping if he met no encouragement, he would ignore them too. So much for sticking one's head in the sand. Her hands lifted to rest lightly on his broad shoulders as she tentatively returned a kiss that tasted very much like Maria's raisin pudding. Jim's silver belt buckle, large as his beefy fist, pressed a cold stamp through her shirt onto her midriff. She thought the kiss quite pleasing, but missing were the orchestras playing, the fireworks.

The duration of the kiss was not overly long, nor was it followed by another. Jim took a step back, resting his hip against the rear of his new pickup truck. He curled his hands over the tailgate. "No good, huh?" he asked, tapping an agitated finger on the metal.

"It was nice."

"Nice, yes. No denying that. But *nice* wasn't what I was looking for. It's the other guy, isn't it, the one in Nashville?"

What could be the answer, when she was not sure herself? "I don't know, Jim." To avoid his intrusive gaze, Korey lowered her head.

Pebbles scraped as Jim Yellowhawk rubbed the sole of his boot back and forth across the ground. In the junipers, a quick wind played mournful music. "You going to waste your best years pining over some guy you can't have?"

"Well, that's certainly a pointed question!"

"'Bout time somebody asked it."

"Look, I probably owe you my life, but...."

His hand shot up to stop her. "Hell, we're not talking about obligations here; debts owed or collected." His jet eyes bore into hers.

"You're angry. I didn't mean to make you angry."

"I'm not angry!" snapped Jim. Then, as he thought about it, a sheepish grin broke over his sober face. "Okay, I am....a little. But not with you. With my false hopes. They won't let me down easy."

Korey touched a hand to his arm. "Please understand. Something has happened inside me, a flame extinguished. I don't know if it can be rekindled."

"I'd give you time, Korey, you know that." He reached out and swept a night-flying insect away from her fragrant hair. "All the time you'd need."

She shook her head. "Don't you see, by waiting for something that may never come, you'd be throwing away the same good years you just accused me of wasting?"

"Aw, Korey...."

"No, Jim, please listen. I care for you, but not in the way you deserve. I'll not trap you so that when the right love comes along, you wouldn't be free to recognize it." Her eyes filled with tears. "It's like I've been hit by a cement truck then pieced back together and some of the pieces still don't fit. You don't want a woman like that. You don't want me."

He had already opened his mouth to protest before her strong last words hit home. They were spoken so convincingly that for a moment he thought maybe she was right. But no, she could not be more *wrong*. He knew what he wanted. He closed his mouth. Tonight was not the time to try to make her understand.

Grudgingly, he said, "Okay, you won this round." He kissed the apple of her cheek before walking to the front of the truck and swinging himself into the seat. Slamming the door, he started the engine and rested his elbow on the frame of the open window. "Just so you know, this is not the end of it. I've been known to fight for what I want."

"I'll just bet you have."

She folded her arms over her breast and stood in his dust until the red tail-lights vanished.

CHAPTER 25

▼

On a warm April afternoon, equipped with nothing more than an overnight bag and a hunch, Marc Bradberry touched down in Albuquerque, sent there strangely enough by Julia Santangelo.

An intuitive woman, that Julia.

Somehow, without asking, Julia had known that Eric's phone call ten nights ago had something to do with Korey Westerfield. Now, as the plane taxied on the runway, Marc remembered Julia's sensible words the morning after. "If there's to be hope for us, you must put the affair with Korey to rest. She's keeping you from me." When he had objected and said the affair *was* put to rest, Julia had calmly brought him up short. "You're wrong. You didn't fool me last night by feigning sleep when I came to bed. You've never before slept so soundly that you didn't arouse to, shall I say, certain stimuli. You have to find her, Marc. I can't live with the suspense. It's not unreasonable for me to insist on knowing where you stand." With that Julia had leveled a gaze across the kitchen table, said simply, "Go!" and left him sitting alone over a cup of untasted coffee.

So he had come. Come with a nervous eagerness that had him jumping out of his seat well before the wheels of the plane rolled to a halt on the tarmac. He cursed the ten-day lapse between Korey's appearance at The High Noon Restaurant and his arrival in New Mexico. Had he been a man of leisure, he would have come nine days ago, but his life ran to the dictates of a business calendar and crucial time had been lost. Had he come all this way to find the obscure trail leading to Korey now stone cold? He would know in the next day or two.

Mentally honing his negotiating skills, Marc sped away from the airport in a leased Jeep Cherokee. He turned left from Gibson Boulevard onto Carlisle and headed for the first stop in his search, Matty Cunningham. Korey's aunt would know where her niece was keeping herself. Getting Matty to reveal that information, assuming she would even let him through her door, could prove the challenge of the decade. He had come armed only with the element of surprise and what sketchy clues Eric had provided. Not much with which to bluff one as sly as Matty. But he had to try.

Disappointment creased his face when there was no answer to the knock on Matty's door. He had prepared himself to spar with her, and the letdown left him limp. He slouched back to the Jeep. Eric and Rae would not be home until late that night. He had a key to their house, opening an option to go there, fix a drink, gather his mental forces for a later meeting with Matty. He *could* do those things.

Instead, he wandered. From Matty's he drove not northeast toward his brother's home in the Sandia foothills, but west. Traveling neighborhood side streets, then congested thoroughfares, he soon found himself in Old Town Albuquerque. Parking the Jeep in a public lot, he walked in the warm April sun to the Plaza Square, uncertain of how or why he had come to Old Town.

Delicious aromas emitting from village restaurants hung in the quiet air, causing Marc's stomach to rumble despite its dyspepsia. His mind more on his mission than his environment, he roamed the village: Past San Felipie de Neri Church, after nearly three centuries its adobe walls still echoing daily Mass; past outdoor vendors, their offerings of silver jewelry sending shards of blinding sunlight into the eyes of passersby; past countless shops, rows of small adobe buildings offering most anything a fanciful heart desired. He saw little of what he passed.

What he did see, in his mind's eye, was Korey as she had been the last time the two of them had visited Old Town. Since that November evening, the seventeen months that had come and gone seemed now like many more. The Korey Westerfield who had strolled with him through these streets had been an innocent, the sparkle of new love as yet untarnished by the discovery that the hand she clasped in hers was that of a married man. Marc tried to purge from his mind the memory of that beautiful night. It was a useless exercise since nearly all the people he now passed were in pairs, and the observation sent his thoughts straight back to Korey. Suddenly he knew why his subconscious had guided him to Old Town: Ten days ago Korey had been spotted here. A derisive smile touched his mouth. The odds, if he were a gambling man, would be more in his favor to win a lottery jackpot than to meet Korey today on the sidewalks of Old Town.

During his aimless walk, a yellow afternoon had turned to purple dusk. Marc shivered as a new-found wind bit through his navy blazer; a paper cup, spun in a dust devil, rattled past his feet. He was tired, and his feet ached. He should leave now, try Matty's door again.

He retraced the shortest steps to the plaza and from there turned onto a narrow brick walk between two buildings, thinking it the way to the parking lot. But to one unfamiliar, the village had become a maze, and Marc instead found himself in a treed courtyard. Lighted water bubbled over large glistening stones in a fountain at the center of the court. In spite of the evening chill, the sound made him want to sit on the fountain's rim, shed his shoes, and plunge his burning toes into the cool water. Bleary-eyed, he scanned the perimeter of the courtyard where the half dozen shops had inviting light burning in the windows. Two women, each with a camera slung over a shoulder and toting bulging shopping bags, came out of a store and, not looking his way, walked past him towards the plaza. He would have followed them, and thus missed seeing the quilt, if their appearance had not drawn his eye in the direction of a small shop tucked in a far corner of the courtyard. He stared wondrously into the window where a spotlight flared brightly onto a quilted interpretation of Enchanted Mesa at moonrise. There was no mistaking the work: red sandstone, mottled lavender sky, golden moon. He knew it to be Korey's even before he walked the depth of the court for a closer look and saw through the clear glass the silver signature medallion hanging from the lower right corner.

He could hardly believe his luck. Suddenly energized, his heart racing, he opened the door to the art-filled store. A bell tinkled, melodiously signaling his arrival. He was the only customer in the tightly-packed shop. Woven rugs, sculptures large and small, sand paintings took nearly every inch of space. The heated confines were suffused with the scent of juniper, a smell that instantly transported Marc to Gran Quivira on a raw November day, a woman beside him, her eyes wet, a hat pulled low over her ears. On the wind, the juniper trees surrounding the pueblo ruins had poured a rich fragrance over the limestone walls. And until now, he had forgotten....

"May I help you, sir?" A young woman, long black hair pulled back from a pretty face, appeared from a back room.

Marc's startled expression lasted only as long as it took him to return her friendly smile. "Yes, the quilt in your window...."

"Enchanted Mesa."

"I find it interesting."

"Here," she said, stepping to the quilt, "I'll turn it so you may have a closer look." With a gentle tug, the large hanging came round on a swivel hook mounted in the ceiling. "One of a kind. Hand stitched, of course. The artist only recently brought it to us."

With hands clasped behind his back, Marc leaned to the piece, pretending to study the expertly stitched appliqués when what he really wanted was to pounce on the opening the clerk had just given him. He stood it as long as he could. His eyes still on the quilt, he said, "The artist delivered it, you say? I assume then that the artist lives here."

"Uh."

Good. He seemed to have caught the young woman off guard.

"Sir, we have a confidentiality agreement with those artists who wish it. I'm sorry, I'm not at liberty to divulge any personal information about this particular artist."

He was loathe to do it, but these were desperate times. He turned on her what he knew to be his most charming smile. "I understand completely. However, since I plan to purchase this piece, I must know it was made by a local artist. You see, I collect from New Mexico artisans only." He marveled at his own ingenuity. In truth, excluding those photos taken by Eric and Rae, he owned not one piece from this art-saturated state. "You wouldn't want me to get this home, now would you," he laughed, "and find MADE IN CHINA stamped on the back?"

The clerk did not seem amused. In fact, she looked offended.

No sense of humor, he thought. "Excuse the joke. I guess it was more tasteless than funny."

"You may be assured, sir, the artist does live in New Mexico."

Marc sobered. Maybe this woman's tight lips would loosen if she thought she were in danger of losing a hefty commission. "It's important to me as a collector to know something of the artist. I may have to reconsider…. You can give me nothing else?"

It did not take long for her to weigh risk against reward. "I really don't know much about her," she volunteered. "In truth this is just the second of her quilts that we have carried. I suppose there can be no harm in telling you she does not live locally, by that I mean Albuquerque."

Now we're getting someplace. "But close enough she would drive here to deliver in person."

She nodded. "A couple of hours south, I think."

Jackpot! Eric had said Jim Yellowhawk had a ranch about two hours south, near Mountainair. This was more information than he had hoped for; he would not arouse suspicion by asking more questions. "You've been most helpful." He handed her a credit card.

"But, you haven't even asked the price."

"I know what it's worth. I'll take it. On one condition."

Her hand halted as she ran the credit card through the scanner. Misunderstanding his intent, she said, "Oh, we have a full money-back guarantee if you aren't completely satisfied."

"No, that's not what I meant. I won't be bringing it back. But, if the artist should happen to inquire, I would rather she not know the identity of the buyer."

This sale had been as strange as it was easy. She handed him a pen and watched as he signed the receipt. She smiled. "Buyer confidentiality?"

"Let's call it that. Now, I'll help you take it down from the window."

Not until she was carefully rolling the quilt in heavy brown paper did Marc take time to inspect the silver medallion. Although stamped with the familiar KRW in the center, the medallion had a different look than any he had seen. As one would absently finger a coin, he turned the silver over. At the bottom, in tiny letters, were the initials JY. Marc dropped the medallion, heard it clank on the counter as a warm flush crept up his neck. So, now the master rancher-sculptor-silversmith was making Korey's medallions! For a blinding instant, Marc's jealousy would not let him see that another stepping stone to Korey had been laid before him.

The clerk, obviously elated over the profitable sale, had become suddenly chatty. Marc pretended to listen as she tucked the silver piece into the parcel, folded the end paper and secured it with wide clear tape. His anger ebbed, and he began to see this latest clue for what it was. He no longer heard the woman's voice. What he heard was the rattle of missing pieces moving together and dropping into place.

✳   ✳   ✳   ✳

The porch lamp switched on, and Marc winced in the white flare. A moment later the door swung open.

"Hello, Matty."

Her face carried an expression less startled than Marc had expected, but she was, nonetheless, taken back. One hand gripped the doorknob while the other, hidden in a cooking mitt, hung at her side. Peering up at him, her gray eyes were abnormally large through the lenses of her silver-framed eyeglasses. "Oh my goodness," she said through a slack jaw.

"Surprised you, have I?"

"You have most assuredly." Her eyes did not leave his face.

"May I come in for a few minutes?"

Matty Cunningham's head bobbed an assent, but she did not grace him with a welcoming smile. "Of course, of course." She opened the door wide.

Marc stepped onto the tile of the softly illuminated foyer. Fragrant smells from the kitchen assailed him and called to mind his unappeased hunger. Matty was obviously preparing dinner, and he knew he should offer to leave and return at a more convenient time. Though entrance to the house had come more easily than expected, he was not about to give ground and invite the probability of next time being turned away. Have her think what she will regarding his poor manners. He would not take much of her time. Whatever she had going in the kitchen could wait.

"Please, Marc, make yourself comfortable." She pointed him toward the compact living room. "I'll be right with you as soon as I turn something down on the stove."

He thought to tell her how delicious the cooking smelled but refrained for fear he would sound as if he had come begging a meal.

Matty called to him from the kitchen. "Would you care for a cup of coffee?"

"Thank you, yes," he called back. "I would love some. The wind has picked up and there's quite a chill in the air." He sat in a low chair and gripped its fat worn arms.

Matty appeared with a steaming mug and a linen napkin. "You drink it with only a few drops of cream," she stated, handing him the cup.

"You remember."

"Yes." She took a chair near his and deliberately folded her hands in her lap.

Marc felt the weight of her gray stare as he sipped the hot brew. A warmth suffused his hollow stomach. Holding the mug by the handle and cradling its base to warm his hand, he raised his head to meet Matty's direct gaze. "So, you must be a little curious as to why I've unexpectedly shown up on your doorstep."

"It occurred to me to ask."

"I'll get directly to the point."

"Always seems the best way."

Watching the woman closely, Marc paused only briefly then said, "I'm here to see Korey." Matty hid her astonishment behind a passive stare, but he noted the rapid flutter of her eyelids. She would not be easily rattled, but still….

"Then you will be disappointed to learn she's not here."

He made her endure his silence while he drank again from his cup. At last he said, "Oh, I didn't mean *here*. Let me rephrase. I'm in *New Mexico* to see Korey."

From the kitchen came the sound of a lid bouncing on a bubbling pot. Matty seemed not to notice. "Two questions, Marc."

"Sure."

"Why New Mexico? And why do you wish to see her?"

Time to play what few cards he had been dealt. "New Mexico because she is living here." He marveled at the cool veneer under which Matty contained her emotions. The old gal knew a thing or two about a game of poker. If not for detecting a nearly imperceptible tightening around her mouth, grave doubts would have been cast upon this new image of himself as a budding pupil of Sherlock Holmes. "And why do I want to see her?" He played another card. "I like to think I can win her away from Jim Yellowhawk."

Dark storm clouds boiled behind those steel-rimmed eyeglasses as Matty shot straight up in her chair. "All right, young man." Her voice was keen as a razor's edge. "What is this game you're playing? Have you no understanding of the pain you've already caused that dear girl? Why, I ought to hog-tie you and, and...."

"Matty, please!" Marc was on his feet, his arms open in supplication. "Listen to me. I'm not so dimwitted that I don't recognize I have no credibility with you. Though it will take time, I intend to change your perception of me. And," he continued with steel determination, "we will begin here and now." He dropped his arms. "I'm in love with Korey. Life without her has been no life at all. I want us to have another chance."

"Another chance?" Matty frowned, truly bewildered. "But how can this be?" Before he could reply, she knew the answer to her own question. Only one thing would explain his coming to her tonight. A drastic event had occurred in his life. Matty was certain she knew the nature of that event. She was calm as she said, "Your wife....she's gone?"

Marc looked down at her from his lofty height. Quietly he said, "Yes. Four months ago. One night she simply slept away."

"I am sorry."

"Thank you." He hesitated before saying what was on his mind. "The death can be easily verified...."

"And for that very reason, I don't doubt you're telling me the truth. However, convincing me that you'll not upset my niece will prove more difficult. Now then, sit down, drink your coffee, and we'll talk."

He did as he was told. "I'll give it to you straight, Matty. I came here tonight deluding myself into thinking I could bluff you into revealing certain things. I see now what a foolish strategy that was. I'm tossing my cards on the table and asking for your help." When he met no immediate resistance, he went on. "I've managed to piece together a couple of things. One, Korey seems to be somewhere in the vicinity of a little town called Mountainair. And two, she has formed an association—I hope a platonic one—with Mr. Jim Yellowhawk."

"No need for me to deny how close you've come, but how...."

"Let's just say I have a source." He smiled.

"Well." Matty slapped her nimble hands on her thighs. "Seems you already know nearly everything. So, why have you come to me?"

"I can stay in New Mexico only two days. As you said, I've come close, but I've not found her. You could save me having to knock on every door from Mountainair to Jim Yellowhawk's place looking for her."

"You've tried other ways?"

"Eric has."

"Ah, yes, your brother, Eric. Your *source?*"

Marc only smiled. "Please understand I'm not here to make trouble. If Korey doesn't want anything to do with me, I'll go quietly. But I'm not leaving until I hear from her lips that she doesn't want me." He drew in a long breath. "I love her, Matty. Will you help me?"

The house quietly awaited her response. Even the kettle on the stove had ceased its chatter. Marc thought he would choke on the silence.

Matty looked at the man across from her. Something showing in his face made her want to believe him. But to do what he asked would mean betrayal. She tried to chase from her mind a picture of herself dressed in the robes of Judas. "I don't know...."

"I'll find her, Matty. You won't stop me. You can, however, make my quest more difficult." His dark brows took an optimistic upswing. "Or you can make it easier."

"So you've come to lock horns with Jim Yellowhawk?"

Marc saw the question as the diversion it was. Plainly Matty was buying time to make up her mind. He thought it prudent to go along. "Let's hope it will not come to that. From what I've heard, he's a man capable of handily defending himself."

"I would say you've heard right."

Marc challenged, "Surely you don't think to deter me through intimidation?" The corners of his mouth lifted.

She admitted candidly, "I'll try anything."

"Come on, Matty," he pleaded earnestly. "Give me a fair assessment of what I'm up against."

"Why, I'm surprised your *source* hasn't…. Oh, don't look so grim. I'm toying with you. And damn if I'm not taking pleasure from it!"

He silently accepted the chiding as his due.

"Korey considers Jim Yellowhawk a close friend," Matty was saying. "Not that Jim is content to have it that way. I've seen them together on occasion. Jim does a credible job of hiding his true affections, but it's obvious to anyone with eyes how he feels about Korey. Whether she's perceived this, I don't know. She and I seldom discuss the subject of men." Matty shot Marc a pointed look. "I'm sure you understand."

With a nod of his head, he acknowledged the merited dig.

"She has worked hard at getting well, Marc. In part that meant not clinging to hope."

"She's over me then?"

"It's been a long time since I've heard her say your name. But *over* you?" Matty fanned her blunt fingers through the air. "Who's to say what lives in the locked corners of a woman's heart?"

"That's why I'm here. To see what lurks in those corners. Matty," he implored, his voice no less determined for its softness, "will you hand me the key?"

A long sigh signaled the aunt's capitulation; Marc breathed a quiet sigh of his own and repressed a gladsome smile.

"Korey is living with a woman named Maria Sanchez," Matty began. "The whys and wherefores you'll learn later. I'll not tell you everything now else I have time to regret telling you anything. Maria owns a small ranch on state road 55 about fifteen miles south of Mountainair."

"Highway 55….isn't that the road to Gran Quivira?"

"Yes. As I recall, you and Korey went there last year. You remember the way?"

"I think so. If not, I have a map in the rental car."

Matty opened her mouth, then paused to study intently the handsome young man now eagerly leaning forward in his chair. "Have you eaten dinner?"

"Uh, actually, no I haven't."

Pushing herself from her chair, Matty asked kindly, "In that case, would you care to join me?"

The inexplicable invitation left Marc nonplussed. Had Matty, after leading him this far, decided against guiding him to Korey's door? But if that were so, surely no misplaced sense of hospitality could induce her to feed him. As she stood patiently awaiting his response, he remembered his manners and jumped to his feet.

She smiled up at him. "I'll take that as a 'yes.' Sharing a meal is such a civilized way to make peace, don't you think? Now then," she placed a firm hand at the elbow of his blazer and steered him toward the kitchen, "over dinner I'll tell you exactly how to find Korey—even draw you a little map if need be—and fill you in on how it came about that Korey is living with Maria." She urged him into an oak chair at the kitchen table. "You look hungry. You like posole?"

"Smells delicious. But what is posole?"

"Oh, hominy and pork and some other stuff thrown in."

Marc grinned. "Hey, I'm from the South. Hominy I know!"

Pulling on the cooking mitt, Matty went to the stove and lifted the lid from a large pot. In the light over the burner, steam rose as a yellow cloud. Marc cleared his throat, and, with lid in hand, Matty turned, looking at him through glasses misted in fog. Water dripped from the underside of the lid onto the tile floor. "Something you want to say?" she asked. With her glasses clearing, she set the dripping lid in the sink and faced the young man who had been welcomed—a surprise to them both—into her warm kitchen. Prepared to listen, she crossed her arms.

"After I see Korey, what will happen between the two of you?"

"Because I'm the one going around giving away hiding places? Oh, at first, as soon as she recovers from the shock of finding you at her door and points a finger of suspicion in my direction, she'll be mad as a bothered bee. Then she'll vent her anger and it'll be over."

"If I could have done this another way…."

"Now, don't fret. You didn't pull anything from me; I gave willingly. And I gave because something tells me you and Korey should be together. Sometimes life needs a little push."

"Thanks, Matty."

"Don't thank me yet. Neither of us knows how it's going to go up on that mountain tomorrow."

The optimistic smile he tried to deliver felt limp on his mouth. In truth he was afraid to think how Korey would react when he appeared suddenly, seemingly from out of nowhere. Apprehensively he said, "You won't warn her?"

"Of course not. I'll leave it to you to take the brunt of her anger, if in fact that's what will be in her mind." Matty came to him and patted his arm. "I'm sorry. I didn't intend to sound mean." Her eyes crinkled into a smile. "I wouldn't worry too much. I know the thought of what may happen tomorrow scares you but don't let that make you underestimate your own persuasive abilities. If you love Korey as much as I think you do, over time there'll come a way for you to set things right."

"I surely hope so."

"But if I'm wrong? Well, that means you're sent packing, and I'm in for a good tongue lashing. In that event, come here tomorrow night, and we'll share a consolation meal." She went to a drawer, rummaged noisily among cooking utensils until she produced a long-handled ladle. "Only then it won't be pork we'll be eating." She gestured with the ladle. "Nope. More likely, if the worst happens, I'll be serving cooked goose."

$$*\qquad*\qquad*\qquad*$$

Having endured a night where anticipation and trepidation had pounded against the walls of sleep, Marc found the morning drive to Mountainair tedious. That is until he reached the flatlands of the Manzano Mountains. There, volatile spring winds, with nothing to slow them, rushed across the mountaintop and brought Marc alert as they buffeted the Jeep and threw sand at the windshield. The blue sky was now closed behind billowing curtains of brown dust. Tumbleweeds skipped on the road ahead, bounced to the shoulder and collected with others to make a low prickly wall along a fence line. Snagged on barbed wire was a plastic shopping bag blowing stiff like a windsock.

Marc silently thanked Matty for her explicit instructions, not the least her caution that he should, on leaving Mountainair, watch the odometer for an accurate point to Maria's turn-off. Notable landmarks provided by Matty—an abandoned barn here or collapsed windmill there—would be easily missed this day. He strained to see through filthy glass and was engulfed by loneliness when the headlights failed to reflect even one living creature. Everyone—every*thing*—had better sense than to be out in this storm, but on he drove, pushed by an urgency that was his alone. Anxious eyes checked the odometer for the umpteenth time. Nearly there. The next minutes would mark his future. His breath drew suddenly shallow and labored; his heart, in expectation, thumped at his ribs.

A battered mailbox, precisely where Matty said it would be, leaped from the edge of the road at mile 19.7. Marc's stomach flipped a somersault. *M. SANCHEZ*, hand painted in white letters and strangely unweathered, flared like neon through the swirling dust to point the way. Marc brought the crawling Jeep to a full stop. After pausing only long enough to draw another breath, he made the fateful left turn.

*   *   *   *

The loud rap-rap-rap on the door so startled Maria Sanchez that she jumped where she sat at her loom. Who would come calling in such a dust storm as was blowing today? Pain shot through her arthritic hips as she stiffly pushed from her chair. The knocking swelled in strength. "I'm coming!" Maria called, though she held no hope she could be heard above the scream of the wind. She shuffled her moccasined feet across the plank floor, almost tripping on a curled corner of a wool rug.

Cognizant of what the world outside could mean were it to swirl into her well-scrubbed house, Maria opened the door only an inch or two and peered out. No one appeared through the slotted space. Then, just as she was about to close the door, a movement drew her eye to the top step of her rustic porch. A tall man in jeans and brown jacket turned an expectant gaze at the door, wind and sand making a froth of his dark hair.

"Mrs. Sanchez?" he called over the noise of the storm.

In this remote area, Maria was unaccustomed to, and did not much like, strangers appearing at her door. She was this minute alone in the house, Korey having gone to the stable to see to Sundancer. It rushed to Maria's mind to slam and bolt the door against this man now approaching her, but his eyes were non-threatening, gentle even, and compelled her to remain as she was. Still, she answered warily. "I am Mrs. Sanchez."

He came to stand over her, the bulk of an unyielding door between them. He spoke evenly and with a hint of friendliness curving his mouth. "Mrs. Sanchez, I'm looking for Korey Westerfield. I understand she's living with you."

With these few words, Maria identified her uninvited caller. His voice carried the same soft drawl she had come to recognize as being unique to Korey's speech. Tagging this man as the disreputable Marc Bradberry only added to Maria's reticence. "May I ask," she said without warmth, "why you wish to see Korey?"

"Korey and I are….uh….old friends, and I thought I would stop in to see her." *Miles from nowhere but you just happened to be in the neighborhood? In a raging sandstorm yet! God, Bradberry, you could have done so much better!* He swallowed dryly.

"Korey is not here."

"But she does live here?"

"Yes." Maria was hesitant. "When she returns I will tell her you came by, Mr…?

"Bradberry. Marc Bradberry."

"....Mr. Bradberry." As she repeated the name, Maria was careful not to let her face show that his reputation had preceded him. Korey must be warned that this scoundrel had found her. She would have the disadvantage if he caught her with her guard down. To hasten his departure, Maria narrowed the door opening so that she was looking at him with only one eye. Wind whistled like a tea kettle through the crack. "Now," she frowned, "if you will excuse me...."

Marc's hope, however remote, of being asked inside to await Korey's return was dashed on the rocks of the woman's stony glare and hard words of dismissal. He clenched his teeth in frustration as he accepted that he had lost any advantage he may have held by confronting Korey unexpectedly. Tipped of his visit, she would surely elude him. Damn. Well, where surprise had failed, persistence might prevail. In parting he said, "Please tell Korey how sorry I am to have missed her." He set on Maria an amicable yet resolute gaze, one he had used with tested success in a great many business negotiations. Keeping his tone cordial, he continued, "Tell her too that I will keep trying until I find her at home." He smiled, and Maria understood instantly why a young and vulnerable widow would fall in love with him. "Thank you, Mrs. Sanchez, for opening your door to me on such a foul day."

She would not be charmed by this man with the dazzling smile. A slight bob of her graying head was her only response to his expression of gratitude.

Not a moment later Marc confronted a closed door.

*   *   *   *

The apparition materialized out of a dust cloud. Even though a ground-hugging denim duster hid the slender form, he knew it to be Korey.

Head bent, wide-brimmed hat deflecting much of the grit, her body pushed against the muscle of the raging wind. She was thinking, as she struggled forward, that when it came time to return to Tennessee, the dust storms would not be counted among things she would miss in this beautiful country. With eyes downcast, she did not see the unfamiliar Jeep parked at the opposite side of the house. Nor, on approaching the house, did she see the man rigidly leaning against the post at a far corner of the porch, his eyes taking in every inch of her progress. She glanced up just long enough to locate the steps, then ducked her head to the wind and mounted the porch.

Here the adobe walls sheltered her from the worst of the storm. Stopping at the door, her back to the steps, she removed her dirt-smothered hat and slapped it against her coat. Weathered deck boards hummed as she stomped thick dust from her boots. She looped the hat string over the door latch and reached to unbutton her coat.

He saw that she wore her hair shorter now, the wind making quick work of tangling the curls. The oversize collar of the duster protected her neck, but he imagined he could see the soft brown flesh at her nape. He planted his hands in his pockets so they could not reach for her. Afraid if he blinked she would vanish, he kept a vigilant gaze on her until his eyes could no longer endure the sting of the dry, abrasive wind. He blinked once, then twice more and praised his good fortune that she still stood before him.

She knew the duster had to come off before she stepped into Maria's immaculate house, but the first button, a thick metal disk, was stubborn, and her slender fingers, stiff from the cold, worked to slip it through a snug buttonhole. Suddenly her fingers stilled; she cocked her head. A whisper had come to her, forming her name. She did not move. Her ears tingled as they stretched to listen. *Fool,* she told herself after hearing nothing more beyond the howl of the storm. She shook her head and resumed freeing buttons. *It's only the wind, teasing you in Marc's voice, as it has countless times before.* She worked down the long row of buttons, bending to reach the last ones below the knee. She straightened, grabbed the coat by the wide lapels, began shrugging it from her shoulders. In mid-motion she stopped, ignoring the coat as it draped halfway down her back. Electricity surged along her spine. Her name. Spoken louder this time. She stood insensible, her feet rooted to the planks.

And then again, this time ringing clearly above the wind. "Korey." Marc tasted the sweetness of her name on his tongue. "….Korey."

Tears already streaked her dust-powdered cheeks when she turned. Her mouth moved, but the wind stripped the words from her lips. A weighty lapel, incited by an angry gust, pummeled her breast. She seemed not to notice.

Planted mere yards from her, Marc stood mute, giving her space and time to absorb her shock. Against his will, his eyes announced what was in his heart.

To escape what she saw there, Korey dropped her eyes from his. She said, "You found me." Unable to control a quivering chin, she swiped her cheek with the back of a hand, leaving a muddy stain where a tear had been.

Marc felt his body tense. He was as a man observing, in a chance of a lifetime, a rare and beautiful bird and wary that his slightest movement would send the bird to flight. Afraid to guess what may be tumbling through her mind, he suppressed a gesture that would invite her to come closer. She stood before him, a waif—flushed, tear-stained face; wind-spiked hair; coat sagging around her ankles. His avowed restraint, mere seconds old, could not withstand the desire to touch her. As if on their own, his arms opened, and his noble intentions were all at once trampled beneath her boots as Korey flew into his locking embrace.

If on the threat of death she had been forbidden to go to him, Korey could not have stopped herself from seeking the shelter of his strong arms. She sobbed without shame or thought of dabbing her tears. She felt the comforting weight of his chin in her hair, the curve of his body loosely fitting to hers, and she cried all the more.

As the time for holding her lengthened, seconds turning to precious minutes, Marc began to think how much having her in his arms seemed like any of the dozens of lusty and euphoric dreams of his past year. And just as those dreams, on his waking, had evaporated, now all that he had rehearsed on this morning's drive fled his mind. From his empty head, came pouring forth those thoughts about which he believed most deeply but which he most intended *not* to say, at least not yet. "My darling, I love you so." Unaware that her crying had suddenly stopped, he hugged her tighter. Had he been mindful of how she would receive his next words, his tongue would not have surged ahead of his common sense. "You're my life, Korey. I want you with me, always."

From the moment she had picked up his voice in the wind, Korey's thought processes had ceased to function. Not once had it crossed her mind to wonder why Marc should suddenly come to stand on this porch. He was here, and beyond that she had not ventured—until now. As his last words penetrated, her addled brain began once more to operate. Under the sagging duster her body grew rigid. Her reddened eyes flared with rage. She jerked free of his tight hold. "Oh! You....you....empty headed...."

Adjectives seemed to elude her, but Marc thought that already she had echoed exactly his own self-description.

In vexation, she stomped her foot. "So you think," she growled, "you can track me down—heaven only knows how—and as if nothing happened can sweet talk your way into my good graces?" A fist swung around as if she might hit him, but it flew wildly above her head, not a weapon but a banner waved in anger. Her voice rivaled the decibels of the wind. "How stupid do...." She coughed on the dust-clogged words. "....how could you possibly...?" Her eyes were dry now, some of the redness gone, and the rage suddenly replaced with something approaching revulsion. Her face paled under smears of dirt, and she backed away from him as if frightened. "Or is it that you've come only to salt the wound?"

Barking at her was not his intent, but in his shock that is what he did. "Korey! How could you *think* such a thing?" Then, like a keen blow to his thick head, the reason for her outrage struck him: Korey could not know the change in his life that had given him freedom to come. He had given no explanation. Only natural that she should jump to the wrong conclusion. In hindsight, he could not believe he had not planned for this before opening his big damn mouth. "Listen to me." But his plea did not stop her backward slide. "Korey!" He wanted to grab her, shake her to make her listen. He said, in a wind-scorched voice, "Clare is dead."

She stopped, stared at him through a fog of dust. One look at his solemn face and it never again entered her mind to doubt the truth of what he said. "I....oh, Marc, I *am* sorry. I didn't know."

"Of course you didn't. Holed up here," he glanced around, "America's Outback, you couldn't have known."

After a pause she said, "Truly I am sorry for your loss. But if you're thinking it can change things....that you and I...."

"No," he lied, swallowing an irrational disappointment that she was not by now all over him, smothering him with wet kisses and declarations of undying love. "I came to ask your forgiveness."

She did not close the gap between them. At last she answered. "I *have* forgiven you." She seemed surprised by this.

Marc smiled. Once more his mind, bursting with eagerness, jumped too far ahead. "Should this give me hope that we can rebuild some of what I so thoughtlessly destroyed?"

Korey bristled. "I *said* I have forgiven. I *did not*, however, say I have *forgotten*." Her look was straightforward. "You broke my heart."

"And my own."

"Perhaps."

He ignored her expression of doubt. It was not his purpose today to waste time sniveling over his own misery. After all, the misery had been entirely of his making, and he had over the past year flogged himself nearly to death with it. These precious moments would be best spent repairing wounds not whimpering over them. He made her an offer. "The two of us....maybe we could mend those broken hearts."

Cool, cautious eyes watched him. "How much do you want from me?"

"Only what you wish to give. Ultimately, I would hope for a restoration of our friendship." When she did not respond, he went on, "A year ago on an airplane bound for Chattanooga, you said I didn't really know you. I'm asking now for another chance to get to know you, Korey." He added humbly, "I'll never again give you cause to run from me."

"Friends only?" She sounded skeptical.

He gave her what he hoped was a convincing nod of his head.

Her face became a billboard of confusion. She looked down at her boots. "Friendship means trust. Without trust...." She shook her head. "It may be impossible to go back after all that's passed between us."

"But can't we try?"

She turned, looked over her shoulder to the haven of the door. He barely heard her words as she said, "I don't know. If it doesn't work out...."

He had no answer, at any rate not one he could say aloud. He could not tell her that what he asked of her today revealed only the tip of his buried desire— that she should one day walk with him as his wife. As incoherent as his mind had been today, it still had more sense than to let him blurt out a disastrously-timed proposal of marriage. There would be a courtship, slow and easy, maybe even disguised. She would need time.... But he had set his sights. It *had* to work; he would *make* it work.

She came around to face him, her eyes glazed as though she had slipped into a trance, the duster hanging from her in a rumpled heap. "What has happened here today.... I have to get it straight in my mind." Abruptly, she stripped off the coat, shook it, threw it over her arm. "I'm going in now." Without looking at him, she turned for the door.

Marc's voice shot across the sand swept porch. "Wait!" If it ended here, he may never see her again. He could not let her go—not yet. As she stood with her hand anchored to the door latch, he spoke to the back of her wind-ruffled head. "May I call you sometime? In a few days? To talk?"

"As a friend?"

"As a friend."

For a time she kept a stiff back to him. But when her head drooped, he wondered with dread if he had asked for too much. Maybe it was going through her mind to tell him not to call, nor to ever again appear at this or any other door behind which she would happen to reside. Above her shirt collar, the nape of her neck was exposed to him, and he saw where the storm had left a deposit of grime. A sudden desire to be present when she bathed the soil from her smooth and slender limbs nearly dropped him to his knees. A flutter danced through his chest, and in spite of the cold, parched wind penetrating his clothes, sweat popped from every pore.

Korey came erect as if she sensed how deeply his eyes probed. Without expression, she turned her head and bravely met his stare. "Call if you like," she said flatly. "But you take the chance that I may refuse to talk to you."

Nothing could have stopped the blinding grin that reflected how he felt about his deliverance. He ignored the grit in his teeth as he said, "A chance I will most gladly take." He came forward two steps but halted the advance when she shrank against the door. From the distance of a few feet, he said, "I'll call you." He thought he may have only imagined her faint shadow of a smile as he watched her vanish behind the sturdy door. With a solid click of the latch, for the second time that day, he had been sealed outside. Instead of showing a frown, Marc's face lit with a grin. True, this was one door she had closed on him. But by not denying outright his request to phone her, she had left open another.

*   *   *   *

Marc's jangled nerves had not let him wait as much as twenty-four hours to call Korey. Much to his pleasure, she had answered in good spirits, sounding slightly breathless as if she may have sprinted to grab the phone. He found her voice to be reserved without being cool. He would be flying home tomorrow, he told her, and could not leave New Mexico without saying goodbye.

To his amazement, she had invited him to again make the drive to Maria's that very afternoon. The storm was over, she said. It was a crisp and sunny day on the mountain. Would he be interested in seeing Maria's ranch?

For a chance to spend the afternoon with Korey, would he ever! But the proposal had left him stunned.

"Marc? Marc, are you still there?" she had asked to a line gone dead.

His affirmative answer had flown out in such a euphoric rush, he knew but did not care that he had come across as a youth just asked to a dance by the prettiest girl in school. That same adolescent had hung up the phone, left his older brother gaping after him, jumped in the Jeep, and driven up the mountain at near-careless speeds.

With the smell of dust in his nostrils, he now found himself strapped to the passenger seat of Maria's range-worn pickup truck, bouncing along a dirt road he would generously describe as a rutted wagon trail. The mountains and desert were there for him to absorb and, as parched soil drinks rain, so too was his arid spirit quenched by the vistas unrolling before him. Surely, he thought, the creator of such rugged beauty would find it a relatively simple task to reunite a man and woman in love.

The woman whom he loved was in the driver's seat, her eyes glued to the road. So far, he had not been the recipient of even one moon-eyed, lingering look. He had not expected to be, was not disheartened by it, but was disappointed nonetheless. Her grip on the steering wheel was overly tight, but to save their skins on such a road, the vigilance was probably necessary.

Quite apart from being churned by the rough terrain, Marc's insides were a wreck. His mind, the authoritarian, was bent on remaining cool and in control so it could responsibly monitor his every move. *Only the most proper behavior today, Marcus,* his mind would remind him. But his body did not give a flip for being proper. Korey's baggy faded jeans and heavy cotton shirt did nothing to bar the memory of what lived and breathed underneath. She had no makeup on her freshly scrubbed face. Her hair blew freely in a wind that funneled through the open windows. She was, in the flesh, the woman who had made her home in his dreams. And she was within an arm's reach. He took a deep breath. Dust tickled his throat. He swallowed.

Korey was saying, as he watched her profile—he could not seem to take his eyes off of her—"Well, it didn't take me long to put two and two together and come up with the answer to how you found me." She glanced at him sidelong as if shying away from his stare. "Let me tell you, once it hit me, I was on the phone to Matty, pronto. After she had her say, I calmed down. I suppose you have Aunt Matty to thank, indirectly anyway, for your invitation here today. She has a way….she made me see some things."

Korey did not explain what she meant by *things,* and Marc thought it best not to ask. Treading softly on the edges of their budding reconciliation, he said, "Asking me here today, so soon….well, you must know it was the last thing I expected."

She smiled. "You arrived here in record time, I noticed." His heart tap danced when she turned the smile on him. Then her face became serious. She said, as if she truly cared about his welfare, "Please don't drive that fast returning to Albuquerque." Her eyes shifted back to the road.

"I won't be in that much of a hurry going back. But you didn't answer my question."

"I wasn't aware you asked one."

"It was implied."

"How come I suddenly decided to ask you here? Well, if you think *you* were taken back, you should have been there to see *my* reaction! I hadn't expected you to phone today, and when you said you were flying home tomorrow, the idea to take you on a tour of the ranch came purely on impulse. But once I'd said it, it didn't seem like such a bad idea."

"And I didn't give you time to retract the invitation."

She glanced his way. "Time enough—if I had wanted to." For the first time she saw the shadows of fatigue under his eyes. "You didn't get much sleep, did you?"

"No. Shows does it?"

"A little. I had stuff rattling around inside my head most of the night. Noisy. Figured you may have had the same problem."

"Yeah. All night."

They had come to a section of road so washed out even the sun-hardened ruts were gone. For several hundred yards the roadway was a series of large eroded boulders, low and rounded like turtles' backs. Korey devoted her attention to driving. The truck rocked, and a nest of keys jangled against the steering column as wide tires rolled slowly up, over, and down the red sandstone.

With the worst behind them and the road leveling ahead, Korey stopped the truck. She turned to Marc, the engine idling, her foot firmly on the brake. "What are we going to do now? We can't take up where we left off, Marc. And we know each other much too well to pretend we just met. So we can't go back, and we can't go forward…. Oh, it's all so pointless!"

She jerked her foot from the brake pedal and gave the truck the gas. The road vibrated through Marc's teeth. He paid no attention to the shadows of clouds frolicking over distant mesas, or to the lone coyote running across the road ahead, or the dust thrown by the truck that curled in on him through the open window. He thought only of Korey and how close he might be to losing her still. He spoke to her profile. "I don't agree. I believe we *can* start over." The palm of his hand skipped flatly back and forth across the thigh of his jeans until the heavy denim burned his hand and he became aware of the nervous fidget. He brought his hand to rest on his knee and lowered his voice to hide the desperation he had begun to feel. "Look, we won't make any demands on each other. No pressure. Half a continent will separate us. We'll have time to design and reassemble our friendship and the space in which to do it."

"Spoken like the consummate architect," she said without sarcasm.

He was comfortable with the ensuing silence, preferring it to having to counter her objections. He remained in the dark regarding her thoughts until she said quite suddenly, "How did it happen?"

"Pardon?"

"Clare. What happened?"

Marc shifted in his seat. "She slept away, peacefully, one snowy winter night."

Thinking of her own mother's suffering, Korey thought of the usual platitude: Clare is at peace; the death was a blessing. But Korey did not speak her mind for fear Marc may mistake her motive. Even now she did not want to admit that in her darkest hours she had wished Marc's wife dead. When Korey said, "I really am sorry," she meant it not only for Clare but for her own evil thoughts as well.

"Yes," he absently replied. Not without some guilt, he remembered the freedom he had felt when Clare was gone. It had been like being released from prison. Liberation—and he had not known what to do with it. After he had buried Clare, he nearly buried himself in pain, self-pity, drunkenness. Clare's family had exacerbated his despair. At the funeral, the self-serving lot gave him the cold shoulder, except when they took turns cornering him, berating him for "ruining our little girl." It was not until he had sobered that he realized how wrong they had been.

Korey had one eye on the road, one on him when he surfaced from the darkness of his memories. Speaking of Clare, he said, "Truthfully, she probably had much less pain in the coma than out of it. Reflecting on her life, which I can now do objectively, she didn't have an easy time of it. I suspect she never was happy with her choice of husband. My ego has come to terms with that. It helps to know that she was so spoiled, so wrapped up in herself, she may not have been happy no matter the man she'd married." He turned away, looked out the side window, spied a spotted brown lizard sunning on a rock of the same color. Marc changed the subject. "Beautiful country up here. Plain to see why someone would choose this place to rusticate....for a while."

"Uh huh," Korey agreed. Was he fishing, she wondered, trying to find out when she would return to Tennessee? She would tell him as much as she knew about her immediate future, but first he would have to ask. She did not want to appear eager. From the corner of her eye, she saw that he was again watching her. Under his scrutiny the flesh on the back of her neck tingled as if he had brushed a kiss there.

Marc lowered his sun visor. Korey's hands, with a firm grip on the wheel, were dark brown in the strong rays of a late sun. She still wore the wide gold and diamond band on her right hand; rainbow stars blinked on the windshield just above the dash as the truck chattered over a section of washboard road. He studied her hands. They were lovely, long and narrow, slender-fingered but not exactly the hands that had touched him in his dreams. With chapped, reddened knuckles these hands had lately engaged in long stretches of outdoor work in warm sun and drying wind. If he turned one over, he bet he would find a callous or two. He recalled how she had shunned wearing gloves when she worked in her flower beds in Chattanooga.

As if flowers had suddenly blossomed in the truck, the scent of petunias was so strong, for a moment Marc could not separate the real from the imagined. He held in his mind, as clearly as if it were in his hand, a picture of Korey that first summer…. He had stopped at her house, caught her coming in from pinching faded heads in the petunia bed, her hands stained and sticky with tangy scent. Nostalgia swept him along, and he began to recognize how much the woman beside him now was unlike the woman of the petunia bed. This woman seemed more self-assured. With the roughened hands, the scuffed boots, a sensible shirt of geometric design carelessly turned back to expose slender wrists, she had a cavalier air about her. But he had to remind himself to look beyond to where he saw that she was still vulnerable—and even more desirable.

As he watched her, it occurred to him that she had come to belong to this country. What if she had made up her mind to stay, to make this her home? Matty had hinted that Korey's time here was temporary. But if not, what would be his chances of luring her away from this life? He wasn't sure if it was the dread that had begun gnawing at the pit of his stomach, or the wild, bumpy ride that had him suddenly feeling sick. The suspense was too much. He had to know. "You planning to stay here….indefinitely?"

There was no small amount of satisfaction in learning *he* was the eager one. She loved him, no denying it, but she had proven to herself she could live without him. She answered his question. "No. But I'm not sure when I'll be leaving." She swerved to dodge a sharp rock protruding from the roadbed. Though his shoulder harness held him fast, Marc instinctively thrust an arm out the window, slapped his hand on the roof of the cab and clung as if the tips of his fingers were suction cups.

"Oops. Sorry. It's that darn heavy foot again. Incorrigible." She flashed him a wayward grin and decelerated.

Marc relaxed, felt his breath return, pried his fingers from the roof.

"Now," she said, "where was I? Oh, yes….about my leaving. No date has been set, but before long Maria will be going to Albuquerque for a hip replacement. At that time, I'll return home."

In his exuberance, Marc wanted to shout "Whoopee!" For two reasons, he took this as the best possible news. One, he would once more have Korey near. And two, it meant she was not, true to Matty's assurances, in love with Jim Yellowhawk. But still leery of scaring her away, Marc tempered his enthusiasm. "I see," he commented simply, then turned away to hide a smile.

Undaunted by his tepid response, Korey continued. "I'm looking forward to going home, to seeing everyone. Especially Tina. She's going to have a baby."

"Oh?"

"I found out last night. Tina called with the news. She's known for a while but didn't want to tell me until the greatest risk of miscarriage was past. You remember she lost their first baby."

Marc nodded. "How is she feeling?"

"Ecstatically happy despite acute morning sickness. And Bryan—when I spoke with him last night he sounded like he was about to bubble over. No telling what he'll be like by the time the baby arrives in October." Korey giggled. "So you see, I have to go home soon. As an aunt in the making, I want to be there to share in this pregnancy. What fun it will be to shop for blankets and rattles, bibs and tiny booties. I wouldn't miss it for anything."

Even his envy of Bryan Goodwin's fatherhood could not stop Marc from becoming infected with Korey's joy. Heart strings hummed in his chest, and at that moment, above all else he knew he wanted Korey to be the mother of his children. The two of them would beget a house full, and, God willing, each and every child would be beautiful and loving, in the image of their mother. A humid warmth instantly suffused Marc's blood. His mind deployed a disciplined army to form a line behind which his body could not reach over to switch off the truck and begin the procreation then and there. Over the noise of his inner conflict, he heard Korey talking. His fevered brain, lagging from battle fatigue, finally caught up, but it was some time before he realized the topic was now Maria Sanchez.

"….sell this place. The cattle and what few horses they had were sold after her husband died. It will break her heart to sell, but it has to be done. She'll lose some of her independence, but she's a spirited woman, and when she has time to adjust to a new life, she'll be happy in Albuquerque."

Marc looked past Korey, out her side window to beyond a distant fence line. "Did I just hear you say Maria had sold her cattle?"

"Yes."

He pointed across her chest, careful to not touch her. "Then what are those?"

She followed his gaze to where fuzzy brown dots seemed to rise out of the sage. "Oh, what luck!" she exclaimed. "Buffalo!" She cut the wheel sharply, sending her passenger rolling into her shoulder. "You're in for a treat, Marc. Jim's herd is a sight to behold."

Marc thought this ride overland smoother than that of the *road* they had left behind. They bumped over flatlands, straddling scrub grass and sage. He jerked this way and that as Korey dodged whole families of cane cholla; with slender, needled arms, the cacti assailed the length of the truck. The sound, like nails raking a chalkboard, turned the skin on Marc's back to goose flesh. "Buffalo?" he asked, shivering. "As in bison?"

"Yep."

Buffalo—Jim. Jim's buffalo! He remembered then that Eric had mentioned Jim Yellowhawk kept a buffalo herd. Thinking aloud, he muttered, "So, this is Jim Yellowhawk's place."

The words drifted through the cab like dust motes in a ray of sunlight. An instant later the truck slammed to a jarring halt. Only Marc's shoulder harness saved him from sailing forward and cracking his kneecaps on the dashboard. "Whew!" His eyes were wide on hers. "What was *that* for?" But he feared she could see in his face that he already knew.

This time Korey switched off the engine. The world was so quiet her ears hurt. "Odd that I don't recall saying anything to you about Jim Yellowhawk."

To Marc's relief she did not sound peeved. Perplexed, maybe. "That's because you didn't. It appears Matty didn't tell you that I knew about Jim."

"No. Seems you've really done your homework."

"Can't take credit. It was Eric."

"Eric!"

"Couple of weeks ago…. He and Rae had dinner at The High Noon in Old Town Albuquerque. Seems you and Jim Yellowhawk chose to dine there the same night."

To Marc's astonishment, the truck echoed with Korey's laughter. "Wouldn't you know," she burbled, wiping a tear from the corner of one eye, "the only time Jim and I went to a restaurant…." Releasing the seat belt, she swiveled sideways, slouched back against the truck door, rested a bent right knee on the dusty vinyl seat, hooked her left wrist over the steering wheel. "I suppose this means Jim and I have become grist for the rumor mill." It was becoming clearer to her why Marc had come: He felt threatened by Jim. Well, perhaps a little jealousy was not a bad thing…. Her laughter had dissolved into an enigmatic smile. "Maybe it's time you told me all about how you came to find me. Apart, of course, from where you adroitly charmed written directions from Aunt Matty."

Marc shoved his rangy legs under the dash and courageously met her waning smile. He began the debriefing: Eric and Rae had taken a series of photos at Jim Yellowhawk's ranch. Marc drew a resurgent smile from Korey when he told her of his many phone conversations with Eric during which they had tried, speculatively, to paste together and make sense of scraps of clues. "….but it didn't take long to discover that without Matty's help, finding you was not going to be easy." Marc purposely omitted telling of his fortuitous stop at the little gallery in Old

Town. He would not yet have Korey know he was now the proud owner of the Enchanted Mesa quilt.

Korey asked, "And what if Matty had refused you?"

"A daunting possibility, I'll admit. It would've tossed a nail in the cog. But if I hadn't found you this time, there would've been other trips."

She knew he was telling her, the same as Jim had, that it was not his nature to quit. His tenacity was as terrifying as it was flattering. His head was tilted, his lips parted, as if he might say something more. Suddenly Korey thought of nothing beyond what it would feel like to have his mouth cover hers. In response, she felt her body ripen. It was then that the warning bells began clanging against her skull. She jerked her back away from its resting place as if the slanting sun had scorched her through the door. Her feet hit the floor at the same instant her hand touched the ignition.

Her lightning moves yanked Marc away from cravings of his own. He came upright, set a hand on Korey's forearm to stop her firing the engine. "Not yet," he said firmly. "There's something else I want to tell you." He dropped the restraining hand.

Korey gripped the steering wheel. "All right," she conceded. She did not look at him, nor did she soften her rigid spine.

"Before you return home, that is to Tennessee, you should hear this from me. You and I agreed once to be completely open. Remember?"

"Yes, I remember." She seemed fascinated with the inert gauges on the dashboard. "Though as I recall, the agreement was a little tardy in coming."

"True enough. Korey, I've been dating someone.... I guess you could say, 'steadily.' A woman I've known several years. I'm very fond of her."

"Ohhh." She drew out the word, her voice shrinking like someone reducing the volume on a radio. To her mortification, it sounded like a moan.

"Her name is Julia Santangelo. The gossip has us all but married—hell, maybe that too. It's only rumor. Julia and I have not discussed marriage. I wanted you to know."

Another woman.... Somehow this did not shock Korey, as if, without forming the conscious thought, she had known he had not gone on to live a monastic life. It *did*, however, surprise her to find that instead of anger or jealousy, she actually felt sorry for Julia Santangelo. The reason for this Korey could not fathom until she turned her face to Marc's solemn but loving gaze. Though no assurances came from his lips, his eyes told her unequivocally that until things were concluded between them, he would not be seeing Julia Santangelo, that as far as he was concerned if a queue had formed for his affections, Korey had moved to the head of the line. Marc had made his choice; the rest was up to her.

She did not know what to do or say. Her back ached with tension. Finally, she dropped her hands from the wheel and leaned to the seat. *Maybe there are no words....* She looked at him across the confines of the small cab. Two people in love and at a loss. One unable to fully trust. One desperate to find a way to merit trust. But miraculously, in a dusty red truck under a late sun turned brass through buttermilk clouds, the past year seemed to melt away. There had been no estrangement, no separation of a thousand miles.

Korey knew if she made the slightest move toward Marc, he would be there to meet her half way. Transcending time and reality, she felt his warm wet lips on hers, felt his hands on her skin, smelled the scent of their lovemaking. On the wind came whiffs of menthol in his shaving cream, papaya in his shampoo, damp cotton in his bath towel. Her mind was alive with teeming memories. Could she send him away, hold a distance between them long enough to get her head on straight? Her eyes lowered from his, and she noticed he had not unfastened his shoulder harness, as if in the absence of self-restraint he were relying on the harness to fix him to his seat. If he would only reach out, pull her to him. One touch, one kiss, and she knew they would be there in that truck on the high desert to watch the sun come up. She suddenly hated him for not taking control, leaving her to find her own answers, yet at the same time, she respected and loved him all the more for doing so.

"Korey?"

"Um?"

"You're a million miles away," he said, as if assured of where she had been because he had been there too.

A purple veil hung in the west where the sun had been. Korey blinked and gazed around as though she *had* just returned from a long journey. "No....I'm right here. I heard every word you said." She cleared a lump from her throat. "It'll be dark soon. If you're going to have more than a glimpse of those buffalo, we'd better get on over there." She added, to a dirty windshield, "I do appreciate you telling me about Julia Santangelo." Korey pulled the shoulder harness across her chest, snapped it into place, turned the ignition key. The truck coughed, roared to life, began to roll. She pinned him with her gaze. "Any future we may have together hangs by a fraying thread from two words: open and honest."

Marc heard two more words: *future...*and...*together.* Rays of hope burned so brightly that it seemed the earth had reversed its spin, and, like a movie run backward, the sun was rising in the west, hitting him fully in the face.

CHAPTER 26

▼

Marc was gone from New Mexico as suddenly as he had come, leaving Korey to wonder if she had seen him only in a dream. One week later, Maria announced that she would have a hip replaced in mid-May. With less than a month in which to prepare, Korey abandoned for now any contemplation of Marc and what his visit might mean to her future.

The house erupted in a flurry of activity. Clothes, dishes, and personal items were packed for Maria's move to Albuquerque. Like a maze, walls of cardboard cartons wound throughout the house. Korey boxed most of her own things to ship to Chattanooga since she had too much to tote on the flight home. As the day for leaving drew near, a pickup truck came and went as Maria's scarred but usable furniture was lovingly given and gratefully received by the family's most recently wedded couple.

Helpful to the last, early on moving day Jim Yellowhawk appeared at the door. Under a cloudless sky, he went about the business of loading Maria's truck. Saying little, he went back and forth from house to truck, carrying boxes stacked three or four high as if the weight were nothing. He expertly stowed Maria's precious possessions, packing the boxes tightly among rolled rugs, then filling a last gap with Korey's two large suitcases.

The sound of the tailgate slamming shut signaled to Maria that it was time, after forty years, to leave her home. With short, shuffling steps, the stripes on her wool shawl outlining her drooping shoulders, she went alone into the house for a final look.

It was then, with no one to see, that Jim took Korey into his arms. For the rest of her life she would remember the kiss. She had known him to be a man of few words; the kiss demonstrated his feelings in other ways. It was almost enough to persuade her to stay in New Mexico. Almost....

Korey broke the embrace and waited for his words of farewell that never came. Then a hand tugged at her arm, led her to the truck. Maria's voice was gentle. "Get in," she said. In the narrow rectangle of the rearview mirror, Jim Yellowhawk, standing motionless in front of Maria's little adobe house, receded behind a veil of dust and tears, becoming smaller and smaller until he was no longer there at all.

Korey stayed in Albuquerque only long enough to see Maria safely through a successful surgery. Then more difficult goodbyes: Maria, Maria's family, Aunt Matty. After hugs, kisses, smiles and tears, Korey too was gone.

She arrived home to a house vacated the week before. Tina and Bryan had eagerly moved into their new home, leaving behind a spotless house, manicured lawn, trimmed rose bushes, and flower beds with soil turned and ready for planting. Though bittersweet, it was good to be home.

Did Marc, among his other attributes, come equipped with radar? He had phoned twice during her last weeks in New Mexico, and she could only tell him she would be home sometime after May 15th. Therefore, Korey was surprised when, on her second day home, she opened the door to a riot of spring flowers presented by a smiling delivery boy. The van in the driveway read **Blume's Blooms**. And it was just the beginning. Over the next weeks, Korey's door became a scheduled twice-weekly stop for **Blume's Blooms**.

Though Marc phoned often, she had not set eyes on him since arriving home. She told herself he did not come because he was too busy, but deep inside she knew absolutely that he stayed away so that their rekindled passion would not overheat and prematurely destroy their newfound relationship. It was clear, however, to everyone but Korey that Marc was paying court. Her self-deception could not last. Every vase in the house stood replenished with fresh flowers, an endearingly witty ode printed in Marc's precise hand clipped to each bouquet. Such lavish demonstrations of affection were impossible to ignore, and, as the thermometer climbed into the heat of early summer, Korey's point of view softened until she finally conceded that being the object of such devotion was irresistible fun.

The third week in June Marc phoned and apologized for having figuratively kept Korey in a closet those months Clare had been alive. Now, to make amends, he wanted to take her to his Chattanooga office "to meet the crew." For the first time, he was offering to open a large part of his world to her. It did not enter Korey's mind to refuse.

Upon seeing her, his smile was so broad as to be blinding, and his eyes held new sparkle. Yet the last two months had changed him: his face was thinner, too much so, and wore added creases where an errant lock of hair fell across his forehead. Though he had recently overtly named their courtship for what it was, Korey suspected her ongoing tepid response was taking a toll on Marc. A mere glance his way made her pulse race, but she carefully concealed how truly thrilled she was to be with him again. Would the day ever come when she could trustingly give her body and soul to his care?

A flood of memories assailed Korey when she stepped into the entry of Bradberry and Associates, Chattanooga Division. Familiar smells—floor polish, leather upholstery, a hint of the receptionist's floral perfume—greeted her in the same way as when she had occasionally spent a night in the room above. But unlike those quiet, solitary nights, the office was now alive with the murmur of voices, the click of computer keyboards, the hum of an air conditioner pouring out chilled air to banish the heat of the 92° day.

She and Marc made their way from the reception room to the spacious room at the back of the office. There, as if she were expected, eight pairs of eyes looked up from computers and drafting tables as Korey entered. Her outward poise belied the inner fluttering at being so obviously on display. Marc proudly showed her off, and Korey gracefully accepted handshakes, returned smiles, and exchanged a few words with each person in the room.

Marc then led her to the tiny kitchen where they found Steven Aymes pouring a cup of coffee. Instead of extending a hand at the introductions, Steven welcomed Korey with a hug. For a moment she was taken back by the familiar greeting, but the grin on Marc's face reminded her that not only were Marc and Steven business associates but good friends as well. The hug was evidence Steven knew the history she and Marc shared. And Steven was so immediately warm, so easy to talk to, it did not occur to Korey to feel embarrassed by the fact that he surely knew what a fool she had made of herself when she had unwittingly been "the other woman."

The ensuing conversation was soon interrupted by a client in search of Marc. Korey recognized Carl Huntington the instant his graying head appeared around the frame of the kitchen door. She had never met him, but being a local business and civic leader—farm boy made good—his picture ran often in the newspaper. Among other enterprises, he was the owner of Huntington Tower, an office building designed by Marcus Bradberry and Associates presently under construction on Market Street. Korey could not guess, as her hand was squeezed under the pressure of Carl Huntington's crushing grip, that before she and Marc departed the office today, she would be commissioned by Carl Huntington to sew a quilt for the lobby of the new Huntington Tower. Since the Tower was scheduled to open in September, Korey knew, as Marc escorted her from his office, exactly how she would be spending her summer.

Her plans, therefore, did not include time away from her sewing. But soon after her foray into Marc's work world, he convinced her to take three days off to visit his family in Nashville. "Fly over with me tomorrow. Mom, Kevin, a couple of my favorite cousins are all dying to meet you," he said, enthusiasm animating his face. "Mom and Kevin know all about us. Kevin knew for some time before....before our breakup, and I told Mom a few months before Clare died. After Mom justifiably stripped my hide, she hugged me close—ah, the unconditional love of a mother—and said, 'Maybe someday, you can go to her.' *Her* meaning you, of course. I did not discourage her optimism, but I confess until two months ago I hadn't a prayer of it happening."

"Ye of little faith," said Korey.

She accompanied Marc to Nashville, setting aside her trepidation about meeting his family. She need not have worried. All fears were allayed the moment she was thrust into their midst. Everyone welcomed her as though she were already a member of the family. She fell instantly in love with Marc's mother. A large woman with silver hair, Barbara Bradberry carried herself erect, wore tailored slacks, silk shirts, and sensible low-heeled shoes. Her gracious disposition matched the sunny weather, and she kept the house in an uproar with an endless string of hilarious, innocuous jokes. "She hears them at bridge club," Marc whispered in Korey's ear one evening. "Not much serious card playing goes on— mainly the gals meet to see who can top the other in the joke department. Lucky for us, this evening she's keeping the bawdy ones to herself."

During her stay in Nashville, Korey slept in Barbara's spare bedroom, an arrangement judiciously made by Marc. In the rare hours when Korey and Barbara had the house to themselves, they used the quiet time to forge a friendship. One such time was on the last night of Korey's stay. The women, sharing space on a wide sofa, talked while eating ice cream.

Barbara said, "I know I'm not responsible for my grown son's behavior, but just the same, I'm so sorry he hurt you."

"It's hard for a woman to find fault when a man falls madly in love with her. His timing was bad, he was out of control, and he withheld some things. I've forgiven him that."

"So I've observed. You'd not have come otherwise." Barbara idly stirred her ice cream into mush. "Marc is the most private of my three boys. He keeps so much to himself. Tell me, are you two planning to marry?"

Korey slipped a cool vanilla-flavored spoon from her mouth. "He hasn't asked me."

"My goodness, I can't imagine what he's waiting for. None of us have missed seeing how much he adores you."

"He's treading very carefully, patiently working at rebuilding trust, handling me as though I'm made of fragile porcelain, much as he did in the early days of our relationship but for different reasons, of course. We're seldom together, the telephone's still our close mutual friend." Korey paused. "He's kissed me a total of three times in the last two and a half months—on the cheek, of all places."

"You're not satisfied with this?"

"No. Yes. I don't know. Within the past year, I've changed in many ways, and Marc's a different person now that he's free of his deceptions. We're getting to know each other all over again." Korey let the last bite of ice cream dissolve on her tongue, then set the empty bowl aside. "He has declared that we are officially participating in a 'courtship.' Since my return from New Mexico, he has sent so many flowers my house has become a garden. He says 'I love you' often and never acts hurt when something inside won't let me say it back. And he's made it clear that he doesn't want my decision on our future to come while he and I are romping in bed." Her face flamed as she realized what she had just said to the mother of her lover, never mind that at the present, the term *lover* was more passive than active. She said to herself: Well, Korey, now that you're sufficiently embarrassed, there's nothing to be lost by being completely candid. "Heaven knows," she said aloud, "the celibacy hasn't been easy on me, but, frankly, I think it's beginning to really wear on Marc."

"Understandably. But don't worry too much about him, dear. He'll survive. Just concentrate now on *you*. Call me old fashioned, but I believe marriage—and no question marriage is what Marc has planned—to be a promise of a lifetime."

"Me too."

Barbara Bradberry's smile was one of encouragement. "When you're ready, Korey, the answer will come." She swapped a puddle of melted ice cream for a cigarette. "I'm down to one a day," she said proudly before lighting it. "I must say," she went on, "I'll be immensely disappointed if you decide against the marriage. In these few days we've had together, I've come to think of you as a daughter. I adore Eric's wife, Raegan, but she lives so far away I rarely see her. It would be so nice to have you here in Nashville." Barbara tapped tottering ash into an ashtray. "Oh, don't pay any attention to me." She squinted into the snaking smoke. "Just an aging mother hoping it will be you who'll become part of my family and provide me with grandchildren."

"You've already made me feel like a member of your family." Korey scanned the warmly lit room. "It's as if I belong here."

Barbara stubbed out the half-smoked cigarette. She smiled at the beautiful young woman she was certain would become Marc's wife. "You do belong here, Korey. And one day soon your head will join with your heart to tell you so."

*   *   *   *

Korey sat cross-legged, not caring that the freshly mowed grass bled green stains onto the seat of her white shorts. Directly overhead, the July sun burnished her hair as she bent to the task of blind stitching together two pieces of fabric. With September fast approaching, the bits and pieces that would eventually become the quilt for the Huntington Tower were rarely out of her reach.

Drowsy in the heat, Marc lay propped on an elbow beside her, a wary eye vigilantly noting the progress of a red ant negotiating the grass's peaks and valleys toward his bare arm. A fish jumped near the shore of the small lake, and Marc, his attention diverted, swiveled a lazy head to watch hypnotic circles expand in the water. In the distance, air hovered in a milky haze above Lookout Mountain.

"You feeling guilty?" Korey asked, smiling at Marc's profile.

"Nope. Not for these few stolen moments. You?"

"No." Korey touched a playful finger to his ribs. "But as you've noticed, I am working."

Marc rolled onto his back, threw a careless arm over his eyes. "We're on office property, so technically I'm *at the office*. Besides, every colony has its drones." For a time he was so still, Korey thought he had fallen asleep. She jumped and nearly pricked a finger when he said, "It's a short walk through the trees to the office. If he needs me, Steven knows where I am."

Taking advantage of the opportunity, Korey paused in her sewing to watch the easy rise and fall of Marc's chest. It was her fault that lately he had been driving himself beyond a mere desire to excel in his profession. A furious work pace diminished cravings of the flesh. So far, the summer had been a sultry one, and Korey, in the context of her musings, was not thinking of the weather. Abruptly she snapped her mind closed to the pictures it was forming. Focusing again on her sewing, she said, "A letter arrived from Maria Sanchez this morning. She sold the ranch."

Marc roused himself to his elbows and looked out across the lake. "That was quick."

"Sure was. Seems she got an offer before the place was even officially listed for sale—at a price she couldn't refuse. Though she misses the ranch, from the tone of her letter, she seems content to be in Albuquerque. I miss it too. The ranch, I mean. And for some strange reason, lately I've had dreams about it."

"What kind of dreams?"

"Nonsense mostly…. I'm there with someone, but the face is indistinct. Somehow, though, I know it's not Maria." Korey shrugged. "Well, if the dreams arise from any subconscious expectations I've had of going back there, the selling of the ranch should put an end to them."

Marc did not comment but kept his gaze fixed on the lake. Two mallards, a drake and his female, flew low, then, orange feet lowered like landing gear, skimmed the surface of the water. Fluttering their wings, they paddled nearer the opposite shore. Marc sat up, reached for a loaf of bread he had brought for such an occasion, tore a slice, pressed it into large pellets, and swiftly overhanded them far out into the lake.

Korey looked up just as the drake, bobbing his iridescent green head, gulped the pieces before the female knew what had hit the water. "Just like a man," she said.

Marc aimed the next throw to give the female the advantage. He smiled over his shoulder. "Better?"

"Much." Korey again strayed to Maria's letter. "I wonder if Maria sold to a local rancher. She didn't mention the buyer, which I thought odd."

"Why?"

"Seems she would have said *something,* especially if the new owner were someone she knew. I don't suppose it was Jim Yellowhawk. He told me once he wanted to expand his ranch. But Maria surely would've said if she had sold to Jim."

At the mention of Jim Yellowhawk, Marc remained silent, and Korey saw that he shifted his weight as if he were suddenly uncomfortable. Clearly Marc did not care to discuss Jim Yellowhawk, nor did he seem eager to speculate on the sale of the ranch. Korey let the subject die, leaving behind an expansive void.

As though they sensed the change of mood on shore, the ducks began to squawk. The feathered pair warily made their way across the lake to be nearer the food source. Sequins flashed as a breeze roughened the water and carried to the mossy bank the odor of fish. Korey absently wondered if the ducks' chatter was love talk or family squabble and was surprised to find she was envious of the apparent simplicity with which ducks mate. For them life would be too short, the call to procreate too great to waste long months choosing a partner.

Weary of sewing, Korey put her work into a tote bag. Marc tried his best not to look at her long brown legs as she stretched them out to further toast in the sun. Korey closed her eyes and listened to wavelets lick the shore. Marc was so quiet she could have imagined he was no longer beside her. She was not at all prepared for what came next.

"Marry me, Korey."

His words struck her like a keen blow to the heart. Eyes popping open, she was at once euphoric and stunned.

Marc took her hand and slowly traced a finger over her lifeline. He lifted her palm to his lips. Her entire body absorbed the kiss, and she wished for the kiss to find its way to her parted lips. But in this she was disappointed; his lean brown fingers merely laced with hers.

At this moment, marriage to this man seemed so right that Korey nearly accepted his proposal. But lingering mistrust once more eclipsed the love she felt for him. Sadly, a shallow smile and a gentle squeeze to his hand became her only response.

"I won't take that as a 'no.'" His voice was gentle but his smile did little to wipe disappointment from his eyes. "The offer remains open. And," he stated with emphasis, "I'll continue asking until I get the answer I want."

Unwelcome tears filled Korey's eyes. Damn his noble restraint! Why, when she seemed incapable of a sane choice, wouldn't he say, authoritatively: "Listen, Toots. Buy a dress. We're getting married. In three days. Be there." But no, he was not one to club her on the head and drag her by the hair to his cave. Instead, he would give her time. Maybe too much time…. Korey swallowed her tears, but her innermost feelings would not be so easily stopped. "I love you, Marc."

For a moment the blush of surprise lit both faces. "I know," he said. Through a widening grin he added, "But it's nice to finally hear it—again." He leaned to her. This time the kiss landed precisely where Korey wished it.

*   *   *   *

It was a promise he made to himself the day he had found her in New Mexico: He and Korey would share a marriage bed or he would never again know the miracle of their joining.

Now, on this muggy August day in a rare moment of reflection, it occurred to Marc just how high was the price of virtue: sleepless nights, irritable days, an increasingly greedy eagerness to slip the bonds of his own prison. And for all that, there had been no reward; he remained unable to net the elusive woman.

Time to face the fact that he and Korey seemed no closer to a wedding this month than last. Worse, these latest barren weeks had tortured him with fresh screenings of erotic dreams in which he found new and delicious ways of making love to her. To save his sanity, he must leap from the dizzying merry-go-round on which he spun. Bruised and aching, he would slink off to tend his wounds and fool himself into believing he could live without her.

Self-preservation dragged him to Korey's door that same August evening. Heedless of how his suit clung to him in the steamy heat, Marc urged Korey to leave the cool comfort of her house and sit with him on the porch swing.

The vacant look in his eyes and the firm line of his mouth told Korey this was no idle visit. She flinched inwardly, guessing what was on his mind. To hide from what was to come, her stomach curled into a hard knot.

Marc felt a tremor go through her hand as he gently took it in his own. In a ragged voice, he said, "I love you, Korey. With everything I have, I love you. But I was wrong to think I'm made of the tough stuff it takes to endure what's going on between us—or more to the point, what is *not* going on. Having you near, wanting you....it's driving me nuts....I can't do it anymore."

Suddenly lightheaded, her words came as little more than a peep. "I'm the one who has brought us to this."

"And you're going to let me walk out of your life?"

She ached enough for them both. "Are you saying that's what you're going to do?"

In a last gasp to forestall his doom, he responded with a question of his own. "Is that what you want?"

Slowly she shook her head. She detested the tiny part of her that stubbornly continued to push him away. Warm, sticky air clogged her lungs as she tried to draw a breath. When tears filled the wide brown eyes, Marc offered her a clean handkerchief. Turning from his disconsolate gaze, she dabbed her face. The words she could not say did painful things to her throat. She pressed her lips together to dam a torrent of tears.

Marc suffered the minutes of awful silence. His dream of bringing Korey to her senses sank along with the sun; together he and the sky turned a melancholy gray.

Beside him she stirred. In a voice soft and small as a child's, she admitted, "I'm scared."

"Heavens, do you think I'm not? Beneath all the wedding hoopla, anyone with a grain of sense is frightened out of their minds when it comes to taking a partner for life. But we love each other, Korey." His warm fingers reached for hers. "That should be enough."

But she did not share his confidence. What was it about her that would not let her grab hold of what might very well be her best chance at happiness? Marc's fine features ran together as she looked at him through fresh tears. She withdrew from his touch and took her frustration and self-pity out on the damp handkerchief she now wrung in her hands.

For him to remain any longer would be futile, and they both knew it. His sincere words, spoken as he stood to leave, cast a glimmer of light along the edges of the wall Korey had erected between them. "I will settle," he said tenderly, "for nothing less than marriage. A lifetime of you and me; home, children. But coercion is not part of my plan." He could not hold back a telling sigh. "Maybe without me around things will appear clearer." His lips brushed hers, and they both pretended they felt no flame. "I won't be waiting by the phone…." Even as he said it, he knew it to be a lie. From this moment the telephone would be his nemesis. "….but I'll be out there, somewhere. All you have to do is find me. That, and come up with one magic word—'Yes.'"

*   *   *   *

As the sisters lounged comfortably on Tina's new brick patio, cool breezes whispered promises of autumn while in the late sun oscillating sprinklers arced rainbows over a thriving lawn. Korey tracked glistening drops of water as they ran down emerald blades of grass. For the first time in weeks, she spoke of what was truly in her heart. "Tina, I've come to a decision."

"Oh?"

"I want to marry Marc."

A grin illuminated Tina's face just before her slender fingers covered her unpainted lips. For a moment Korey thought Tina would cry. But any tears that lurked were instantly swept away in a rush of words. "Oh, Korey, how wonderful! I was afraid you would never get to this. And now." Tina bobbed in her chair. "So many plans to be made…."

Korey motioned with her hand. "Hold on just a minute. Better put a damper on that excitement."

Tina's smile faded. "Hey," she said, her spirits taking a dive, "I'm not looking into the face of a happy bride-to-be."

"Only because I'm not one. Marc doesn't know. We haven't spoken in weeks."

There were no barbs in Tina's tone as she asked, "And why is it I'm hearing this before the prospective groom?"

"I tried to tell him."

"Tried?"

"This morning.... I called his office. He's traveling this week. I didn't ask where to reach him. This is too important to be discussed on the phone. Next week is the private party for the opening of the Huntington Tower. Since my quilt is now hanging in the lobby, I'm on the guest list. Marc will certainly be there. I'll tell him then."

"But, Korey, that's another eight days."

"I know. But it will take me at least that long to summon the courage. Look at me—I'm shaking like a leaf just thinking about it. My mind keeps asking these stupid questions: what if, while I've been 'soul-searching,' he has changed his mind; what if, while I've dilly-dallied, he's given up hope and taken up again with Julia Santangelo; what if...."

"Oh, stop it! What man who's crazy in love would do that? Not Marc. After just five weeks, he wouldn't chuck everything he's gone through this summer to prove himself. Why, I'll bet the poor man's first waking thought each morning is that this would be the luckiest day of his life if you showed up knocking at his door."

Korey's eyes softened. "Do you really think so?"

"I don't doubt it for a minute and neither should you. One long look into those gorgeous green eyes, and my bet is you'd find love's gold mine." Tina lovingly patted the kicking baby inside her growing tummy. She smiled wistfully. "Marriage, motherhood—Korey, these things don't come neatly wrapped, tied in pretty ribbon and with a lifetime warranty. Marry Marc. Give each other beautiful babies. And please don't waste any more time doing it."

*   *   *   *

That her back was to him in the cavernous lobby teeming with guests mattered not a whit. He spotted her the instant he entered. Throughout the day his head had hoped she would not come, while in opposition, his heart had hammered in anticipation of this moment. Marc felt his neck grow warm under his collar as he observed Carl Huntington hanging on her every word—that is, when

Carl was not running a lecherous eye along the elegantly understated black dress that was, from neck to ankle, her second skin.

His irritation hidden behind a convincing smile, Marc mingled with the crowd. Chatting his way in a wide sweep of the room, he remained aware of Korey's every move as he deliberately stayed to her blind side. Over the fluffy white head of Carl Huntington's butterball wife, he did not miss the small diamond sparkle at Korey's ear as more than once she turned her head to glance in the direction of the building's main entrance.

Politely extracting his arm from Dora Huntington's bird-like grasp, Marc wove his way to the quilt hung with distinction high on a lighted wall. He plucked a glass of champagne from a passing tray and sipped without tasting. Korey moved among the guests. From the shadow of his brow, he watched as a circle of men—bachelors all, damn them—swallowed her. Jealousy spun him to the wall; he raised his head and pretended to study the quilt. Rising to him above the buzz of the crowd, Korey's sweet laughter pricked his pounding heart. Staring blindly at the abstract display of color above him, his mind slipped away from the party to a place of solitude where he saw, like snapshots jumbled in a shoe box, images of Korey as she once was—when she had been his. Marc took refuge in this world apart until a tingle of awareness climbed his spine. A voice said near his ear, "Well, what's the verdict?"

He kept his eyes to the wall, but his thought was not for the work of art, only for the scented woman who had come to stand at his side. "Beautiful," he said. "Absolutely beautiful."

Full ruby lips smiled in triumph. "I almost crippled myself with this one. Too much work; too little time." She thrust a gnarled hand under his nose, hoping to elicit a chuckle. It worked, and to Korey there suddenly seemed to be more air to breathe in the vaulted room.

"Maybe you've earned some time off," he suggested.

"I plan to take some." For the first time in six weeks her eyes looked into his. "Look, could we find a quiet spot, some place where we can talk?" In anticipation of an affirmative response, she discarded her champagne glass on a nearby table.

Though nothing in her expression hinted at her purpose, in Marc's mind the solicitation presaged a turning point. Whether the new direction would fulfill his desires he could not guess. Fearing the unknown, he hesitated.

Refusing to wilt as she waited under his inquisitive gaze, Korey clasped her restless hands together. Shallow breaths floundered in lungs that seemed to have collapsed. She used the agonizingly slow moments to congratulate herself on the wisdom of choosing to wear a dress long enough to effectively sheathe her knocking knees.

At long last Marc lifted his eyes to scan over a sea of bobbing heads. On the opposite side of the lobby was a vacant alcove near the elevators. He set his champagne next to hers, then, resisting the impulse to place a possessive hand at her waist, he guided her by an elbow across the marble floor. In a semblance of privacy, they huddled behind a pillar, and, as their own silence grew, the echoing voices of the many revelers faded to a distant hum.

Korey leaned a hip against the marble column; the cool unyielding stone served to prop her up much more reliably than her quaking knees. She thought to plunge in with, "Let's get married," but something was wrong with the timing. So she watched him as he watched her, until finally, trying not to sound perfunctory, she said, "How have you been?"

"Busy."

If he stuck to one word replies, this was not going to be easy. But after the way she had behaved, should she expect otherwise? Because of her, an entire summer squandered…. His eyes did not stray from hers, and Korey saw that Tina had been right: no mistaking the unconditional love in those beautiful green depths. And there was also fear. The discovery that he was as frightened as she, quieted her own trembling. "I've missed you terribly," she said.

The softly spoken words seemed to work magic. Marc shifted his rigid stance, leaned toward her, pressed a flat palm on the pillar above her head. His suit jacket fell open to display at her eye level a broad chest clad in a crisp white shirt. She looked up to return the warmth of his smile. A jolt of electricity leapt between them, so tangible that to Korey it would have come as no surprise to find they were the center of a shimmering blue aura. She did, in fact, suppress the urge to reach up to feel if every hair on her dizzy head were standing on end.

"I've been thinking," she said in a voice low but sure, "September is such a fine month for a wedding…."

For a breathless moment Marc was afraid to trust his own ears. But with the spread of Korey's effervescent grin the truth came home. Marc held up the colossal stone pillar on the strength of one arm as the rest of his body ran to mush. As he pushed himself erect and took her eager hands in his, only two words rode on his sigh. "Oh, Korey." Too awash in flooding emotion to smile, his face was sober as he rocked back to peer around the curve of their trysting place. He surveyed the lobby, brought his gaze back to Korey. "I hate crowds," he declared bluntly. "Let's get the hell out of here."

"At this moment nothing would please me more, but," she resisted his tug, "shouldn't you spend some time with Carl Huntington first?"

"My darling, I've spent months with the boor, culminating in being trapped in this place all afternoon helping him prepare for this wingding. Believe me, I won't be missed." Marc ogled her from head to toe, a leering grin adorning his playful mouth. "No, the real question is....will he miss *you*?"

So Marc had seen Huntington's eyes take their rude liberties! Little wonder then that he viewed the client with disparagement. No one stopped them as Korey gleefully allowed Marc to pull her by the hand through tight clusters of guests, out the soaring glass door, across a granite esplanade to a slatted park bench set among ornamental trees and mounds of yellow chrysanthemums. The oak bench reflected the white light of a boulevard lamp while in the night sky low copper clouds rolled above city lights.

Pleasantly cool air bathed Korey's warm flesh as she paused with Marc beside the bench. Beneath her breast, her heart broke free and began doing handsprings. Like an excited, uninhibited child, she had an overwhelming urge to jump up and down and clap her hands together. Before she could act on the wild impulse, she was swept into powerful arms. Marc's heart pounded against her breast as his mouth swooped to hers. Korey's skin radiated heat where his hands roamed her body. Time was measured in whispers, touches, and sighs. Between hungry kisses, *I love you* fell from their lips like sweet fruit from a tree.

Before passion's fever drained him of his last grain of sense, Marc recovered sufficiently to remind himself that he and Korey stood outdoors under a street lamp and, therefore, were not unlike two mannequins on display in a lighted shop window. Raising his tousled head, he grinned impishly, secured Korey's slender waist in a vise grip, and, lifting her feet off the ground, whirled her in broad circles along the esplanade.

"Marc!" she giggled, struggling for breath. "Put me down, my head is swimming!" On one final spin several strangers passed in a blur. With hands clutching his neck, she pulled herself to his ear and whispered self-consciously, "People are watching."

"Let 'em watch," he invited, not the least abashed. But in deference to his bride-to-be, he gently set her feet on the ground. Studying her face at close range, he asked, "When?"

Korey tilted her head. "When?"

"The wedding."

"Of course," she said, still recovering her stolen breath, "the wedding. Soon....arrangements must be made."

She saw the glint in his eye just before he said, "Korey, let's run away and get married."

"Run away? You mean....elope?"

"That's exactly what I mean. Just like a couple of hot-to-trot kids."

Above steepled hands she had pressed to her lips, her dark eyes were held by his. Why not? The unconventional proposal had instant appeal. Her family would want only her happiness, would not feel slighted if there were no ceremony to attend. After all, they had been through one wedding....

Marc's voice came from the midst of her thoughts. "I'm flying to Albuquerque in four days. Come with me, love. We'll marry in New Mexico."

"Who could refuse such an enchanting proposal?"

"It was my intention that it be irresistible." He paused, then asked, "Would you object if I made the wedding arrangements?"

"My, my," she chuckled. "You *are* being unorthodox. And why is it I have the feeling this has been tucked up your sleeve for quite some time?" She went on as if not expecting an answer. "I would be pleased to relinquish all responsibility for the planning. In what now seems like another lifetime, I was privileged to have my one elegant affair with all the pomp, expense—and frayed nerves. All I desire now, my darling, is to be your wife. The *how* does not matter." She smiled pertly. "In other words, mister, the job's yours." Korey stepped into his loving embrace, thinking that she never again wanted to know the desolation of life without him. Her elated giggle was muffled as her forehead rested on his chest.

"Four days....time won't go fast enough."

"My suitcase will be packed."

Marc glanced across the street to where his sporty but not always practical red Miata sat at the curb. With a feather's touch he placed a finger beneath Korey's chin and directed her gaze to the small car. Laughter colored his voice as he said, "Hey, lucky for me, I don't have to bring a ladder!"

CHAPTER 27

▼

"Where are you taking me?"

Marc smiled indulgently. "You ask too many questions."

The winding road and familiar landmarks all pointed the way to the Sanchez ranch. But Maria no longer lived there…. Only yesterday Korey visited Maria in Albuquerque, and not once through the joyful hours of reunion did Maria mention the ranch. Korey too avoided bringing up the still tender subject. So now what possible reason would Marc have in making the ranch their destination? She said to him, "You are aware, of course, that your elusiveness invites questions."

"You'll have answers soon enough."

For a long stretch of road Korey was, if not pacified, at least silent. But Marc asked the impossible to expect his companion to complacently remain mum when at last he switched off the car engine at the door of the adobe house that had for so many years belonged to Mike and Maria Sanchez.

"Ma-arc." Korey addressed him as though the name were two syllables. "What are we doing here? You know Maria doesn't own this place anymore."

"True. But I know who does."

"You do?"

"Yes."

"Who?"

"You."

"M…me?" It came out like the cheep of a newly hatched bird. "Why, that's ridiculous. Where did you get such an erroneous idea? Who in the world told you I bought Maria's ranch?"

"No one told me anything. It happens that I bought the ranch—in June. And now, my love, I'm presenting it to you. As a wedding gift."

Korey's mouth formed a perfectly round **O**. "This," she spread her arms inside the restrictive space of the car, "as a gift?" Slowly she seemed to digest his words. "And what do you mean you bought the ranch in June? In June you didn't know we would be married. In fact," she stated as if he needed a reminder, "as of this moment, we have only a license to marry in New Mexico. We've been here three days and there has yet to be a wedding."

"Mere details. All of which," he announced confidently, "are being taken care of, so don't you worry your pretty head about that." Sunshine reached in to warm his leg as he swung the car door open. "As to making the purchase before I knew you would make me the happiest man alive…well, somewhere in the recesses of my mind lived the belief that if I bought this ranch, it would follow that you would eventually come with the package. Self-fulfilling prophesy."

"But you were taking such a risk."

"Was I?" He studied her face. "I don't think so. Oh, I admit there were moments when I doubted my fiscal acumen, but regardless, I knew the ranch would one day be yours whether or not you agreed to marry me."

"You're talking nonsense."

"No, I'm not. I bought it for you, Korey. My fondest hope was that I could give it as a wedding gift. But if not…a gift is still a gift, no strings attached."

Her eyes glazed as if she were peering into a dream. Tears of gratitude dotted her flushed cheeks. "You are the most generous, caring man….and me with only a gold ring to give."

Kissing away her tears, he said, "I have you, my love. I ask for nothing more." He kissed her again. "Now, let's take a tour of our hideaway."

With recovered poise she accepted his hand as he came around to escort her to the front door. But she could not refrain from making a sensible observation. "Won't it present problems to run a ranch from a distance of a thousand miles?"

His answering smile exuded confidence as he dropped a shiny brass house key into her palm. "A practical question but unnecessary. We have only the house and twenty acres. I sold most of the land. To a neighbor."

The key paused in the lock. Korey looked up in surprise. "Not to Jim?"

"None other than Jim Yellowhawk. He jumped at the offer. Said if he couldn't have you, the land was the next best thing."

"He didn't really…."

"Actually, no. But he did say to tell you the land was still yours to ride. It seems Sundancer is pining for you. May not be the only one."

Korey dropped her gaze, fiddled with the stubborn latch. "So you and Jim have become….friends?"

"I wouldn't go that far. But we have spoken on the phone. The first time I called he was not terribly pleased to hear from me, but he did me the courtesy of not slamming the phone down in my ear. In the end, he eagerly accepted my proposal to sell him the bulk of the ranch. At the time, however, he didn't know I intended the house as a wedding gift."

"Does he know now?"

"Yes. And I'll give him this….he's not a sore loser."

Her hand stilled. "What do you mean?"

"No good denying that he had an eye for you, but there seem to be no hard feelings. I hear he's found himself a girl. He'll make a fine neighbor and will watch our place when we're not here. I've learned he's a man of his word. I trust him."

With Marc looming over her, the chiming of wedding bells in her head seemed to drown out all thought of Jim.

Until she stepped into the dim shade of the house.

There, in the center of the room, on a low, fashionably rough-hewn table, stood a carved alabaster buffalo.

"A wedding gift to you from Jim," Marc said quietly as he stood back to watch. Korey respectfully traced a finger over the translucent stone. "He said you seemed to have a particular fondness for this sculpture."

"Yes." The tears returned. "I had hoped to buy it some day. Oh, Marc, all of this in one day—it's too much." Nostalgia seemed to cock its finger and beckon her farther into the room. The fragrance of piñon, indelibly scorched into the fireplace, mingled with sun-warmed adobe in the uncirculated air. The scent of dry wool still told of Maria's years hunched over her loom. Overlapping the familiar were fresh smells of wood veneer, lacquer, and new upholstery. In bewilderment, Korey's teary eyes drew a blurry line across brightly dyed sofas and chairs. "But Maria left no furnishings," she said hesitantly. Her arms reached to encompass the room. "Where did all of this come from?"

"Rae. With carte blanche she had the time of her life spending my money! I hope you approve."

"Approve. It's splendid. I could not have done as well."

He came to her and took her in his arms. It was then, as he held her close, that her eyes fell on the Enchanted Mesa quilt filling the wall between the fireplace and the door.

Marc felt a pang of loneliness as his arms emptied and Korey drifted to the draped wall. "This too?" she asked in a dreamy voice. The feel of tiny stitches under her roving finger brought to mind the countless winter hours spent in companionship with Maria as they both had patiently bent to their tasks. "Rae bought this too?"

"No." The old floor chirped under his weight. Then his warm breath was in her ear and the comfort of his arms came from behind to cinch her waist. "I found it in Old Town, last April. The moment I saw it, I knew I couldn't walk out of that shop and leave it behind."

"It looks at home here. As if it were made for this wall."

"It was. It could never hang anywhere else."

She rotated smoothly in his arms, on her toes, like a ballerina. Her kiss was ripe with yearning, and when it was finished, she slipped her hands deeply into the back pockets of his jeans.

The next kiss seared his eager mouth. "I can see," he said breathlessly, "where this is heading. I promised myself we would wait...."

"Phoo." She pressed him close, kissed the point of his smooth chin. "We *did* wait. Through the longest, hottest summer of my life. No more waiting."

"You're sure? Because in another ten seconds I may not be able to let you change your mind."

"My dearest love," she murmured through kisses trailing downward, "I have no intention of changing my mind."

*   *   *   *

"Korey.... Korey." The whisper echoed through her sleep. A playful hand ruffled her curls. "Wake up, sleepyhead."

She roused and rolled onto her back. The voice was both gentle and familiar, and she was not alarmed. Forcing her heavy lids up, she stared into Marc's face only inches from her own, his smile illuminated by light spilling into the room from Matty's hallway. Her eyes went to the window, noted the blackness still shading the curtain, then slid to the green numerals on the bedside clock. Her sleepy face puckered. "It's 4:35 in the morning. What are you doing here at this hour?"

His grin reassured her he had not come bearing some sort of ill news. His spicy aftershave tickled her nose as he leaned closer and whispered, "There is something I want you to see, something special that must be witnessed at sunrise.

We need to get you up and dressed because it will involve a bit of a journey to reach our destination." He left her and headed for the closet.

She stared at his back, dumbfounded. "Wait a minute," she said, propping up on her elbows. "You sneak in here and expect me to jump out of bed and follow you into the night?" She snapped her fingers. "Just like that?"

"For the record, I did not *sneak* in. I arrived honorably. Matty let me in the front door. And," he threatened from the shadows as his hand grabbed the closet doorknob, "if you *don't* jump out of that bed, I just might take a notion to jump into it with you!"

"Hush! Matty might hear you."

"Well, are you getting up or am I hopping in?" He ogled her through the grainy light.

Under the blankets, her knees formed a mountain as she sat up in the bed. "I may," she said, stubbornly, "entertain the idea of getting up if you try being a little *less* forceful and a little *more* cooperative and tell me where in the world we're going."

"Please, Korey, don't make me spoil the surprise. You won't be disappointed, I promise."

"Oh, all right. But this had better be good." She shoved the bedcovers aside, swung her bare feet to the cool carpet and stood, wiggling her full cotton gown to the floor.

"It will be," he assured her, grinning at the prim gesture of modesty and wondering how this could be the same temptress who had so successfully seduced him only hours before at their ranch house. "Now, though you look mighty fetching, I suggest you get into some street wear. We're leaving here in thirty minutes. I'll choose something for you." Flinging open the closet door, he pulled the cord on the overhead bulb and disappeared.

Korey shuffled across the hall to the bathroom, gladly closing the door against the repellent scrape of hangers traveling back and forth on a metal rod. Twenty-five minutes later she emerged showered, shampooed, and her face adorned with minimal makeup. Her bedroom was empty; she heard voices coming from the kitchen. The co-conspirators sharing a cup of coffee, no doubt.

Marc had left a small lamp burning and her clothes spread across a smooth bed. Knowing the September air to be chilly at this hour of the morning, she first worked a pair of opaque tights up her legs. Dressing by rote, she next shrugged into a creamy silk shirt, followed by a skirt of ankle-length crushed velvet. A vest of matching turquoise floated onto the silk shirt. She rummaged in her jewelry travel case for her favorite turquoise and silver earrings.

Leaning to a mirror, her eyes caught her reflection as she slipped the ear wires through her lobes. It came to her, as the tips of the secured earrings brushed her shoulders, that this entire ensemble was the one Marc had bought on their first trip to Albuquerque almost two years before. During the year of her separation from Marc, the outfit had hung in a plastic garment bag, banished to the back of the guest room closet in the house in Chattanooga.

Korey smiled as she stepped into turquoise leather boots awaiting her beside the bed. A year ago who would have guessed she would now be dressed in the very clothes she had sworn she would never again wear. Instead of a painful reminder of love lost, his purchases were now a token of love renewed. Could it be Marc had chosen them this morning for that very reason? Plucking the last item from the bed—a wool poncho in a bold turquoise and magenta plaid, woven for her by Maria—Korey lovingly draped it over her shoulder. She adjusted a sagging bra strap, buffed a smudge of lipstick from a tooth, switched off the lamp and breezed into the kitchen.

"Good morning, all," she gushed.

Matty Cunningham managed with effort to keep her own high spirits under wraps. She simply cast her niece an innocent smile and said, as if it were not at all unusual for three people to gather in her kitchen at five o'clock on a dark morning, "Good morning, dear."

With a near empty cup of coffee nestled in his hand, Marc said nothing as Korey stood beside his chair. He looked up at her, his mind on little else but that of his beautiful bride.

Korey's hands went to her hips. "Well, Mr. Bradberry," she said feigning impatience, "as you can see, I'm ready. If you can tear yourself away from this tete-a-tete, I believe my thirty minutes are up."

Marc came readily to his feet, reassuringly squeezed her hand, then wrapped his free arm around Matty's shoulders, planting a noisy kiss on her rosy cheek. Matty placed in her niece's free hand what appeared to be breakfast in a sack and wordlessly hugged Korey to her ample bosom. Korey saw, as Marc led her past Matty and out the door, that her aunt's eyes were shining. The tears signaled that something momentous was set to occur, but Korey asked no questions for she knew they would go unanswered.

She derived a tingling pleasure in the bizarre events of the morning but kept her bubbling curiosity in check even after she and Marc had boarded a helicopter and flown up and over the lighted city. Conversation was limited to Marc and the pilot shouting succinct phrases over a constant whop-a-ta, whop-a-ta, so Korey nibbled on a Danish pastry from a paper sack and trusted herself to Marc's care no matter how strange it all seemed.

In the gray light of the emerging day, she began to distinguish towering mesas. Soon neon strips of pink and orange backlit the eastern horizon. Above, in an indigo sky air-brushed in violet, stars still twinkled with diamond brilliance. Korey had never witnessed a more spectacular dawn.

As the helicopter swooped west, the mesas began to show their ruddy complexions in the rising morning light, and Korey, from her unique vantage point above the mesa tops, marveled at the spectacular scenery. It crossed her mind to envy the birds that enjoyed this same view as a matter of routine.

The mechanical bird in which she flew dropped in altitude; for a disconcerting moment, it seemed to Korey that the red mesas were rising swiftly from the ground to meet her. In a vestment of purple morning haze, one massive rock, as though it had elbowed others aside, stood alone as guardian of a valley floor.

Enchanted Mesa.

For nearly eighteen months, since she was last here with Marc, Korey had purposely avoided setting eyes on the mesa's sheer sandstone walls. In reflection, she now understood how difficult it had been to let the tumultuous memories of that visit lie undisturbed within Enchanted Mesa's primordial stone. Before her musings could take her so far as to wonder why Marc had brought her to this place on a clear September morning, his strong voice spoke to her above the noise of the rotor.

"You're thinking, of course, that I have completely lost my mind."

"It was beginning to occur to me....," she called back.

Marc took her hand in his, bridging the gap between them. "You've been a terrific sport about this. I'm not so sure I would've been as pleasant if someone dragged me out of a deep sleep for a predawn foray into the unknown."

"I suppose," she smiled tolerantly, "it would depend on whom was doing the dragging." Their descent tugged suddenly at the pit of her stomach, and her eyes flew to the forty acres of mesatop that loomed large beneath them. She was stunned by what she thought she saw there. "I must not be as awake as I thought." She pointed through the glass and asked in disbelief, "There are *people* down there?"

He stated calmly, as if it were the most natural event, "Yes. Three. Dropped off just minutes ago."

"But who? Marc," her voice strained above the noise, "what is happening here?"

"A wedding."

"A wed.... You can't mean...."

He leaned over and sealed her open mouth with a kiss. After a moment he said, into her ear, "Happy wedding day, love."

It was evident Korey was incapable of speech, so Marc took the opportunity to offer an explanation. "Those people with their clothes flapping in our breeze are our witnesses, my brother Eric and his faithful wife Rae, without whose assistance I never would have been able to pull this off. Because of the type of work they do, they have contacts that granted us special dispensation to land on this landmark of the Acoma Indian Reservation. They also knew who to call to ferry us out here at this hour. With Eric and Rae this morning is the Reverend Ronald Sandoval, a childhood friend of Rae's who conveniently happens to be a fully ordained minister. So there you have it, my love." He patted the breast pocket of his dark blazer. "Marriage license here. Everything arranged. Right down to Eric having in his pocket the wedding bands you and I bought two days ago. In a matter of minutes after this bird sets us down on that rock, you will become Mrs. Marcus Bradberry. I trust you know how much I adore the sound of that."

She spoke so softly he could not hear her through the noise of the landing. But his heart nevertheless swelled with joy as he read her soft, full lips: "Everything is perfect. I've never been happier. I love you, Marcus."

*   *   *   *

He wrapped a protective arm around her shoulders and snatched her against his side as if in fear the wind gusting around the rotating blades would sweep her from the top of the mesa. Then the helicopter lifted and was gone.

Korey turned a wide eye on her beloved.

Still pressing her to him, he grinned down at her. "You're wondering how we're going to get off of this pile of rock as man and wife."

She admitted aloud that until now, when their only way off the mesa was but a speck on an orange sun, she had not thought that far ahead. "But," she added, "since this is the most unorthodox wedding, I can only assume you will have us all rapelling down the 430 feet of these precipitous walls!" Hiding a grin, she turned her head one way, then another. "Where are the ropes?"

Marc looked at the beauty who would leave here as his wife and roared with laughter. "A pity I didn't think of that. Much more creative than whirlybirds returning in twenty minutes to lift us off." He buried his laughter in her fragrant hair.

Oblivious to the three shivering figures watching patiently from the far end of the mesa, he kissed her soundly, then said soberly, "We have both traveled our share of rocky roads. But everything has its price, Korey, and we have paid dearly to stand here today. For that the reward is all the sweeter." He warmed her chilled hands in his. "I won't presume to guarantee smooth roads from here. But this I do promise: no matter what lies ahead, no matter the external forces that may batter and bruise us on our journey, trust me to love and cherish you as much as any man has ever loved and cherished a woman. As this rock on which we stand is timeless, so is my love for you."

A chill wind whipped her skirt around her boots. She shivered and pulled her wool poncho tighter. Before he took her in his arms, Marc wiped a single tear from her cheek. Her hand rested on his hard chest and was warmed by the strength of his beating heart.

"And now sweetheart," Marc said as he waved to the wedding party, "let's stand before the Reverend Sandoval."

Korey only smiled, not daring to open her mouth for fear the tears would flow. She snuggled her hand inside his jacket and found his waist at the same moment he embraced hers. Together they began the walk over crumbling sandstone to where they would take their vows.

*   *   *   *

On steady wings, an eagle soared above Enchanted Mesa, the lone witness to five people huddled in the rosy dawn. Unobserved, the regal bird circled once, twice. Then it glided east and disappeared into the risen sun.

978-0-595-38575-1
0-595-38575-3

Printed In the United States
44891LVS00007B/75

9 780595 385751